On The
Nature
Of
Magic

MARIAN WOMACK

TITAN BOOKS

On the Nature of Magic
Print edition ISBN: 9781803361345
E-book edition ISBN: 9781803361925

Published by Titan Books
A division of Titan Publishing Group Ltd.
144 Southwark Street, London SE1 0UP
www.titanbooks.com

First Titan edition: May 2023
10 9 8 7 6 5 4 3 2 1

A CIP catalogue record for this title is available from the British Library.

Printed and bound in Great Britain by CPI Group (UK) Ltd, Croydon CR0 4YY

CONTENTS

PROLOGUE

They would be dressed as fairies, planets, stars, bound tight to ropes as they soared up, up all the way to the glass ceiling to be enveloped by the light. It would still be there when she closed her eyes, tiny green dots floating behind her eyelids.

The ropes and the levers would start working, and the dancers would fly up, performing their daring pirouettes, their arms and legs forming delicate shapes, love doves that would entrance the movie audience.

Yes, she knew it then: that night there would be nightmares. They were like clockwork, always after seeing the lady dancers floating in mid-air for the camera, everyone silent at the studio, intently following their progress, only an old piano shrieking somewhere, and *le patron* giving directions, a grin on his face. That was all everyone wanted, to please *le patron*; but his grin brought no relief to anybody. At least not to her. In bed, when she was trying to sleep, she would still see it when she closed her eyes, the green light that had covered the dancers. And the dreams were awful. They would always be populated by the same strange creatures, beasts out of a fairy world but awfully wrong, twisted: tall boys made of clay and sticks glued together, gentlemen in expensive outfits, which crumbled into tatters when she got close, wicked women who talked to the dead. Who were these strange people? Why did she have these strange dreams?

She remembered the first few times she saw Star Film Studio. It was impossible to believe it, a building completely made of glass like some oversized orangery. There was a complicated system that moved curtains one way or another to maintain a measured quantity of light. There were ropes and levers that lifted the dancers. The ropes helped *le patron* create his illusions; her aunt's job was to render them invisible among the costumes. There were always ladies flying in *le patron*'s movies. Fairies bathed in light. He would be giving instructions, if he wasn't operating the camera himself. But on many days there were visitors in the studio, and he would show them around. Investors, her aunt would whisper. These two had come often, a tall man and a petite woman fashionably dressed. The man sounded English, but his wife was definitely French. She had been an actress herself, someone commented; there she was now, trying on a decorative headpiece, laughing and chatting with the dancers. Philothée wondered if one day she would be as beautiful as that woman, if she would be able to chat to strangers with such confidence.

She had always been a shy girl, fond of a book, hiding behind her glasses. Her aunt had pressed her mother to let her make the journey from the country, for *le patron* was looking for more dancers for his moving pictures. Any pretty girl would do. And if she was something she was pretty, with her big blue almond eyes and her blonde hair and her little doll face. That was, if she removed the glasses, which she would have to do. As it happens, if Philothée had wanted anything in her short life it was to see Paris, which she imagined full of books. And so she came, and so she now was starting her apprenticeship, observing the lady dancers, for soon she would be one of them. She had misgivings about this, all the excitement of the idea burning itself out as soon as she confronted the deed, which always seemed to end in dancers with distorted faces, a strange demeanour as they came back down and were freed from the ropes: unhinged, like life-size, broken dolls.

And then there was Paris itself. She had expected lightness and laughter in every street, only to find a city of darkened corners and thousands of strangers who did not look at each other once, as if they all shared an awful secret.

She soon found that the vast avenues and fanciful buildings were indeed hiding another reality after her aunt took her to a 'religious' meeting, where Philothée discovered another world sitting below our own, one of middle-aged ladies holding hands in darkness, sitting around a table that turned by itself as it provided messages from the Beyond, oddly grinning faces following the movements of this unnatural occurrence; and all that followed by watery tea and stale pastries in the parlour, as if what had just happened was part of a normal day.

'Don't be scared, child,' her aunt had advised. 'What you have seen is a miracle.' And Leonie would make the sign of the cross, and kiss the medal of the Virgin Mary that hung from her chest. And then, at home, she would do even stranger things, like lighting a blue-black candle, and studying by its darkened light the peculiar symbols on a piece of paper. Philothée did not know what to think, except that Leonie, with her grey-white hair and her distorted expression, worrying over the difficult words of her blasphemous prayer, resembled a witch. A horrid thought. At night, when she went to bed, she would hear Leonie still chanting under her breath, something that sounded almost like a Christian prayer, on the edge of being a prayer, that was no prayer Philothée had ever heard.

That morning she had been helping her aunt, distributing silver organza bows on each hand that happened to come within reach, the dancers running around in a frenzy. But still she saw it, their dull faces, as if they had been dancing their very souls away.

The ladies expertly arranged the last few elements of their costumes. Everyone knew what was required of them, or rather they ought to know, if they valued their position: *le patron* did not expect anything less than perfection. Soon, they would all appear exactly on their marks, which some young assistants were now crudely drawing on the wooden floor with thick white chalk. There was no time to waste on divagations. Behind them, the carpenters were still hammering the craters on *le patron's* Moon. Meanwhile, there were hats and feathers and short bits of clothing changing hands and thrown over quickly-coiffured heads, and even being repaired and sewn and cut at this late hour, a cacophony of voices competing to make themselves heard. And, despite the apparent confusion, the proceedings would occur exactly as was expected, in that oversized glasshouse that was in fact a smoothly run machine.

The dancers were being ushered along now, helped by studio dogsbodies to carefully climb the *papier-mâché* set, positioning themselves on top of the Moon itself.

A call for attention, and everyone scrambled to their required positions. She quickly got out of the way. Behind an oversized demon's head, she peered into the colourful scene. The ladies were arranged as if for having their picture taken, and indeed *le patron*'s camera now appeared, pushed from both sides by eager helpers. Lights were switched on and adjusted, a huge heavy beam, white and yellow, dispelled the shadows. The ladies stepped inwards, and the harnesses were brought forward.

She liked this moment very much, the endless energy that ran through the place right before shooting a scene.

What she did not like was the next stage of filming.

Soon, the light would engulf the dancers, and they would dance as they ascended, a green halo shining around them. And they would start floating: hands, arms, legs, flung in all possible directions. Everyone was praising Leonie, even the visiting couple. Her artistry was incredible.

Leonie enjoyed the favour of *le patron*. And why not? She happened to be one of his oldest and most loyal workers, and her work meant that the dancers wore the most wonderful creations, with none of the levers and ropes visible under the folds of their ornate costumes. Philothée had noticed how, the morning after each séance, *le patron* would call her aunt into his office, and he would speak to her with interest. Leonie enjoyed the favour of *le patron* – and so it was soon that Philothée enjoyed it as well.

But she would not dance that morning after all, the first time she had been due to. She had not been able to sleep again, the faces and the loose limbs of the dancers worrying her mind. But the moment she feared would not come to pass, not now or ever. She did not know it, but Philothée had been chosen for an even greater task.

She was holding the package for dear life. It was rectangular, and small enough to be carried in her hands. It was also very light. But she had been told repeatedly to guard it carefully, as it was extremely fragile.

Le patron's office had been out of a nightmare, with his affiches on masonic lodges and telekinetic theatre performances, its upright palms and his disembodied *papier-mâché* heads on shelves surrounding the room.

'You need to give this to Madame Mathers personally. Do not leave it with anybody else. Understood?' And then, because he must have realised he was sounding stern, he tried to smile. He was still wearing his black-and-white make-up, and he looked strange.

'Oui, Monsieur.'

It was the first time she had climbed into a hansom cab, which would take her all the way to the centre of Paris. She felt special, as *le patron*'s brother Gaston held her hand and helped her ascend. The Mathers building was located at 1 Avenue Duquesne, a normal Parisian street close to Les Invalides, bathed in the mild afternoon light. But the light was already waning, and Philothée could divine the shadows among the cracks of the city. But as soon as she walked into the entrance hall, everything became dark, unrecognisable. The dark wooden walls had fantastical creatures carved on them. She climbed the staircase to the first floor, and rang the bell.

It was a long time before somebody opened the door, and the woman who did so was the same elegant actress who had laughed with the dancers that morning. Philothée could now see her more closely, her dark eyes and jet-black hair, tied back and piled up in the latest fashion. She showed her the package, and mumbled her errand.

'I am Madame Mathers,' the dark-haired lady said. 'Would you like to come inside? Have a little something before you go back.' An elongated hand, encrusted with more jewels, more rings and bracelets than Philothée had ever seen, took the package and ripped apart the brown paper to reveal nothing more than an old and tattered-looking book.

Philothée explained that she had been told to go back to the flat she shared with her aunt, and that she couldn't stay.

'Ah! I am sure we can take you there later on. Please, come in.'

Inside there was an unexpected green profusion of plants, little palm trees and huge aspidistras competing in their race to reach the ceiling. A huge balcony, an interior glasshouse, shone at the end of a narrow series of chambers, inundated with pile upon pile of fantastical objects, terrifying sculptures, and books: more books than Philothée had ever seen together in her life.

'Oh! I see you have found Hathor,' Madame Mathers said, for Philothée had stopped in front of a statue. 'She is the light that helps us reach the Beyond.' But Madame Mathers was wrong, for Philothée had stopped to admire the books lying about, had not even noticed the Egyptian goddess. The books were mostly in piles, in disarray, occupying corners, covering chairs, and hiding a sideboard in the dining room.

They reached the orangery-balcony, so small in comparison with Star Film Studio, and Madame Mathers told her to sit on a couch, and she was abruptly left alone.

Philothée wondered who these people were.

Madame Mathers came back; this time her husband was with her.

'Thank you for bringing back the *grimoire*,' he said. Philothée had no idea what that word meant, but she assumed he was referring to the book. 'I am Samuel and this is my wife Moina. Have some refreshments before you go back.' Moina was next to him, already putting down a tray on an ottoman. Philothée noticed it had only one cup. 'I am sure we will meet again,' he said, and he left after shaking her hand.

Moina Mathers sat down next to her, and watched as she drank her cup. They chatted a bit about the scene that *le patron* had filmed that morning, and then she called her a hansom cab. Philothée had never been inside one before that day, and now she had been in two. All her excitement returned at once, all those feelings of yearning mixed with fear that had brought her to Paris. She sensed again the possibilities of the unknown floating in the air.

That night she wondered again who these people were, this time out loud, as her aunt wanted details. But Leonie seemed ecstatic that her niece had been singled out to help *le patron* with this particular errand, and kept fussing over her. To Philothée, it was like when they shot the flying scene at the studio: it all had left a peculiar taste in her mouth.

1

BEYOND THE VEIL

London, 13th March 1902

The woman on the stage jerked horribly, her neck bending to breaking point. A loud crack, the collective gasp of a full theatre. Her head hanging, falling to its side like a rag doll's. Eliza could feel it, the dark energy that now hung above the audience, the shared fear. The power that descended over the small auditorium, keeping everyone enthralled.

On stage, the terrible vision, a woman shifting and jerking, a woman who ought to be dead.

Eliza was sitting in the fourth row. She was a woman in her twenties, with the healthy countenance of people who take good books along for lengthy walks. She was wearing a pretty set of skirt and puff-sleeved jacket of a fashionable light grey with no frills of any kind, an amethyst brooch in the delicate shape of a forget-me-not her only concession to fashion. The brooch was a loan from the friend who was with her, who had explained that the stone in question helped with clear thinking, and brought spiritual peace; Eliza merely thought it pretty.

She had recently cut a new fringe, which got in the way, and she had to keep pushing it to one side: she was trying her hair up in a new low bun.

The friend sitting next to her was Helena Walton-Cisneros – spiritualist to the higher London society, detective to those in the know – her mentor, her teacher, her business partner. The woman, generous enough to refer to Eliza as her associate, took notes frantically, her pencil scribbling on a small silver-bound paper holder that hung from a chatelaine on a silver chain around her waist, a present from her grandfather. The beloved object had been customised for Helena's unique needs: instead of a pair of sewing scissors, a diminutive magnifying glass; the contents of the sewing kit substituted for the tools of an experienced lock picker. She was a handsome woman, younger than her worried countenance and flashes of grey hair, already whitening in places, seemed to suggest. Her clothes were curiously subtle, appearing to be both in the latest fashion but not flashy, as if they had been designed by an experienced seamstress to allow the wearer to enter any building, and access any situation, without looking out of place, which indeed they had been.

Eliza had to admire her cool detachment: Helena had presented the evening's entertainment to her as an opportunity for research, and that was what she was doing, while Eliza herself had started, to put it mildly, to panic.

Eliza had looked at Helena for a moment, and when she looked back towards the stage new horrors awaited her. The woman on stage was now floating in mid-air. There was no doubt: the unnatural posture of her head and limbs suggested that she was dead; but there she was, still opening and closing her darkened mouth, a monstrous attempt at communication. As the commotion behind Eliza gathered intensity, she was finally able to pose one simple question: how was the illusion possible?

'Someone in the audience is in danger,' reported the woman's aide, a short man situated close enough to the floating nightmare to receive her intermittent messages. His voice wasn't particularly strong, and he was making no special effort to project it, as if he preferred to force his audience to keep up. Or, thought Eliza, her rational mind now fully recovered, as though he were attempting to dispel any suggestion that an act, a performance, was at work. It struck her, how rational thinking seemed closely – perhaps uncomfortably – aligned to thinking cynically. The man insisted on behaving in this casual manner, as if he and the dead woman just happened to be passing through, and, touched as they were with the ability to receive messages from beyond the veil, had decided to stop and help this particular group of people. No doubt this was another trick, to add truth to the act.

Eliza had to hand it to them, the cleverness of it all. She didn't need to look around to see the conflicting emotions in every single member of the audience. They had all come seeking a miracle, looking to be touched by the inexplicable. Seeking contact. A loved one. A certainty of their wellbeing. Anything at all would do. And yet, they were stirring in their seats, repelled by the means by which this miracle was enacted.

'Someone whose name begins with the letter M,' the short man continued. 'A Maria? Yes. A Maria.' The floating nightmare, still opening and closing her dark mouth, her blackened puffed-up tongue on show, was trying to communicate an 'M'. Meanwhile her aide had now produced a handkerchief, and strived to look as surprised as the rest of them, and as repulsed. As if he himself were not in on the deception.

The name Maria lingered over the auditorium. A sudden recognition sparked somewhere at the back. A gasp, clearly audible, cutting through the silence. The commotion, already brewing, grew louder. It seemed that the woman called Maria – if indeed she was there – and those around her, her friends, family, or even those simply sitting in close proximity of the lucky winner, were coming to terms with this sudden contact with the Other World. They had come seeking this, of course: what else would induce them to part with a good portion of their weekly wages? But now that it was really happening, even by association, they would have preferred to be elsewhere. Some people were turning around, nervously considering whether to get up.

Eliza marvelled at this dichotomy. It was one of the things that Helena referred to as the 'psychology' of the sitters, of the clients, of everyone who came seeking understanding, at times when understanding was impossible to parse.

In fairness, the floating woman would have repelled anyone. Even from her position in the fourth row, Eliza could now smell her overpowering tomb-like stench. It was not surprising that even the short man was the colour of a sour lemon, and looked about ready to surrender his most recent meal to the wooden floorboards. Eliza looked at Helena again. Her eyes were on the stage, half closed, a gesture Eliza now recognised well: her mentor was trying to work something out. She looked down at her notes, then back at the stage again. Interestingly, Eliza saw that she had drawn diagrams, a pulley-activated contraption, and scribbled a couple of mathematical formulae next to it. There were arrows as well, indicating the movement of three cones of lights, reflecting from a crude square that Eliza assumed must represent a mirror. A huge question mark next to it all had been pressed against the page, no doubt indicating the frustration of the detective searching for an elusive conclusion. Eliza wondered what the numbers meant. Looking at the stage, what could Helena be trying to work out that she couldn't?

'Quiet, please! Mademoiselle needs to concentrate!'

Reluctantly, people folded back into their chairs, and turned diligently to face the stage, like children instructed by a stern professor to pay attention to the lesson. It was ironic: that was exactly why Helena had insisted that she should come tonight, knowing only too well how much Eliza despised these public demonstrations, so they could carry on studying what she called 'the Method', which seemed to include everything from the unconscious make-believe they had at times encountered, to the deliberate attempts to mislead the credulous, to what Helena rather annoyingly insisted on claiming as the 'true supernatural', which to Eliza was nothing more than a puzzle whose solution had until that point somehow eluded them both.

It took Eliza a few seconds to interpret the small chaos at the back: apparently someone, perhaps the woman about to communicate with the dead, had fainted. How quaint, she thought, and wondered cynically if this 'Maria' were not in cahoots with the two people on stage.

Once everyone had resumed their seats, and some semblance of order was restored to the proceedings, Mademoiselle Carrière went back to her business of waking the dead from their eternal slumber.

Even if Helena could work out how some elements of the performance were put together, as if she had been privy to a secret rehearsal, there were still moments, far too many, in which she had to recognise the artistry behind the proceedings. She was capable of following the logic behind the changes in the highly creative and effective lighting, of seeing which effect was deployed at which point, and why; and she could even make an educated guess as to how some of the hidden mechanisms must be operated. She had to admit it: the elevating and casting down of the sparse furniture would have appeared comic if it hadn't been used for a particularly uncanny effect. Objects seemed to float unsteadily, as if about to crash against the wooden stage. The eerie voice modulation was perhaps necessary given the setting, although Helena had witnessed far scarier performances where mediums employed child-like voices for their grimmest pronouncements, which she had found to be highly effective. To resort mid-performance to an aide, as if the medium had lost the capacity for communing with her audience, was even more so. Indeed, she fancied that she could follow the orchestration, and admire it.

Such certainties had been welcomed until now, allowing Helena a sense of security. It was comforting to possess this knowledge, to see behind the well-rehearsed spectacle. And still... She had to admit it: there were some blind spots in today's particular riddle. She wasn't solving it for its own sake: it was more than an intellectual exercise, a way of keeping herself trained, appraised of the latest fads at work in the art of deception. She was also trying to answer some questions, for Eliza, and also, crucially, for herself.

Helena had felt compelled to attend Mademoiselle Carrière's performance after hearing the extraordinary reports that circulated around London. Some of them hinted at quite incredible and eerie physical changes in the medium. She was particularly interested in observing this; the artistry at work had meant that even friends more versed in these illusions had sworn bafflement. It had been extremely difficult to secure a ticket, let alone two tickets. Even harder had been to convince Eliza to come to the theatre with her. She had to frame the whole outing as some sort of scientific experiment, which in truth it was, although Helena was curious as well. Her associate, on the other hand, seemed to be the only person in the whole of London with little or no interest in the performance. She had managed to bring her at last, and now hoped that Eliza had been at least duly entertained, with any luck even baffled. Later, once they had the chance to discuss the proceedings, probably in one of the afternoons that Helena kept free in order to instruct her protégée, she would be happy to confide to Eliza her own theories. The explanation of how such or such moment had been orchestrated by Mademoiselle Carrière's team was sure to be welcomed by the young sceptic. And yet, she had at present no idea of how she would explain some of the most unsettling moments of the evening.

In short, there were quite a few things that even she, with her ample knowledge of all things false, had not been capable of furnishing with a plausible explanation. She had no idea, for example, of how the medium on the now well-lit stage was managing to change her size, let alone to shrink her very features, which in turn made her neck look longer, as if it were gradually elongating. Helena thought of Alice in Wonderland, curiouser and curiouser, her neck opening out like a large telescope… The woman must have been a very good actress to create that particular illusion. Or was it all nothing more than a sly mixture of mirrors and intricate lighting systems? Whatever it was, the illusion that the woman was a plastic thing, a doll that was now proceeding to extend her limbs and her neck, monstrously and at will, was something that surpassed even her own ability as a connoisseur of on-stage illusionism and spiritualist fraud. The strangely grown creature, now almost reaching the ceiling, a clever play of unknown effects, shadows and plain fear, was now pointing to the back of the auditorium, ominously aiming its elongated finger at the lucky chosen woman, Maria. Helena felt Eliza shivering next to her, and she could see it in her friend's features, everything that was transpiring in the audience: admiration, uneasiness, fear.

It was becoming more and more difficult for Eliza not to gag. The stench descending from the stage was unbearable. People in the first few rows were covering their mouths and noses with anything to hand; some ladies had fainted, and others were getting up and were in the process of leaving the theatre.

'*Mesdames et messieurs*, if you please!' the short man pleaded from the stage. By now everyone was starting to get into a sort of frenzy. Although most of the members of the audience remained in their seats, it was obvious that the evening was getting out of hand, its rhythm now moving as fast as a runaway horse; as soon as someone had dared to get up and flee, their movements and demeanour had changed the mood of the theatre, a new plasticity which meant that everything was accepted now.

'*Mesdames, s'il vous plaît!*' It was clear that the short man thought his pleas would become more effective in his native tongue. *Not in London*, thought Eliza.

Then, as if on cue, Carrière mutated again, moving from the deathly pallor she had exhibited until that moment to a green hue.

'How on earth…?' Next to her, Helena could no longer contain herself. And Eliza understood that the veil had finally been broken, as well as the pretence from her mentor of being able to follow the tricks, unmask the deceitful. It was clear that Helena was as surprised by this strange chain of events as everyone around them. Eliza could hear screams now, as the lady on stage ballooned out of all proportion, as wide as the stage, with the short man exiting left in a fearful hurry that didn't bode well. Carrière was now pointing at the audience, and, around Eliza, the mood shifted once more. She could now sense pure panic. If those responsible for the spectacle did not stop it, they would start a riot. Eliza had to give credit to the French performer: she looked menacing now, with her impossibly elongated limbs, her green countenance, her cavernous diction. How did she manage all that at once? She was obviously a superior actress, worthy of a Shakespearean play. She would have made a rather fierce witch in *Macbeth*.

'Everyone! Stay calm!' A different voice, a commanding tone.

The police? At the Alhambra?

Eliza hardly believed what she was seeing. A young man advanced, dressed in the practical and sturdy brown favoured by the less wealthy members of Scotland Yard, cutting through the crowd, shouting instructions right and left. He was followed by a retinue of similarly clad gentlemen, albeit older than him, which rendered his commanding attitude even more impressive. They were escorted by at least thirty bobbies, maybe forty. It was impossible to say.

'The Jacks from the Factory are here!' someone shouted. And all hell broke loose.

Eliza could not believe it: the police were indeed raiding Mademoiselle's performance.

'Come. Now.'

Helena was getting to her feet and, amidst the commotion, directed Eliza to follow her to a wall, where she pushed until a door slid aside, cut into the theatre's décor: a panel that Helena seemed to have found miraculously; or rather, as Eliza suspected after knowing Helena for some time, that her friend must have known was there by her usual secret means. Eliza was confused. Were they hiding?

'We will see everything from here,' was all Helena would say.

See what, exactly? Eliza found herself inside the cavernous and dark labyrinth of the back of the theatre. But, within seconds, the police seemed now to have extended their octopus limbs everywhere, and they were beginning to swarm the back corridors and passages as well. From the main auditorium, Eliza could now hear a different, older voice, no doubt the young detective's second-in-command, asking for the audience's collaboration, pleading with everyone to stay in their seats; and, finally, the same handsome and powerful voice of the younger man in charge again, a voice more suited to an actor than a detective, confident and absolutely in command of the whole operation, and loudly declaring that the show was over, for everybody to remain calm, and that the whole company was to be taken into police custody for fraud.

'Damn! How on earth did *he* know?' Helena exclaimed. He? Who was this *he*, wondered Eliza. From their side lookout, Eliza could see that Helena's eyes were fixed on the young actor-detective. Presently, a bobby put an axe to the fake walls built as part of the décor, unveiling ropes and levers. Humiliatingly, Mademoiselle Carrière was still tied to one. Helena's look was difficult to parse. Angry? Tired? Or simply about to lose her temper, judged Eliza. She hoped Helena was planning to confront a small Scotland Yard army.

'Do you know him?' she ventured.

'Do I know *him*?' snorted Helena. 'Do I know *him*?' she repeated, unhelpfully. Whether she did or not, she seemed obviously put off by the mere presence of the man, imposing in his demeanour. Eliza could now see him clearly: he was tall with elongated blue eyes that seemed to end in a question mark, and expressive eyebrows. His chin was pointy and his mouth twitched as he commented on something with another of the policemen present. Eliza recognised that his attractiveness was as much due to his pleasant features, so unusual in the Yard, as to his command of the complex situation. She guessed he might be one of the many Scotland Yard men that Helena knew from before their acquaintance.

'That man, my dear, is a veritable nuisance!'

The policemen had now swarmed past their hiding place and adjacent corridors, and soon Helena found her chance to intercept him, Eliza following closely behind.

'Mr O'Neill, if you please!'

The young man turned to face them and, to Eliza's surprise, let out a long sigh, rolling his eyes under the longest strawberry-blonde lashes Eliza had ever seen on a man.

'It is *Detective* O'Neill, Miss Walton.'

'And it is Miss Walton-*Cisneros*, Detective.'

They both stared at each other for a couple of seconds, enough to make Eliza feel that they ought to get out of there before Helena landed them in police custody.

'I guess there is no need for me to ask what *you* are doing here...'

'Oh! By all means! Allow me to illuminate you, *Detective* O'Neill. I am conducting scientific research.'

The man chuckled at this.

'Miss Walton... *Cisnegos*...' O'Neill mispronounced, making Eliza flinch. Was it really so difficult for her fellow Englishmen and women to remember the correct pronunciation of Helena's surname? It wasn't as if London society was free of its Cholmondeleys and St Johns, its *Chumleys* and *Sinjuns*. Eliza hated these situations, making her feel protective towards her friend. The man was still pontificating. 'As you know, I have already had an opportunity to express in the past what it is that *I think* your research can achieve...'

'But, *Detective*, if you allow me...' Helena seemed to be trying, very hard indeed, to hold her face in a non-cynical smile. 'This is my associate, Miss Eliza Waltraud.' To his credit, Detective O'Neill smiled courteously in her direction, although he did so while keeping an eye on the comings and goings in the little theatre.

'A pleasure.' They shook hands.

'The thing is, Detective,' Eliza detected a change in Helena's tone and felt relieved: they would not end the night in a cell after all; although Detective O'Neill seemed to be expending his whole resources of patience on them, 'Miss Waltraud and I have been studying this particular performance today, and, let me reassure you—'

'What? Are you now going to say that Mademoiselle Carrière really levitates? The whole thing is a hoax and, as they are charging money, it is also fraud, plain as daylight.'

Eliza doubted the legal veracity of the man's statement, but was at a loss as to how to intervene.

'But, in this case, my observations—'

'I apologise, miss, but I really have to abandon our conversation here. I would strongly advise you to leave this to the professionals from now on.' And with that he left.

'How dare he?' Helena was incensed. 'I'll bet we have far more experience than he does in these matters!'

'And still, my dear Helena…'

'What?'

'He is probably right.'

'Eliza, pray tell me, have we not watched the same performance tonight?'

Eliza could not help it, and gave a more forceful response than she had intended: 'But the police found her crane system! We both saw it!' She refrained from pointing out that Helena herself had been drawing ropes and levers while trying to understand the performance on stage.

Helena despaired. Until recently, she had not called herself a detective, at least not openly. A network of mostly female clientele, friends, allies, built over a number of years, had made it possible for other women in need to find her, and to seek her services. All this was about to change. Helena was about to take a step she had never imagined possible with the opening of her own detective agency, a firm which would specialise in solving cases for women who found themselves in trouble of any kind. Due to her knowledge of spiritualist fraud, and her growing understanding of the supernatural, she hoped one day to be able to intercede for women who had been accused of committing fraud themselves, at least when she suspected that they were being wrongly accused. Usually, it was the female mediums who suffered from this kind of accusation. Usually, it was the majority-male Society for Psychical Research, and their close ally, the Golden Dawn, who publicly accused them. The organisation supposedly conducted scholarly research into séance phenomena, but instead was bent on 'exposing' fraudulent mediums, who – nine times out of ten – turned out to be women.

Helena's investigations had made her realise how so often women's safety, the difference between being sent to the madhouse or not, depended on how men interpreted them, read them. It wasn't so much about losing one's reputation as about losing one's freedom, and, in the most extreme cases, one's life. The zealous work of the Society for Psychical Research was clearly at fault here, with their insistence on the unreliability of female experience. But who was telling the truth, and who wasn't? Many times, it was a matter of interpretation, of who decided to look at you, of the preconceptions they used, of how they decided to frame the narrative that explained what they were seeing.

In the context of a séance, or even a performance like the one they had just witnessed, when the same men who had given testimony against a medium had paid for seeing those same marvels they did not believe to be possible yesterday, it would be considered a positive result that a woman levitated, or climbed the walls like a reptile. However, as soon as their intentions had changed, those same men declared themselves disgusted by the display of those uncanny powers.

The whole thing was profoundly unfair. The manner in which the overzealous SPR members collected huge folders of 'evidence' and 'documentation', sometimes no more insightful than the fact that a male witness voiced his suspicions... it was enough to make anyone disgusted. These old-fashioned mediums, she knew too well, at times indicated the presence of their spirit guides by manically laughing; the line between supposed 'raving' behaviour and accepted mediumship-related deportment had always been thin, and the SPR knew how to capitalise on it. Once the 'deal' was broken, and someone fell out of favour, it was a free-for-all, a wild hunt. It was so easy for those men to label a medium they did not like or who refused to play by their rules as 'mad', a trickster.

Was that what had transpired that evening? Had the SPR put the Yard on to Carrière and her entourage?

Ironically, the creation of the SPR had signalled the need to separate the fraudsters from the real thing, its remit precisely to preserve this *reality* of spiritualism, winnowing its true practitioners from the tricksters. Its mere existence, therefore, suggested a belief in the supernatural. Things had veered aside at some point, intentions had shifted, the SPR becoming a tool for its members to retain control over the occult community. No matter how well-meaning its earlier iteration had been, it was clear that it had now grown into yet another device to keep the women of the spiritualist community under control. This infuriated Helena. She had studied their reports, a fascinating and disgusting read in equal measure, which gave a chilling insight into these men's minds: the manner in which women were forced to 'perform', or 'work' subjected by the men present, who relished in physically holding down their legs and arms, four bear-like men encroaching on a tiny five-foot woman, so as to prevent any cheating, the possible activation of any supposed hidden mechanism. The practice, as extended as it was intrusive, was disturbing to Helena, a violation. Understanding these cases had led her to the opposite side of the spectrum regarding her own understanding of the paranormal. For she had to admit it: the mere recognition of fraudulent mediums implied that there were instances in which the powers these women displayed were real. And the sceptic Helena ceased to exist.

Was it really so difficult to understand that a woman may be the real thing, but may equally need to feign supernatural powers sometimes? That the supernatural was not something that could necessarily be commanded to appear exactly after supper, when the rest of the world demanded entertainment? That women like La Carrière needed to make a living, to keep warm, put food in their bellies? It seemed increasingly difficult for Helena to suggest these and other nuances of their world to Eliza. Her friend seemed to stubbornly insist on seeing everything in black and white.

On the way home in the hansom, after leaving Eliza safely in her rented rooms, Helena had some time to herself to reflect on the events of the night. She was furious at O'Neill's ignorance, and arrogance. Not only did he not understand why some measures were at times needed, even by the most experienced mediums, but, even worse, he had absolutely no desire or intention to educate himself. She thought that some hope remained with Eliza; she knew there was absolutely no hope for people like O'Neill. As far as Helena was concerned, this alone marked him out as someone suspiciously aligned to certain parties, the Society for Psychical Research coming firmly to mind. Since when did Scotland Yard storm theatres in the middle of a performance? The whole thing stank of the SPR's tactics. If the SPR and the Yard got in cahoots, from now on O'Neill, and others as ignorant as him, would continue to dictate the future of female mediums, based on little more than preconceptions and stereotyping.

And Eliza? It was becoming ever more obvious that their partnership, which, at the beginning, had seemed such a great idea to them both, was at the risk of turning sour even before they truly started. Helena feared that she should have gone to see the medium backstage after the performance, insist on acting as her advocate. But the truth was that she was unsure what she would have achieved. Tonight had been their first attempt at studying her methods and, unfortunately, she only had suspicions at this point that the act was at least in part genuine; suspicions and not enough proof, or indeed any kind of proof. True supernatural actions were much harder to confirm than fraudulent ones. She studied her notes, and realised she could not have done much for the woman. Still, should she ask the hansom driver to go back? Had they really arrested the medium, was she now in police custody? What were O'Neill's true intentions in raiding the theatre?

It did not bear thinking about, that horrid man. But what was happening to her? She felt anger after each one of their interactions, but also a strange desire to get him to understand... what, exactly? She herself was still coming to terms with this new uncanny reality becoming more and more apparent: the inexplicable existed, the supernatural was real. And it had been present in that shabby theatre. It did not matter if the medium had been suspended from ropes and levers. Other things had happened as well, inexplicable to modern science. But whether O'Neill would listen or not... And tonight, finally, Helena had realised how much his interventions and methods aligned with the SPR's.

And, as she thought this while sat in the hansom cab, she saw herself go there—

She's walking among the people in the theatre foyer, excusing herself, talking in a slow voice with someone, being conducted down a badly lit passage, facing a door, and, behind a little door, the stage, and Mademoiselle Carrière turning, floating in mid-air, a ray of light pouring from her chest, blinding the audience...

Helena opened her eyes, the hansom cab's jerking motion bringing her back. She didn't know or want to know where the images came from, what they were saying to her. She felt ill-prepared at present for this new development. She ought to be careful; this was now happening more often, these *visions* – she did not dare call them premonitions; and anyway, if they were premonitions, she had absolutely no idea what they could be foreshadowing. What she knew, beyond a shadow of a doubt, was that she could never tell Eliza about them. And she wondered, was she really going to open a detective agency with somebody she was keeping secrets from?

It took her a minute to realise that something from the vision had lingered, as aspects of dreams sometimes do; a smell, a feeling.

A noise, in this case.

Helena still could hear it, the little funeral bells, chiming their endless ominous tune, each of their peals a reminder; they had been in the vision, they were still here, in the actual world, as if showing the flimsy gossamer of reality, the volatile borderline, that separated them both.

Through the window, London. The *clack clack* of the horses on the paved road helped centre her. The world seemed unreal, she thought, as the hansom cab came in and out of the lamplight, advancing through streets and alleys where children were being born and old men were dying, at that very moment; turning corners where people were getting murdered, leaving behind taverns where women were using their wits to survive, and all that happening at the very same time, the energy of the city emanating hope, evil. And, somehow, Helena partaking of it all, sensing it all inside, for her senses were always more acute after one of these visions. She now knew how to make the most of this, if she tried very hard, of the lingering effects of her own private moment of wonder. She closed her eyes again.

She saw the sea, for some reason. Margate, perhaps, where she had spent a childhood holiday with her grandfather. She saw horses running. Women together, chanting, not just any song, but one with meaning and direction. Modern witches, in Edwardian England? Why not, she thought. And still let her mind wander even further, into those recesses that anyone would avoid, where fear resides. And then she felt it, very closely indeed: more fear, not too far off. A puddled street, violence, pain, and her mind's eye racing towards the commotion. A young girl, one street to the east, feeling lost, bewildered, frightened, beaten black and blue by a hag. With all probability, the woman who sold her every night to passing strangers. Fear always got to Helena; it was the one constant emotion her newly acquired powers of predetermination never missed.

Helena opened her eyes.

'Driver! Stop here.'

And there she went, directly onto the scene, half hidden round a filthy London corner. She was armed with her umbrella, a detachable blade shining inside it. She also carried a revolver with her at times, a fact she had never shared with Eliza. But she judged that the umbrella would suffice. Helena approached the scene decisively, umbrella up and ready to strike. Nothing was needed in the end: as soon as her tall imposing figure emerged, the old woman fled, leaving the child covered in blood and tears over a urine-stinking floor. Helena lent her a hand:

'Are you hurt? Can you stand?'

'Don't worry, miss, I am fine.'

'Do you have a place to go to?'

'Yes, my brothers are waiting for me.' And she fled. Then, after she had run for a bit, she turned, as if she had forgotten something, and shouted back:

'Thank you, miss!'

Helena sighed, and walked back to her hansom cab. She climbed onto her seat, told the driver to set off, and let tiredness take her, dozing into oblivion.

2

WALTON & WALTRAUD, INQUIRY AGENTS

15th March – Morning

The sitter was waiting for her in the conservatory, among the Japanese fans, the flowers and ferns in the jardinières. Helena's entry wasn't unplanned: the sitter had been taken through the connecting doors into the main room where the readings were conducted, and left there to wonder about the smells of the myrrh burning, the mind-clearing holy basil tea burning sweet inside her mouth. Those senses awoken, the sitter was given a chance to consider the ornamentation around her.

Helena's house was a new-build in a fashionable area on the Surrey side of London. As the clean red brick of the construction, the delicately laid front garden, the newly laid stone road anticipated, she had preferred to adopt a modern look for her décor. Brought up by her maternal grandfather, a Cambridge classicist with more penchant for accumulating dusty books than elegant vases, she had had enough of the frilled profusion of the previous century, favoured by the aunties, great-aunties and housekeepers that had kept house for the widower in succession. In quite a rebellious spirit, Helena had adopted a much more contemporary style, favouring the cream and pastel colours of the new century over the dark and heavy drapes of the last, with crawling ivy patterns covering the wall in symmetrical greenery. On the bookcases, blue and white china was mixed in merry profusion with other more exotic decorations from Helena's travels. A bust of Aphrodite, a gift from her grandfather, was prominently displayed, along with a couple of phrenology heads and an upstanding palm. On a Morris chair there hung a Spanish shawl, the only detail that denoted Helena's Andalusian heritage. It had beautiful parakeets dancing on pink flowers and among leaves. It was modern, scandalously so even: the expensive item would not have graced the shoulder of a Spanish grandee, but rather of a piquant dancer on stage. The French doors offered a vista of the large garden, and, on the line of the horizon, London emerged in a haze, its towers and chimneys pouring the eternal smoke of industry into the sky.

Had the sitter got up and wandered to the communicating sliding doors, they would have walked into a rather different scenario. The wall in the adjacent room displayed a dark and foreboding map of London, ominous with its snake-like twisted river. The map, a fresco she had commissioned nearly five years ago, was the remnants of Helena's old life. She remembered fondly when she first had it painted, how horrid it had looked to her grandfather, how much it had aided her investigations. It had turned out to become more than a fixture; it had been the beacon of an important era, an era in which she had honed her detection skills, built a not quite hidden reputation. It had had the power of making her feel as if her whole life was as twisted as the river on the wall, that she could go no further than its imaginary curves. Now that her future was fresh, new, the darkened map ought to be painted over, and she would welcome instead the leaves and flowers and trompe-l'œils that would further the impression of these rooms as an earthly paradise. But she was reluctant to do this: getting rid of it would be an important symbolic act for her, but the darkened map was far too useful in her investigations, and she was rather fond of it.

Still, most of the tools of her trade were being relocated somewhere else, the first time Helena would work outside of her own home. Her book collection had been dismantled, and some of her bookcases were now empty and had been painted over, from a dark cedar to a shiny white.

The decluttering had been a mere practicality. The missing items – comprising not only books, but also maps, reference guides, catalogues of the London Library at St James Square, the Rolandi foreign books library off Oxford Street, and the Patent Office Library, together with several editions of the red book, medical directories and registers, *Debrett's*, *Whitaker's Almanack*, as well as numerous travel guides and atlases, Ordnance Survey maps, a stenograph, and other small scientific apparatuses – had all been carefully wrapped in silks and transported in sturdy wooden crates to the brand new offices of Walton & Waltraud, Inquiry Agents. The new haunts were located in Marylebone, not too far from Helena's beloved University Women's Club, the site of so many encounters with prospective clients, a home from home where she had found perhaps less friendship than she had expected, but decidedly a common purpose with others of its members, namely the advancement of women in all areas of society.

Helena emerged now, wearing the kimono she favoured for her readings, to find the sitter in place, sipping her tea. The sitter was a woman slightly older than Helena, with carefully coiffed blond hair where some disordered white streaks shone through like rays of the moon, big blue eyes with almost white lashes, and a knowing smile. Helena welcomed her, an Andalusian peace greeting recently incorporated into her routine, the bow and light touch of her joined palms to her forehead decidedly setting the scene. She then proceeded to draw the flaming burgundy curtains, mounted over the French windows exclusively for the effect they gave, the early rays of light painting the room red through them, transforming it into a sacred and intimate space.

Every reading was now a test for Helena, but this one was somehow even more special. She offered the cards to the woman, placing them in the middle of the large round table between them. The table was covered by a colourful quilt, a present from a grateful American client. It depicted, rather pointedly, the tree of life, and the archetypal imagery consistent with the motif.

The lady separated the cards three times as instructed, and Helena regrouped them in the correct manner. She had some trouble manipulating them in her small hands; the French-produced Hermetic version of the Marseille deck that Helena had incorporated into her readings was a tall deck of thick cards. Helena then attempted her favourite spread, an old-fashioned pattern known as 'shining light in the darkness' that seemed to suffice for these occasions.

'No,' said the woman, with a smile. 'Why don't we keep it *even simpler* this time?'

Nodding in agreement, Helena drew three cards only. She sighed momentarily: the scarcity of the elements could in fact play to her disadvantage if she aimed to produce an effect. On the back of the cards, the Greek god Hermes, holding his winged staff, brought heralds from the Other World to their earthly realm.

Helena turned over the three cards, and they all appeared in their reversed form, which she immediately disliked. The *cavalier de baton*, or knight of wands; the ten of swords; and *Le Monde*, the bull, the angel, the eagle and the lion, all holding a book, one at each corner, making the world revolve.

The three reversed cards faced the sitter; Helena felt slightly dizzy looking at them upside down. The *cavalier*, reversed, lack of trust. The ten of swords, one of the fiercest cards on the deck, pushing against the flesh of the dead man that had surrounded to their power; reversed, a change in the sitter's perception, an acknowledgment of past deceptions, and a desire to move forward. *Le Monde*, reversed. When things do not go according to plan.

It was an acrid spread, impossible to sugar-coat in its dark simplicity.

And, Helena reflected, those meanings, pretty much out

of a book, would not suffice the woman in front of her. So she started modulating her breathing, allowing those signs to wander inside her, the bright colours of the deck, greens and blue and red; the images and the symbols dancing in her mind together with those meanings: mistrust, deception, acknowledging failure. Helena knew there was no point in trying to force it. Her inner eye would open, or would not.

The little funeral bells started chiming then, and she lost herself in the exercise.

The door opened further, and she saw the images, and she saw the meanings, as the story weaved itself into being in front of her eyes, a shining thread of knowledge that was telling her exactly what had happened, and what was meant to happen. Helena fell into a trance, jerked her head backwards and started reciting the words:

It's been so hard to overcome this feeling, so long has it taken you not to blame yourself for the past. You wonder if you did not know, how could you not see it coming. Didn't you, really? The force with which the betrayal crashed at you, like a wave. You knew it. You knew of its coming, eventually, and have wondered often what made you accept it for so long. When did you know that things were not entirely as you had expected? And how did you make yourself pay for those lost years?

She regained consciousness as suddenly as she had lost it, unaware of what had happened, except that she found herself a little out of breath. Aurora was watching her intently, as she straightened herself on the chair. A silence opened between them, until eventually Aurora spoke:

'Bravo! I must admit I am mystified by how deep your eye has managed to go this time. And with such a simple spread! Mind you, there is nothing "simple" about stripping a reading to the basics. But you know what I mean. This is an unquestionable improvement, my dear.'

Helena could not help a short smile. Aurora, her friend and mentor, had stopped clapping, and was now lighting a pink cigarette with a golden filter, the bleak revelations of the reading pointedly ignored.

'I am astounded,' she continued. 'What unstoppable progression. I have never witnessed anything like it, except perhaps for Crowley becoming a Magus! In a matter of a few months you are becoming more than proficient.'

'My dear Aurora,' Helena began, 'I would not presume to have made such colossal advances without your help. I was so confused when we met. Now I am finding some clarity at last.'

'Well, it is very kind of you to say. But the merit is definitely yours. You are an excellent pupil.'

'You know that I enjoy the research, and reading these books you have lent me has helped so much.'

'Oh, dear, not the books again!'

Helena looked up, a crooked smile on her face. She had not been able to restrain herself. She knew well the conversation that would ensue.

'Meaning?' she asked anyway.

'You know exactly what I mean.' Aurora blew out a white cloud of aromatic smoke. 'It is all very well to consult those tiresome guides and read the experiences of others, learning from previous card readers, blah blah blah; all the wise men and women – definitely more women, mind you – who came before you, and so on and so forth. But the *real* work, as I will never tire to tell you, is done within ourselves. The real work begins once we put all those dusty books aside, and learn to allow our inner eye to wander deeper. The symbols on the cards are only a guide, Helena – they may direct you to the right door to open, but it is you who opens it.'

Helena had a reply ready.

'You know I don't wish to challenge any of that. I know there is some truth in your words.'

'Some?'

'But you know perfectly well that I have, in the past, been rather successful by limiting myself to reading the symbols, and studying the "dusty books", as you call them.'

'Tut, tut! Not exactly. I can believe that there may have been two or three occasions when you have allowed the current of inner knowledge to direct you. That you might have reached, almost, that state of grace in which you finally let knowledge overcome the tedious interpretation. You have opened the doors on your own, I have no doubt of that. But that is only because your ability was already there; you were always meant to do this, Helena. You are finally learning to let go of the tyranny of the word and wade into the river of knowledge you were always meant to find. Those are the readings that are successful, those are the readings that bring us closer to the truth.'

There was a pause while they both drank their basil tea.

'I will even say that the power of intuition, the clarity, afforded by the cards should help you find answers in your... other endeavours. I would encourage you to ask the cards whenever you are stuck, or find yourself at a crossroads.' Helena knew Aurora was referring to her career in detection.

'I do not deny that everything is becoming... connected somehow.'

'Hmm,' Aurora made an appreciative noise while sipping the hot tea.

'But,' continued Helena, 'even if I admit that the cards are helpful at times, I still think that certain activities need to follow a "proper" method.'

'What is more proper than this?'

Helena did not reply, partly because she did not have a reply. She found incidents like the one two nights previously difficult to explain, even to Aurora; how her newly found 'intuition' had guided her, allowing her to help somebody. This went against everything that Helena had believed in only a year ago; this went against the Method. And now she found herself trying to bring together both things, but also having to convince someone who did not want to be convinced.

The two friends had one more cup of tea together, the discussion moving over well-trodden ground until it was time for Aurora to go. They agreed to meet the following day at Aurora's shop, an establishment that sold antiquities, close to the British Museum. Helena knew she had to be thankful to Aurora. It was all part of their relationship: Helena did what she was told, seeking the path of knowledge; but she still enjoyed her protestations, resisting a little. Presently Aurora left, and she was left alone with her thoughts.

But the tide was changing for Helena, that much was clear. The supernatural could not be denied any longer. Her recent experiences had opened her mind to accepting the grey areas, the liminal and the unexpected, even to the point of admitting her own abilities, even to herself. There was some power that had been striving to break free for many years, perhaps since the moment when she was a child and heard the bells for the first time, mournfully chiming as Helena's dead mother emerged from within the shadows of her nursery room. Once she allowed this memory to emerge, other feelings took over, among them the overwhelming one of drowning into the unknown. She had sought help then, and Aurora had responded. Helena's very wandering into her shop had been in itself an admission that she was out of her depth, and more than mere chance. Aurora truly believed Helena's steps had been directed there by some hidden force.

Until the previous year, Helena would have sided with the sceptic, placing herself firmly within the community of debunkers of the 'supernatural'; but the death of Victoria had thrown the whole of London into a whirlpool of dark possibilities. Then she had gone through a case, a case that had forced her to rethink her whole outlook. Still, it all felt wrong somehow; the inexplicable felt distasteful among the electric lights, motorised cars, desk telephones. Aurora had taught her to resent her static, book-led card readings, forcing Helena to abandon her usual self-imposed control. They felt stilted, untrue. She had accepted the new dogma, but not without a struggle. There had been an early reading in which she had *had* to force herself to let go. With each card, she had been trying to remember what she had read, sometimes conflicting analyses, how to understand and interpret the different symbols. It had all been too much, and she had fainted. She heard them, the little funeral bells. But something had changed. She finally understood: once all one could learn from books was processed, interiorised, it was possible to allow the mind to find the answers freely. Sure, the book-learning entered into the mix. But the mind wandering, a sort of mind travel of sorts, did it all. It was like learning a new language: at the beginning one was forced to memorise lists of words, make diagrams containing verb tenses and declension, learn new grammar rules by heart. Eventually, one could maintain a conversation without these aids, the various meanings and guidelines coming to one's help without the need to force them.

Helena now saw the cards as doors, leading towards vistas, new landscapes, sometimes beautiful, sometimes dark and menacing, where true interpretation lay, waiting to be found.

While she put away the cards after her reading to her mentor, Helena considered everything that had happened in the past few months. She had not come to Aurora merely seeking help with her cartomancy. She had been trying to come to terms with her shifting idea of the truth, how at times it had not lain in indisputably natural phenomena, but in the most unexpected places. She was trying to let go of her scepticism; but accepting the true nature of certain things was nothing if not difficult.

She did not cling onto her previous beliefs for the sake of doing so. If anything, Helena was trying to accumulate more arguments with the remnants of her resistance: she herself had someone in her life who in turn needed to be convinced; that not everything was magic, and not everything was fraud, but that indeed, most of the time it was both, or a little of each. That the truth, which was their job to uncover, was something more slippery, more in-between, instead of either one or the other.

Eliza did not approve of these theories, and had no problem in communicating her misgivings. The young woman epitomised all that Helena's method was lacking: the scientific approach, the eye on the latest inventions and developments, the understanding of the impossible or strange that already existed within the natural world. But, what to do with those things that could not be explained away with observation, testing, scientific parameters? Increasingly, it had been more frustrating to Helena how Eliza refused to let anything slip through the cracks. Their reaction to the show they had seen together, the one sabotaged by the infuriating Detective O'Neill, was a case in point. They had both watched the same phenomena, and yet their interpretations of what had happened on stage seemed to be so different as to be almost opposed. Helena could understand Eliza's reticence; but, if there was anything that she, Helena Walton-Cisneros, palmist to London society, knew about, it was the conflicting dynamics of pretence, and in particular the endless struggle between the real and the invented when performing the supernatural.

For a number of years now, Helena's real work had involved solving mysteries, mostly in London, where the majority of her clients came from, but often travelling over the south of England, East Anglia, as far as Scotland, in the pursuit of truth. The majority of these early mysteries were grounded in the cruelty of mere human beings, proving that one did not need a ghost or a goblin to stir problems. Her career had been entirely unexpected, even for her. At one time, Helena had hoped to receive an education, and had been supported in this by her grandfather. Alas, that had not ended well. Her dreams of becoming a doctor one day had been shattered, and it had been her ability for detecting that had put an end to it.

Early on, even before she had chosen detection as a possible career, she had found herself involved in the search for a missing child. And, as it happened, Helena had managed to locate the whereabouts of the child before anyone else, including the Newmarket constabulary. Faced with the raised eyebrows and bewilderment from the policemen involved in the case, from the newspapermen, even from bystanders, she had found an easy way out, a manner in which to disguise her industriousness and good brains, when the mother of the child had explained that Helena had seen where the abducted child was hidden 'in a dream', exercising some kind of crude (or, even better for a woman, innate) act of divination. Helena saw it immediately: everyone who had been involved in the case, the authorities, the constable, even the child's family and neighbours, now understood everything; there were no awkward questions put her way, and everybody was content. These things happened, especially in such rural areas, where the flimsy boundaries between superstition and the real world were made of gossamer. Everything had become very easy then, and Helena had seen a clear path ahead of her: she could help people, women in particular, whose worries were so often dismissed. She would just need to do a little bit of pretending to avoid incurring the suspicion of the police. By that time she had known that she was good at locating missing objects, solving awkward problems, deducing the truth among the lies. Now she realised this all could amount to more than a mere party trick.

Her involvement in the disappearance in the fenland town, while still a student at Girton College, had brought her into prominence with the authorities for all the wrong reasons. She was invited to leave the college, her chance of joining a London teaching hospital all but shattered. But Helena had not remained idle. She had found her way into a profession she enjoyed and was good at; or, rather, this profession had found its way into her life, as she preferred to see it. And, in a society that could not bring itself to accept, or even look kindly upon, women's professional ambitions, she had needed a plan, a sort of alibi – and so she had worked ceaselessly to gain the trust of London's society by forging a space for herself within the spiritualist community, as a cover for detection. It had been a convenient disguise, and she had always been scrupulous in not engaging in any deliberate deception.

She had limited herself exclusively to card and palm readings; the two things, she rationalised, that she could read about and learn how to perform by following a sort of method. She had not deluded herself; these were not sciences in the usual way. But, nevertheless, she had been dutiful in the perusal of her studies in both topics, and devoured every single book she could find on the subject, progressively becoming quite proficient in the understanding of the symbols in front of her. After years of study, she knew herself capable of interpreting them fairly accurately. Still, she had felt guilty at times. This also changed. She found she had what she would admit was a natural ability. She studied contentiously. But, of course, Aurora would say that she was already attuned, even then, to the deeper currents of knowledge that she was now getting to know. And Helena, in return, would have to admit that perhaps that was the case. She had fought it so hard. But wasn't it true that, at times, meanings had come to her seemingly out of nowhere? That her sitters were overwhelmed by the accuracy of her findings? *The cards never lie* was her mantra, then and now. But how did they communicate these truths? Through her dutiful study, or through her 'gift'?

The Method was nothing other than a way to reshape these new learnings; everything practical she had learnt detecting was part of it, everything inexplicable ought to be taken into account as well. Needless to say, Eliza had problems with this.

As people strove to leave behind the darkness of the Victorian era, it seemed that the new century was still not able to dispel all shadows, even after the widespread adoption over recent decades of that miracle, electricity. That energy, which had seemed magical to so many, and which was instead based on solid scientific principles, was a good example of the difficulty in breaking apart both sides of this duality in people's minds. What was magical, what was governed by science? And how to know? It still troubled her, how much human beings depended on perception, at times on their emotions, first-hand reactions to an event, without leaving any room for reason at times. During the last year and a half she had been in contact with and had the opportunity to learn a lot about this eerie new world, and even more about herself. All those years when she had been reading the cards, how much had been the carefully curated meanings, the colourful symbols, the creation of an atmosphere, the psychology that she intuitively knew how to use with the sitter in front of her…? And how much had been a true understanding, a deeper current of energy and meaning she had been able to tap into, even before she recognised it herself? The little bell that announced her dead mother all those years back, chiming again from the ether?

15th March – Later

In the sanctity of her home Helena reflected on what had happened at the Alhambra, at least before Detective O'Neill had disrupted the gathering. She had her notes and diagrams quickly drafted in the theatre in front of her. She could pinpoint several of the tricks that had been used on stage, such as use of lights and mirrors, and even levers, which could make almost any illusion possible. But of course, there had been other things that she had witnessed that she did not understand, could not understand: how had the medium elongated and contracted her limbs, for example? This, far from troubling her, as it would have a couple of years ago, made her now eager for more knowledge. How to communicate this to Eliza? How to make her understand that there was some veracity in this world beyond the veil, and that it was their duty to acknowledge and study it?

Helena gathered the tarot deck again. She placed the cards on a messy heap on top of the little round table. She moved them around, trying to empty her mind. She noticed that Aurora had left her cigarettes. Why not? She got up and lit one, the sweetness of the tobacco impregnating her insides, and sat again.

The spread would be about Eliza. She gathered the cards, shuffled them. She found and placed the four Queens in front of her, in her deck the *Reyne de Baton, Reyne de Deniers, Reyne de Coupe, Reyne d'Epée*. Wands, golds, cups, swords. Which one was Eliza for her? She let her mind wander a short minute. Her hand shot to the Queen of Wands: wise, open-minded. Not quite. Her hand moved along, this time to the Queen of Swords.

She placed the Queen in the middle, spread the cards: the one over the Queen blocking her; the one placed right below, her ultimate goal. She placed the line of four cards to the right of the central Queen, indicating the actual situation. She placed the last three to the Queen's left, indicating the path that Eliza would need to take.

It wasn't going to be easy. There would be obstacles in the way. But, somehow, looking at that spread, Helena knew that they would find common ground at the end. But for that to happen, Eliza would have to suffer.

There was sorrow, and acceptance. *La Papesse* occupied certain space in the spread as someone to respect, but also rebel against. Helena felt a bit of shame, as she saw herself occupying that space. Another prominent card for the narrative weaving was *Lamoureux*, The Lovers. Helena knew that Eliza still pined for her lost love, and she sensed the inner turmoil, the pain. Either Eliza was still suffering, or she would suffer anew.

Helena felt again as if she was trespassing, and guiltily gathered the cards.

From the beginning of their acquaintance, Eliza had possessed a serious resistance to things happening right in front of her eyes. Helena remembered the case in the Norfolk fens where they had first met, the case that had also marked the beginning of the end of her own scepticism, the case that had changed it all. Helena was sure that Eliza had been present during its resolution, when a complicated ritual, one that Helena could not have enacted alone, helped her unveil the truth. But Helena's own memories of the situation were hazy, and Eliza herself claimed not to remember anything of what had happened: a truly selective cloudiness of her recollections. Helena had the feeling that at times her friend protested too much.

'Miss Waltraud is here.'

The housekeeper's words brought Helena back into the room. Her tarot deck was still spread all over the reading table.

'Well, Dotty, don't make her wait. Please, bring her in.' But Eliza was already crossing the threshold. 'My dear, I thought we were due to meet at the agency this evening. Something must be preying on your mind to have forced the journey to the other side of the Thames.'

Eliza Waltraud's smile froze as she took in the contents of the room. She was considering the books, and the colourful Marseille tarot cards, and even the little notebook with Helena's prim annotations.

'I didn't know you were still doing all this.'

'"All this"?'

'The cards. Working with Aurora.'

Helena sighed.

'Aurora is of the opinion that my work, as you call it, has barely started.'

'Is that so?'

'There now, must we quarrel? You know perfectly well that I am only seeking enlightenment.'

'Yes, but are you? It seems very strange to look for it in some colourful painted cards.'

Helena bit her tongue. 'Is this really about the cards? Why don't you tell me what's really bothering you?'

This time it was Eliza who let go of a long sigh. She sat heavily on the ottoman.

'I have done what you asked: the meeting with the two

ladies. It has been arranged: they will come to the agency office tonight. They are scared to leave their rooms by daylight: they insist they are being followed.'

Helena knew that doing this had been truly difficult for her friend.

'Thank you.' As soon as the words left her mouth, Helena saw that something was still bothering Eliza. 'What else is troubling you? You can tell me.'

It looked as if now it was Eliza's turn to bite her tongue. However, after a moment of uncertainty, she spoke.

'Please, don't take this the wrong way.'

'I won't! You can say anything to me. We are partners, fifty-fifty.' Even as she said it, Helena could feel the weight of the lie. Eliza's family history was complicated, and she had not been able to contribute much to their common enterprise. What was more, the only one with real experience in detection was Helena. However, she was being sincere. Meeting Eliza had been providential, and had shown her at once what her method was missing: the modern take of science. In brains, and in quick understanding, and in proposing alternatives that half the time would not have been obvious to their clients, Eliza was her equal, if not her superior.

'Can you please explain to me again why we are seeing these two women?'

'This is an important case, Eliza.'

'In what way?'

'Well, for once, they obviously need our help. Did you have a chance to read the article that I gave you?'

Helena meant a succinct page in the spiritualist monthly *The Open Door* that had made Miss Moberly and Miss Jourdain's adventure, or incident, infamous, known far and wide. She passed over a leather folder, her casebook, containing the main pieces of evidence, cuttings and notes about the case. Eliza glanced again at the account as reported by *The Open Door*:

A WALK INTO THE PAST – The Extraordinary Case of the Women Who Saw The French Revolution More than 100 Years After It Happened

———

Two women tourists walked into the gardens of Versailles Palace in 1901, where they found themselves looking at scenes from the Versailles of 1789. The beautiful Marie Antoinette was painting in the gardens. They were witnesses to a past age.

From Our Special Correspondent. Oxford.

⌒

BAFFLING CHAPTER!

The Amazing Incident occurred to two English women. Their experiences form one of the most baffling chapters in the history of psychic phenomena. They are Charlotte Elizabeth Moberly, daughter of the late Bishop of Salisbury, and for 10 years principal of St Hugh's College, Oxford, and Miss Eleanor Jourdain, her deputy. Miss Moberly, whom I saw in her house in Oxford, explained: 'We travelled to Paris,' she said, 'as tourists, and one afternoon went to see Versailles. Near the little Trianon we came upon the extraordinary sights and sounds we now know belonged to the 18th century. Beyond a queer sense of oppression, we noticed nothing extraordinary. Only when we returned to the spot did we realise how different everything was. We remembered seeing a bridge over a ravine. There is no bridge or ravine in 1901, but there was, we have discovered, in 1789. We saw soldiers. And their uniform, we found, was the uniform of 1789. We had seen a grotto, and again there is no grotto in 1901, but in an old map we found the grotto was marked. In the garden I had seen a woman painting. Now I am certain it was Marie Antoinette.'

Professor John Woodbury, new president of the Society for Psychical Research, Sir William Barrett, its chairman, and Sir Oliver Lodge, all have testified as to the lack of verisimilitude in the details put forward by the ladies.

Helena hoped that Eliza would start to get an idea of the two women's predicament once she read of the involvement of the Society for Psychical Research. Indeed she had:

'I understand that the SPR is trying to discredit the ladies. But, why us?'

Why us indeed, thought Helena. It would be difficult for her to convey all her hatred for the SPR if Eliza did not feel the same way. She wondered if her dislike for the organisation was misplaced. Still, she ought to try.

'That article was the first. The first planted seed, we can say. This one is from the *Oxfordshire Weekly News*, less than two weeks later.' Helena passed over another document. The mocking was merciless:

> One wonders, in view of such fantastic scenes, exactly what the two ladies had for dinner the night before – the heaviness of French cuisine having been an unremitting problem for the delicate English tourist of the fairer sex.

'You can see it, crystal clear. Once the SPR threw the tiniest speck of doubt over their experience, it was a free-for-all: Miss Moberly and Miss Jourdain risk becoming a laughing stock, thanks to our dear friends in the SPR.'

'I see that. But again, what I fail to see is why any of this is our problem.'

Helena could not believe what she was hearing. Still, she assumed that Eliza had not made the connection clearly in her head.

'Eliza, my dear friend. Surely you can see. These two ladies are connected, at the highest possible level, with female education in this country. Oxford, for goodness' sake. If there is even the slightest speck of doubt about their word, let alone their judgement – or if you want me to be melodramatic, their sanity – it is not only they themselves who are in trouble, but the whole cause of female education as well.'

'In that case, don't you think that they should not have put themselves in such a precarious position? Why on earth did they speak publicly about this?'

Eliza was right. It did sound like the women were somehow seeking recognition for their adventure.

'I am just not suré we should meet them,' continued Eliza. 'Why start the agency by aligning ourselves to this kind of publicity?'

'We will be discreet in our investigations. And what if there is a perfectly normal explanation as to what happened to them after all, one that does not mean they are necessarily lying?'

By the time Eliza left she seemed, if not convinced, at least a little happier. Helena herself did not know what to think, or even if she was doing the right thing after all – what Helena had not shared with Eliza was her appetite for this kind of adventure, for debunking hoaxes, for investigating cases where the lines between the real and the unreal were murky, and her hope that their detective agency would specialise one day in looking precisely into this kind of occurrence. Her business partner would not have understood.

Interlude

They picked her up in a hansom cab, Samuel and Moina Mathers, accompanied by a young man whom they presented as Édouard. Moina explained he was in Paris to consult the Comte d'Ourches's ten-thousand-book library on magic. Philothée was instantly intrigued by this statement, but Moina assumed she preferred to discuss the new clothes she was wearing that her husband had obtained for her. The talk about the books and this mysterious library stopped. Suddenly, Moina turned to Édouard:

'Pray tell me, is it true that le Comte's house is filled with broken furniture from spiritualist levitations?' The young man laughed, but said he had not seen anything to confirm that statement. He and Samuel Mathers started an agitated discussion about the benefits of Kabbalah and magic, defended by Mathers, over occult medicine and alchemy, defended by the younger man, while Moina ingested some Russian balm, the newest fashionable drug among the most elegant ladies.

Philothée was by now no stranger to these exchanges. Acting as secretary to Moina and her husband, as well as serving as their conduit with *le patron*, she had wandered the city transporting books, letters, delicate ornaments wrapped in shreds of paper, hailing hansom cabs between their new address at the suburb of Auteuil and the Studio, buying *Hashish d'Orient* from an apothecary on the Rue de l'Ancienne-Comédie for the rituals, or collecting occult objects from *antiquaires*. She was used to the large paintings of Egyptian deities that decorated the Auteuil villa, or at least she was not intimidated by them any more, and was fully conversant with the couple's ongoing strategy to bring the 'Cult of Isis' to the masses; she and Moina had been working hard on the performance that the Matherses would soon bring to the Théâtre de la Bodinière. Mathers and his wife would appear in full regalia – white robes with leopard-skin capes, thick gold bracelets and conic hats symbolising life purified from above, all these put together by a Leonie ecstatic to be included, whereas *le patron* had helped them secure the theatre. They would invoke the goddess, lotus in hand, while a young woman in a long white robe gave herself with passion to the Dance of the Four Elements. The dancing, the performance, was an inescapable part of the ritual.

Putting everything together had meant weeks and weeks of exhausting work, and tonight was meant to be a well-deserved treat. Philothée noticed how Moina's smiling face went between her own and young Édouard, now passionately arguing in favour of mesmerism, Mathers for once agreeing with him, and she understood something: Moina had been thinking of her when she had invited him. Sadly, Philothée thought he looked like a toad.

After these months, and all her comings and goings in her endless working hours, she had also got to know the city better. They were not far away from the racy atmosphere of the Chat Noir, the conflation between the Rue Victor Massé, the Boulevard de Clichy and the darker corners of the ninth arrondissement, where one ought to be thankful if a night out like this one did not bring something like syphilis as an unwanted souvenir.

Eventually they arrived at their destination, and Philothée felt a shiver. She was now used to outings with the Matherses not following their expected patterns, but this was something else. The door of the place where they were going to have dinner – it could not be called a 'restaurant' – was framed by two skeletons holding scythes, completely painted in black, and the windows were also shut with black-painted wooden boards.

'Welcome to the Cabaret of Death!' announced Samuel Mathers. Édouard descended from the hansom, and did not look back to help her. She made her own way down, Moina coming at once to lock arms with her.

'This should be fun!' she piped up.

Philothée had heard about these places, but she had never been to one. They crossed the threshold to find tables and chairs, and people animatedly chatting, and drinking, and eating, a scene that would have made one think that they were in some kind of eatery. Albeit one decorated with skeletons and skulls, a mountain of them covering one of the walls, chandeliers made with bones, and doors into the deepest recesses of the place made to look as the gigantic open mouths of fantastical creatures, their pointy teeth climbing down from the door frame, almost grabbing the tips of their hats. But when she looked more closely, Philothée saw that the tables were not tables, but coffins. She was by now used to her bosses' eccentricity, but this was a bit too much, even for her curious mind. It was not the first time she had felt this way; but she knew Leonie thought it a great honour, and she was handsomely paid.

'Come! Come!' She followed Moina, who was indicating a table, or coffin, in a corner, where several people were already sitting. As soon as they were settled, wine and beer flowed around, followed by a plate of strawberries, of all things. They were shiny, sticky. Two girls in front of her shared one in a long kiss, one of them pretending to faint, and everyone laughed.

'The strawberries are bathed in ether,' somebody explained. She quickly put the strawberry she had taken back. She might try one later. After she had sat picking at the food for a while, for she had lost her appetite, Moina came to talk to her again, about moving to the house in Auteuil.

'It will be so much more efficient, for all of us!' It was a well-rehearsed argument, and Philothée was running out of excuses. She had tried to argue that her aunt was elderly, and needed her around. But this had only meant that the Matherses had had a talk with a mortified Leonie, who had assured them she would be very happy indeed to see her niece settled with them. 'You could catalogue our books!' It was nothing if not very tempting.

Later that night, the party found themselves in another hansom, this time in the company of the two girls who had shared the strawberry. They took the place of young Édouard, whom they had lost in the action, leaving him in animated conversation with a member of the Society for Esoteric Studies at Rue de Trévise, where most Masonic fraternities had in recent months coalesced around the Librairie du Merveilleux bookshop. Édouard and his interlocutor had been screaming at each other their competing visions for a materialist world of mass production and mechanisation, Darwinian evolution and geology's implosion of the biblical time frame: they both agreed a new Hermetic view was needed, 'High Science, that is to say, Hermetic Magic!'; what they could not agree upon, alas, was what form of Hermeticism should bring this about, as they both thought their own version was the one that needed to be chosen. It was a discussion as old as time itself, or so Philothée thought, as she had heard it under different guises on many an occasion in the past few weeks, animating almost any meeting.

At some point she noticed that the hansom was not going in the direction of her home as she had expected at this time of night, and that indeed it had passed the appropriate turning.

'We have gone past my aunt's apartment,' she said.

'You are coming with us tonight, *ma cherie*,' announced Moina. Samuel smiled, and the girls giggled, sharing some Russian balm with their hosts.

The hansom cab stopped in a street next to the Seine, and they all alighted. Samuel directed them to an unassuming door, which he opened with his own key. There was an overpowering stench, and the women covered their mouths and their noses. Samuel went into the dark hole, and they descended after him into a rough and wet stone corridor, as narrow as yet another coffin. They could only hear the flicker of fire, and follow its yellow light, warm and inviting. There was nothing else down there. It was as black as death.

It was a first time for this as well, thought Philothée as she descended into the catacombs. For a few minutes, they existed only within that cone of light: everything ahead of them, and behind them, dark as a tomb. But at some point there were faded noises and chants, not dissimilar to those in Leonie's 'religious' group, and a light flickering further ahead, its unsure orange glow suggesting a path.

Following it they arrived into a small circular opening, where five or six other people were already gathered. They received the newcomers with a curt nod. They were given the choice of sitting on some rocks by the wall, or of standing and being part of the Mass. The girls immediately said they wanted to be a part of it, and Moina hugged them, and said they ought to prepare. This 'preparation' consisted of donning a white robe and injecting something that Moina had brought with her inside her gold-plated syringe. Philothée went over to the circular wall and sat. Then she noticed somebody else, lingering in the dark corridor that had led them there.

She stood up and moved quickly along the circular wall. The dull figure was a white, lifeless shadow crawling in the darkness. She could not see more than the white line getting ahead. With a jerk, the whitish robe moved up, climbing up the wall to the corner where it met the ceiling, making a guttural sound all the while. Philothée closed her eyes and shook her head. It must be a trick of the light. Behind her, the members of her party chanted. Ahead of her, a humanoid figure was jerking and stretching their limbs and head unnaturally, and moving like a lizard on the wall.

She looked back: everyone in her party was now deep into their chant, talismans in hand. She was on her own. Whether there had been somebody there or not, she could do nothing for them. She would indeed get lost forever if she was to venture into those tunnels alone. She had been probably mistaken anyway, she thought. It was too dark down there. It must have been a trick of the light.

3

TWO FEMALE SCHOLARS

London, 15th March – Evening

Miss Moberly and Miss Jourdain arrived at the appointed time at Walton & Waltraud. The office was not yet completely organised, with the remnants of painting and decorating jobs still waiting to be cleared by the entry hall and the landing. The rooms smelled faintly of wood varnish and of the tepid gas fire that had been installed a week earlier. Several wooden crates, containing most of Helena's research collection, were lying around in labyrinthine profusion. Despite the chaos of books and papers waiting to be organised, most of the shelves were still empty. They had recently installed a modern 'oil-can' – a Stromberg Carlson candlestick telephone, a much more versatile machine than the wooden boxes that hung from walls all over London. This kind could be placed directly on a desk. But it had not come cheap.

Helena considered the rooms around her. It still gave her a small thrill to turn the key and enter the reception area, moving though the wide corridor, on one side a wall composed mostly of windows that let in some scant light from a back alley, on the opposite wall the newly fitted library, this corridor leading into the main office, where two desks sat facing each other. Aspidistras had been carefully placed to give a welcome feeling, and paintings were waiting to be hung on the walls.

A muffled rustling sound announced another's presence. It could only be one person, no one else yet being in possession of a key.

'Eliza?'

'Here.'

Eliza emerged from the shadows at the back of the office, her dishevelled low bun and new fringe a welcome sight; Helena could not have abided a ghost in her new ultra modern offices. Still, she could not help but notice that her friend was a bit paler than usual. Eliza did not say how long she had been there, and Helena did not ask.

'It's finally coming together.'

'It is nice, yes. Although that daunts me a little.' Eliza chuckled, pointing at the crates with books and archival material. It had ended up being rather more than either of them had expected. Helena was glad that the awkwardness of their previous conversation seemed now behind them. She thought it was a good moment to explain her idea of looking for a collaborator, someone who was more than a secretary, who could also do some cataloguing and archival work for them as well as light office duties.

'Perhaps even research. It will be wonderful to have someone back here, gathering information for us, so we can concentrate on making our enquiries.'

'That is a wonderful idea! However, I don't think it will be easy to find someone fulfilling such specifications… That look.' Helena was smiling, and had started casually flicking through a box of files. 'You already have found someone?'

'I still need to meet her formally. But yes, an American lady. I understand she arrived recently to the country, and sought employment in one of the antiquarian bookshops on Cecil Court, not successfully, I am afraid. Before she came to England she worked in the New York Society Library.'

'Impressive! How did you come to know about her?'

Helena took a moment in replying.

'Mutual acquaintances. I suppose the rare books world and the spiritualist community do on some occasions collide.' She felt it was not the right time to mention that it was Aurora who had told her about Miss Jocasta Webster. One more secret she was planning to keep from her partner, to add to the others.

At that point the ladies they were expecting arrived and were duly welcomed into the main room. Two chairs had been procured from a stack in the small room near the entrance, where they were waiting to be distributed around the rooms, some destined to sit in front of the desks, all in general mismatching each other. The ladies were invited to sit down, while two more chairs were placed opposite them for Helena and Eliza.

During the awkward arrival, the procuring of the chairs, and the first few exchanges of conversation, Helena took a moment to consider the two ladies. They were both of short stature, middle age, and what society usually defines as 'respectable'. Helena, however, was trained to look further. One of them was carrying a reticule slightly longer, heavier-looking, and definitely squarer than the usual ladies' bag, and Helena recognised immediately, in kinship, that the woman did not leave her rooms without carrying a book or two about her person. The other lady had heavy ink stains on her old-fashioned lace gloves, although apart from that the two women were the very image of neatness. One of them was wearing a pair of glasses on her nose, and the other had her own hanging from her neck. They also looked slightly more fashionable than teachers, an air of prosperity that Helena recognised from Oxford and Cambridge. The visitors' pale countenances, sign of a life spent in libraries and study rooms, glimmered in contrast with the darkness in the office's unfinished corners. After the introductions were made, Helena felt for the first time the thrill of receiving visitors at last at Walton & Waltraud, Inquiry Agents, all the previous moments of doubt that had pried into her mind in the last few hours vanishing as if by magic.

'We are so happy to welcome you both,' Helena began, 'Miss Moberly, and Miss Jourdain. Can we offer you some refreshments? A cup of tea? Or a sherry, perhaps, judging by the hour.'

The two women looked at each other. One of them, Miss Jourdain, offered a shy reply:

'Please, I am Charlotte, and this is Eleanor,' said the elder of the two, smiling. 'And thank you, it would be nice to have a cup of tea, if that is convenient,' she said, signalling the chaos around them. Eliza got into motion, and headed towards a little room adjacent to the reception area, where the usual materials for producing small meals and refreshments were kept.

'Please make yourselves comfortable. Miss Waltraud – Eliza – will return momentarily with the tea,' said Helena. And then: 'I apologise for the state of the place. We are not yet open for business, not as such. I am afraid you find us at a very particular moment, with things almost finalised, but not there quite yet. In fact, you are our very first clients. Thank you so much for coming all this way to see us.'

'Oh! We are honoured.'

'However…' started Eleanor, unsure. 'Excuse us, but we were told that you had… rather long experience solving mysteries. I hope I haven't offended you.'

'Not at all. Yes, that would be correct. I have been "solving mysteries" for a few years now. But people usually came to me by recommendation. This will be the first time that I have an office dedicated to this.'

'I see. Well, I am sure we are exceedingly grateful for your assistance, and hope that you will be able to help us.'

'I certainly hope so.'

Even with the atmosphere visibly more relaxed, and the ladies' mood considerably improved after the arrival of the tea, nonetheless the usual pleasantries did not seem to extend to making conversation. The two ladies looked tentatively around them, as if unsure of what they were doing there. Helena felt that she needed to say something else: it looked as if they were not going to tell their story, unless prompted. Helena knew this behaviour very well. Sometimes, even people who sought help still needed a nudge to let go of their fear. Besides, after their public humiliation, the two women had reason not to trust them, or anyone else for that matter.

'Since we have already ascertained that you are our very first clients, may I ask, how did you come to know about us? We haven't even gone public, as they say.'

The ladies looked at each other, unsure. Eventually, Charlotte offered a rather unexpected reply:

'We have... a mutual acquaintance. Your grandfather and I met a few years ago, while on holiday in Switzerland.'

'Oh! Goodness, that is certainly unexpected.' Another thing to thank her grandfather for, thought Helena. The list was becoming long: after he had helped handsomely with their costly new premises, he was now sending clients their way.

'We reconnected not so long ago. He came to Oxford to give a lecture recently.'

Miss Jourdain gave a short account of this encounter, a college garden party, where croquet had been played and lemonade consumed. Helena privately thought how happy she was to have escaped the life of academia; although, if she were to be honest with herself, sometimes she still felt a pang. Had she had the chance to finish her studies, she would have worked as a doctor as her primary occupation, but nonetheless she had always imagined that she would have also taught other young women. In a way, wasn't that what she was doing with Eliza, passing on whichever little knowledge she possessed to help others? What would young women need to know in order to become detectives? she wondered. What would a detection school for ladies entail? It wasn't an entirely fanciful idea; perhaps it wasn't so hard to imagine such a prospect. Who knew what awaited them both beyond the horizon.

The tea had been brought in on a tray, which became a small auxiliary table as Eliza dextrously proceeded to unlock four little legs. Tea and milk and sugar had been procured to everyone's taste, and the ladies visibly relaxed after a second cup. Would they be willing to confide in them more now, Helena wondered.

'Thank you very much for the tea, Miss Waltraud, Eliza.'

Eliza was quiet; it was obvious that she was going to leave Helena to take the lead. As they had not talked to each other yet about how the dynamics of their partnership would unfold, Helena was relieved.

'We have been of course following the – rather unusual circumstances surrounding the incident,' she offered. 'I am afraid I am still struggling to understand. Could you perhaps explain it to us a little bit further?'

'We are not sure how to start,' Eleanor said, 'to tell you the truth.'

'Why don't you explain to us exactly what happened to you at Versailles, in your own words?'

The ladies exchanged glances.

'It was last summer, so quite a few months ago. We had travelled to Paris for a short holiday, and decided to spend an afternoon visiting Versailles.'

'And what happened there?'

Charlotte put up her chin in a clear defiant gesture.

'We saw Marie Antoinette.'

'You mean you saw a ghost, perhaps?' offered Helena.

'No, I am afraid that it is rather more complicated than that... We *think* we travelled in time.'

Helena heard Eliza humming next to her. It was a small sound, almost imperceptible, but there nonetheless. Helena thought she knew what it signified. She made a mental note: in the future, they ought to debrief before seeing a client in order to show a united front. She hoped the ladies had not detected the doubt implicit in such a noise.

'Miss Walton, Miss Waltraud. We know how this sounds.'

'Please, you can be honest with us. In fact, we need you to be honest with us. How did this... journey into the past occur? Did you suddenly find yourselves in the past, or did you walk there, or did you cross a door of some sort, perhaps?' Another sound from Eliza, connected to this last suggestion, that Helena could not exactly place. Why was she not quiet? They risked losing their very first clients. 'And, more importantly, how did you return to the present?'

'Perhaps we ought to be a little more precise. We did not actually step *into* the past... rather, we looked into it,' explained Charlotte.

'Exactly! As if through a painting, or as if we were seeing it in a toy theatre,' piped in Eleanor.

'It all happened... in a quiet way.' It certainly was a curious remark. Helena moved her head slightly, inviting Miss Moberly to expand it. 'We were walking in the Trianon gardens. Have you been there, Miss Walton?'

'Once, a long time ago. I was a child, travelling back from Spain. We stayed a few days in Paris. I have been back many times to Paris, but haven't made it back to Versailles.'

'Well, the profusion of bushes make it almost impossible to move around, to see ahead. Everything seemed normal to us; but, at the same time, there were some changes, almost imperceptible ones, so small—'

'Changes that we both felt,' concurred Eleanor. It was clear that they were used to talk in this manner, finishing each other's sentences, or rather completing each other's thoughts.

The women went on to explain in this manner, alternating who explained what, how the light had suddenly become duller. Another humming sound from Eliza. Another sign of something that Helena could not place. She had to intervene.

'Eliza, please, would you mind terribly taking notes? I trust there is a pad somewhere.'

Eliza obediently got up and started rummaging through the heaps of materials on one of the new desks. She returned momentarily with a pencil and a fresh blank notebook.

Helena saw Charlotte's expression change, frowning now, as if she was looking for the exact words. The lady twitched on her chair, and became more animated, as she strived to convey the oddity of what had happened. Helena could imagine her displaying a similar demeanour while teaching a lesson.

'Suddenly, it looked as if we weren't in a real garden anymore, but a garden in a painting, hanging on the wall of a gallery,' she continued. 'The light became dull, and it all looked greyer, somehow. Do you know those painted decorations they use in the theatre? Everything ahead of us now looked like that.'

'You suddenly had the impression that, if you extended your hand, you would just touch a stage decoration,' Eleanor ventured. 'One that had been used in many plays, completely drained of colour.'

'Exactly!' commented Charlotte. This exchange seemed rehearsed to Helena, as if it had been repeated a number of times, and learnt by heart. But that didn't mean anything suspicious: she imagined that the ladies had spoken many times in the past few months about what had happened to them.

'I can understand the place becoming... duller. And a number of things can explain that. You just mentioned the change in the light,' started Helena. 'What made you think that you were looking into the past.'

'Well, we saw people, and buildings that are not there.'

'People?'

'Yes, Miss Helena. Dressed in a manner that did not make sense, until we found reproductions of the old uniforms of Marie Antoinette's private guards. Then they were all there.'

'The lady dressed in old-fashioned clothes, and the soldiers, who looked like something out of a play.'

'Exactly, then it all made sense.'

'And once we checked old maps, and old guides, we could locate the strange building and the bridge we had seen behind them as well.'

'A window had been opened in front of us, Miss Helena,' put in Charlotte.

'What we had in front of us wasn't our world, or rather our time, anymore. It looked like a half-finished sketch, half-formed shapes and figures. Unreal. Not proper. Not here and now,' concluded Eleanor firmly.

'I see.' They were all silently considering this last exchange. Whatever had happened to the ladies, it was clear they were not lying. And they believed implicitly in the explanation they themselves had given to their experience. And yet, a window into the past… Helena could only guess at what Eliza was thinking.

'Pray, tell me,' continued Helena. 'Even if you were looking into the past, somehow, what makes you think that the lady you saw was Marie Antoinette?'

'We recognised her later on, from one of Vigée Le Brun's famous portraits.'

'It was clearly the same woman, but dressed unexpectedly. Dressed like a washerwoman – no, dressed like a rich lady would as a washerwoman.'

'It sounds confusing, I know. But, you see, Marie Antoinette used the Petit Trianon to play at being a farmer's wife! And she did pretend to wash little items of clothing and so on.'

'Yes, exactly. She played at being poor, and then shouted, "Let them eat cake!" All very sad, if you ask me.' It was the first time that Eliza had spoken, and the other three women looked at her.

'Very well,' continued Helena. 'What happened then?'

'We simply continued walking. It was all very unpleasant; we could not find the path. And then, it was suddenly there.'

'We pressed on, until we saw a group of tourists.'

'Everything was back to normal. The sun was shining again. The grass was green, not greyish. Our adventure had only lasted a short amount of time. No more than ten minutes.'

'I see. And what did you do once you were back in England?'

'Why did you go public?' Eliza cut in. Helena would need to have a conversation with Eliza. She was trying to get to the same question, but her protégée wasn't being very delicate in her approach. Interviewing clients, witnesses, even suspects at times, was half the battle. It needed to be done properly: there was an order, and a manner in which people felt themselves opening up to you or not. Pushing them down the negative path was the last thing they needed.

'All we wanted was to conduct a scientific investigation, Miss Eliza,' responded Charlotte, rather defiantly. 'That is why we tried to involve the SPR. But they dismissed our story.'

Still, dismissed would have been enough – why ridicule the ladies instead? Helena suspected that, had they been *Mr* Moberly and *Mr* Jourdain, their claims would have been taken much more seriously.

'And what do you expect us to do?' Again, Eliza was leaving delicacy on the doorstep, preferring instead to get straight to the point. Helena intervened:

'What my associate means to ask is whether you would like to hire our services to help you find the truth, or to prove that you were right. And, let me tell you, we will be exceedingly happy to assist with the first, but I am not sure we could do so with the second. The reason, you see, is simply that... not that we don't believe you, heavens, no! Only that there are many reasons why you may have encountered what you encountered, some of which may not be aligned with the explanation of... opening a window into the past, or experiencing some... uncanny distorted-time experience?' Helena said this looking directly at Eliza. She was trying to find a scientific idiom to discuss the incident.

'It's called a time-slip,' put in her protégée. 'A small distortion of time, losing time and not knowing how, for example. Or... this.'

'A time-slip, thank you, Miss Eliza!' beamed Eleanor.

'Once we start investigating,' continued Helena, 'we cannot anticipate what it is that we are going to discover. I cannot, from the onset, simply "agree" with your view of the events. I can only try to find the version of events that sits most closely with what really happened. And it may be possible that you will not like what we find.'

She felt Eliza visibly relax next to her.

'Miss Helena, if I may. Let me reassure you there. Whether we saw Marie Antoinette or not, I am sure you understand that, at this point, that is the least of our considerations. Our main difficulty now is the reaction of the SPR. We approached them as fellow scientists. Who would have anticipated such vindictive behaviour on their part?' Helena was vigorously nodding now, as Miss Charlotte voiced her own feelings. 'They at first tried to ridicule us, but now they have turned openly hostile.'

'You must understand,' said Eleanor, 'it has not been easy for us to achieve our professional goals. Charlotte here, she is very modest, but she happens to run one of the few Oxford colleges for ladies. I myself am proud to be her deputy. Our reputations are at stake; perhaps too the reputation of the institution we represent.'

'We were betrayed. There was what you might call… a leak, you see. We reported our incident to the Society for Psychical Research – in confidence, you understand – in the perhaps naïve expectation that they would help us uncover the truth. I am afraid that the papers got hold of the story, and they are of course misreporting everything. We need to set the record straight.'

'As scientifically as possible.'

It was impossible to know what Eliza thought, but all of this resonated with Helena deeply. Her own dealings with the SPR did not leave room for doubt: the society was determined to undermine any report that came from a woman, and to fight ferociously for their dominance of the occult scene. Scoring a hit off the chair of an all-female college master and her deputy, striking a blow at their credibility or reputation, would be an excellent opportunity for the SPR to re-establish their distorted idea of the status quo. Helena looked briefly at her partner. Eliza gave a slight but definite nod.

'Very well. It would then be most helpful if you could provide us with a full account of your experience. Would you be willing to put something in writing for us?'

The two ladies exchanged a singular look. One of them extracted a couple of pages from a little case that rested on the floor between their chairs. It was a sensible leather file case, of the type that writers use, and closely resembled the ones used by Helena as casebooks. Eleanor passed the pages over to Eliza.

'These are our testimonies. We wrote them separately, not looking at what the other put down, not talking to each other in advance.'

'A very sensible, scientific way of doing things,' approved Eliza.

'Thank you,' said Helena. 'May we make copies to incorporate into our casebook? And do you mind if I ask you a few more questions?'

'Keep the notes; we have made other copies ourselves. And please, ask your questions.'

'Perhaps the most obvious one, is to know if either of you have ever experienced anything that could be classed as…'

'Paranormal?' asked Charlotte.

'Well, yes.'

'Well, one of us must admit that she possesses… some unexplained skill in premonition, if one can put it in an idiom we can all understand. But she… Well. I am talking about myself. I can assure you I have tried very hard to ignore them all my life. My family is of Huguenot descendancy, you see.'

'Whereas I am the seventh daughter of a seventh son,' said Eleanor. 'My mother and grandmother were true Scots, and they both reported a similar gift to my friend's here, together with visions of things that eventually came to pass to both of them, to our family in fact. My family has always been sensitive to ghosts and apparitions, but at the same time, we have always tried to keep an inquisitive, scientific mind, and not let ourselves be overly excited by any of this nonsense.'

'So you are both believers and non-believers, if I can put it that way,' said Helena. 'You both have experienced things that cannot be easily explained, but at the same time have tried to rationalise them, or if you can't do that, ignore them.'

'My dear, we both fear the occult terribly!' started Charlotte. 'We take as many opportunities as possible to preach against occultism to the world. It is morally corrupt, they prey on the weak and the vulnerable, and, if they were to be studied, they would probably be the result of some kind of physical manifestation we hardly comprehend at present.'

'Basically,' interjected Miss Eleanor, 'we do not trust stories of apparitions and paranormal phenomena, and in fact they awaken a singular distaste in both of us.'

'Which is why we are both unimpeachably reliable witnesses, as must surely be clear. Though, we both do share one particular interest with these... occult societies.'

'What is that?' asked Helena.

'Mesmerism.'

Helena's heart sank, and she wondered if Eliza was going to make another dismissive noise at this; she knew well her associate's position on mesmerism. Eliza gave no credit to the 'science', which suggested an invisible fluid impregnating the universe, one that could be manipulated to cure certain diseases; she, in fact, did not believe it a science at all. Were the two sensible ladies in front of her prepared to believe in something like that?

Helena felt she had all she needed for the time being. It was time to end the interview. She stood and offered a smile. 'I thank you both for coming, and for your written testimonies. We will be in touch. Eliza, I was wondering if you would be so kind as to escort Miss Eleanor and Miss Charlotte back to their hotel.'

Helena gestured to the main door. Eliza got up immediately, but the two ladies hesitated.

'Is there a problem?' asked Helena.

'Well, you see, we think we have been followed here. In fact, we think we may have been followed for some days now.'

'We can leave using the service staircase. Helena, I trust we have a key to that side of the building?' asked Eliza.

'Certainly. Let me fetch it.'

Helena went towards the new cabinet built below the shelves in the main office, and found a metal hoop thick with many keys of different sizes. After procuring what they needed, Eliza and the two academics got up, but the ladies still seemed to hesitate.

'I assure you both it is safe to leave this way. And Eliza will make sure that no one is situated at that entrance of the building.' Helena felt happy to have trained her associate in the basics of surveillance, but also knew from experience that their adversaries were usually not so incredibly thorough as to cover all possible exits. Women, underestimated at each turn. However, the ladies were still not moving.

'There is something else, Miss Helena.'

The ladies were exchanging glances now, obviously considering whether they could trust them with a further piece of information. Helena sighed.

'Miss Jourdain, Miss Moberly. This partnership is not going to work if you are not entirely open with us. I assure you, you can trust us.'

'Very well. But I am not sure at all how to explain it,' Eleanor said. The two ladies exchanged worried glances once more.

'The thing is,' Charlotte began, and they both resumed their seats. 'I fear the SPR is not the main problem, but the *visible* problem.'

'I am not sure I follow.'

'Well, you see, they have taken a public lead in discrediting us. But they are not the main organisation that has harassed us.'

'Right after our incident, we got an invitation to attend a meeting, here in London,' Eleanor elaborated. 'We had not yet made the Versailles incident public, you see. This meeting, which turned out to be something very different indeed, took place on the twenty-third of September.'

Helena shifted uncomfortably in her seat. 'The Autumnal Equinox.'

'I see you are acquainted with the Golden Dawn, Miss Walton.'

'I am afraid I am. And I have been following their close alliance with the SPR with interest for a while. May I ask what happened on that occasion?'

'We were picked up from our hotel, in rather a luxurious carriage.'

'That's right. And as soon as we arrived at Mark Masons' Hall on St James's Street, where the meeting was to take place, we were treated as valued guests.'

'This in itself was unexpected. We did not know these people. They did not know us.'

'We were suddenly surrounded by amiable faces, smiling people. A couple started asking, rather pointedly, about the incident at Versailles.'

'We had hardly spoken about it! It was little more than a month later. Our accounts were private.'

'We had no idea the invitation came from the Golden Dawn. We frankly thought it had been dismantled, after the scandal last year.' Eleanor was referring to the incident in which two adepts had been accused of abusing a young girl in the course of a ritual. Helena had feared that the scandal had not dismantled the Order, just sent it underground, where it remained under the protection of the SPR. 'We would have never attended otherwise.'

'They wanted to know everything that had taken place in Versailles. They kept asking if we had been in touch with a certain Mr Mathers in Paris.'

Samuel Mathers, a Freemason, had been one of the two founders of the Hermetic Order of the Golden Dawn, only to have his powers revoked, and be forced to remove himself to Paris, where he was trying to start another temple. That was all Helena knew.

'We had never heard of this person,' put in Eleanor.

'They were incredibly interested in our experience.'

'And how did you react to this interest?'

'We wanted nothing to do with them! We left, and refused to answer their questions, or to share our experiences with them in any way.'

'That was partly the reason why we decided to go public, searching for a scientific explanation to our experience. You see, it suddenly seemed to us that to keep our knowledge as occult risked making it more valuable.'

'We discussed it for a long time, and finally came to the conclusion that the only way to keep this kind of people away was by making it all public.'

'I see. At the time you received the Dawn's invitation, had you spoken about your experience with anyone apart from the SPR?'

'Indeed not,' said Charlotte. Helena and Eliza exchanged a knowing look.

Eleanor continued: 'We were not aware of their connection with the Order. As far as we knew, the SPR has had, until now at least, a solid scientific reputation in dealing with these issues.'

Helena acknowledged this with a curt nod. She thanked them profusely, and indicated to Eliza that it was time for them to leave. The ladies exited the premises by the back route, escorted by Eliza, and Helena was left alone.

After they left, Helena sat for the first time at her new heavy wooden desk, reflecting on the encounter. She thought how curious it was that her grandfather had sent the ladies her way, and wondered whether they were only going to receive clients in this manner. Were the advertisements she had paid for in

The Lady, or *The Illustrated London News*, not going to be seen by anyone? Sadly, these were the only two periodicals that had deigned to carry the note for a female-led detective agency.

She would have time to worry about all this later. Now there was work to do. This was an intriguing case, and she wondered whether they should concentrate on investigating the sudden interest from the Golden Dawn in the ladies – even, perhaps, digging deeper into its connection with the SPR – or whether this would prove to be a far more complicated matter, in which travelling to the Petit Trianon, to Versailles, to see the place for herself would be needed. Could she perhaps go to Paris and come back in a couple of days? She looked at the crates of books and notebooks and maps, and considered all the work that needed to be done. She was the only one who understood her filing system. How was she going to investigate an affair in Paris, or even in London for that matter, while the office was in such chaos? Suddenly, hiring someone with cataloguing and archival experience, with research skills if possible, had topped her list of priorities. Fortunately, Aurora had already arranged a meeting with her one prospect for the following morning.

But going to Paris seemed unavoidable. Some work in situ ought to be required, especially if Mathers had been mentioned. She wondered if Eliza was ready to go herself, to take over this line of inquiry on her own. No, it was too soon. They should go together. Helena took out a fresh sheet of paper, and started making lists of what ought to be done.

Number one was to get a sense of the general reputation of the two ladies in their local town. She ought to make enquiries at Oxford. Number two was finding out as much as possible about the Trianon, and perusing the ladies' statements. Whether what they had experienced was a real supernatural phenomenon or not, whatever had happened there might resolve the further question of the Golden Dawn's interest in them. Hopefully, she would find natural explanations for their supposed 'time-slip', and free them from being doubly harassed: firstly by the SPR, aimed at discrediting them, and secondly by their accomplices, the Golden Dawn, which was probably looking to tap into… what, exactly? She did not know enough of the Dawn's rituals and aims in order to answer that question. That became the next item on the list. Who knew about the Dawn? In this case, the answer was obvious.

She went towards the crates, and started looking for a street atlas of the capitals of Europe, and a guide to Paris. It would not be amiss to gather more historical information about the Trianon gardens, and she resolved to go to the Round Room at the British Museum as soon as possible. In order to find these items, she had undone the crates a little, and several things now cluttered the floor: her trusted *Bradshaw's Railway Guide, Post Office Directory of London,* and a medical dictionary. Her working materials were too sensible, she feared. Whatever knowledge she had of the Hermetic Order of the Golden Dawn had been acquired privately; there were no records at all, and their rituals and hierarchy were shrouded in secrecy. Luckily, or unluckily, as she hated the idea of preying on her friend's privacy, there was someone who could help.

Aurora had escaped what could only be described as a toxic relationship with the Hermetic Order, and one of its Inner Circle members. As far as Helena knew, she never spoke about it to a soul.

Aurora and the Dawn. The very name, Aurora, meant dawn in Latin. Helena knew the use as a common name in English dated back some time, maybe two hundred years, but in Mediterranean countries it had been adopted much earlier, derived in some cases from the Roman occupation. It was too much of a coincidence: Helena knew that the names of the members of the Dawn were Latin monikers at times. Was Aurora an assumed name, not her friend's real name? It could not be: Helena did not imagine she would have kept it if that were the case.

Just as Helena was considering how she was going to approach the subject with Aurora, how she was going to ask for her help understanding what the Dawn may want out of the two ladies' experience, there was a loud crash out on the landing.

Helena jerked, her heart jumping inside her chest.

She opened her drawer – at home she kept a small revolver there. Alas, this drawer was still empty, of course; and the small revolver she had recently started carrying about her person had been left at home. She made a quick mental note to change this, and to sew a secret pocket in all her skirts and dresses in order to carry it always.

But at present there was nothing for it other than finding something else to protect herself with. She got up slowly, trying to make as little noise as possible, grabbed the first thing she could find – her umbrella – and walked towards the door, all the while trying to remember where the wooden floorboards creaked.

She opened the agency door slowly. It was dark. The landing was seemingly empty. She was taken aback by the pungent smells of new wood, paint varnish and oil lamps. The noise outside was not loud but clear, the hubbub of a street in the hours when everyone was making their way back home. The light coming in from the streetlamps helped her see the source of the crash: several crates and iron buckets left by the painters had fallen to the floor.

'I'm sorry, it wasn't my intention to startle you.'

The voice was unknown, female, and sounded tired. Helena wondered who might be lurking on the landing of a business not yet opened.

'Who are you?'

'I apologise. The lady downstairs said there was a detective agency on this floor.'

Their sign, 'Walton & Waltraud, Inquiry Agents', had not been delivered yet, and there was no indication of what happened in those offices. So this person had been making enquiries about their purpose. And this person, whoever she was, was not showing herself. The hallway was mostly in darkness, and seemingly empty.

Helena readied herself, her umbrella poised. Painfully slowly a woman emerged. She was short and pale, with frizzy yellow hair, and a countenance that showed she had not slept much recently, heavy shadows beneath her eyes.

'Good evening,' Helena said, trying to keep her voice steady, and quickly putting the umbrella behind her. The young woman in front of her wasn't a threat.

'Good evening.' Despite her pallor, the woman looked real enough.

'Are you looking for anyone?'

'That depends. Is this really a detective agency?'

'That is right. My name is Helena Walton-Cisneros. I am the co-founder of the agency. And you are…?' Helena extended her hand, and the visitor took it.

'Miss Carmina Lowry.'

The name rang a bell, but she could not place it. Perhaps the daughter of a well-to-do family, perhaps a connection with a piece of news, or even a scandal, that she may have read of in the papers.

'How can we be of help, Miss Lowry?'

As she spoke, she gestured the young woman to enter. Miss Lowry hesitated, but eventually crossed the threshold. Helena felt a shiver up her spine: she remembered a recent book she had read, that well-received and gruesome novel by Bram Stoker, in which inviting an unknown creature to cross a threshold proved particularly dangerous. Miss Lowry, whether she was a woman at all, an apparition, or even a demon out of some Irishman's imagination, who could tell, was now looking around her, considering in quite a human way the crates and the empty bookshelves, and the general air of disuse about the place. Her small nose twitched at the sharp smell of newly painted walls and cabinets.

'I have to apologise; we are not yet open for business, you see. At least, not officially. Do you need a detective agency?'

'I need help.'

'What seems to be the matter?'

'But, are you…?'

'The detective? Yes, I am.' She was happy that Miss Lowry did not flinch at the notion. Helena had gestured to the chairs previously occupied by Misses Moberly and Jourdain, and the young woman now sat down.

'Please tell me, how can I be of help?'

Miss Lowry did not speak for a second. Helena thought that she looked extremely unwell.

'Are you alone?' It was a strange question. But Helena sensed she had nothing to fear.

'Yes, I am alone. Are you hungry?' Miss Lowry shook her head in negation. 'Then please allow me to offer you something to drink. Tea, or perhaps something a bit more fortifying.'

Helena opened a new bottle of brandy, which was waiting to be decanted for visitors. She found two glasses in a wooden crate spilling with hay and poured drinks generously. Miss Lowry accepted one with trembling hands, and murmured a hardly audible thanks. They both drank.

'I am sorry to appear like this, unannounced. The woman downstairs…' She was probably referring to Mrs Matthews, who was employed to keep the entry areas of the building clean, and who worked most evenings. 'The woman downstairs said that you help women. That was what decided me to come up. I was curious, I guess.'

'Well, is it only curiosity that is troubling you?'

'Not exactly. To be completely honest,' Miss Lowry paused, 'I am in mortal danger.'

This sounded certainly dramatic.

'Why don't you tell me everything, from the beginning?' Helena looked carefully at the visitor. She could not sit straight, like a little child, and kept twitching and flickering, looking around with big, wide eyes. There was more, of course, that could be deduced from her appearance. Still, Miss Lowry seemed uncertain as to how to start her tale. 'I can see you have been abroad recently,' observed Helena.

Miss Lowry looked startled by this.

'How can you possibly know that?'

'Your bonnet. It is very much the latest Parisian fashion, and still largely unavailable in this country, due to the French milliner's strike. Have you been to France, perhaps?'

'That's correct.'

Helena thought how interesting it was that everyone she had dealt with that night had a French connection. Still, it was the neighbouring country after all. Most of her compatriots came and went to Paris for all sorts of reasons at all seasons of the year, more than to any other foreign place, with the exception perhaps of India and Ceylon. She had heard of an increasing number of young people who decided to try their luck in the subcontinent for some reason. Still, Paris was Paris. The woman in front of her was likely an artist of some sort.

'I have been in Paris for just over two months. I have just returned home.'

'What you were doing there?'

'I was visiting a friend.'

'What does your friend do?'

'Or did. She is probably dead, Miss Walton.'

Miss Lowry had delivered this with aplomb, almost detachment. However, Helena could see through this: her late-night visitor was also moving her eyes left and right, never posing them on Helena's; and she could not help moving her two knees together repeatedly. She looked the very image of a child that is called by the headmistress upon some real or imaginary mischief.

'I am sorry to hear that. What makes you think that?'

'She has disappeared. Vanished. And now they are coming for me.'

On hearing this, Helena kept her expression neutral. She merely refilled the glasses, while further considering the woman in front of her. She was obviously telling the truth, and she looked incredibly scared. She kept twitching her hands obsessively, looking furtively around herself at the many shadows in the empty rooms. She had not looked directly at Helena once.

'Miss Lowry, when did your friend disappear?'

'About a month ago.'

'I am sorry your friend cannot be located at present, Miss Lowry. I trust you are aware that the Paris gendarmerie is excellent? I have myself been involved with them on more than one occasion in the past, and I can assure you they are really thorough in their work.'

'That may be the truth, miss, but at the moment they don't seem to me to be doing nearly enough to locate Emily.'

'In that case you have come to the right place. I am going to need you to recount everything, from the very beginning. It is of the utmost importance that you relate what you know about your friend's disappearance, and please do not leave anything out, even if you suspect it is a useless or irrelevant piece of information. I have all evening, and I will need to hear it all, from beginning to end.'

'I went to France to visit her. Emily is an artist; she's at art school. While she was there, she took a job in the studio of a theatre owner.'

'And what did she do for him?'

'Well, this theatre owner also makes those funny lightshows that they put on sometimes between performances.'

'Do you mean moving pictures?'

'That's correct.'

'I see. And what did your friend do for this man?'

'She was helping him colour the pictures, patiently hand-painting them frame by frame, so when he shows them in his camera-machine it creates the illusion of being in real colours. It is quite magical.'

Miss Lowry was not showing any signs of excitement as she shared this piece of information.

'And why did she take this job?'

'It was just a little job so she could pay for her studies, and live in France. Her parents did not want her to be an artist. They had disinherited her, you see.'

'So,' Helena tried again. 'Your friend was in Paris, colouring film reels by hand for this man.'

'Yes. Quite the illusion.'

Helena thought she knew something about illusions, about performance, about pretence. However, moving pictures. That was definitely something new.

'And where does she live in Paris?'

'Well, she does not live in Paris, exactly. She rents a little house in the outskirts of the city in a suburb to the south, one of the last train stops. It is cheaper that way, and she is halfway between the city, where her art school is located, and Monsieur Méliès's movie studio.'

This was interesting. Helena got up at once and went to her books. She found what she needed in the crate of oversize publications: a French atlas, complete with a detailed double-page map of the southern environs of the French capital.

'Can you please give me an indication of where she lives?' she said to her visitor. Miss Lowry stood up and walked over to where Helena had opened the atlas on the floor. Helena now noticed that she was short, and plump in a matronly sort of way. Miss Lowry would have been a good governess, if it weren't for her nervous twitches. Her guest said she was not exactly sure, but pointed to a general area with her finger.

The area Miss Lowry signalled was peculiarly close to the location of the first mystery of that evening, the gardens at Versailles.

'This is silly,' said Miss Lowry. 'You cannot drop everything and just go to France. But if you could please give me the name of anyone who could help me, I would be very thankful.'

Helena did not understand: if this person did not think she could do anything, why she hasn't asked for the name of someone in Paris to help her? It was clear the woman had needed to talk to someone about the situation, unburdening herself as soon as she was given the chance, which in Helena's experience indicated one thing: some form of guilt.

'Well, there is a very happy coincidence at play here.'

'What is that?'

'You are not the first person who came looking for our help tonight, Miss Lowry. As it happens, we have another case to attend to, and it is also in Paris. I cannot reveal more to you, of course, but I can assure you I can accommodate your needs.'

'My needs?'

'Well, of course. You want to know where is your friend, isn't that so?'

'Yes.'

'In that case, I believe we can help. Do you know how she disappeared?'

Miss Lowry's friend had been crossing a populated bridge in Paris, heading to her art class, when a couple of thugs had come towards her, and, by all accounts, seized her in plain sight, in broad daylight, put her in the back of a cart, and ridden away with her.

'That is the scariest thing, Miss Walton. They took her with total impunity. They weren't scared of being stopped or questioned. Imagine how powerful they must be.'

'That is very perceptive of you, Miss Lowry. Can I ask what do you do?'

'I am a writer, Miss Walton.' Helena had suspected it by now: if not an artist, perhaps a writer, or a reporter; certainly not a governess. It was obvious that Miss Lowry was used to looking beyond the surface presented to her, not unlike a detective. It was also clear she had a few quirks about her that only an artistic person possessed. Still, she would be a valuable witness.

'Do not worry, Miss Lowry. I will help you. But I need to know: why do you think your life is in danger?'

'Because of the letters.'

'The letters?'

'I think they may know that Emily wrote me rather detailed accounts of her life in France. I fear there must be something in them, something that she was not meant to tell me, and I wasn't meant to know. And I think they are following me, Miss Walton. I think someone followed me here.'

That would explain why Miss Lowry had entered the building. She had been probably looking for a place to hide herself, and then, on hearing there was a private detective agency, had decided that this had been providential, and, having nothing to lose, and no one to turn to, had decided to go upstairs.

Helena walked towards the window, but did not look directly through it. She placed herself on the side and lifted the curtain imperceptibly, trying to keep undetected from the street. She hated to admit it, but Miss Lowry was correct.

'Do not be alarmed, but I am afraid you are right. There is a man down there, rather strategically placed to intercept whoever leaves our building.'

Miss Lowry got to her feet, visibly scared.

'Please do not worry. I will make sure you are safe. But you have to trust me. We can exit the building undetected, that is no problem. We will use the service exit. And I know a place where we can spend the night. You obviously cannot go back to your lodgings. You must come with me right now. I will do what I can to discover what is happening, and you will remain in a safe place until I do. How does that sound?'

'It sounds extremely generous of you, Miss Walton.'

'Please, call me Helena. I will need your address, and the key to your house. I will send my associate tomorrow to fetch a bundle of clothes for you, and anything else you may need. And, of course, the letters themselves. You will need to leave them with me. Are you carrying them about your person?'

'No, they are in the room I am renting. But they are hidden.'

'Where?'

'Under a loose board in the closet.'

For the second time that night Helena sat down at her newly built desk, this time to pen a note with instructions for Eliza. She asked her associate to first gather necessity items and clothes from the given address and put them in a suitcase, and also to retrieve a bundle of letters, which she explained how and where to find.

'Is there anything else you may need from your room, Miss Lowry? It is possible you will not set foot in it for a couple of weeks.'

'In that case, there are notebooks on the bedside table.'

'Your diary?'

'No, I don't write a diary. Haven't for years. They are my novel in progress; the work of the last two years of my life. They are extremely important to me.'

'Indeed.' Helena added the new instructions to the note, and wondered for a moment if she wasn't overpromising: taking not one but two cases, not in London but abroad, when they were still not fully operational, could prove to be among the least sensible things she had ever done. But, when she envisioned opening the agency, this was exactly what she had hoped she would do, to have a place that would not turn women away, that would believe them, would take their worries seriously. She had to help Miss Lowry.

Of course, there was another explanation for Miss Lowry's presence at the still unopened agency: she had been the very person following the Misses Moberly and Jourdain. After seeing the proximity of the two locations, the two mysteries, this seemed more than possible. In that case, Miss Lowry worked for the SPR, or the Dawn, or both. But, then, thought Helena, why reveal her hand in such a manner? Why enter the agency at all; why mention the disappearance of her friend? Did she get involved in something unwillingly; did she now regret it? Did she see the agency and Helena's existence as providential, a way to escape from a situation that had made her remorseful? Or was she indeed in danger, as she claimed?

Whatever the case, Helena was sure of one thing: Miss Lowry might well be working for the Dawn, but she was also frightened for her life.

4

CHAFFINS'S ANTIQUE COLLECTABLES

15th March – Later

There was no doubt about this: Miss Lowry looked petrified. Either that, or she was a very superior actress. It took one more generous brandy to convince her to leave the office with Helena. Despite Helena's reassurance that no one ever kept an eye on their service entrance, Miss Lowry only agreed to leave once the detective offered yet another means of escape. Armed with a gas-lit lamp, both women descended into the very depths of the building, the smells of earth and rot competing here with the new paint and varnish upstairs, where Helena guided them through cavernous tunnels filled with abandoned broken furniture, empty glass bottles and general rubbish, into the basement of an adjacent building, whose back entrance they used as means of escaping.

The Method would have suggested a singular dual psychology in this client. She was hesitant about everything, while, at the same time, wanting to be convinced, to be given reasons to trust this stranger that was Helena. It was clear to the detective, who could read the signs like an open book: Miss Lowry looked as if she had taken a huge load off her shoulders by simply sharing her story with somebody.

'In truth I do not wish to return to my room. I know they will find me there,' Miss Lowry now admitted, as they finally climbed into a hansom.

Who were 'they'? Helena wondered. This would be the first order of business. She leaned forward and gave instructions to the driver:

'Montague Street, please.'

Next to her, Miss Lowry seemed to catch her breath.

'Where is that, exactly?'

'You will be safe there, trust me.'

'In the middle of London? Next to the British Museum, the most visited national collection in the world?'

'It is the safest place I know.'

The hansom stopped on the street where the museum is located, but further along, at the corner where Great Russell Street turns into Montague Street. Helena paid the driver and gestured for Miss Lowry to follow her. They went around the building, a rather quaint detached house on the corner facing Great Russell Street, which did not look like a commercial premises, but rather some kind of respectable dwelling.

There was a shop overtaking both front bay windows, although in the dark Miss Lowry could not read the name of the establishment. She quickly followed Helena, who was gesturing for her to move quickly and out of view. They took an alley adjacent to the building, and knocked at a back entrance. In a few seconds a tall blonde woman with furious streaks of white in her hair and ice-blue eyes opened the door.

'Helena! Whatever are you doing here at this time?'

'Aurora. I apologise for the intrusion at this late hour. May I present Miss Lowry? We are in need of help, I am afraid.'

'Well, in that case, come in at once!'

Miss Lowry feared that the blonde lady, whom Helena was now introducing as Miss Aurora Chaffins, had not been particularly taken with the idea of their invasion. However, it was soon clear that both she and Helena shared a friendship in which questions could always be left for later, and help was readily given. The woman transformed instantly into a figure of welcome, fluffing cushions and pillows, throwing blankets on an ottoman and chairs, and quickly producing what looked to Miss Lowry like Eastern European pickles and an unidentified crimson drink. A small glass of the liquid was thrust into her hand as Helena explained their predicament. Miss Lowry took a sip, and choked.

'What *is* this?'

'*Pacharán*, a kind of sloe gin. A Spanish delicacy, in honour of our friend here,' explained Aurora, gesturing towards Helena, who had now removed her boots and was putting her feet up on the chair she occupied, demanding a second glass. Miss Lowry managed a smile, but the last thing she would have called the drink was juice.

'Delicious,' she said politely.

Ten minutes later the three women were sitting around the fire in Aurora's cosy private sitting room at the back of her shop. Miss Lowry was looking around her as the two friends discussed the plan for the coming days. Helena's associate would bring a case for Miss Lowry the next day. The sitting room seemed to open into a small kitchenette, and a spiral staircase led to the only bedroom above, a storage space where Aurora also had her bed and other pieces of furniture, and where Miss Lowry was going to sleep. To her protestations of where Aurora would sleep in her turn, the shop's owner signalled a rather tattered-looking ottoman, and assured her that she had slept there on many an occasion, and that it was perfectly comfortable, thank you very much, so there was no need to worry on her behalf.

Mina Lowry could see colourful tarot cards, phrenology heads, astrology charts hanging from the walls, and bookcases groaning with books chiefly on these subjects. A book called *Aetherial Travels Beyond the Imagination* was too big for the shelf, and lay on the floor, propped against the ottoman. Everything was colourful, comfortable-looking. An odd smell emanated from a little silver slipper-shaped burner, cloudy blue smoke rising from its tip. Aurora addressed the newcomer in a much more relaxed tone than on arrival, placing a calming hand on her arm:

'Miss Lowry, you will be completely safe here. No one can see what happens at the back of my shop. You are very welcome to take the room upstairs for as long as you need.'

'I don't know how to thank you.'

'No need for thanks,' Aurora assured her with a smile.

Later, after an improvised supper of cold meats and warm spiced wine, and after an exhausted Miss Lowry had been shown to bed, Aurora and Helena sat downstairs to discuss recent events.

'What do you think?' asked Helena.

'I think that coincidences like this one do not normally happen outside of penny-novels.'

'Quite.'

'Then why aren't you suspicious?'

'I know, I know. It is highly improbable that our first two cases are in Paris; but, if anything, this situation has pricked my curiosity more.'

'Curiosity killed the cat.'

'Only because the cat wasn't paying enough attention.'

Aurora laughed at this.

'So, what are you thinking?' insisted Aurora. Helena let out a long sigh.

'Well, it's obvious, isn't it?' Helena lowered her voice to a whisper, and the two friends sat very close to each other. 'Miss Lowry must have been following the misses. What this means also seems obvious: she either had been tasked by the Dawn to do so, or she suspects them to be complicit in her friend's vanishing. I can see no other explanation. And still…'

'And still she put herself in your hands, when she knew you had just seen the two ladies, and would reach this conclusion yourself. That points at her desperation.'

'I agree. She is obviously frightened, and her need for help seems real. I believe it also points to how out of her depth she must feel with whatever she has become involved with.'

'There is something else, Helena, I am surprised you haven't noticed. But perhaps you have.'

'What are we talking about now?'

'It is obvious, my dear. Our Miss Lowry seems to have another problem.' Helena frowned, and Aurora offered, rather unexpectedly: 'She seems to be... under the influence of something. I am sure she partakes of some substance or another with regularity.'

Helena thought about this for a moment. It explained the physical twitching, the nervous darting eyes, the heavy bags under Miss Lowry's eyes. Aurora was, as usual, correct.

'In any case,' continued her friend, 'Miss Lowry seems to be keeping too many cards up her sleeve, don't you think? You have always told me that an investigation can only progress if you base everything on the truth.'

'And yet, we have just crossed paths. I am a stranger to her. And she came here with me, followed me here. She is alone. If she is lying to anyone, I believe it is more to herself than to me.'

'That's certainly one way to see it. Why don't we...' Aurora got up and crossed the room to find her cards inside a drawer in her desk. Aurora's cards were oversized, with dark patterns, and they were dog-eared and even dirty after years of use. Without saying anything she laid the cards carefully, so Helena could follow the spread. One for the past, two for the present, three for the future. Or rather—

'What spread is that?'

'Oh! I am just answering a question. It is a permutation of a normal one.'

'What is the question?'

'I'm not getting a straight answer. But, do you see this Seven of Swords here? It means there is something in her story that doesn't quite add up. That much we already knew.'

'Well, the cards are clear: she is definitely not telling me everything…'

'But the point, dear Helena, is not that. The point is, *to what extent* is she not telling you everything? And what exactly is she lying about?'

16th March – Morning

When Mina woke up, it took her some time to remember where she was. She could hear a faint thread of words spoken downstairs, and smelt coffee. She could not stand the liquid, and preferred tea herself; recently she recoiled at any unwanted smell. She would feel better as soon as she had taken a drop of morphine from the small bottle that she carried hidden in her bosom, the known calm descending upon her. She stood up, suddenly scared, and crossed the room to her handbag: the large bottle she used to refill this little one was still there, she saw with relief.

For the first time it dawned on her what she had done, and she felt uneasy again. How had she ended up sleeping in the back of a stranger's shop, of all places? She suddenly felt out of place, not sure that she wanted to go downstairs. But she also feared being rude, her childhood manners kicking in, and so she eventually did, cautiously navigating the rickety staircase.

'Good morning, Miss Lowry.'

'Good morning. Please, call me Mina.' In the morning light the room looked different, much smaller than it had seemed when blanketed by shadows. The objects and books lying around were strange and shiny and multi-coloured, and seemed to have multiplied in the light of the new day.

'Miss Chaffins…'

'Aurora, please.'

Mina was staring at an oversized golden beetle lying on the floor. Aurora immediately got up and took it.

'Excellent! You have found Pit! I thought I had lost him.'

Next Mina's attentions were caught by a rather large purple stone sitting on a side table, which shone differently depending on how she moved her head. The effect was hypnotic.

'What exactly do you sell in your shop?'

'Oh, this and that. Antiques, for the most part. But I find that my clientele has, as well as unflinching good taste, of course, a certain penchant for the uncanny, the inexplicable, the occult.'

'Oh!'

'There is no need to look so shocked,' said Helena, stretching out of a small sofa where she had obviously slept. 'Aurora provides goods and items to a large number of curators from the museum. After all, most of the exhibits have some ritualistic component, as I am sure you know.'

Mina had not sat yet, her eyes taking in as much as was possible to do, considering the profusion of items in view. She now stopped in front of a small shelf perched on the eastern wall of the rooms.

'And what is this?' Mina had found Aurora's altar.

A huge-breasted goddess with a protruding belly was surrounded by what could only be interpreted as offerings of all kinds: flowers, walnuts, sticks with blossom flowers, and even tiny bowls containing a white liquid that looked like milk. Was this woman some sort of witch? Except that witches only existed in stories, not in London in the brand-new twentieth century.

'What's all this for?'

'The altar? Mostly protection, I am sure you will be happy to hear. Religious faith. After all, most religions have syncretised all kinds of pagan belief into themselves, over time.'

'My grandmother was a committed Anglican,' Mina began, 'but she had an unflinching belief in fairies, although she thought them much darker than we are led to believe by children's tales. I think that, whenever I write about them, I am very much influenced by her constant warnings against them as I was growing up. Come to think of it, there were sheela-na-gig in our local church, and no one seemed to think that was strange.'

Helena and Aurora looked up with obvious interest: it was the longest thing Miss Lowry had said, and the first thing she had shared about her herself.

'Miss Lowry, why don't you join us?' asked Aurora, indicating the table set for breakfast. The young woman did, muttering her thanks.

'It is even more pronounced in Spain, let me tell you,' offered Helena, as she buttered her toast. 'The Catholic Church only managed to introduce itself by cannibalising all sorts of pagan rituals. Even the festivities of today, like the Corpus Christi processions, come directly from Roman and Celtic festivals, and are modelled and adapted from them.'

They chatted for a while in this manner. It was clear that their guest was interested in folklore and history, Helena sensing that common interests were bringing Miss Lowry and Aurora together.

Presently, there was a knock at the back door. Miss Lowry jumped in her seat: it wasn't shop hours. But Aurora got up with a smile, as if she were expecting someone, and opened the same entrance they had used themselves the previous night. She greeted the visitor warmly, and Miss Lowry visibly relaxed again.

Aurora returned to the sitting room with a young black woman, who was wearing a blue dress of the latest fashion and a particularly handsome turquoise bonnet that matched her obviously expensive reticule. She also had a little pair of glasses hanging from her neck on a pretty gold chain.

'Helena, may I present Miss Jocasta Webster? She is the young lady I was telling you about the other day.'

'How you do? I am very pleased to finally meet you.' The visitor was obviously American.

Pleasantries exchanged, it transpired that Miss Webster had been seeking work among the antiquarian and rare book trade in London, and that was how she and Aurora had come to meet.

'Miss Webster trained in the Columbia School of Library Economics, and worked at the New York Society Library upon graduation.'

'That is fascinating, Miss Webster. Visiting New York and its libraries is high among my list of desires to fulfil in my lifetime.' Miss Lowry piped up in high excitement. Aurora gave a significant look at Helena, her pale-blonde eyebrows raised to the sky. Oh, Aurora, Helena thought. She decided to intervene in the conversation:

'What did you do at the New York Society Library, Miss Webster?'

'Oh, a mixture of cataloguing and administrative duties. Receiving visitors. Assisting scholars with their enquiries.'

'Do you enjoy research?'

Miss Webster's face transformed as an ample smile illuminated her features.

'I adore research. In fact, that was the main attraction of library work. I enjoy cataloguing books, in particular rare books and incunabula. Finding their provenance. Establishing their unique traits. But solving the tiniest of queries for readers, now that can be fascinating. Almost like detective work.'

'Indeed!' exclaimed Aurora. 'I think you and Helena will get on like a house on fire.'

'Miss Chaffins told me you are in need of an archivist…?'

'Well, that hardly cuts it, Miss Webster. I require someone to catalogue my newly relocated library, help with occasional filing, and answer our telephone, as well as attend to visitors to the premises. But I am not looking for a mere secretary. Your resumé frankly surpasses anything I might have had in mind. But I guess it is fair to say that my business is of a rather particular nature.'

'How so?'

Helena took a sip of her coffee before speaking – it was all still quite new, even for her:

'I am opening a detective agency. I have a partner, another lady. We want to be a port of call for women in distress.'

'That is fascinating!' said Miss Webster.

'Well, at the moment, the agency is not much more than a chaos of books on the floor in our new offices, as well as many archives and files that I have accumulated over the years – I have been doing this work before, you see, albeit from my home. And I am afraid that transporting everything to the new premises has made it all a tiny bit more muddled.' Miss Webster had been offered coffee, which she now sipped, while nodding at Helena. 'But then,' continued the detective, 'organising those items, although important, is not the only thing, not by far. What I really need, Miss Webster, is someone who can assist us whenever the need for research arises. Which, let me tell you, is very often. Sometimes we need to check a fact, or find information about a particular person, or a company, perhaps. And it may happen that we are in need of that information while working a case in Norwich, or in Essex, far away from London, my books, and its many libraries and archives and civic records repositories.'

'I see. Well, let me reassure you I would be more than capable of helping you with everything that you have described.'

'There is also the need for absolute discretion about all of our activities, of course.'

'I understand. You will not need to trouble yourself on that account, Miss Walton-Cisneros. Perhaps you would like to see my letters of reference?' Miss Webster was already putting a hand inside her reticule, but Helena stopped her.

'That will not be necessary. Your experience is just what we're after.'

Miss Webster smiled at Helena, and, in turn, at Miss Lowry, looking at her directly and disarmingly with her dark eyes.

Miss Lowry felt a sudden jolt inside her. Miss Jocasta Webster was one of the most beautiful women she had ever seen.

'Thank you, Miss Walton-Cisneros. I am sure the work will be as interesting as Miss Chaffins assured me it would be.'

'I am exceedingly pleased! We ought to celebrate.' Aurora got up, and served hefty shots of liquor into everybody's morning coffee and tea. Miss Lowry, fearing the previous night's experience with the *pacharán*, pretended to have forgotten that her cup was there. Miss Webster was looking at her again, and she felt herself reddening.

'When can you start?' continued Helena.

'I can start immediately.'

'Can you come by this afternoon?'

'Absolutely.'

So Helena was hiring Miss Jocasta Webster. Miss Lowry smiled with the rest of them: the possibility of seeing Miss Webster again had improved her strange morning greatly.

Later on, back in her assigned quarters, Mina reflected. She had told Aurora that she needed a rest, just to have some time to herself and think.

She still shivered when she recollected the events of the previous night. She had acted on pure instinct, without thinking much about the consequences: one of her less pleasing traits, she knew. This impetuousness had been costly for her in the past. It had cost her, if nothing else, her most important relationship, and the loss of the love of her life.

It was too late to regret her actions now. What was done was done. She thought of how naïve she had been to put her fate in the Dawn's hands. She had hoped to get the truth out of them about Emily, but this had not happened – what a fool she had been. Her motives had not been that pure either: she had been promised everything she wanted, the moon and the stars. Now, due to some absurd, childish reaction – the need to come clean, for goodness' sake – she had placed herself in the most precarious position possible. She knew what she had done took the hardest sanction, but there was nothing she could do: her actions had turned the wheel in a completely different direction. New characters would emerge, new plots would develop.

All she could do was wait to see what may come of her decision to trust Helena Walton-Cisneros. And hope that the Dawn's hounds did not find her, for if they did then she was as good as dead.

While this was taking place, in a different part of town, Eliza Waltraud was looking quickly over a letter delivered early that morning by the canal and tinker network, one of Helena's most trusted street associates. She was quick in realising her improvement at using the cipher she and Helena had devised, and decoded it quickly. After memorising the address, she put it in the fire as they had arranged they would always do. She then finished her morning tea in a long gulp, grabbed her buttered toast between her teeth, put on her coat and hat and set off from her rooms, wondering who the mysterious new client was.

The messenger had delivered the note inside a little box that also contained the key to the client's room. The box was wrapped in the monogrammed paper of Chaffins's Antique Collectables. This had brought a definitive distaste to her mouth.

Eliza found a hansom in the street, and arrived at the address twelve minutes later. She found herself facing a tenement building with the faint sign of 'Hotel for Ladies': peeling paint, no reception on view or any sign of being anything other than a house with keyholes in each bedroom, with the larger rooms divided into two or perhaps three, chamber pots under every bed that each tenant would empty through the window, one of those places with a perennial smell of cabbage soup and decades-old dust about it. From the inside of the building came wailing and cries, the smell of cooking, and a faint stench of something she did not want to identify. She went up the stairs, not without a small shiver that she deliberately ignored. As a general rule she disliked badly lit stair passages, something she would need to overcome if she was going to be a detective. She was surprised that this notion did not seem fanciful to her any longer, when a few months ago she would have recoiled at calling herself that. Luckily, she would not be required to climb up to the last badly lit landing: the room she was seeking was on the first floor, to the left. Room number nine. She turned the key in the lock and opened the door.

Eliza went directly to the closet to gather the letters. She counted to the third board from the left, and indeed it slid aside as Helena's note had said it would. Inside, a bundle wrapped in a scarf, which she undid to reveal letters both dog-eared and newer looking; the correspondence clearly spanned a considerable period of time.

Eliza felt the prickle of alarm before she could even understand why. This was what, in the Method, Helena called 'growing instincts'. So it was true: instincts were something to reckon with in their profession, and she was somehow acquiring them.

She had heard something, and her brain made her stop what she was doing before she could understand why. And what she had heard were slow, heavy footsteps: a working man's, a dock man's footsteps; the sound of strong, sturdy boots. In a hotel exclusively for young women. And now these heavy footsteps were stopping right in front of their client's door.

She slid the board back into place, and just had time to crawl under the bed before two of the heaviest-looking boots she had ever seen started pacing around, inches from her hiding place. Judging by their colossal size and the fact that they could crush her skull with little effort, she guessed that the man must be quite tall and sturdy. As he moved away towards the window, she inched forward and risked a glimpse upwards. He was rough-looking, another nameless thug among the very many for hire in the city. While he was looking down at the street, Eliza surveyed the man, and noted his smell: the newcomer had brought the stink of the tavern in his wake, the smell of factory fumes and the tepid humanity of the docks; he could have come from a number of places. Even more important was to commit his face to memory. But she had to retreat back to her hiding place, as he stopped considering the street and went back to inspect the room. The thug started moving objects, dropping them on the floor as he discarded them, ripping open drawers; eventually he made his way towards the closet itself, where he gathered the clothes and threw them on the floor too, near where Eliza was hiding and holding her breath. He was methodically, and silently – a small but significant detail, which brought to Eliza's mind the notion of a certain professionalism – trashing the room, no doubt in search of the letters. As the objects flew around her, Eliza covered her mouth to suppress any noise: she did not dare entertain the thought of what might happen to her if this man found her there.

Right after leaving Chaffins's, Helena had taken a hansom cab to the station and jumped in the first available train. Later that morning she was walking down Broad Street in Oxford. Every time she came to the city of dreaming spires – she had no idea why it was called this; in her experience Oxford ought to be called the city of gargoyles – she visited her favourite place in town: Blackwell's bookshop. Fortified and happy with her bundle of purchases, she acquired a last-minute greeting card at the counter, featuring Alice from the Lewis Carroll novel proclaiming, 'It's no use going back to yesterday, because I was a different person then.'

After Blackwell's, Helena made her way across the city to the suburb of Jericho. She knocked on the door of a small two-bedroom cottage. A robust-looking woman with a thrilling shock of red hair opened the door, in a silk dress far more elegant than the woman's profession might lead one to expect. She had often been stopped when entering academic buildings, had it patiently explained to her by orderlies that there was no picnic going on there, and that perhaps she was looking for a dress shop instead. She was good-humoured about it; although Helena knew that, behind the frills, there was a strong-willed woman who had been known to organise the local suffragettes. To be fair to the orderlies, even other women had at times been known to reach the wrong conclusions as they judged the frills and expensive lace; that is, before they were faced with her formidable mind. Beatrice Gaskill merely liked both frills and scientific research, as she was fond, albeit frustratedly, of explaining to all and sundry.

'Helena Walton-Cisneros! Dear me. Do tell me, to what do I thank for this visit? What brings you to my part of the world? Gosh, I hope it's not serious; last time I saw you, you were working a case…' was Beatrice's greeting, and she immediately gestured to her friend to enter.

Helena and Beatrice knew each other from their time at Girton in Cambridge, a place Beatrice had despised – it was no surprise she had ended up working in what was known as 'the other place'. Beatrice's role comprised chiefly of teaching girls in the couple of women's colleges. She was a trained botanist, but taught them everything connected to science.

'My dear friend, how are you?' They hugged. 'Indeed you are correct, and I have to apologise: I have just started working on a case,' said Helena, as Beatrice directed her through the house. 'We will see each other in non-working circumstances at some point, I promise.'

Beatrice laughed at this.

'It doesn't bother me at all. You are always welcome. I myself have little time for social calls; it is all work and work and then more of it.'

As they came towards the back of the house, where the conservatory presided over a large garden that sloped down towards the river, Helena saw large piles of student notebooks to mark. She had also spotted the usual mixture of scientific textbooks, education treatises and the odd suffragette chapbook lying open on a settee.

Every single inch of the conservatory was covered by plants of some kind, leaving only a little space for a sofa and a coffee table, and a larger table covered with test tubes and test lamps and a bulky microscope. There was a musky smell lingering in the room. Here was where Beatrice undertook her research – no laboratory in the town was open to a female scientist, not even to one of her brilliance. How sad it was, Helena thought, how much of mankind's progress was lost by denying itself brains as brilliant as her friend's. Like shooting yourself in your own foot.

Beatrice received the greeting card with Alice on it, and, laughing, propped it against a pile of books on the table.

'I wonder what the Reverend Dodgson thought of his sudden literary fame.'

'Maybe I should ask him the next time I find myself in a séance,' was Helena's reply. Beatrice laughed at this.

'How good it is to see you, Helena. Please, have a seat. We can have some refreshments, and you can tell me what brought you here.' Beatrice was known for a no-nonsense attitude, and it was just what Helena needed.

'I am here because I need information.'

'You could have written a letter?'

'It is of a rather delicate nature. Also, much quicker to face the steam train. I should be back in London this afternoon. I had a very early start.'

'I see. What kind of information are you looking for?'

'The kind that it is hardest to get, at least for an outsider: local knowledge, mostly. Maybe some gossip, if possible. I have a couple of new clients, pretty much from your side of the woods. You must know them, as you work in their college from time to time, if I am not mistaken. Miss Moberly and Miss Jourdain.'

'Indeed I do! There are very few of us lurking about here who don't cross paths and become acquainted at some point.' Helena knew that her friend was referring to female scholars. 'Besides,' she continued 'they are two important voices for the advancement of female education among these venerable walls,' she explained, moving her arms vaguely to emphasise either her house, the town of Oxford, or perhaps the whole universe. 'So, I take it you are getting involved in their little adventure?' It was clear that their current predicament was now common knowledge.

'I am. They have asked for my help, and I feel somehow compelled. Precisely because of what you have just said. They are two important figures, and their reputations are systematically being shattered.'

'Perhaps it is fair to say that they have themselves helped shatter them a little? You don't believe it possible that someone travelled in time and saw Marie Antoinette while tourists in Paris.' It wasn't a question. As always, Beatrice liked getting directly to the point. Helena noted she had not rung for the promised tea yet.

'Time-slip, I believe it is called,' said Helena. 'Not time travel, not exactly.' Her friend suppressed a chuckle, badly.

'What is the difference?'

'A time-slip is a displacement in time of short duration. Almost as if some place, or energy, is out of tune, and you either are transported there briefly, or you lose time and can't account for it, or simply a window into the past opens, and you can peer into a vista from long ago.'

'And this is what happened to them, they had a… vision of the past? Do you mean like postcards, or those new motion pictures everyone talks about?'

'Yes, that seems to be the case.' Helena thought how interesting it was that Beatrice had compared the two ladies' experience with watching a film. This had not occurred to her before, but it certainly made sense. They had themselves liked it to a theatre, that was true. But she could not mention the other mystery they were preparing to look into, as that would break her client's confidentiality, but she made a mental note of the connection that the two ideas had sparked in her clever friend's mind.

'So the two ladies suffered one of these time-slips? Understood.'

'So they say. And, to answer your question, I neither believe nor disbelieve their account. I have simply agreed to look into the reasons why they think they saw Marie Antoinette in the Petit Trianon, and have been very clear that my findings may point to completely reasonable causes as to why this happened.'

Beatrice was nodding at this. She still had not rung for tea. Her friend was as absent-minded as Helena remembered.

'And what is it that you would like to know?'

'General information, the kind of reputation they had prior to this. They are both academics; it is somehow out of character for someone whose life revolves around learning to find themselves in the predicament they are in.'

'Indeed,' was the short reply to this, a reply far too short for her friend. Helena thought she had to say something.

'Beatrice, is everything alright? It seems that you are not very comfortable with this conversation.' She paused. 'I am sorry to have come unannounced. I am perfectly happy to have tea with you, chat about the weather, and head back the way I came.'

'Ah! The tea. How very rude of me.'

Beatrice now popped her head around the conservatory door and called her maid, a young moody woman with a sullen expression who came to receive her orders and left the room with much huffing and puffing. After she had left Beatrice said:

'Look, to be completely honest, and I hate to tell you this, they are thought of locally as… a rather eccentric pair.'

'Which kind of eccentric, exactly?'

'The kind that are thought of as fantasists.'

'Oh.'

'Exactly.'

'Is that all?' Helena felt compelled to ask. She sensed there was more, and that Beatrice was simply tiptoeing around the facts.

'I guess… there was an incident.'

That was it, what Beatrice had been dancing around, wondering whether to mention it or not.

'What kind of incident?' Helena saw her friend's expression, and wished she did not have to ask.

'A student. She was having the most awful nightmares.'

'Up in the college?'

'Yes. They all lived together in a little house somewhere. This was during the earlier days, you see. There weren't that many female students around yet.'

The sullen-looking young woman reappeared now, and set down the tea things on the little table with a heavy thump that sounded like a protestation at having to perform such menial ritual.

'Thank you, Mary!' Beatrice almost shouted as Mary closed the door loudly behind her.

'What happened?'

Beatrice started serving the tea.

'Do you believe in ghosts, Helena?'

Helena let out a long sigh and a nervous laugh. 'That is a big question.'

'Do you?'

'Perhaps I do,' she replied, fixing her friend with a look. She realised it was simpler to own up to it than to feel embarrassed about it.

'Well, I am not sure *they* do!'

'What do you mean?' said Helena, sipping her tea. The water was cold; it had obviously been boiled early in the morning and not reheated, which explained how quickly it had been brought.

'The girl said her room was haunted. She was scared out of her wits.'

'And?'

'The misses did nothing. The girl ended up drowning herself.'

This was devastating news for Helena. She sipped her cold tea, or whatever it was, out of politeness.

'They refused to believe her? Or perhaps did not want anything unsavoury to be connected with their beloved college? Who knows.' Beatrice had served herself a cup, but she was not touching it. She grabbed a biscuit that looked papery and thin, put it on her little plate and forgot all about it.

'I imagine that would have been problematic for them...' Helena offered.

'Problematic? They had to hush the whole thing up! The whole college could have closed after a situation like that, even before it had started properly. Frankly, Helena, I am not sure how they managed to survive the whole sad affair. I bet it was because no one in either town or gown cared much yet about these female colleges that were starting to pop out like mushrooms here and there, and therefore no one even remembered they existed.'

'I see. So, in your opinion...?'

'They don't strike me as particularly reliable witnesses. Mind you, this is between you and me. They employ me from time to time to deliver science lessons to their wards,' Beatrice said, one eye twinkling, a short, unsure smile dancing on her face.

'Don't worry. Everything you have told me remains between

you and me.' Beatrice looked relieved at this. 'I am really thankful, Beatrice, truly I am.'

Next they discussed the infamous *Open Door* article. Were the ladies in fact unreliable witnesses to their own adventure? Had they suffered a collective hallucination, or a fever? Or had they indeed been honest about the incident, and there were other reasons why they became confused? Beatrice was helpfully pointing at possibilities, a gas leak somewhere. Mushroom spores impregnating the air. Anything. It was clear that her usually open-minded friend seemed to have problems accepting the realities of windows opening into the past. Eventually, they were both fishing for other, more mundane topics: life in London versus life elsewhere. The weather, unseasonably hot for the time of the year, and so on and so forth.

'How rude of me!' Beatrice presently said, opening her arms wide, finally taking a sip of the beverage, for it could not objectively be called tea. 'How is your agency going? And your associate? How is she taking to a life of detection?'

Where to start?

'I think we have a good partnership, as we both have different specialities. She is more scientifically minded than I am. Whereas I… well, I am prepared to look into a time-slip to start with. The problem is when two people have completely opposite inclinations. I am afraid it strains our professional relationship at times.'

'It seems to me you've had a hard year, my dear.'

Helena thought that 'terrifying' would be a much a better adjective.

'The thing is, Helena, the way I see it, Eliza is a Darwinist, as clear as day, whereas you are shifting. You are more open to all sorts of things.'

'And what about you?'

'Me? Ah! I am a proud Utilitarian, of course. I seek to find knowledge that will bring the greatest good to society. If you think about it, isn't it wonderful that women can now believe in so many different things, and form their own ideas? I believe that this kind of intellectual difference ought to be celebrated. After all, we all share the same goal: to understand humanity and save it from chaos.'

Helena hoped her friend was right.

Interlude

Leonie had been gone for a few hours to one of her meetings and Philothée was alone in the flat. She had come to visit her aunt, they had drunk tea. She had asked after some of her belongings, and they had discussed life in the Studio.

She had been living in Auteuil for a couple of weeks now, in the Avenue Mozart, number 87. The property contained a private residence, a substantial garden, and the 'temple', a large hall that was accessed by an imposing marble staircase. 87 Avenue Mozart had quickly become the basis of the so-called Independent Group of Esoteric Studies, and lectures, conferences and workshops were run out of the premises. The plan was to expand into the profitable publishing business, something Samuel's spies had assured him that the London chapter of the Golden Dawn was keen on. The first book which was being sent to print was titled *L'ésoterisme dans l'Art*, and had been prefaced by none other than Georges Méliès, *le patron*. Since opening their doors to the public, and indeed to some minor Hermetic Orders, Moina Mathers and her husband were closer than ever to their ultimate goal: becoming the centre of a spiritual movement that merged theological doctrines with the transformative power of the arts, the artist becoming as important, or nearly, as Samuel, the leader. People who came to Auteuil had to conform to this vision. In exchange they obtained instant access to books, journals, discussions, as well as meeting places and even new members. The move to the suburbs had been a success.

Philothée rarely came into the city; when she did it was usually on the Matherses' business, or to visit her aunt. She was only back to gather a few of her possessions that had not made it to the villa. She had everything she needed in Auteuil, including a new wardrobe, and books aplenty. But she had come to Paris with a small suitcase, containing photographs of her mother and her sister, a knitted blanket from her childhood, her school bible, and other small comforts that she had not wanted to leave behind. When Moina had suggested they would send someone to get her things, she had hoped all of these would come in the trunk; but the trunk had arrived mostly empty, except for a few items of clothing, all these few sentimental objects left behind. After her aunt had left her, Philothée looked for her battered case and started packing. Leonie had tried to convince her to accompany her to her meeting, but Philothée had said she needed to get back immediately to Auteuil, though not without promising they would go together some other day. Leonie had kissed her on the head, and she had left.

Once Philothée was done, she looked around the apartment once more. The view was into a courtyard, but it was pretty one, a couple of almond trees giving the illusion of looking into a park.

A memory surfaced of talking to her mother, who was showing her a letter from her sister Leonie in Paris. There was an unexpected opening in her place of work, the reason being that some of the girls who had worked for her boss as dancers, all of them pretty girls – mind you, much less pretty than Philothée, she had written – had suddenly stopped coming; nobody knew where they were. After this, the letter explained, other dancers had said they did not want to come, and so everyone had been asked to try and find someone suitable. Everyone who was a trusted employee, as Leonie was.

Now, some months later, Philothée was trying to remember how she had interpreted these words, read out loud in their small parlour over the well-known round table, her mother's tea things mismatched but still pretty; her mother had a knack for pretty things, she had always had it. There had been nothing sinister or suspicious about the words themselves, about the letter, except perhaps the statement that other professional dancers were now refusing to work for *le patron*. Now *that* was interesting. The distorted faces and the loose limbs now came to mind, and how the women who descended from the ceiling after the flying illusion needed to be helped back into their changing rooms.

Philothée left the apartment, and instructed the hansom driver to carry her small case to the cab, and he helped her in. They set off.

Paris was showing off its loveliest colours. This was the kind of unexpected autumnal light in a spring evening that made one wish for colder nights and sitting with a book near a fire. It would be many months until that happened. *Would she still be with Moina and her husband?* she wondered. Autumn nights were Moina's favourite, when the separation between the seen and the unseen, the revealed and the occult, life and death itself, diminished, and, she claimed, unexpected portals were opened that allowed us to peer into the unknown.

In the light of what she had seen at Star Film Studio, Philothée was forming a theory of her own. She was embarrassed to recognise the fact, but the truth was that she hadn't given a single thought to the dancing ladies since she had swapped the Studio for the Mathers villa. And yet. There was one explanation that tied it all together, and it was that the dancers had not just stopped coming to work for Monsieur Méliès, but rather that they had disappeared altogether.

She still had some work to do before going to bed, and the little case she had brought with her was forgotten in the hansom cab, so upset she felt with where her thoughts were going, running like a wild river in her mind. She returned to her cataloguing of Samuel's alchemical equipment: the old crucibles and alembics; the aludels and retorts scattered on the large solid mahogany desk; the framed Rosicrucian engravings and the jewel-encrusted talismans. She worked until she felt exhausted, ready to go straight to sleep.

But sleep, alas, did not come. Philothée woke up and went out into the main reception area, where she knew there were hashish pipes lying around, and she got enough to prepare a small one, hoping it would help her enter into oblivion. Ten minutes after laying it down, she became conscious of somebody else in the room. But it was herself. She was conscious that she was lying on her back in the house at Auteuil; she was conscious of the heavy wooden furniture, the walls encrusted with occult tomes she did not yet understand, the heavy English drapes Samuel favoured, and herself, lying on her bed. She was scared for a second she would not be able to come back into her body, and saw her face from above, strangely blank, the vacant eyes as distorted as the dancers'.

And then she woke up, cold and drenched in sweat, shivering, exhausted and scared. As if she had not slept at all in a decade.

5

THE GHOST OF
CHRISTMAS PAST

16th March – Afternoon

E liza had not felt this upset for a long time. Helena would
have to listen to her now. It was one thing to accept that
her associate was the professional detective, and to defer to
her on matters of procedure; it was a very different thing to be
thrown into this mess, into danger.

She had the letters in her bag. She had not dared look at
them. Once she was in the client's room, as instructed, she had
retrieved them just in time, before the thug had arrived. At least
twice she had feared the man would break the bed or toss it
over and find her there. Miraculously, this had not happened.
Did Helena not realise that she could put Eliza in danger
sending her there? She had spent the morning putting two and
two together in her head. If she had been sent to retrieve the
clothes and other items for their new client, it must have been
because the new client could not go back to her own dwellings
safely. If that was the case, why then had Helena sent Eliza into
the wolf's mouth without warning her?

She reflected on all this as the hansom cab took her later that afternoon to the agency. Through the window, the commonplace images of a normal day like any other; the sun was shining as well in a mockery to her spirits. She was mentally bruised, but alive, and the fact of how close she had been to getting hurt was by far her least reason to be angry. For she had retrieved the letters, and she had hidden under the bed, and only later, a long time after the man had gone, had she crawled out, and found a case, thrown into it some clothes that she now collected from the floor; and only then something, a lingering smell, or a memory, had slowly awakened. And then she had it in her hand, the very shawl that she herself had knitted, so long ago. *Mina*. It was not possible. Had Mina given it away, to a charity perhaps, after their relationship ended? She had it then, a horrid moment of realisation, and had unbound the letters from their wrapping to read who their recipient was.

Her heart had missed a beat, stopping for what must have been little more than a second inside her chest, but one that felt like an eternity.

She confronted with disbelief the loved words, the name repeated slowly so many times, in darkness, in intimacy, in love, only to be lost forever: Miss Carmina Lowry, *her* Mina. That was their mysterious new client.

How could Helena do something like that to her?

Now in the hansom, she extracted the bundle from her canvas bag. She was too much of a professional to look at them, but held them there, expecting to feel something more than shock and anger. Perhaps she was getting to a point when she could move on, who knew? The cab jolted on a stone-paved alleyway, and the bundle fell from her lap. Distracted, Eliza bent over her knees in the moving vehicle and clumsily gathered the letters, much as she had seen Helena gathering and mixing the tarot cards, forming a small heap. With no little difficulty, she climbed back onto her seat, and folded the letters into the shawl. They had arrived in Marylebone, and she paid the driver. As she went up to the agency, she realised how tired she was, an enormous tiredness, as if she had just swum across the Atlantic. Going home, having a bath and changing her ripped clothes had not helped much. She was still bruised: a small cut on her cheek that she had not noticed at the time, but that must have appeared when she hid under the bed in a hurry, was refusing to heal and she could feel it seeping droplets of blood. She quickly wiped it now with her hand, opened the door, and went directly to her desk without saying anything to Helena, who was looking through crates of books and files. Eliza sat heavily on her chair.

'Eliza, do you have the letters?' was all her greeting.

'Yes. I have the letters.'

'I am trying to arrange things a little for Miss Webster,' Helena started. 'She is stopping by now, and my trip to Oxford took longer than I expected…' Only then did she look up, and notice the cut. 'Oh dear. What has happened to you?'

'Let's say I wasn't the only one who knew where Miss Lowry…' the formality of the loved name was hard on her mouth, stacking itself right at the top of it, '… who knew where Miss Lowry was staying.'

'This is entirely my fault. I should have foreseen this, I should have anticipated that this could happen. I am so, so sorry, Eliza. Are you hurt?'

'No. Yes. Only my pride. This is nothing,' she said, gesturing towards the small cut.

Helena looked as if she did not understand. Eliza thought she would have to lay it all bare, and she felt increasingly ashamed. But she must, or the truth was bound to come out in a much more awkward situation, if that was even possible, whenever she needed to interact with Miss Lowry, Mina, for the purposes of their investigation. She hated that Helena had put her in this uncomfortable position, but she ought to speak.

'Look, Helena. What you have done is not good at all; this is not a partnership at the moment. And I—'

'I know, I know. I truly am very sorry, I've been a fool, and I hope you forgive me. But still, I am glad you are unhurt. How did you manage to escape? Did they see you?'

'I crawled under the bed in time. It was a man. And no, he did not see me.'

'Thank god for that! Good thinking.'

But he was destroying the room, he could have flung the bed aside at any moment, Eliza thought and did not say.

'I am not referring to putting me in danger,' struggled Eliza, 'or how close I have come to being harmed today, although that is bad enough. I am talking about accepting cases without consulting me first.'

Helena raised her eyebrows, but did not say anything.

'Look, I – I know Miss Lowry.'

'You know her? Carmina Lowry?'

'*Mina* Lowry.'

The penny dropped. Helena's eyes widened in disbelief, and she covered her mouth with her hand.

'Goodness… Yes, that is rather unfortunate, I agree.'

Unfortunate was a big understatement. If there was one person, and only one, in the whole universe Eliza did not want to cross paths with, it was her former lover, Mina.

As Helena knew, their parting had been acrimonious. And Eliza's part in it had been rather less edifying than she liked to remember. In other words, Mina had been entirely justified in leaving her. Still, she had hoped they would not need to meet again. Eliza went on to explain this.

'I am sure you understand, Helena, that, with Mina being someone from my past, I don't think I can be involved with the case.'

'I see.'

'But also…' Eliza was clearly fighting with her emotions. She got up, walked a couple of paces, sat down again. 'There is something else. Look, Helena. I am beginning to wonder whether we can work together at all, if you are just going to go ahead and make all sorts of decisions by yourself, when we had agreed we would always take them together.'

'You are absolutely right. And I apologise, unreservedly. This is all rather unfortunate,' Helena said again. 'But you also have to admit that it is a terribly sad coincidence. Who would have thought it possible that Mina, of all people, would end up coming here, of all places? I obviously did not know it was her.

And to be perfectly honest with you, Eliza, she thinks her life is in danger. I could not have turned her out of the door even if I had realised who she was. I imagine you would have done the same.'

She was probably right, although Eliza was cross about this as well.

'Can I show you something?'

Helena pulled over an atlas of France, and pointed towards a circle, drawn in pencil, comprising a large area outside of Versailles, with large Xs dutifully marking two locations.

'These two places are less than a mile apart.'

'I see. But I fail to see why this is relevant.'

'Eliza, may I ask, when was the last time you spoke with Miss Lowry…? With Mina.'

'About two years ago this last Christmas.' Mina had left her for good on Christmas Eve.

'I see. And do you know where she has been since? Or, rather, where she was recently?'

'No. Why would I?' Eliza was now looking from Helena to the map. 'Do you mean…?'

'Exactly. Miss Lowry was staying with a friend in the outskirts of Paris, a friend who works here.' Helena placed a finger over the first X.

'What is there?'

'Georges Méliès's moving-picture studio, Star Films.'

'How is that connected to…?' But Helena was already showing the little distance between the two exes on the map. 'And this place is…'

143

'Less than a mile from Versailles, where the misses experienced their uncanny little window opening into the past.'

'This is not possible,' said Eliza.

'I know.'

'It's too much of a coincidence.' Eliza was now getting animated.

'Aurora thinks the same,' said Helena, and immediately regretted it.

'Of course she does.'

'At least we both agree with her on something: there are no coincidences, not this big, anyway.'

'What are you saying, Helena?'

'I've got a theory. But at present it is only a suspicion, I have no evidence to support it yet.'

'I'm all ears.'

'Do you remember how Miss Moberly and Miss Jourdain said they were being followed?'

'Yes.'

'In my note I had no time to explain how I came to meet Miss Lowry.' Helena explained now how Mina had arrived on the landing after Eliza and the two ladies had left the building.

'Are you implying that it was Mina who was following them? But why?'

'I've no idea. But it is the only explanation I can think of for her showing up at our door right after them, and the fact of their two mysteries happening within less than a mile from each other, in another country. Both parties showing up here on the same night; two cases, knocking at our door on the same day, both tracing back to the same place. Gad, Eliza! We are not even open for business yet!'

'I understand.'

'Eliza, I really am sorry about what has happened. I had no way to know that Miss Lowry was... is your Mina. But, even if it had dawned on me, I don't think I could have said no to her, especially when I fear that these two cases may somehow be connected.'

'But how, Helena? How can they possibly be connected?'

Helena related everything Mina had shared with her, about her friend being taken in plain sight, the absolute impunity with which it was done.

'Miss Lowry fears for her life. She suspects that the letters contain information that someone is after, or wants to keep secret.'

'These letters...' Eliza unwrapped the bundle.

'Exactly. Our next task will be to go over them as carefully as possible.'

'I don't know how I feel about doing that.'

'I understand. Why don't we divide things like this? We need to know more about Miss Lowry's friend's daily life in Paris, more about her occupation, and all of that. So I will study the letters, talk to Miss Lowry, try to get to the bottom of her connection with the misses; meanwhile, I will ask Miss Webster to find some information for us, on Georges Méliès and his film studio.' After the first shock of their conversation, Helena had gone back to moving crates and piles of books. Eliza now came to join her.

'So… you will deal with Mina?' Eliza was starting to blush.

'I think that, at present, we need to make sure Miss Lowry trusts us, so we are going to need Aurora's help.' Helena let this sink in, and then continued. 'I will have to prevail on her to keep our guest in her shop a little longer.'

'Are you going to ask her directly if she was following the misses?'

Helena thought about this. Presently, she said:

'It is obvious to me that Miss Lowry is hiding some information, and that we do not know her motives. But I also believe that the basic reasons why I decided to take on her case do apply: she is in danger; she is very scared. She probably is right that the information contained in the letters is relevant, and potentially lethal. She has trusted us with the letters.' Helena had stopped moving crates and sorting books in piles while delivering this. 'This at least means that (a) she does not know what this information might be; and (b) from this is it implied that we can trust her, inasmuch as she has trusted us with the main piece of evidence that can keep her alive. So, answering your question: I also don't believe we should force any kind of confession, or connection. It will play to our advantage to keep quiet about our suspicions.' She now resumed moving the crates and books once more.

'I see,' was all Eliza said.

'Eliza, what do you do you know about moving pictures?'

'The same as anyone else. I have been to see a couple. Not my favourite thing. I prefer a good concert any day.' She seemed relieved about the change of topic.

'Okay. Well, I may have someone who can help us. An old acquaintance of mine, Alice Guy. She moved from somewhere in Switzerland to Paris to work on these pictures. I helped her find lodgings. I will write to her at once. We also need to go over the maps and guides, and get a good sense of the locale, before we decamp there—' Eliza abruptly stopped moving books to look in shock at Helena. 'Dear Eliza, going to Paris has become our number one priority.'

'I see. In that case, I can leave tomorrow.'

'What? I am sorry, but that is out of the question.'

'Why? You said it yourself: you need to look into things here, and keep an eye on Mina. And your Miss Webster is going to compile information for us. So that only leaves one question: what about me?'

'I beg your pardon?'

'What am I supposed to do, what am I contributing to this case? If one of us needs to go to Paris, then I will go to Paris.'

'Have you been to Paris before?' Helena asked.

'Only once.' With Mina.

'Look, Eliza, whereas it is true that there are still some things that need looking after here, I think it will be best if we both go to Paris together.'

'Why? There is no need to delay our investigation. I can go now, you can come and find me there later on.' All this translated as one thing, whether Helena trusted her or not. She could see her considering the situation.

'Very well, if that's what you want.' Eliza was pleased. Helena continued, 'I am hoping that you will be able to stay with Alice, so I must send her a telegram. Now, Miss Moberly and Miss Jourdain's written accounts. We need to study them closely before you go. And you can leave Mina's letters to me.'

'What are you expecting to find?'

'I am not sure, but it will be good if we get something that connects it all. Anything. I will keep you informed.'

'There is one more thing, Helena. This man…'

'Yes! I forgot. We need to make a likeness as soon as possible of him. Did you get a good view of him?'

'Mostly his boots. Well, I did see his face, but only quickly. We better do that first, or it may go out of my head.'

'Eliza, you know what I have said about exercising your memory. It is paramount that you cultivate an almost photographic memory. You need to do everything you can to achieve this. Commit long poems to memory. Even better, learn a new language.'

'Yes, yes. I will probably need to spend tonight revisiting my French.'

They both smiled. It was good feeling that they were again focused on the same aims. Eliza had no idea if Helena truly trusted her enough to let her go to Paris on her own, but she was pleased to leave London as soon as was possible, certainly before she was thrown into Mina's company.

'Anyway, what I wanted to show you was this.'

Eliza took a programme from the pocket of her skirt and passed it to Helena.

The SPR Discovery Series of Talks & Exhibits. Helena had seen this before, the series of scientific talks and exhibits sponsored by the SPR, and, of course, the Hermetic Order of the Golden Dawn, their main public outing together as allies of a certain kind. Thick black and red programmes had been distributed everywhere in London.

'In the commotion the thug created, it fell out of his pocket,' explained Eliza.

'And? These are all over town.'

Eliza spoke tentatively: 'Well, he... he didn't look the type to have an interest in scientific talks.'

'Of course. I apologise. Point taken. That is perceptive, Eliza. Good instincts.'

Eliza beamed. They looked over the programme carefully. It must have had a hundred different events listed.

'This is impossible. We will never find him; we cannot cover so many events.'

'We'll worry about it later. Let's do the likeness.'

Their method had been devised by Eliza herself. She had made a catalogue of types of eyes, eyebrows, mouths, noses, shapes of faces. It had taken a long time. Then, they had commissioned a commercial artist to produce drawings of each one of these elements on strong paper. They opened a case – the system was designed to be portable – and they chose different versions of facial expressions according to Eliza's memory. They worked on this for a while. Once they were done, they had a good likeness of the man in question: round-faced, rugged-looking, heavy eyebrows and small black eyes, very much like a villain in a children's book.

'Yes, that is him. I have no doubt.'

'Now *that* is impressive!'

Both women turned to the door, where a young woman was standing. Eliza had never met Miss Webster, and, in the face of such elegance, her instinctive reaction was to stand up courteously. The woman regaled her with a wide smile. She was tall and expensively dressed.

'I apologise – the door was left open.'

'Miss Webster! Please, come in. I am so happy that you made it. This is my associate and business partner, Miss Eliza Waltraud. Eliza, this is Miss Jocasta Webster, our new archivist.'

'How you do, Miss Waltraud? It is I who is happy to be here. And thank you once again for hiring me. Where do I sit?'

There was a bit of a scramble moving crates and finding chairs, but eventually the desk in the main library area was vacated, and Miss Webster's impressive resumé commented upon, including her time as junior under-librarian at the New York Society Library, or her achievements as female chess champion for New York State. Eventually, the young woman took off her coat, revealing a waistcoat to match her skirt, fastened over a white blouse; she immediately went towards the crates, and took charge of proceedings. She stopped from time to time to analyse the different shelves the carpenters had built, and shortly declared she would 'get on with it' if that was acceptable. Half an hour later the first books were up, and there were piles of papers organised in the middle of the room, in preparation for housing in archival boxes. All the while, Miss Webster wrote furiously in a large inventory ledger she herself had provided.

Eliza's instincts were indeed developing rapidly, for she was wondering why someone who dressed so expensively could possibly need a job of this kind. She noticed one more thing: Miss Webster had a man's fob watch hanging from the lapel of her waistcoat. Rehearsing her detection skills, she concluded that this was a significant piece: it seemed to Eliza that Miss Webster was the kind of woman capable of donning what she wanted, even wearing a male accessory; however, the old and rusty fob watch did not match her chic clothing. Her father's? Or a brother's, perhaps?

'She is extremely efficient,' commented Helena as the piles of books metamorphosed themselves, once on the shelves, into the one thing greatly admired by a detective: order. 'I think we have done enough for one day, don't you?' she said to Eliza, but got no reply. 'Why don't you go back home? I can tackle Miss Lowry's letters on my own. Besides, we both need a rest.'

Eliza nodded with a brief smile that rather suggested her inner pain than any joviality. Helena reflected on how much an open book her younger associate was, when a life of detection implied a certain amount of pretence.

They said their goodbyes, and Helena was left with Miss Webster. She had dreaded dealing with the book chaos, and was happy to see the sorting finally happening. She had to be on hand to answer a couple of things, but mostly Miss Webster was getting on splendidly on her own. When she realised she would not be needed by her new recruit, Helena set to work as there was no time to waste: things were progressing at a dizzying speed. Noting down step-by-step approaches to given problems, the current list of necessities to advance this particular investigation was now getting awfully long. When it was time to leave she took the bundle of letters with her: it was a good idea to take them home, for she could put them in her safe. Perhaps it would not be a bad idea, she thought, to have a safe in the agency. She took a pencil, found the to-do list, which was already three pages long, and added the word 'Safe' at the very end.

17th of March – Morning

They reconvened in Eliza's rooms. Her trunk and cases were packed, waiting by the door for the driver of her hansom to arrive later that day. They had the misses' accounts laid out in front of them. They sat at a little round table that seemed designed to play cards on rather than for the business of investigation, and Eliza provided hot mugs of coffee.

Then they read.

Miss Moberly's Account of her Visit to the Petit Trianon on 10th August 1901

It was August last year. Miss Jourdain and I were on holiday in Paris, and we decided to visit Versailles. Neither of us had been there, or knew much about the place.

We took the early train and, upon arrival, spent a considerable time inspecting the many rooms and galleries, and then stopped for a rest in the Galerie des Glaces, enjoying the morning breeze that entered through the opened windows. The sweet smell of flowers invaded it all; it was overpowering. I took it as an invitation, as if the gardens were calling us. I suggested to my companion that we should go and see the Petit Trianon, which I knew to be a little farm where Marie Antoinette kept lambs, churned butter, and did other domestic chores to amuse herself. The notion of pretence was interesting to me: why would a queen have a need for such a place?

We found its location in the Baedeker and set off. The sky was a little overcast all of a sudden: the sun had hidden under some clouds. We reached a little copse, and, looking at the map, decided that was the way to follow. After reaching a long lake, and passing the Grand Trianon to our left, we took the path we thought was the correct one.

What happened then is difficult to describe. The truth is that an extraordinary depression overcame me, which deepened, in spite of every effort on my part to shake it off. I must stress there was absolutely no reason for it. I looked around me, at the trees and the lane, and I felt as if things were not meant to be there, or made no sense somehow. I was anxious that my companion would discover the sudden gloom upon my spirits; I did not know then, and would not know until we talked about it, many days later, that she was feeling some deep repulsion for the place, as if her body was alerting her most powerfully that we ought not to be there.

'Feelings of repulsion?' commented Helena, interrupting Eliza's reading. 'They did not mention any of this yesterday.'

'Indeed they did not,' confirmed Eliza, who was now thinking: had the ladies had a bad dinner the night before like the papers had suggested? But all she said was: 'Shall I continue?'

'Please.'

In front of us was a little wood, and inside this wood, we both saw clearly a man sitting. The ground was covered with dead leaves, and the place looked shut and otherworldly. Everything seemed unnatural, felt unpleasant; even the trees behind the building were flat and lifeless, like a wood worked in tapestry: an image, instead of a real place. No wind stirred the trees; everything was unnaturally still. The trees were simply there, as in a childish embroidery.

My whole body started to shake, as the man got up and walked in our direction. He was handsome, but looked as lifeless as the place around him; he reminded me of an old picture. I was in shock, I could not move. It was as though a demon walked towards us. He had the jaunty manners of a footman, and wore a livery. I also remember that he wore buckled shoes. As he got closer, he stopped right in front of us, and, for a second, it seemed that he was talking to us through a darkened mirror, or perhaps we were looking at him through a window. He said nothing to us. His whole demeanour was saddening, and I started feeling as though we had somehow trespassed within the public gardens, as if we ought not to be there, as if something was wrong.

Miss Jourdain, who was holding onto the Baedeker for dear life, got hold of my arm, and she cried, 'Look!' I hardly knew what she referred to, except that there was a bridge behind the man, and that this bridge was not in our guide's map. How was that possible? The only thing to do was to press on. We reached an open meadow, the place was deserted. Was it possible that none of the dozens of visitors who had walked around the palace had desired to walk through the gardens like us? The whole place felt wrong somehow; the light cast a sombre look upon everything. I started feeling again the overcoming dread, as if we were looking into another garden, or in a mirror version of our garden. As if a timeless window into another world had opened there for us.

'A timeless window into another world...' Eliza stopped reading. Helena noticed she was shivering.

'Whatever is the matter, Eliza? Do you want us to stop?'

'No,' was all she would say.

She continued reading:

The feeling of dreariness was particularly strong here. We saw a lady sitting on the grass, wearing a light summer dress with a bodice, and a light muslin tucked in it, as with the fashions of old. We first thought she must have been a tourist, but her dress was so old-fashioned. She looked at us with pure hatred, as if we were intruding in a private moment, and as if she had power to force us out of there.

By then, we could not understand anything that was happening to us, except that instinctively we took each other's hands, and,

155

*after seeing some brighter light showing at the other end of a copse,
we walked there resolutely, neither of us sharing her misgivings
with the other. We came through to the other side of the copse, and
there was a sudden change: everything seemed alive, and not as if
we had been walking inside a lifeless simulacrum of life. We came
into a path, and there we saw a little carriage carrying some other
tourists. We looked back – everything was normal now.*

*The carriage drove us back to the Hotel des Réservoirs in
Versailles, where we had a remedial tea. Neither of us confided
in the other our impressions of the otherworldly afternoon; we
would do so only days later, when, armed once more with the
Baedeker, we would march on, this time ascertaining that its map
was correct.*

*We went back at least four times, but could not find the
meadow, the bridge that we saw behind the man in old-fashioned
robes. We also did not experience again the feeling of looking
through a window into another world. Maps and engravings
and many plans that we have collected since, visiting libraries,
archives, antiquaries, all show a clear discrepancy between the
Trianon with the bridge and the meadow, and the Trianon now,
without them. The question therefore that we dare to ask is not
what we saw, but when we saw. A very particular question,
and one that we cannot comprehend or satisfactorily resolve
at present.*

*After tea we walked back to the station, looking on the way
for the famous tennis court. We were back in Paris in time
for supper.*

Helena's casebook was open on her mahogany desk. It was filled with all sorts of information, including letters, photographs and maps of Versailles, of the English Garden, of the Trianon itself. First, they had read the account by Miss Moberly; now they tackled Miss Jourdain's account. Needless to say, although written separately from her friend's, it resembled it nearly word for word, especially her impressions, her feelings, the increasing dread that the experience had created for her.

Miss Jourdain had written:

'For a whole week we never alluded to our strange walk. Whenever I thought about it, the same feeling of dread and unnatural oppression came over me so strongly that I could hardly recollect our visit. One day I said to Miss Moberly: "Do you think that the Petit Trianon is haunted?" to which she responded immediately: "Yes! I do!"'

'So, they had discussed the incident before putting down their statements. That is not very scientific,' Eliza pointed out sharply.

'Much later, I discussed the story with my elder brother, and we agreed that such experiences made little impression upon us, and that, if only the people involved in occurrences like this would take the trouble to investigate them, thoroughly and honestly for themselves, they could be quite naturally explained. He suggested *lightly and in fun that maybe we had seen the Queen as she saw herself in her times of play in the Trianon, and that it would be interesting to know whether the dress described was the one she used when she went there to play lady-farmer.'*

'I cannot help but notice,' Eliza began, 'that the ladies contradict themselves at each step: they insist on not believing in these things, on wanting to use a scientific method to investigate them, and on not being clearly disposed to believe in this kind of event, while at the same time their accounts are filled with...'

'Sensations, feelings,' offered Helena. 'Dread, fear, incomprehension.'

'Exactly. Look, they both allude to being lost. They might have *felt* lost as well. Let me check one thing.' Eliza looked quickly over the guides and plans of the gardens that Helena had procured for her to take with her, and announced: 'I suspect that the ladies might have stumbled upon the Temple de l'Amour or the Belvédère: it has a "hidden" bridge, which crosses over the river. It is not on the tourist trail. I wonder if they stumbled upon this, precisely by "getting lost" and leaving the tourist trail behind,' she concluded.

'Goodness, what a mess! Is it all going to be so simple to refute?' asked Helena, half joking.

'I was thinking the same,' offered Eliza. But she was also thinking, why had Helena insisted on taking the case?

There was something else: the two ladies had noted the importance of the date of their own adventure, a date of violence, which could suggest a haunting in the palace. It could be a coincidence, or it could throw new light on the Moberly–Jourdain incident:

> 'On August 10th 1792, the Tuileries Palace was stormed. The royal family managed to escape in the early morning to the hall of the Legislative Assembly, from where it was possible for them to hear the massacre of their servants and the Swiss guards at the Tuileries. From the hall the King and Queen were taken to the Temple.'

'A date charged with meaning,' said Helena darkly. 'However, that does not prove anything.' Eliza nodded in agreement. But Helena was thinking, was it possible that the ladies had seen ghosts, rather than opened a window a take a peek into the past? She could not speculate out loud about this, not to Eliza, and knew she needed to tread lightly.

Helena now shared what she had learnt in Oxford. Eliza whistled.

'My goodness! Are the ladies of sound mind at all?'

'It certainly bears being collected in our casebook. It speaks to their character.'

But Eliza was not really listening. She had gone very quiet. Eventually she said:

'Look, it is not ideal. We both know it. But we will be in constant communication.' She was referring to her going to Paris on her own. 'Besides, you will come and join me soon. Miss Webster can help us with the research from here. And Aurora can look after Mina.'

'I should have asked Aurora to come with you.'

Eliza laughed: 'I'd much rather go by myself, believe me.'

'Are you serious? I know you don't like Aurora, but surely—'

'It is not a question of liking or disliking,' interrupted Eliza. 'I don't trust her.'

'Why not?'

'Have we not said that we would approach everything with detachment and scientific zeal?'

'And when have I not done so?'

'Helena… what we have just read, and what you found out in Oxford, all this is worrying me a great deal. It is difficult not to come to the conclusion that becoming involved with this case doesn't make much sense at all.'

Helena said nothing, just let her speak. In many ways, this was worse. But she carried on: 'It is almost as if we are not fully in control of our investigation anymore, but that other people are influencing our thinking.'

'And you think this person influencing our thinking is… Aurora?'

'I am worried, that is all.'

'Worried about what?'

'Worried that you are showing too much of an inclination towards the supernatural lately. You have been doing more than attending séances and psychic performances, Helena. I know that something else is happening.'

Helena wondered if it was the moment to share her secret. The chiming bells, the premonitions. Going into a trance when she read the tarot cards. But she needed more time. Instead, she said:

'Eliza, to me, all of these things form part of the same research, part of the Method.'

Eliza sighed.

Helena continued: 'You have to trust me. We do agree on the fundamentals: proof is needed in order to believe in certain things. All I am doing is trying to find this proof.'

'So do you still think we should look into this strange matter? When you spoke of opening a detective agency, I pictured something different. Solving complicated murders. Finding missing people. Unmasking famous thieves.'

'We can still do all those things, Eliza! But I don't see why you are so resistant to looking into this. It is, after all, no more than another mystery. Going to Paris will help us build a picture, if nothing else, of what may have happened to Mina's friend. And you know what I think: this case is somehow related. We don't know how yet, but we need to look into both. Find proof of their madness, if you must!'

'I see.'

'This is what the Method consists of, Eliza: building a picture; drawing it, stroke by careful stroke. I do not expect that everything you find out, or everything you do, will turn out to be relevant, or irrelevant, or even exonerate the misses. But, nonetheless, scratching these items off a list, as it were, even if it closes off byways that we thought might bring us answers, will highlight the true occurrences that are connected with our two mysteries, if only by a process of elimination.'

Eliza considered this. Eventually she spoke.

'Very well. I've got my marching orders.'

'There is something else.' It was clear that Helena had tiptoed around this for a while: 'Since you are not going to be here, I need to ask.' Eliza raised her eyebrows. 'I need to know more about Mina. You know her, intimately. I hope you understand that it would help us immensely, since she is not being entirely open with us, to have some idea as to her possible motivations.'

'What do you need to know?'

Helena had thought about this in advance. In fact, she had hardly slept considering this conversation. She could only ask Eliza a few questions; it wasn't fair otherwise. She wanted to know what were the most important things for Mina; had she ever shown any inclination towards the occult, and if so, had Eliza known her to ever join an occult organisation in the past.

'Well, I guess publishing her book. Mina's career is... non-existent. She is a wonderful writer, but has been rather unlucky.'

'How important is it to publish for her?'

'Oh dear. Even while we were together she had been trying for years, and was rather desperate. She would have sold her soul in exchange for getting published, believe me.' This was rather interesting. 'And about the occult, oh yes. She believed in fairies and such. We used to argue a lot about this. And no, I don't think she ever joined a society, other than writers' groups. At least while I knew her.'

'Thank you, Eliza. This is very helpful. There is one other thing, though I am not sure how to put it delicately... Did she ever partake, to excess, of opium, laudanum, morphine? Anything of that kind?'

'Not at all. Not while I knew her, at least,' said Eliza with finality. Helena did not elaborate but simply thanked her.

'Let's go over Paris then, please,' she asked. 'I can't believe I am agreeing to this.'

'It is not your decision, it is mine.'

Helena wondered if Eliza was putting on more of a brave face than she felt. But she wasn't going to back out now.

'Very well. Alice will meet you at your arrival. She has arranged lodgings for you in the hotel where she lives. She will also take you to Star Film Studio, and introduce you to Méliès. Is he connected with the Dawn at all? We need to find out. *Do* visit the Trianon; it is important that we also gather our own impressions *in situ*. And go to Miss Emily's cottage. Alice assures me she will be with you at all times, so you will not be alone. That is all.'

Eliza seemed confused.

'That is all? You don't expect me to solve this before you join me?'

Helena seemed bemused by this.

'It is not a matter of expecting or not expecting. Your trip is one of information gathering, and, if we are lucky, getting proof of our possible theories. But we will need to get all those theories together. I won't expect you to do much more on your own; it would not be fair.'

Eliza wasn't sure how she felt about this: was Helena being protective, or patronising?

'And please, Eliza, even if you don't believe yourself to be in danger, even if you don't believe in fairies at the bottom of your garden, for God's sake, be careful.'

17th March – Afternoon

As soon as she was by herself Helena made a quick decision: Eliza had been brave taking the lead with the Paris trip. Surely Helena could also face her own fears.

She telephoned Chaffins's at once, and had a short chat with Miss Lowry. Although it was a Tuesday, the shop was closed for the day and Aurora had gone to fetch some more items from 'somewhere in the docks'. Helena knew exactly where Miss Lowry meant: a warehouse where her friend bought items sometimes, in front of the Isle of Dogs by the Thames. She talked a little more with Miss Lowry, who sounded in good spirits, and even mentioned that she had been writing a little.

'It is so peaceful here. Again, I am really thankful, Miss Walton-Cisneros.'

'Oh, please. Call me Helena.'

'Then please call me Mina!'

Helena grimaced, biting her tongue: she would need to come clean with Miss Lowry, Mina, as soon as possible, about her partnership with Eliza.

'I am really pleased for you,' she said for now. 'I should come and visit soon, I may have a few more questions to put to you. And I know that not being able to leave premises freely can be wearisome at times, when indeed I must ask you to stay indoors for the time being.'

'Don't worry on my account, Helena. I have been thinking about getting on with my writing, and these conditions are perfect – there will be no distractions! Also, Miss Webster has been to tea.' Interesting, thought Helena.

After she had put the phone down, Helena went into the street and called a hansom cab. If she had enough money, she knew exactly what she would want to acquire for the agency: a motor-car. For now, that was little more than a dream.

London was its usual hubbub of activity. On route, Helena had some time to herself to think. She had really made a blunder with Eliza, and hoped she could be forgiven. She felt embarrassed by the whole thing. Poor Eliza. It was all her fault. She did not relish the task ahead either: she knew Aurora was more than reticent to discuss her past connection to the Dawn. She wondered whether she was on the way to hurt another friend, and hoped not.

In truth, she was looking forward to talking with Aurora, and hoped that her friend and mentor would help her connect the few pieces, so few, already in her possession. She hoped that she could provide her with information about the comings and goings of the Golden Dawn, something, anything, that might explain their interest in the Trianon incident. But there were other things she was hoping to discuss, of a more personal nature. Her visions were becoming more frequent now, and she suspected that Eliza had begun to realise that something was going on. Why had she been so keen on going to Paris at the earliest opportunity? Had she wanted to put the English Channel between herself and Miss Lowry, or between herself and Helena?

She found Aurora inside the warehouse, exactly as she was expecting. Her friend greeted her with an expression of 'look what the cat dragged in' that made her smile.

'I really had to see you, sorry to blunder in like this.'

'On the contrary! I value your opinion, what do you think?' she said, showing her two small figurines of a feminine deity, which both looked much the same to Helena.

'They are pretty…?'

'Oh, goodness! You are hopeless!' They laughed. 'Well, at least we can go and have lunch together. Mind you, the last thing I want is to leave young Mina alone longer than necessary.'

'Very prudent. Thank you. I just talked to her on the phone, she says she is planning to do some writing.'

'Yes, that is good news; an artist cannot stop doing what they must. Anyway, what was it that couldn't wait? Why have you come all the way here? And why that look? No one is dead, I hope?' Aurora moved deftly among crates and boxes half opened, and requested to know the price of one of the little statues.

'I find myself once more in need of your expertise.'

'My expertise in occult matters?'

'Something a little more specific, I am afraid.'

Aurora looked quizzically back at her. Then, 'The Golden Dawn,' she said, rather perceptively. 'Ah.' Eventually, she looked about her, and obviously deciding there was nothing of note there, she added: 'Indeed. Shall we eat lunch first? I think that conversation requires to be fortified with plenty of food and drink. Your treat, of course. Then I can tell you everything you want.'

'That sounds perfect, thank you, Aurora.'

They found a little shop that would sell them pies and pints of ale, and they sat overlooking the river. It was an odd lunch for someone as dainty as Aurora, who kept picking out the tiniest crumbs of pastry and taking them to her mouth, as if she were scared of taking a proper bite of the monstrous thing.

They started discussing the weather, of all things, both commenting on the unseasonably warm and dry March they were having, which seemed to have pushed all Londoners out from the flea-infested abodes into the street like lizards. Some brave souls were even trying to bathe on the murky and dangerous river. The conversation soon moved on to a plant that Aurora had bought on leaving the warehouse. It was only St John's Wort. Helena knew her friend had been searching for another 'magical' plant for years, an elusive species, credited with curing leprosy.

'It is a bit of a legend, you know. We don't really know if it exists or not. It's a mystery. But several accounts place it in Siberia, in the middle of the tundra.'

Helena knew the reason for Aurora's interest: back at her flat, on the mantelpiece, a blond man, in the prime of his youth, looked very seriously into the camera. He was holding a book and had a pipe in his mouth, which made him look absurdly like a child in fancy dress. It was Arthur, Aurora's long-dead brother, who had succumbed to leprosy while on his grand tour twenty years previously.

'It all sounds so mysterious. Are you after its scientific or... legendary properties?'

Aurora chuckled.

'Well, my friend, a bit of both. Look, all the properties I expect to extract from it, I assure you, I would have read about in anthropological books and in travelogues. But frankly, I don't care as long as leprosy can be finally eradicated.'

Helena had some occult knowledge herself, after all. She offered: 'Didn't Blavatsky mention magic plants in *Isis Unveiled?*' She smiled widely as she helped herself to the ale. It was warm. Aurora laughed.

'No doubt she was trying to justify her fondness for smoking hashish pipes. In some cultures,' said Aurora, 'the soul wanders through a door, or a portal, in order to find the healthy version of the self, and bring it back. That is what the plant is meant to do, according to the anthropological accounts: to transport you there and bring you back. Who says that is not what happens when we drink a medicine?'

They continued to eat in companionable silence, as much as could be eaten of the pies, whose insides looked suspicious to say the least, like all good London pies did. They were both making a very good pretence of being interested in the comings and goings out on the river.

Eventually Helena said: 'Aurora, the truth is, I have never really asked you about the Dawn.'

'About the Dawn? Or about *me* and the Dawn?' the older woman smiled. 'My dear, that is, as we say in my village, yesterday's newspaper, only good to wrap today's fish. The truth is, I never amounted to much. I had no patience with their strict rules. I am not talking only about the rituals, mind you, but about all the administrative organisation as well. It really was a bit too much for me.'

Aurora went on to explain that, in the first years, the Golden Dawn worked almost like a college, with a very serious hierarchy of learning alongside tedious, complex rituals.

'I am talking about the most strict kind of magic that you can imagine! Nothing was left to chance: a tremendously technical kind of magic. Completely void of the intuition that you know I greatly favour.'

'I can see how that would not have been to your liking.'

'Mind you, perhaps their reasons to want to get to grips with everything in a thorough manner were not too bad… The major tenet of dispute among all these societies, clubs, and occult whatnots? The very definition of 'occult', my dear friend, is that which we cannot see, and these societies sometimes just want to see. So the question is, do they aspire to knowledge alone, or to do something with that knowledge?'

'To do something?'

'Power, Helena.'

'I see.'

'That is all I can really think of that may be relevant. But don't worry, I will help you get to the bottom of things. What else are friends for?'

'Thank you, Aurora.'

'So, let me think. Both your mysteries originate in Paris, correct?' Helena nodded while sipping her ale. 'Right, Paris. So we know, of course, that Samuel Mathers, co-founder of the Dawn, lives there, at least since he was deposed, exiled."

'That's all I know,' explained Helena, 'that he was expelled from the organisation. What can you tell me anything else about him?'

Aurora obliged. She went on to describe a charismatic man with many interests beside the occult, including politics and sports – he was apparently a keen fencer – who had spent his adult life creating his own system of ritualistic magic, which was to become the Inner Order's rituals. 'He was not only full of fresh ideas, but he was the brains behind the Inner Circle, of all these rituals that we see now. I imagine how unhappy he must have been to be given the boot from an organisation that he so carefully crafted.'

Aurora explained that Mathers had fought ferociously for control of the Dawn. There was a race to find something capable of increasing the power of their magic rituals.

'Mathers believes that some substances, not too dissimilar to Blavatsky's pipes, ought to be taken before rituals, as they give moments of… illumination. The theory is that certain states of intoxication might create spiritually significant moments.'

'Substances?'

'This constituted a major rift, my friend: some were concerned that, even if these substances are effective to detach the soul from its material envelope – your physical body,' Aurora helpfully translated, 'the results are artificially produced, and not as valid as true transcendence. Hence the terms *"fantasia"*, or *"somnambules extatiques"*, used to explain them. And there is one more issue at stake: I am sure you are aware of how highly valued the idea of temperance is for Woodbury and his associates.'

'I can see how abstinence from toxic substances would speak to the SPR's ... obsessive discourse on the need for "purity" in the occult milieu,' put in Helena. Aurora nodded. 'What did Mathers think these substances would do, exactly?'

'Well, what is a person who dedicates herself to the occult really doing? Straining to see the unseen. Call it whatever you want: detaching yourself from this world, engaging with your non-material entity, looking beyond the veil. A section of the society certainly placed their hopes in substance-induced states to effectively remove these barriers.'

'Did any of this work, to your knowledge?'

'Not really. Mathers flew to Paris, and there he is making his own experiments. Mind you, Mathers was being faithful to the main principle of the Dawn, to use some form of "scientific method" in the pursuit of occult knowledge.' Helena looked up. This sounded interesting information to pass on to Eliza. Aurora continued: 'What is the difference between the Hermetic Order of the Golden Dawn and any other occult organisation? That they want to unveil the occult "scientifically".'

'Yes, but do they really?' Helena asked. 'I thought it was all pretence. You know, to have "scientific" arguments to defame women spiritualists.'

'Oh, the blessed ignorance of youth!' cried Aurora. 'Things are more mixed up than all of that; you of all people, ought to know this.'

'You are right. But, for the sake of argument: how would you convince someone scientifically minded of the possibility of using science to unveil human consciousness?' Helena put in. She was thinking of Eliza.

'Easily. I would ask them: what is the single most relevant scientific discovery of our times?'

'I don't know... Mr Darwin's theory of evolution?' she offered.

'Very well,' continued Aurora. 'Even Mr Darwin himself had his brushes with spiritualism, and consulted mediums.' Aurora recounted how Darwin had approached spiritualism in order to understand his daughter's death decades before. 'She was only ten years old, and apparently she suffered a long agony, poor thing. Darwin and his wife saw mediums, and even attended a regular circle of séances.'

'God, that is truly horrible.'

'So, the Dawn. Let us not forget that the earlier, founding members, all Mathers's little friends, were mostly scientists,' continued Aurora. 'William Crookes. He discovered thallium. You know, that poison that is so effective on rats.'

'Charming.'

'William Westcott was a coroner; and not just any coroner, mind you, but the crown coroner!'

'Alright. So, they believe in the supernatural, *and* also in scientific method and research.'

'Exactly. Occultists are somehow convinced that the scientific method will demonstrate that human consciousness is alive after death. They are willing to achieve this by whatever means,' Aurora summarised. 'Beyond the veil, like I said. Looking there.'

'And how would substances help with all this?'

'"Scientific revelation", they call it. And the substances themselves "technologies of transcendence".' Aurora laughed. 'Everything very scientific. It would appear that their complex and tedious magic was not giving them what they wanted after all!'

Helena was now taking notes in the little notebook she carried with her.

'But no, answering your question: nothing of this seems to have made any difference in Paris. Not to my knowledge, at least. So, when their substances did not work for them, they moved on. I think what they are trying to find now is some form of energy to aid in their rituals.'

'Energy?' asked Helena. This was unexpected.

'That's right, to enhance them.'

'What for?'

'I don't know – world domination? What do these societies truly want, Helena? Power. Power here, in this world, not in some occult realm.'

Helena gave her a quizzical look.

Aurora continued: 'The Magus – that is the main leader, or head – looks to extend his powers over all aspects of creation, both in the material world and in the spiritual dimension.' Helena flinched, and Aurora explained: 'That boring "Astral Plane".'

Helena nodded, and Aurora continued: 'That is the theory. In practice, all they desire is tangible power here, of course. Occult societies are, after all, little more than boys' clubs,' she concluded.

Aurora kept pretending to eat the unsavoury pie for a while. But Helena had lost her appetite. She was thinking of Mina's addiction, new connections and answers to questions appearing in her mind. What did this narrative mean? Had Mina become addicted in Paris, while engaged in ritualistic magic with Mathers? She now asked Aurora:

'So what do you think the Dawn wanted with my two scholar-ladies?'

'Now, that definitely beats *me*. Mm. Explain to me again, what did they say happened to them, in their own words?'

'The light changed, everything became dull around them, as if they were on a stage.'

'And then?'

'A window opened, and they saw a scene that they interpreted to be in the past.'

'A window, hmm. What about... a portal?'

'A portal?'

'Look, Helena. To the Dawn, there are few things that produce more energy than a displacement in time, space, or indeed opening a portal. If you open a portal, and this portal opens into the past... that's a bet that pays off hugely. I imagine the amount of energy that you would produce would be vast.'

'Wait, you said the two factions of the Dawn, Mathers and the others, were now occupied with finding an energy...'

'Not occupied! Fighting, my dear. And yes, a *powerful* energy.'

'A portal or door?'

Aurora nodded.

'I wonder how I could find out more about portals,' Helena found herself wondering out loud.

'Well, with wonderful Siberian shamans, my dear! They know all about portals. And I happen to know that there will be one of them in London the day after tomorrow,' Aurora announced with a smile.

'A Siberian shaman? in London?'

'That's right. Haven't you seen the programme for the SPR Discovery Series?'

'Yes, in fact I have.' It was funny how sometimes all the paths and all the thoughts and all the visions led to the same place, and somehow everyone seemed to be attuned to the same insights.

'Why don't you come with me to see him perform?'

Helena thought for a moment.

'Why not?' she found herself saying. She had always shunned SPR's public events, but perhaps she would learn something. About portals, about energy, or even about herself.

'That's settled, then. If we cannot go all the way to Siberia, at least we can let Siberia come to us! The day after tomorrow, we will be there.'

After her meeting with Aurora, Helena decided to stop by the new offices, where she found Miss Webster diligently going through the crates of books, forming piles, and even, she saw happily, completing the work on some of the shelves. After only a day under her care, the collection looked purposeful, and the place already felt less abandoned, more lived-in.

'Good afternoon,' she greeted the librarian. 'Your progress is astounding,' she indicated the shelves.

'This is a very impressive reference library, if I may say so. It must have taken you years to put it together.'

Helena walked towards her desk, and left her bag and her bonnet there.

'Sorry, I am still catching my breath,' she said, as she sat on her chair.

'Do you need anything? Water, perhaps?'

'I am okay, thank you. And yes, it has taken me a while. To tell you the truth, I had no idea there were so many books and files! They were distributed around my house; only when I started packing them to bring them here did I realise the volume of the collection.'

'It tends to happen, doesn't it? Sometimes you leave books together and it seems that they multiply of their own accord.'

They laughed.

'Can I ask, how do you know where are they going to go?'

This question animated Miss Webster, who immediately went to her desk and retrieved a notebook.

'I wanted to discuss that with you, exactly where everything is going to go. As I see it, there are four major strands to the collection,' Jocasta started explaining her plan for the organisation, together with a carefully drawn plan of the library areas.

'This is all most impressive. I am truly thankful. Once everything is in place, it's going to be very easy to find what is required. Unlike in my house!' Helena laughed. 'Sometimes I had to go up and down the stairs several times because I could not remember where a file or a book was,' she explained. 'This is almost flawless, and it seems to come so naturally to you.'

'Well, I have been trained, after all. And, as a librarian, I must admit that I find the idea of creating order out of chaos very rewarding.'

'That is not dissimilar to detection, do you know? Though you deal more with books, and we deal with people, and psychology and emotions.'

Jocasta smiled. 'Yes, I noticed that the psychology collection is vast. But, you see, what I practise is a new method of classification. We don't have medieval libraries in America like you do here, with that custom of allocating for each item a set place on a shelf, and guarding them with a heavy chain. The books need to move, and be flexible, as they change in relation to one another, talking with one another within the collection. Very much like people do.'

'That is fascinating.'

'When you stop determining a set space, and instead place each book according to their relationship to one another, you get so many surprises! For example, your psychology books.'

'What about them?'

'They are in clear dialogue with your books on the occult. And there are even more of those.'

Helena said nothing. Jocasta continued:

'And you can certainly apply this to people, as well. Do you ever have the feeling that a person does not belong with the group of people he is with, has nothing at all in common with them?' Helena did not miss the masculine pronoun, and wondered who Miss Webster was referring to. 'And don't you feel like you desperately want to help them find a better group?'

'I think you have just defined detection for me.' And then she added, 'Why have you come to England exactly, Miss Webster?'

'Oh. I...' she seemed to be looking for an appropriate answer. 'It is a long story.' And she would say no more. But Helena thought how surprisingly their professions aligned with one another, and wondered whether Miss Webster's future at the agency would not develop into more clearly defined detecting endeavours, something she seemed to understand almost naturally.

'Miss Webster, if I may. We make a point of keeping an up-to-date file with our current addresses, in case we need to communicate something urgently. Can you please let me know yours?'

The American woman looked up, her face unable to suppress the inner turmoil the innocent question had posed.

'I am afraid that I am between places now,' was all she would say.

'It's not a problem,' said Helena, smiling. Privately, she made a note of this detail.

It was time for Helena to settle to her own work for the remainder of the day. She pulled out from under her clothes a chain around her neck – its tip a small key – and used it to open one of her desk drawers. From there she took out a brand-new leather-bound notebook. On the first page it was inscribed: 'The Method'. She opened the next page: it revealed an index of sorts, which had been reworked and scribbled over to accommodate all the new annotations. The list read:

Main Tasks:

(1) Research:

(1.1) Initial Information Gathering: This constitutes the first necessary step into any investigation. It can involve talking to witnesses, visiting libraries, public records, private archives, consulting old newspapers, etc. Another way involves questioning witnesses: when doing this, in the preliminary interviews we need to keep them on our side, even if we suspect they are deceitful. Only later, as the investigation advances, can we reveal our hand with whatever suspicions we have had.

(1.2) On-site Detection: Whenever possible, it is imperative to look for clues in places relevant to the investigation. Surveillance of suspects, following suspects. Entering buildings under false pretences. For this, disguising oneself is a very good way of gaining access; performance of roles when necessary (e.g. servants).

(2) *In-Depth Research* [*To be completed*]

(3) *Preliminary Deductions:*

(3.1) *Determining Motive: This would typically lead to the identification of one or more suspects.*

(3.2) *Gathering Proof: Here, bear in mind that it would be possible to be proved wrong! Prepare for this eventuality.*

This was as far as she had got. There was much to add, both to the sections already depicted and in new sections – she had not started working yet on the Moment of Resolution, when things start falling into place, and a plan needed to be created to unveil the truth and catch the culprit.

She turned the page onto another section, one that Helena had not dared to tackle yet. It was tentatively titled 'On the nature of magic for the purposes of detection'. She had very few notes in there, chiefly about having premonitions that pointed to a path; or the value of the tarot cards to bring clarity with their readings; or even the hypothetical use of spells and good-luck charms. It was all very innocent, she thought; not an inch of anything dark or uncanny in view. And still, she felt it would not sit well with Eliza. She closed the notebook and put it back in her drawer, and locked it, wondering if she was doing so forever.

INTERLUDE

It was always going to be Moina, the person she would take her fears to, the person who would betray her.

Samuel had not been pleased with Philothée. What was she saying about Georges? Georges, who was their friend, who had done so much for them, for the movement. First, helping them get a theatre to disseminate their message, far and beyond. Later, he had helped them establish themselves in the suburbs, and had brought people, and, more importantly, had helped in other ways that Philothée could not possibly understand.

But Philothée had been sufficiently clear to Moina: she did not trust him, and did not want Leonie to continue working in Star Film Studio. She had never seen Samuel Mathers so incensed after he heard this:

'But Georges is a true artist, touched by the Divine!' Philothée knew what it meant: in the Matherses' opinion, Georges could do no wrong.

And Philothée had heard this before: art was a divine gift, and a conduit to divine experience, and the work of the creative imagination was akin to magic. Under this principle, the Artist was Magus; but Samuel Mathers aspired to be the only Magus. He alone wanted to have power over all Parisian factions of the Golden Dawn. Her question now was: if art was so important for the movement, was it more important than people?

She knew Georges' work was important. And she had not come with any accusation; she had just needed to understand. What exactly went on in the studio, what her aunt was exposed to, day after day.

Philothée thought she knew why the Matherses were in debt with Georges. She had seen him, many times, filming. First, he filmed the performance at the Théâtre de la Bodinière, then she saw him filming small scenes with Moina around the gardens in the villa. And then, there he was, a constant presence in each Mass, his noisy camera grinding away at the back, hardly noticed among the chanting. She did not know why this was important in Samuel's scheme of things, but it obviously was.

'I am sorry. I… I must have been mistaken.'

Instantly she saw it, Moina's smile of relief, as she went over to caress her husband's arm.

'You hear, Samuel? She was just mistaken.'

'I hope she was,' he said with finality, and left the room.

Moina looked like she wanted to say something. But at the end she simply extinguished her cigarette in the glass ashtray, and left after him.

Philothée had been standing in front of the window, and now sank down onto the window bench. She was shaking all over. She had been a fool. She had been naïve. And she would need to watch her step from now on. Being honest with herself, she knew she would need to escape soon.

6

GASLIGHT GHOSTS AND ELECTRIC FAIRIES

Paris, 18th March 1902

The Hotel Lirriper was an abomination in brick and mortar. Confusing vines and leaves in twisting green metal formed a gate-door that seemed to indicate the way into Hell. An entrance hall that reminded Eliza of a cave, with sharp-edged protruding decorations superimposed on its walls. Windows placed 'artistically', which meant they looked out of shape, out of order. This art nouveau style was intended to represent youth and vigour, to conjure up a new kind of beauty. Eliza was not a fan.

All the same, knowing that she was to stay in a building like this brought an unexpected pang: Eliza was sure that Mina would have enjoyed the place greatly. Her former companion had been very partial to all those sinuous lines and flowing organic shapes. She believed the style replicated a walk in the park, perhaps, or a dive into wild nature. She found it all so colourful and romantic. She would once even have said that her very favourite piece of art had been Alphonse Mucha's theatrical posters drawn for the Renaissance Theatre, promoting the performances of Sarah Bernhardt. Eliza had travelled to Paris with Mina a couple of years back to see the Paris world exhibition, but mostly to see Sarah play the role of Hamlet: to them it had been the culmination of everything they had believed in, hoped for: that a woman could do that. Anything was possible, and there would be no end to the female revolution.

Now, Eliza was back in Paris, alone this time. It pained her more than she had expected when she accepted the assignment from Helena – no, when she insisted on the assignment. She hoped this was not a mistake; she was already apprehensive to have gone into the unknown alone.

If Mina had loved art nouveau, to Eliza, the notion of twisted vines climbing up walls and floral-looking lamps had ominous tones. She interpreted the décor not as if she was walking into a park, but rather as if she were entering a dark forest you could get lost in, or even worse, the gigantic nest of some otherworldly insect. The thought made her skin crawl. She wondered whether she would be able to sleep inside the building. But Helena had made the reservation for her, and insisted on the discretion and general well-positioned nature of this hotel for their purposes.

'Have you investigated a case in Paris before?' Eliza had asked.

Helena had smiled.

'My investigations have led me across the Channel twice before. But I know Mrs Lirriper from much earlier on. Believe me, she understands exactly how to accommodate our needs.

She would be a useful ally. If I remember correctly, she has numerous contacts within the gendarmerie, were you to need their help at any point. Her late husband was a policeman. And Alice lives there.'

Mrs Lirriper, Helena explained, had started the hotel to house gentlewomen travellers as a means of survival when she had been widowed.

'When Alice was in need of lodgings, I sent her there. I think it may be very useful to stay with her. She is our door to Méliès, but I am sure she will be helpful in other ways.'

'How do they know each other?'

'She has collaborated with him from time to time, and even participated in a few recordings of his moving pictures. Alice has been trying to raise money to make a film of her own for some time.'

And so it was settled. Alice Guy was to meet her at the station. She turned out to be an exceedingly well-dressed woman who favoured trousers and who today wore an attractive black and white striped blouse with bell shoulders. She introduced herself as a theatrical worker, and shook Eliza's hand vigorously.

'But I am sure you know exactly why Helena contacted me. No worries on that front; I know Monsieur Méliès, and you will be able to meet him soon,' she explained in impeccable English. 'Shame about Helena, not coming for the moment,' she continued. 'How is she?'

Eliza froze. For a second, she realised she had no idea how to answer this question. She murmured a 'well, busy' that could mean anything, and they set off. But the short interaction had bothered her: had she really worried so little about her business partner recently to not be able to give an honest and meaningful reply? She felt a pang of guilt.

Once in the hansom, Mademoiselle Guy offered some more information about their destination:

'Look, the Lirriper can be odd at times but I hope you will be comfortable there.'

Eliza smiled for a reply. Once they arrived at the hotel, they were received by the owner, who seemed cold and close-lipped at first, even as she explained that she was exceedingly happy to see Eliza, and that she was extremely fond of Helena, even hinting that the detective had helped her in the past in some professional capacity.

'Let's go see your room, you have time to rest before supper.'

Eliza followed her thankfully. Mrs Lirriper conducted her to a room on the third floor of the establishment. It was small but well-kept, immaculately clean, and it got a good deal of light coming in from a window into the inner courtyard of the building. It was sparsely furnished, but it had a sturdy writing desk on a corner, as per Helena's instructions.

'I hope this is convenient.'

'It is perfect, thank you, Mrs Lirriper.'

'Why don't you get settled, and I will bring you some tea in a minute?'

Eliza did not need to be told twice. As soon as she was sitting, her things having been put away with the help of a maid, the casebook and writing materials ready on the desk, Mrs Lirriper appeared with tea and refreshments on a tray. And, when Eliza went down for dinner, Mrs Lirriper insisted to Alice that she would make the introductions herself. Alice stayed where she was, hidden behind the satirical pages of *Le Figaro*.

Miss Laura Winningham and her twin sister, Miss Maureen Winningham, travelled to Paris for the season, and always stayed at the Lirriper. They were a pair of Scottish matrons, who introduced themselves as 'retired'; Eliza wondered from which endeavours, and was curious, but refrained from asking, as she did not want to appear rude. There would be plenty of opportunities to enquire about their profession, as Eliza knew how people were thrown into each other's company in hotels like the Lirriper. Miss Frances Lamont was a writer.

'Well, I call myself a "ghostly writer", if you take my meaning,' she explained, with a nervous smile.

'Do you mean that you write ghost stories?'

'I mean that I am the ghost that hides in the shadows, and writes other people's memoirs and books for them. Busy politicians, fashionable poets, spiritualist mentors. And of course I charge handsomely for it.'

Eliza had never heard of the concept before. Miss Lamont was in Paris conducting interviews with a famous courtesan, the Queen of the Demi-monde, 'But born in Peckham, of all places!' Afterwards, she would return to her cottage in Surrey – bought with the proceeds of her hard work, she explained with obvious pride – to write the sensationalist tome.

Señorita Bustelo was a Spanish dancer – and, Alice would later gossip, a spy – who lived permanently on the premises.

The peculiar collection of female talent was completed by Alice, the only Frenchwoman in the group. 'Miss Bustelo and I work together sometimes,' she explained. 'We both have some sporadic assignments with the Robert-Houdin theatre. If you want, we can get you tickets for a performance while you are here,' she offered.

'Thank you. That would be wonderful.' Alice had already explained to Eliza on the way to the hotel that the Robert-Houdin theatre was owned by Georges Méliès, and that he usually showed his movies there.

Eliza was quickly warming to the surroundings that she was going to call home for the next few days, her first ominous impressions, brought about by the aesthetics of the place, receding in her mind. She was, however, dreading when she would have to mount the dark mahogany staircase at the end of the convivial evening: it was an absurd twisting affair that tried to resemble vines and branches, but that in her head could equally be the limbs of some fantastical creature, crossed over from another, less charming realm. She tried to dismiss the thought. She would have to get used to the look of the place. And to thoughts of Mina.

After supper, it was coffee and *beignets* in the sitting room, with something a bit stronger for Eliza and Alice. Conversation flew swiftly among the ladies. Outside, the rain fell stubbornly, causing in Eliza a certain nostalgia: not for England, she reflected, but for the person who remained there, forcibly kept in her past, and now, so inexplicably connected to her again. She wondered, would she ever see Mina again, talk to her?

Until now, only Helena had interacted with her, keeping Eliza out of view. She felt trepidation at the thought that, sooner or later, Mina would be told of her connection with the case. Would she be angry? Or had Eliza been forgiven? The past mirrored those decorative vines of the fashionable new art, a beautiful but insidious reminder that could at any moment threaten her present reality.

'This is a rather modern style of architecture. Has Mrs Lirriper been here long?' Eliza inquired of the sisters.

'We understand she got the building quite cheaply; that it was abandoned right after construction.'

'Why is that?'

'Several workers died; the architect killed himself while it was still being built. Many thought the building was cursed!' The sisters chuckled, their smiles conveying approval for Mrs Lirriper's excellent business sense. But Eliza did not see the fun in the revelation. Typical of Helena, she thought. Throwing her into some uncanny place. She almost wished that the haunting, if there was to be one, would manifest itself soon and be done with it.

Miss Lamont lit up a pipe and read the newspaper, while the others moved their conversation to the inclement weather, as a veritable storm now roared outside.

'You must be delighted to be already here. I am sure the Channel is not at all calm tonight,' suggested one of the Misses Winningham.

'Don't be silly!' snapped her sister. 'The Channel is many miles from Paris. For all we know it may be delicious weather out there.'

'Hmm. I doubt that is true, dear.'

Eliza smiled vaguely and moved her mind away from the conversation. She drank her excellent coffee, which had been served in tiny cups of translucent porcelain. It was inevitable, she reflected, that talk among newly acquainted people would keep to trivial issues. Spring was late arriving; the weather did not settle. The ladies surrounding her, who had come to Paris in search of nicer and warmer prospects, were duly disappointed. It was dismal, unusual weather for that part of the year, and they all agreed their disappointment was right and proper. Eliza thought of how hot it had been in London in the days before she took the boat, and reflected privately on how every year the seasons were getting a bit more muddled up. She had worried about this in the past.

Outside, as if echoing Miss Laura's assertion, the furious elements continued roaring, a sound like the throes of a storm in the high seas, something completely out of shape with her idea of Paris, and with the part of Paris where they were situated, in the gentle suburb of the twelfth arrondissement.

Still, Eliza could not help wondering that the ladies in front of her, enjoying the warm fire and their hot cocoa, coffee and port, carefully avoided commenting on the other noise-related disturbance, one that worried Eliza far more than whether the roof of the Hotel Lirriper would resist the assault of the elements: from one of the upper floors, Eliza could hear the unmistakable sounds of furniture tumbling down to the floor, rapid footsteps, a stomping and kicking of doors, breaking of glass. It was evident that the noises were being made in one of the upper rooms of the building. At last, the agonised cry of a young woman was heard and Eliza could abide the situation no longer. She got to her feet exclaiming:

'We have to do something!'

To her dismay, the four women looked at each other with nothing other than amusement. Miss Bustelo broke into a small laugh.

'Do not laugh, Mariana. It is the first time that Miss Waltraud has stayed here,' one of the twins said.

Eliza was confused. 'Are you telling me that you are used to this?'

The twins exchanged a knowing look.

'My dear, I can assure you, there is nothing at all to worry about.' This was the other twin. Not knowing who was speaking unnerved her greatly, but now was not the time to consider this. Eliza was still standing, wondering whether to run up the stairs, at a loss as to why none of the others had reacted like she had. Miss Lamont pressed her pipe between her teeth, her broad smile reminding Eliza for a moment of the Cheshire cat in *Alice in Wonderland*.

'Well, ladies. I am afraid that my conscience does not allow me to sit here, enjoying the fire and this reviving port, and do nothing.' Eliza walked resolutely to the door, and ran up the stairs without thinking, and immediately knew two things: the noise of the fight came from the top floor, the attic, and her reaction had surprised not only her after-dinner companions, but also herself. Her collaboration with Helena until now had been of the intellectual rather than the physical kind. Having contrived to conduct the assignment on her own – anything better than enduring the tiresome company of Aurora – she knew that resolute moments such as this one would occur far more often. The idea was welcome: she could force it all out in action, all her sadness, all her fury, all her miserly nostalgia for her lost life with Mina.

Following the noises, and avoiding Mrs Lirriper on the way, who opened and promptly closed a door at Eliza's coming, she ended up at the bottom of a narrow staircase, at the top of which loomed the attic door. Breathless now, she propelled herself up the stairs, and, just as she was going to beat on the door with all her might, the noise stopped, as suddenly as it had started. Eliza stopped in her tracks. She could hear nothing now, no cries, no sobbing, no dragged chairs or broken vases. Nothing at all.

Still, that sudden absence of noise was even more disturbing. Eliza knocked on the door. Silence. She knocked once more, but still she could hear nothing, only the scurrying of rats here and there, which seemed to suggest the impossible: there was no one in that attic room.

Flashes of a London home, servants' quarters, a mystery they had investigated the previous autumn, went through her mind. Helena had then suggested a paranormal version of events, which Eliza had known was simply impossible. Unfortunately, she had not had the chance to prove her theories.

There was nothing else for it. Tentatively, she pushed at the door, and found it unlocked. She entered into a long attic room, lit sadly by the yellow light that poured inside from the streetlamps. She had not had the good sense to bring a candle with her, and it was obvious that the old-fashioned gaslight did not reach that part of the building.

Still, all that she could see through the dim light was nothing at all – no furniture, no broken glass, only some boxes, goods and chattels covered by white linen sheets, which had obviously not been disturbed in years.

Never had Eliza experienced heartbreak as powerful as she did right there, not even when she saw Mina pack her belongings and leave their cottage in the pony and cart. An absolute sadness crept over her, a black well opening inside, a void where no happiness, no love, could ever live. A feeling she'd not encountered anywhere else in the house. She knew, unmistakably, that those rooms had seen dark times. She could accept her instincts; what she could not accept was the notion that this darkness was bound to repeat itself. It was clear that Helena had sent her to stay here as a test, or to teach her something, as she probably believed that the Lirriper was haunted. If that was the case, Eliza would prove her wrong.

'You ought to feel blessed, dear. Not many can hear her.'

'Blessed?'

'They say she went mad up there. But nothing was ever proven, no one was ever found guilty of anything. Charles Dickens himself was interested in the case, the aunt who convinced the young husband to end his wife, the poison, the attacks of madness, perhaps provoked, invented. The character of

Rigaud in *Little Dorrit* is loosely based on whatever happened here, so long ago now. So very sad.'

The Miss Winningham who had just spoken, that Eliza thought could perhaps be Maureen, was absolutely right: sadness was the exact word. However, she noticed there were already flaws in this narrative. She said:

'Miss Winningham, if I may: If I am not mistaken, *Little Dorrit* was written in the 1850s; I thought you explained before that this building is only a few years old.' She didn't want to embarrass the lady, and was careful to sound as scientifically minded as possible, and as if she herself was perhaps not entirely sure of these dates.

'Oh! Is that so? Oh dear, I am sure you are right,' offered the old lady weakly. Still, Eliza thought, remembering the staircase mystery: she needed to gain their confidence, she needed to play along a little, if only while she gathered information. She was very proud to have remembered this, in lieu of rushing to dispel everything in an agitated speech. Instead, she said:

'This is terrible beyond words. Has this event recurred since you started coming here?'

'Oh yes, absolutely,' the other miss piped up now, obviously much happier with the turn of the conversation. 'It must have been four years ago that we first reserved rooms here.' This ought to be Laura, she thought.

Eliza sipped the strong brandy that Mrs Lirriper had poured for her. At least this time there were answers, instead of bemused looks.

'Her "madness" seemed to be manifested in that way you just heard, very violent attacks,' continued one of the sisters. 'But, as with all these stories, there is more than meets the eye: they were provoked by frustration, by sadness. She knew no one would save her. She was left up there to die. Locked up and alone. A case, and more common than we tend to accept in society, of a healthy mind driven to madness. There is no doubt about it.'

'No doubt. We know the case well. We have studied it,' said her twin.

'From our medical perspective.'

'Medical perspective?'

'Miss Laura and Miss Maureen here were doctors. Up in Helensburgh,' announced a proud Miss Lamont, as if the achievements of the two ladies somehow were due to her own ministrations.

'The poor woman,' continued the other twin. 'She must have suffered terribly. How else could such events remain fixed in time, and so powerfully in a space?'

'Do you think that is what is happening up there? I mean, you are doctors…' The notion hung in the air, unsaid. Were these scientifically trained women allowing for a supernatural explanation to the noises? One of them offered:

'It is true that, at present, there are no natural laws to explain these occurrences, but perhaps there will be someday.'

Eliza could only manage a non-committal smile, and sipped her drink.

'We all have heard her, many times. Mostly on stormy

nights like this one. I am writing a treatment about her,' announced Alice.

'A treatment? What is a treatment?' asked Eliza, still thinking for a moment of medicine.

'It's words, like a play,' explained Miss Bustelo. 'But you don't speak them. You act them – like this, and this, and this,' she continued, pantomiming an exaggerated face of happiness, of sadness, of fear. Eliza looked on, confused.

'The *cinématographe*!' insisted the dancer.

'Oh! Sorry, I have not seen many of those.'

'Let's hope we can remedy that while you are here,' noted Alice with a smile.

Eliza contemplated the inside of her glass, the brandy moving in circles as her hand moved, circles in which her mind was trying to draw, as usual, Mina's face. Recently, she had feared she was forgetting Mina's features. The thought worried her.

The women around her were silent now, all soft stories to be told around the fire after a good dinner now dead on their lips after the night's true revelations. No one said anything for a few minutes. Only the storm outside could be heard. The wind roared, forcing the flames inside the fireplace into strange dances. Eliza's mind was now filled with her recent experiences more than she wanted to admit, all the ones since meeting Helena, and she felt an undetermined heaviness pressing on her heart.

Miss Bustelo and Alice said their goodbyes and left for their work – Eliza was still not sure exactly what it was – at the Robert-Houdin Theatre, renewing as they left their promise of procuring some tickets for Eliza if she so desired. Eliza excused herself shortly after, she was after all still tired from the crossing, and went up to her room. It was located right below the 'haunted' attic, it seemed.

18th March – Later

Dear Helena,
I arrived in Paris earlier today. The channel crossing was rougher than the last time I was here

'with Mina', she wrote, and immediately blotted over with black ink.

It seems odd to write that I have been here before, for it truly feels like a completely different place, and a lifetime ago, rather than only a couple of years.

So much had happened since then, so much had changed. Coming to Paris to undertake this particular investigation had somehow forced Eliza to look at the city anew, as a different place, not for walking around as a tourist, having fun, but for hidden, uncanny things. Eliza had no idea how to put all those new impressions in her letter, so she continued instead:

I know you advised me to keep to myself during an investigation, but perhaps I am more of a social animal than I thought, and the truth is that I soon found a companion for the journey: a Miss

Tilley, bound for Brussels, where she is going to be governess to three children. An intelligent, fun and capable woman, it pained me to see her beaming at her good fortune after securing this position, one that is so obviously beneath her many capabilities. Myself, I could only wonder at the notion that there are so many women in the world whose little opportunities in life mean they are forced to work for others, and live with other families, as their only possible means of support. We said our goodbyes at the Gare du Nord, exchanged addresses, and promised to keep in touch.

Even now, only after a few hours in the city, Eliza wondered if she was going to be true to her word, for she had already sensed that ominous things awaited her, things that she would call 'wonders' so as not to call them terrors. Now that she was finally here, she could not conceive of sitting down over innocent cream-colored paper to recount sightseeing and other useless pleasantries. For the truth was that she feared things would prove to be even stranger than she and Helena had anticipated. Had she embarked on a wild-goose chase? Was the Moberly and Jourdain mystery truly connected with Mina's story? She wished she had been allowed to talk to Mina after all: in her view, Helena was being far too kind, and her ex-lover had a lot of explaining to do, for the notions in their casebook now appeared nothing short of fantastic, strange and dark.

But I digress. Suffice to say that I have made it to the Hotel Lirriper, as you arranged in advance. I am sitting down to look over the notes you have so helpfully put at my disposal. Tomorrow

I am meeting a friend of Alice's at the Brasserie Montparnasse, someone who also worked with Mina's friend. I will report back promptly afterwards. I am very much looking forward to hearing her version of events.

Your friend and colleague,

Eliza Waltraud

Eliza sat for a minute considering the note. Then, she decided to add a postscript:

PS: Not that I am complaining, I hope; after all, I have come here to investigate possible paranormal occurrences. But I cannot deny that I would have been much happier if you had told me in advance that the Hotel Lirriper was, of all things, haunted – if that is what is happening here, which I truly much doubt.

As it happens, my first night here has been most eventful.

As soon as she finished writing it, she realised how childish she sounded, and she crossed out the whole thing. Now the expensive writing paper was soaking in a huge black stain. Cursing herself, Eliza threw the letter in the paper-basket and started writing again.

Having finally managed to pen a letter, Eliza tried to sleep but kept wondering about a number of things she didn't know: for example, how many cases Helena had solved before meeting her, how many people she had helped before they had set up their business together. She reflected on the many unknowns she was collecting about her associate's past. Helena used to pretend to be a palmist and cartomancer, in order to gain access to places and people, so she could carry out her detection. Very few knew how to hire her detecting services. Spiritualism was a kind of cover, at least, back then. 'Pretending' was perhaps not the correct word, and indeed she felt it would be unfair to draw her in those terms. However, Helena had clearly been a sceptic, yet since they met, she seemed to have become increasingly more accepting of certain ideas, which to Eliza was a worrying development.

Eliza had met Helena only about a year ago, in the spring of 1901, which was surprising considering how quickly they had stumbled upon their shared enterprise. Helena had been working a case trying to find three missing girls, whereas Eliza had been trying to uncover a mystery of her own: the disappearance of the tern population in the countryside around the cottage she inhabited. The backdrop for these were one and the same: an eerie part of the Norfolk coast where at times it felt as if they were treading upon two different realities.

Fate had thrown them together, as Eliza was connected to the area. However, Eliza had gone quickly from acting on the fringes of it all, at times not fully aware of Helena's discoveries, to playing a rather more important role in the proceedings. Recalling it all made her skin crawl. She had fancied herself an amateur scientist in those days, something that now struck her as ludicrous. However, the things they unveiled, and the readiness with which she had accepted the most unfathomable occurrences – for example, she had been ready to believe in the existence of a parallel realm, only accessible through some portals, and had even engaged in 'portal magic' – made her now feel embarrassed, upset with herself. No doubt she had been prone to some kind of mass hypnosis, or even mass hysteria, taken in by the atmosphere surrounding the mysteries, the curiously off-kilter setting, and of course Helena's shifting views.

She did not like reminiscing of those days. But the truth was that she valued Helena's friendship by the end of it all, and when the detective offered her the possibility to be the 'reasoning head' of their Cerberus, to add some balance to the uncanny cases she normally confronted, she thought she had found her calling. How wrong she had been. Eliza now would give anything to go back to those innocent days of amateur pseudo-scientific investigations – was 'counting birds' even a form of science? – alone in her cottage. But she felt duty-bound now to Helena, who had invested a considerable amount to start their joint venture. Nonetheless, she had no delusions: Helena was moving more and more out of her area of influence; and she herself, quite simply, could not accept that the 'supernatural' was real, that problems could not be solved by applying a solid scientific method, grounded in reality.

At the time of the Norfolk mystery, Eliza had been taken by a project, now abandoned: a biography of an American woman of science, Eunice Foote, a woman who had been forgotten by history. Foote had written a paper on the circumstances affecting the heat of the sun's rays and carbonic acid in the mid-1800s, only to have her discoveries presented for her by a male colleague at a meeting of the American Association for the Advancement of Science, her findings repackaged by a different male scientist, years later, in England, and said male scientist later credited with being the first one in history to look into these occurrences.

It was too much to bear; Eliza had hated the unfairness of it all. It was also a project that spoke to her two passions, writing and science. At the time, she had entertained the idea that counting terns or musing around old volumes of scientific journals in public libraries was a form of scientific endeavour. In truth, she could not even have attached the label of 'amateur' scientist to her persona, for she had not read enough, done any independent study, nor reflected enough.

This was what she did, continuously: create narratives about herself that weren't based on anything solid. That was why she had abandoned that project; she knew that now. That was also why Mina had left.

It was painful to remember it, even now. And no doubt pining for Mina, who had been gone a few months before encountering Helena, at a time when Eliza's loneliness was unbearable, had helped her bend whichever sense she still had over to the fanciful, the improbable. She must have felt the need to help someone, especially another woman, to erase the guilt of her treatment of Mina.

Losing Mina was her fault and hers alone.

Mina, who had been used and abused by a fellow writer,

her ideas stolen, her imagination shattered and remade into digestible pieces that someone else had used to form into the literary success of the season. Mina, broken at the unfairness of it all. Mina, called childish, self-centred, by Eliza of all people, when all she had hoped to find was love and support in an impossible situation.

No, there was no doubt about it: Eliza had exactly what she deserved.

19th March – Morning/Afternoon

After a restless night, during which Eliza dreamt of getting lost in a French formal garden, she spent the morning perusing the casebook, in preparation of her conversation with Alice's contact. This would be the first time she interviewed a witness on her own, and she was feeling nervous: her breakfast, which she had requested to be brought up, sat hardly touched on a tray.

At the appointed time she took a cab and directed the driver to take her to the Brasserie Montparnasse. The place was ridiculous. As soon as she entered into the establishment, Eliza felt as if she were descending into a hellish fairyland, an overly floral realm inspired by the tiresome art nouveau.

'Dear God,' she said, rolling her eyes. At once she heard English spoken, first to her left, then to her right, followed by German. A cursory look made her realise that the majority of people in the restaurant at that time of the day were tourists.

The Brasserie was organised in neat rows of little tables, sitting very close together, fitting at least fifty or sixty of them, and the place was packed. It was difficult to see through the waifs of smoke, to hear anything over the continuous crackle of laughter. Why were people on holiday invariably so happy? It was beyond her understanding. Then she had another thought: when had she become a grumpy old maid? At least she knew the answer to that.

When she was starting to despair, tired of straining her neck, she finally saw Alice getting up and signalling from a table.

'Eliza! Here!' She was alone.

'Where is your friend?'

'I am afraid she could not make it.'

'Why not?'

Alice took a second to reply.

'I think she is scared.'

'Scared? Of what, exactly?'

'I'm not sure. She was conveniently vague about it, said she did not want to meet us "in public", and,' Alice gestured around them, 'it is very public around here. Sorry, I should have thought about that.'

'I can understand. Is there any other place where we can meet her?'

'She has left Monsieur Méliès's employment now, and is working in a bookshop. She suggested we go there at closing time.' Eliza thought about this.

Alice indicated the two china plates and coffee set at the table.

'Would you like some tea and pastries? I am afraid that is all there is to be had here at this hour of the day. They are a bit dry, but perfectly adequate. I fear it may not be pleasant, talking to Millie. Let's fortify ourselves first.'

Eliza thanked her, and bit into one of the small biscuits. Sadly, Alice was right: they were dry and papery in her mouth, with a streak of old jam that had somehow solidified and stuck to her teeth. She thought about tea and pastries in some of London's most popular teashops and mused she would have never been served something quite like this there.

'And did you ever cross paths with Miss Peters?'

Alice shrugged.

'Not really, not substantially. The problem is that their work was conducted in a workshop where I really had no reason to go. I never interact with the printed rolls of film. And she hardly ever ate with the rest of the workers.'

Eliza sighed. This was going to be difficult. She ought to visit Emily's cottage at the earliest opportunity.

'What can *you* tell me about Méliès?' she asked, gulping some tea to help her swallow. Alice flinched slightly. 'Helena said that you have collaborated with him on occasion.'

'I have worked for him, yes. Look, we don't really share many artistic beliefs. He is one of those Parisian aesthetes, who basically believes in the triumph of art as artifice, in complete separation from nature. I had to work *for* him. He is incredibly prolific, and I need to raise money for my own productions. And he gives me regular work at the theatre, mostly with the lighting and other things backstage. It may not come as a surprise to you to know that I find it much harder than my male colleagues to find investors for my work.'

Eliza could well believe this.

19th March – Late afternoon

Eliza had stayed in Paris for the first time in the summer of 1900. She and Mina had visited churches and one or two picture galleries. There were numerous expeditions to the shops. In a fancy arcade Mina had bought notebooks and writing paper, of such quality and at such cost that she joked she would never be able to use any of it. They made no excursions of note, as the World Exhibition of 1900 was happening, and they spent most of their time there. They made a lovely discovery during one of their walks, the English book section at Galignani, at the Rue de Rivoli. They spent many a happy hour looking among their tables, getting lost in the adjacent chapel-like little rooms. They had bought a copy of *Alice in Wonderland* in the bookshop, a French edition they would never read, or at least Eliza hadn't: Mina had taken it with her when they had confronted the awful task of separating their books.

Now, Alice and herself were going to Galignani. Of course, thought Eliza, who now seemed resigned to have her heart opened again at each walk, with each vista, in each place she visited. She felt the world was conspiring against her, instead of simply admitting to herself how similar were the experiences of English visitors to the City of Light, how closely connected were the places where they all spent their waking hours.

Millie Jenkins had been the only English-speaking worker for Monsieur Méliès, and Alice explained that, if Eliza played her cards correctly, she could in turn become the 'new Millie' for a short while.

They arrived at the Rue de Rivoli. As she entered the bookshop, Eliza almost thought she could smell Mina's scent. She was confused, because she could not possibly remember it after all this time. And then she saw her, her frilly yellow hair and freckled countenance, browsing among the tables piled high with English language books. This could not be. Alice was walking directly towards Mina. The young woman unbent; and then Eliza saw that it wasn't Mina, thank goodness. It was probably Miss Jenkins.

Eliza was nearly frozen on the spot. What was wrong with her? With an abominable pressure in her chest, she took a breath, and approached Miss Jenkins with a *bonjour* that almost stuck in her throat.

'It's nice to meet you, Miss Waltraud. It's time that I close the main door; would you both be so kind as to wait for me at the back?'

They did as they were told. They could hear the little bell ringing one last time as the door was forced shut, and the main electric lights dimmed, until all that was left was a shadowy yellow light. Presently Millie joined them and indicated they should step into a small room at the back full of boxes and envelopes and a packing station. Pointedly, she did not invite them to sit.

'Thank you so much for agreeing to speak with me.' Eliza stopped for a second, and gathered her thoughts. Helena had not been impressed with her performance when they interviewed the Misses Moberly and Jourdain, and she had had no qualms in expressing this. Eliza knew that Helena's words were true, and she was hoping to have learnt from the experience. 'I understand this may be difficult for you, but I would like to ask you a couple of questions, if I may.' She saw Miss Jenkins visibly relaxing. The woman looked at Alice, who was also nodding reassuringly. 'If at any point you don't want to reply to any of my questions, or simply would like me to stop, you just have to say the word.'

'Yes, thank you. Ask away.'

'Alice has told me that you were employed by Monsieur Méliès until recently.'

'That is correct.'

'What did you do for him?'

'I worked in his office, mostly.'

'Doing what, exactly?'

'Monsieur Méliès employs three girls as secretaries and typists, but I was the only one of the lot who knew English. I was in charge of writing and answering letters in correct English, and filing all documents in English as well. When I met him, the first day of the job, he explained that the work would consist mainly of this, and that his brother Gaston, who deals with the American side of the business, knew very little English. Together they had the idea of hiring an educated English woman to assist with all the paperwork and correspondence in English.'

'Do you mind me asking, what brought you to Paris?'

'I came as governess to a child, but to be honest, the work did not suit me in the slightest. There was much more child-minding and much less teaching than I had been led to believe.'

Eliza continued, 'Was the job at Star Film Studio hard in any way, or unpleasant?'

'No harder than other office jobs, I guess. At the beginning it was alright. Until strange things started to happen.'

'Strange things?'

'Tell her about the vanishings,' intervened Alice. Eliza's ears pricked up.

It had all started about a year previously, at the beginning of the summer of 1901, shortly after she started working in Star Film Studio.

'The Glass Doll House, as we call it.'

'Why do you call it that?' asked Eliza.

'You'll see,' replied Alice. 'I'll take you there tomorrow.'

Millie continued: 'Things started getting decidedly peculiar. First, one of the flying ladies—'

'Sorry, excuse me, what do you mean, "flying ladies"?'

'You know, fairies, floating stars and such. Méliès uses them a lot in his movies.'

'Yes, they are Méliès's trademark,' remarked Alice. 'Georges's movies tend to include a celestial flying woman. She can be the moon with a woman's face, or a star. And sometimes he includes fairies.'

'And these *femmes-étoiles*! *Mon dieu*!' cried Millie. 'They are like goddesses, holding the stars up. It is quite pretty.'

Eliza nodded encouragingly, letting the other women speak.

'One of them, she started acting very strange.'

'Strange in what way? Can you be more precise?'

'Like she didn't understand anything, didn't even respond to her name. Like she had turned into a shadow. And then she stopped coming.' Millie sighed. 'And it wasn't only her. One dancer after another. After they danced for a while, after they had been stars or fairies for a while, they all ended up becoming dumb. Not replying, not understanding. Until one day they weren't there at all.'

'I see,' Eliza replied.

'What happened then?' intervened Alice.

'Then the other dancers started to get spooked, and stopped coming.'

'How many stopped coming?'

'Three that we know about.'

'Look, one of them had a very poorly mother in Brussels, the other one kept saying she was going to elope with her rich boyfriend. No one can really be sure that this isn't what happened. The other we don't know,' intervened Alice.

'And what did Méliès do when dancers did not want to come to work in the studio?'

Apparently, Monsieur Méliès had started going to the neighbouring villages, Montreuil and Versailles, in order to find girls willing to act in his movies. He had even asked some of the members of the crew to help him find suitable girls, as pretty as possible, and petite enough to fly on the ropes.

'Eliza,' this was Alice again. 'I can corroborate all this. Méliès used the dancers of the Théâtre du Châtelet and the Folies-Bergère in his movies, but nobody wants to come and dance in his movies anymore. He also asked me to find him girls.'

'The gendarmerie came around and everything, to dig up a little field close to the studio! It was so demoralising for everyone.'

Alice explained that Millie had handed her notice in two weeks later, and that Méliès had not found a replacement yet.

'As soon as I got Helena's letter I suggested your name,' said Alice.

Eliza nodded to Alice, and to Millie she said: 'I don't know how to thank you for talking to us.'

'You can start by promising me you will find out what is going on in that place.'

Eliza smiled inwardly, remembering Helena's warning that she was not expected to solve any mystery, only to gather information. She could not promise this to Millie, and felt useless. Instead she said:

'I will do all in my power to get to the bottom of this.' That seemed vague enough to her, but Millie smiled for the first time. Eliza continued. 'I understand that they work in a different workshop, but did you happen to meet another English lady working there colouring the films? A Miss Emily Peters?'

'Yes, of course. Emily.'

Eliza felt excitement rise within her, but she had to keep her emotions in check in front of the witness, as per the Method. She tried to sound calm when she asked:

'Did you speak to her often?'

'Not really. But we chatted sometimes about how different life was here from how it was back at home.'

'Do you happen to know of Miss Peters' current whereabouts?'

'I don't. Sorry. Didn't she have an American gentleman friend?' she asked. 'I'm sorry, I did not know her well. And then she left work one day, so suddenly! I assumed she had gone with him, to America perhaps.'

This was interesting in itself. Millie was not aware that Emily was missing at all; she simply thought she had left the studio. And who could this American gentleman be?

'Thank you for your help, Millie, it has been most illuminating.'

As they were preparing to leave, Eliza thought to ask:

'You have explained what your job consists of – what I don't quite understand is why Méliès has so much correspondence in English. Is he trying to sell his movies abroad? I tried to see his work in England and they were not easily available.'

'Oh no, it is the opposite, in fact. He has the most dreadful time trying to stop his movies *from being shown* abroad, especially in America.'

'What do you mean?'

'When Monsieur Méliès' movies are shown in America, it is always because Mr Edison has made a copy without his permission, and poor Monsieur Méliès does not earn a penny! Mr Edison gets all the money, you see.'

'Really?'

'Oh yes! That was the main part of my job: filing and correspondence relating to the feud with Mr Thomas Edison.'

19th March – Evening

Alice had been as good as her word, and had procured Eliza a seat in the second row of the stalls of the Robert-Houdin theatre that evening.

Eliza had been surprised on arriving at the Boulevard des Italiens to discover that scenes from Méliès's movies were being projected above the entrance of the theatre, a rather clever way to attract the clientele. Added to that, a man dressed in a livery shouted to passers-by:

'Entrez, entrez, mesdames et messieurs. Venez voir le merveilleux kinematograph de Monsieur Méliès!'

She tried to enjoy the first twenty minutes of the production, a visual spectacle like none she remembered. Even in London she wasn't a theatre regular; Mina had loved the theatre, and her last outing had been with her to the Egyptian Hall as a Christmas treat. This had happened mere days before breaking up. She crossed the threshold with a pang: she would need to get over herself soon. She could not be thinking of Mina at every turn, on every corner. Somewhat surprisingly, Paris was opening more wounds afresh than London, a city they had frequented more often, had done. She blamed the novelty of travelling, the strange new vistas, her senses pricked by the unknown. She was trying to enjoy the performance, as much as it was possible, without losing her wits about her this time, which required huge amounts of concentration. There was a strong smell of cigarettes and unwashed flesh that was particularly pungent, even more so than she remembered in the vaudeville theatres, which Eliza normally avoided for this very reason. This was entertainment for the masses.

The offerings of the Robert-Houdin centred around *pantomimes lumineuses*, a kind of short magic-lantern act; displays of automata; and lavish illusions, choreographed with elaborate decor and profuse tricks of the light: the man in front of her could not really be levitating on a solid piece of rope, no matter how much her fellow theatre goers were gaping and clapping. Even after bearing witness to performances such as Mademoiselle Carrière's, Eliza still believed too much in the sanctity of physics to consider this a real possibility. She was, however, knocked askance by one act in particular. A life-size portrait of a woman appeared on stage, and the accompanying magician initiated his illusion by calling upon spirits to help release her, to bring her back. Eliza could not believe what she was witnessing: little by little, the woman gained solidity, until what was inside the portrait was, or appeared to be, a living woman who walked out of the frame. The illusion was complete: the woman had turned from painting to flesh.

Eliza felt confused, as if something had gone wrong in the world. How many trap doors, pulleys, mechanical devices and elaborately engineered contraptions had been necessary to make that miracle possible? She was sure she had looked carefully, convinced she had not lost sight of the portrait, and still she had been deceived. It was cleverly done, she had to admit it. She wished Helena had been there to see it.

Something came to mind, and she followed the thought, something rolling at the tip of her tongue... There it was. Hadn't the Misses Moberly and Jourdain explained that their timeless window opening into the past had looked like a sort of animated painting? Could they have been subject to a trick like the ones at work here?

During the interval people did not get up, but stayed mostly in their seats. Alice had been very particular before leaving her, instructing her to do exactly that. The lights then dimmed almost entirely, and an eerie darkness crept over the stalls and the boxes, finally engulfing the stage completely, while the heavy curtains opened slowly to reveal a large white canvas. She had been expecting this, and knew which illusion she was about to see. At last, the auditorium went completely dark, and somewhere at the back someone started hitting an out-of-tune piano.

The cone of light, directed from somewhere at the back of the theatre, started flickering, as shadowy images appeared on the white canvas.

The new movie was the latest production by Méliès' Star Film Studio to be shown in the theatre, a rendition of *Barbe-Bleue*, or Bluebeard, which ended with the killing of the hideous man. But this only happened after nearly ten agonising minutes – it was the longest of such offerings Eliza had ever encountered –

in which women had been shown hanging from ropes, dead, of course, but also resembling marionettes, under the inescapable control of some evil force. They were either suspended in mid-air, completely immobile, lifeless, or vanishing in and out of the young wife's nightmare.

Earlier in the film, a series of oversized keys had danced playfully, to the laughter of the audience. There had been other moments of raucous laughter, most clearly when one of the cooks at the wedding breakfast had fallen headfirst into the soup from which only his clothes were fished out, his body now incorporated into the brew, a crude joke. Eliza cringed at the maddening cheers, the audience laughing so hard that it brought tears to their eyes. But the whole movie had an eerie, unsavoury tone, a warning to women of their fate – to be used and chopped to pieces, or otherwise disposed of when no longer needed.

Eliza tried to recall what she knew about the tale. Mina had been the expert in fairy tales, but at least living with her she had some fleeting recollection. The original story had been collected by Charles Perrault as early as the seventeenth century, she thought, and was a warning against women's curiosity. Of course, thought Eliza, for what else could men be scared of?

As for women, it was clear what they were scared of. The young woman does not want to marry Bluebeard, but his father forces her to do so after being given a tour of his many riches, forcing her to sign the marriage certificate.

There was another figure, moving in and out of the narrative too, the fairy godmother. But she was a cruel figure, who was rather critical of the young woman. She was on her knees, crying, and the fairy godmother seemed to be saying that she had to accept her fate. At the end, when Barbe-bleue had been defeated, the fairy godmother reigned over the final tableau, sparks pouring from her chest. Eliza felt she had seen this before, this kind of figure with rays of light pouring from her, but she could not put her finger on it. Where had she seen this image before?

The evening continued with the rest of the programme, and as things advanced there seemed to be a sense of excitement in the audience, as if the best was yet to come.

The room went dark again, the piano started, and Eliza twisted uncomfortably in her seat as a cone of light reappeared, shadowy images starting their tentative flicker. Then an image formed on the screen, a title page announcing 'L'Homme à la tête en caoutchouc. Star Film, Geo. Méliès Paris'.

The show was about to begin again. At least this new film proved much shorter, almost simplistic.

A man appeared on the stage, or rather on the white screen; he was moving around what looked like a kitchen, perhaps a rudimentary laboratory. He walked up and down, considered his instruments, and finally placed a table in the middle of the room. The sizes were all wrong, and only after a second Helena remembered this man was not on the stage, but that she was looking at a moving picture, and the man was a projection onto the white canvas, a ghost of light.

A head appeared atop the table, a head without a body, but moving; the mouth and the eyes were powerfully gesticulating.

The man now took a pair of bellows from a corner of the room, attached them to a tube, which Helena now saw the moving head was connected to, and started pumping.

It was the best illusion she had ever seen; so simple, and at the same time so effective. The head on the screen was ballooning up, then ballooning down again as the man playing the scientist released air, then pumped it back up again; it was all done as if in child's play, with a deliberate light-hearted tone.

And then the head exploded.

There was some brutality in the idea, and it took her a few seconds to catch up with the reactions around her, so different from her own: people in the theatre were laughing wildly, some of them had begun chanting, '*L'Homme à la tête en caoutchouc! L'Homme à la tête en caoutchouc!*' She imagined they had seen the short film before. She certainly did not want to see it ever again.

Eliza had not said much during the walk back to the Lirriper; she did not feel able to engage Alice in small conversation, and she felt unprepared to talk about the show in particular, or the French *cinématographe* at large. Alice started chatting then, perhaps to fill the silence.

'So, what did you think?' she said, referring to Méliès's strange offerings to his theatre audience. 'They are not like moving pictures by the Lumière brothers, not at all.'

'Who are those brothers?'

'The inventors of the *cinématographe*, of course. Although this is contested. There had been things happening at the same time in America as well, and in Britain, mind you. Many people have developed their own cameras after the Lumière brothers, so there are questions of patents as well.'

Eliza thought that a patent was certainly a reason to kidnap, or even kill somebody.

'Are they the ones who film people leaving a factory?' she asked.

'That's right. They recorded a lot of these kinds of scenes in the earlier days. Before anyone had thought about the ability of movies to tell stories,' she explained. 'What you have seen today, and what Georges excels at. That is why I was interested in working with him in the first instance, even if at times his movies make me sick.' This pricked Eliza's curiosity intensely: perhaps Alice shared some of her misgivings as well, even if Eliza could not articulate quite yet what exactly had made her feel queasy. Alice continued: 'Believe me, I have no time or stomach for fairies,' she explained, 'but I am interested in finding the narrative potential of this. He even has a name for it all, *l'expression spectaculaire*.'

Spectacular shivers, rather, thought Eliza. 'Why do you think his movies make you sick?'

Alice sighed. 'All his star-women, celestial-women, fairies, butterflies, even planets Millie was talking about. They are immobile, docile, decorative, always at the mercy of the men. It is perverse. He once – I remember this movie. I was utterly disgusted.'

'What happened?'

Alice was now speaking perhaps more reluctantly than Eliza had expected:

'He wanted to show a magician creating a human doll by taking dolls' parts out of a box, and then, using substitution splicing – it is a technique, I shall explain later what it is – turn it into a woman. And then back again into a doll, and put the pieces away. I said no way, I was not going to help with this. Living dolls! Doll women!'

Eliza did not understand. What was Alice talking about?

'I'm sorry Alice, I'm not sure I follow.'

'Don't you?' Alice stopped, looked left and right before she spoke again: 'He is spreading these ideas about women, normalising them. He is creating stories that a woman is a disposable thing.'

This made Eliza shiver.

Eliza had been eager to learn about Monsieur Méliès, as a first step into the case. What she had witnessed, however, had wildly exceeded any of her expectations. Until that moment she had had a very limited idea of what moving pictures could achieve. She had not been particularly interested in the invention, because she had not seen the point of looking at a scene in a park, or people walking around, or similar everyday occurrences that you could either already see in real life, or perhaps through another medium, such as photography. But Monsieur Méliès's movie had shattered her preconceptions: this new medium could offer so much more, a kind of realistic magic, a dark idea if there were any, as far as she was concerned. And, if Alice was right, with a unique power to manipulate which stories it put into people's minds. This was a far more dangerous proposition.

She was speechless, still trying to process it all. And coming to terms with how unsettled it all made her feel.

The streets of Paris were a mixture of the electric lights, remnants of the World Exhibition two years ago, and the shadows that the very lights now made more abundant, in contrast with the illumination, a dichotomy which left Eliza feeling enervated. Despite the overwhelming displays of phantasmagoria in the programme, the magic lanterns and automata, the magician who had read the audience's mind, she had sensed that the projection of the short film had been the main event of the evening.

Once they were back in the Lirriper, they said goodbye and went to their separate rooms. Eliza was exhausted, but still she tried to put down in writing the events of the evening for Helena. She now wondered whether she should also explain her feelings. Although this wasn't very scientific detecting, the Method included at times the slippery notion of 'instincts', and she wondered whether this would fit within that.

The film had affected her deeply. Because it had been so long, lasting nearly ten minutes by the theatre clock, she had felt immersed in the experience, she now realised. The length was no doubt a well-designed trick to control the audience. What Alice had said was intriguing, worryingly so. Until now, she had had no idea that the new medium of moving pictures could be used in this manner to build narratives, to tell tales. All she had seen were the short-duration recordings Alice had referred to, of people walking in Oxford Street, perhaps, or else climbing aboard and descending from trams, running out of the way of horses and carriages; pictures of barges packed to the sky with goods commuting up and down the Thames.

In truth, she had not seen much point to it, especially when transportable photography was becoming so advanced, when words could be used perfectly to describe any given scene down to the last detail. Add to that how unrealistic the people looked, with everyone moving slightly quicker than in real life – Alice had explained this was due to the number of frames that the recording machines used per second, which rendered it all a bit comical.

This was definitely something different, and, as far as she was concerned, worrying, Alice was right about that. If there was something that working with Helena had shown her, it was the importance of stories, how much it mattered who controlled the narrative. She thought again of the cruel image of the cook falling into the soup. She realised why people in the audience had laughed so hard: Méliès had decided to present that death as a joke. He had controlled, no, he had manipulated, the audience's understanding of this moment.

Something with that kind of power was deeply unsettling: into whose hands would it fall? To be used in which way? In this, movies were not too different from other forms of technology. She had often reflected, secretly hoped, that the new advances in science were occupying the role previously played by superstition and religion, even by magic, in older times. Up to now, she had imagined this to be a good thing. Now, she was not so sure. In a way, acts of 'magic', like the ones in that very theatre, resembled science and technology more and more everyday. The transition from manual to automated production was happening in front of their very eyes, and electricity itself was the new technology fated to finally dispel the shadows. Or was it? In her own opinion, the streets they had traversed on their way back to the hotel were teeming with *more* shadows, if that was possible, the contrast between the dark and the light almost unbearable. She had found the streets impossibly dazzling, as she was used to the more sedated illumination of London. But she knew those old-fashioned methods belonged to a bygone era. Soon, London itself would have to adopt... this. Would the shadows be dispelled for good, or would they just grow and multiply? Who knew?

She remembered now something that she and Mina had encountered and found amusing: the figure of the 'electric fairy', or *fée électricité*. It had been during their visit to the World Exhibition. There had been something about this written in the exhibition guide book. She remembered seeing the volume downstairs, in the Lirriper's parlour. She threw on a shawl and went into the corridor. The gaslight was dimmed on the walls, increasing the shadows. She shivered for a second. But she knew that ghosts were not real, that the supernatural was not real. Nothing would make her change that idea. She went down the stairs, careful not to make a lot of noise in the quiet house. She found the parlour empty. On a bookshelf were some tattered old tomes of the kind that are always in this kind of establishment – the guide book was where she had last seen it. She looked through it patiently, until she found the passage:

The supreme ruler of the 1900 Exhibition is Electricity, the brilliant young fairy who endows modern industry with two important features: movement and light!

She had to admit it: despite her unexpected doubts about the modern scientific miracle of electricity, one thing that was clear was that she had felt safe enough to walk back with Alice to the hotel instead of taking a hansom cab, something she would not have attempted in dimly lit London under any circumstances – if it was easy to disappear in London, it was doubly easy for a young woman to do so.

Her conversation with Millie earlier that evening resonated in her head: where did those vanishing ladies go? And why it was always women who vanished?

7

THE GLASS DOLL HOUSE

The Glass Doll House looked more like a giant greenhouse than a movie studio. It was erected on the Méliès family property at Montreuil, just outside of Paris. Alice had given Eliza the general description. Seventeen metres long, six metres wide and six metres high, these specific measurements were identical to Méliès's theatre, and equipped with movable panels, trap doors, ramps, pulleys, cranes, even sets. Still Eliza had not expected this, even after hearing descriptions of 'an oversized orangery'. It looked slightly unreal, as if the glass structure could collapse at any moment. According to Alice, it was built like this to allow as much light in as possible.

'He has no artificial lighting, except in the workshop areas; nothing to illuminate the scenes. He only uses daylight.' It seemed, however, that Méliès had decided that the Doll House wasn't enough to create his elaborate illusions. 'He is building a second studio now; he calls it Studio B.'

They approached the structure and even from afar, the hubbub of people at work was apparent. Alice continued:

'Méliès is involved in everything. He writes the scenarios, supervises the construction of the sets, which are based on his own elaborate designs, he designs the lighting, arranges the action and sometimes – to top it all – even acts himself!'

'That must be exhausting.' And potentially control-seeking, Eliza thought.

'He and his brother Gaston even draw the movie *affiches*.'

'*Affiches?*'

'Promotional posters.'

Alice went on to explain that, even if most of his illusions derived from his theatre work, Méliès had also started developing many new cinematic techniques. He had got bored very quickly with what the theatre could offer, and was now a firm believer in the possibilities of cinema.

'I guess the Robert-Houdin proved to be a very limited space for showcasing his genius – he has created a massive number of illusions and tricks for the theatre. Some people say twenty, or even more, in ten years.'

On top of the entrance, the motto of the Méliès company was prominently displayed: *Le Monde à la Portée de la Main* – 'the world at your fingertips'.

'So, he is some sort of genius?' asked Eliza.

'Pretty much.'

Great, thought Eliza. How on earth she was going to lie to this man's face about what she was doing here was beyond her. She started to lose her nerve a little. Still, she was here now, and they were expected. She would have to pull herself together. Hopefully she would only need a couple of days of snooping around the studio to have enough to report to Helena.

Somebody bumped against her, shouting something in French that she did not catch. Eliza turned around to apologise, and jumped in shock. Despite the elaborate costumes, all actors and dancers were dressed in different shades of grey, the same colour as the decorations around them, with white and black makeup covering their hands and their faces, their heads also powered white, with heavy grey eyeshadow, which made them look like faded ghosts. The ghostly man she was now facing shook his head and moved on.

'Why these colours?' She had imagined Star Film Studio as much more colourful. She noticed she was still catching her breath a little. The whole thing made the place look like a tomb.

'Oh! That's because of the filmstock: it is orthochromatic, so the colours don't come up right. It is much better if they are painted over,' explained Alice.

So that's what Miss Peters, Emily, did. But, despite already knowing that Emily painted the frames, Eliza had assumed that the scenes were also shot in colour anyway. Seeing things as they really were, as if a whimsical mask had been removed, made her think that this was, behind the scenes, a far different affair from what people were led to believe, with illusions, or rather deceptions, needed. There was a peculiar sadness about the grey decors, the actors made up in black and white, the monochromatic place.

'Look, there he is, checking his *moulin à café*.'

'Excuse me?'

'Coffee grinder. That's what he calls his *kinematograph*, on account of how noisy it is.'

Eliza looked in Méliès's direction. He was very much in the midst of things: a great number of workers were gathered around him, listening carefully to his instructions. Méliès looked like an affable man, who cultivated a funny moustache, probably due to his work as an actor. But all those smiles, even the cuteness indicated by his camera's pet name, could be cultivated, forced. Eliza thought of how queasy watching his two movies had made her feel – there had certainly been something off about them.

A great number of people were moving around, going about their business. Building materials were on the floor, scattered here and there. She could see bits of décor, women being fitted with extravagant grey costumes, half-opened automata. She would later learn that these were routinely scavenged by Méliès for pieces.

As Alice had explained, most of the girls had a flying motif attached to their elaborate grey costumes; a star, or wings, sprouting from their backs or heads. It was clear that Méliès was still working on perfecting his favourite symbol according to Alice, that of the 'amazing flying woman'.

Méliès was now approaching them, a beaming smile on his face, arms extended to embrace Alice.

'Alice Guy! Thank you, thank you! You have found me an Englishwoman, if I am correct, and thus you have saved me!'

Alice smiled. 'Georges, can I introduce Miss Eliza Waltraud? Miss Waltraud, Georges Méliès.'

'*Enchanté!*'

'A pleasure, monsieur.'

'Have you been long in Paris, Miss Waltraud?'

'Not really. But I am hoping this will be a long visit,' she lied. 'I am very thankful about the opportunity for work, sir.'

'Please, it is me who is thankful. My little office is growing in chaos, and something needs to be done. My affairs with America are by no means diminishing, and if I don't employ someone soon, things are going to explode, like an overfilled balloon! Please, allow me to show you around. What do you think about our little studio?' asked Méliès, indicating the proceedings around him.

Eliza noticed his twitchiness, the way he could not stop moving. It was as if he were going to start dancing all of a sudden.

'It is a truly remarkable place. I have never seen anywhere like it.' Eliza was being honest, and Méliès beamed.

'Allow me to take you to the office, where you will be working most of the time.'

They followed him. He indicated, more vaguely than Eliza had expected, the stages where the decorations were placed, and the rails for the camera to move around it. Some obvious cranes and pulleys were on view, but Méliès did not refer to them, like a magician who did not want to give away his tricks.

He was opening doors to different sections, rooms which were moveable instead of fixed, showing where the seamstresses were located and where the carpenters kept their tools, and even quite a large room filled with *papier-mâché* leftovers from previous productions. Everything had a magical air, as if those planets, with their uncanny anthropomorphic faces smiling back at her, could start talking at any moment. Eventually, they came upon the office, a small room that mirrored the seamstresses' area on the other side of the building, where a man got up from among piles of papers and desks to greet them.

'Miss Waltraud, may I present Gaston Méliès, my brother?'

'How do you do?' he said. 'If I am not mistaken, you have come to help deal with this!' he said, signalling the chaotic room. There were papers to sort and file, piles and piles, all over desks and on the floor. 'I am exceedingly thankful. *Bonjour*, Alice!'

'How do you do? And I will certainly do my best!' Eliza looked uncertain as to the mess. She suddenly thought of Miss Webster, and wished she was here. 'I should perhaps explain that my background is in scientific studies.'

Georges and Gaston exchanged a look, clearly delighted by this.

'My dear Miss Waltraud! That is music to my ears. I should perhaps explain a little of what your job will entail, if you allow me.'

The filmmaker went on to talk about camera specifications, parts, construction, and, in general, the whole process of how ideas became movies.

'When I realised I wanted to make movies, my first intention was to purchase a *cinématographe* from the Lumière brothers, but this was met with resistance. So I had to travel to London instead, where other machines were being produced at the time. I purchased a machine from Robert William Paul for the sum of 1,000 francs. Robert Paul's machine is called an *animatograph*. Then I came back here, and performed a large number of improvements on it, using mechanical parts found in my theatre's storeroom, at times using pieces from my own automata.'

'Please, you will have to excuse me, but how is this relevant to the job I'll be doing?'

'My dear Miss Waltraud, I only found out much later on that Paul's camera was, in fact, a copy from Thomas Edison's Kinetoscope, the American inventor. Edison may not have been happy about this, but his own invention was itself based on a previous inventor's ideas, so he could not prevent this false Kinetoscope from being manufactured in England.'

This was impossible to follow. Should she be taking notes? How she was going to remember it all to report back to Helena was beyond her.

'All of this complicates matters exceedingly, especially when we are having problems with Mr Edison regarding patents and copyright,' clarified Gaston.

'You see, Miss Waltraud,' noted Georges, 'the majority of my correspondence in English deals with my dispute with Mr Edison. I am afraid he has decided, quite unilaterally, it seems, that he is the only person who has any right to benefit from showing motion pictures in America, and hence, he simply cuts the frame with the Star Film logo and sells his own copy. He distributes them there, getting all the money for himself, and not caring at all that *we* made them.' Eliza noted he was getting more agitated as he recounted the feud. 'I am sure that, with your scientific training, it will be easy to get you up to speed on the particularities of the different machines, so you can appreciate the issue, understand it correctly, and write authoritatively. I feel it is providential that you are here.'

'I am happy that you think so, sir. I can assure you I will do my best,' she replied, feeling her heart sink. She had thought she was going to be employed for some light secretarial duties, but all of this sounded ten times more complicated. The sooner she found out about Miss Peters and the other vanished ladies and went back to London the better.

'What you see there,' interceded Gaston, indicating a group of numbered cardboard boxes, 'is a detailed archive discussing this issue. Not only about distributing our movies in the US without giving us any credit—'

'Or any money!' added an incensed Georges.

'—but also issues of patents that need to be dealt with in the US and England. I am afraid that my English doesn't seem to be good enough to deal with all of this competently, Miss Waltraud.'

'Of course,' continued Georges, now getting animated, 'from a mere patent point of view, as his camera was based on another, and the *animatograph* included quite a large number of improvements, the original from which I built was quite different from his first invention. What is more, my own camera-projector is also considered, if I may say so, a huge improvement as well. I therefore patented it. It now seems that Mr Edison has taken issue with this, and he seems quite immobile in his intention to continue distributing unauthorised copies of my movies without giving us any credit.'

It was dawning on Eliza exactly how patchy, and complex, the legal situations arising around the new art of filmmaking were. It was clear that everyone seemed to have borrowed from everyone else – hadn't Alice explained how the Lumières, in turn, had been inspired by Eadweard Muybridge's photographs of horses in movement? However, as a detective, was all this worth pursuing? Could there somehow be a connection with the disappearance of Miss Emily Peters in France? She would need to write to Helena for counsel.

And then she remembered: she wasn't in Paris to solve anything, not even to reach conclusions. Her only role there was, as per the Method, 'information gathering' to send back home. Before arriving in Paris, she had felt undermined by this, as if Helena had not considered her good enough to do much else. Now she started to see how important this was, how potentially complicated, how valuable. She would content herself with reporting as accurately as possible on the feud, one more piece of a puzzle that was gaining, in her mind, gargantuan proportions.

'We are hard at work on the most important movie we have ever produced, Miss Waltraud, our little *Trip to the Moon*,' continued Georges. 'This will be the film that will prove, beyond any doubt, that cinema ought to become something separate at last from the between-the-acts entertainments shown at the vaudeville, and that it should make the impossible possible, the real and the fantastic overlapping so seamlessly that the fantastic becomes the real!' Eliza shivered at this notion, but she managed a nod and a weak smile. 'In short, this production is proving particularly complex, Miss Waltraud, and extremely costly as well. I would hate for Mr Edison to get even one bit of benefit from all our hard work.'

'That rascal!' said Gaston. 'Please, *excusez moi*, mesdemoiselles.' The issue clearly affected the two brothers deeply, and, perhaps, the future of Star Film Studio itself.

Eliza was thankful to find that Alice was still around at lunchtime: she wasn't feeling confident enough yet to start talking with the rest of the workers by herself, and preferred a chance to observe them first from a distance. They were working their way through a simple meal of thick-cut bread and a potage of pulses and cabbages that was more delicious than Eliza would have imagined.

'I do make a point of eating here as much as I can,' explained Alice. 'The food is very good. It comes directly from the kitchen in the family house,' she said, pointing through the glass wall to the Méliès's family home, a sumptuous white mansion that sat one field beyond.

Eliza nodded. However, she had more pressing matters on her mind. She had brought a blank notebook to her first day, a notebook that was now filled with explanations as to the developments of the different *cinematograph* machines.

'It seems incredible,' she started, 'that someone can simply snip a couple of frames and benefit from something they haven't done. Is there no system in place to guarantee any kind of authorship? Simply looking around the studio for ten minutes, you could see it is a massive undertaking, and a costly one.'

Alice nodded, her mouth full of potage: 'Georges has other problems, believe me,' she said when she could speak, and taking a drink of the rather good wine: 'He cannot keep up with his competitors here in France, either.'

'Why? It seems to me he knows exactly what he is doing.'

'Oh yes, he knows what he is doing. And he knows how to do it – that is his problem. His way of making movies is so complicated that he only produces a couple of them per month, you see, whereas others produce a dozen. This is what happens, I suppose, when you are making these elaborate flights of fancy,' she noted. 'Georges is an excellent theatre owner and producer, with a flair for putting together really great spectacles. But I gather that all his business acumen will not prevent him from needing to spend a lot of money to make his movies.'

'Do you think that he could be looking for a way to produce films quicker, and cheaper?'

'That would certainly be a quick solution to many of his problems. But how to achieve this? Unless you can make the ladies fly for real,' Alice laughed.

But Eliza did not laugh. She was not sure what she had meant with her question, but somehow darkly her mind had gone towards the idea they had discussed the previous night, of making women disposable. Some notion was being nurtured in her mind, but she could not put it correctly into words.

'Alice,' she said. 'I am not sure what I am getting at here. But the movies I have seen made me feel…'

'What?'

'Queasy. They made me feel queasy.' Eliza did not say it out loud, but she was wondering whether this was information worth passing on to Helena in her letter. 'Do you have any idea if this is what he intends to achieve? I mean, it cannot be… It has to just be me. Everyone else in the theatre was laughing.'

Alice nodded. 'You said that his movies made you sick, but something tells me you weren't referring to the same thing.'

Alice looked left and right, leaned closer to Eliza, and lowered her voice.

'It is more than that, Eliza.'

'More? How?'

'There were rumours, years ago.'

'What kind of rumours?'

'About a movie that made people not just sick, but violent.'

Eliza could not believe what she was hearing.

'Violent? But how?'

'I am not sure. The movie was lost, it's still lost. Some people thought that the movie was Georges's.'

'Did they have any proof?'

'Only that he has always been so willing to experiment with what he can do, to push further than anybody else, to see what truly can be achieved.'

Eliza stopped eating, and in fact could not have another mouthful. The lunch hour was soon over after this, and they returned to their different tasks, Eliza to the office with Gaston, who had not stopped to eat anything, and Alice back to the workshop where the automata were being dismembered in order to reuse their parts in the many levers and contraptions.

Eliza spent the rest of the afternoon thinking about this mysterious movie. Could a movie really make people violent? Was that even possible? She suspected it was. Her reaction even after only seeing the 'funny' movies that Méliès produced were a case in point. Could it be that he had been implicated in the past in something far more sinister, something that had served, perhaps, as a rehearsal of the effects he was striving to produce now in a more refined manner?

That night, back at her desk in the Lirriper, she started by writing her general impressions of the Méliès brothers, both knowledgeable and proud of their work, while bitter due to the money they were losing because of Edison. She then went on to explain as best she could the issues of copyright regarding the camera-projectors themselves. The summary of the invention of the machine was rather labyrinthine and difficult to follow at times, but Eliza wrote a careful timeline for Helena, hoping it would be helpful, but not knowing if it would be.

Helena had been warning her precisely of this, of not reaching any precipitous conclusions on her own. She had to admit it: information gathering was a far more difficult occupation than she had allowed herself to believe.

Paris, 21st March 1902

The next morning Alice was not needed at the studio, and Eliza made her way on the little train out of Paris into Montreuil on her own. She could still feel the rush of surprise on arrival when seeing the glass building, which she now thought a crystal palace in miniature, something out of a Russian fairy tale. She went inside and directly into the office. It felt strange to enter without Alice's company, as she was sure that no one knew yet who she was. However, the morning seemed even livelier than the previous day, with people coming and going everywhere, and no one challenged her. Should she mention this to Helena, the lack of security in the Studio? Probably it did not matter to their current endeavours: Miss Peters had been taken in the street.

She entered the empty office: no sign of Gaston. She could see him from the door, however, chatting animatedly with two girls in costumes, pale stars with floating organza wings. They were due to shoot that morning, and the energy of the place was chaotic; everyone seemed to be in a sort of frenzy. She imagined that, now that she was here, Gaston would not spend much time pretending to answer and read correspondence in English.

She looked around. Where should she start? The cabinets were bursting with papers, there were piles everywhere. Working for Méliès had presented itself as the perfect cover to have access to his employees, as surely they were the ones that could offer information about Miss Emily Peters. But the records ought to help as well, and perhaps this would be the only occasion when she was going to be alone in the room. She opened the cabinets containing the staff files. Peters, E. Nothing, nothing at all. Emily Peters did not appear there. Was she searching correctly? She looked for Alice Guy under G. There she was, a short form with her name, contact address, and how to pay her (in cheques, weekly). This was nothing if not odd. Had someone removed the file, perhaps to cover that Mina's friend had worked at the studio? There was only one way of knowing this: to look for the file of one of the missing dancers. She had not asked Millie for their names. She cursed herself for her beginner's mistake.

Presently, she heard a shriek, followed by shouting in French. She peeped outside of the door. The girls were gone, and so was Gaston; everyone seemed to be concentrating in one spot. Her curiosity pricked, she went to have a look at proceedings. Surely understanding the mechanics of the studio would prove useful.

The ladies dressed as stars were being filmed, all connected to harnesses and ropes. Only some straps were visible, and she imagined that most of them, which would take them up into the ceiling, painted to resemble the night sky, would be concealed in their elaborate costumes. Presently, le patron, as everyone called Méliès, shouted something, and everyone stopped what they were doing, their last-minute touches here and there, and disappeared from the shot; people crouching on the floor, on their knees, some of them simply lying on the wooden floor. Two sturdy men were now on each side of the shot, out of view of the camera, holding massive ropes. She looked up: the ropes went all the way up into a crane system that looped down again, and connected directly with the dancers. She remembered the theatre performance Helena had taken her to back in London, the levers and cranes that had been revealed by Detective O'Neill. But in that case they had been concealed, and these ropes were now in view; the only things hidden were their connectors to the dancers.

Piano music began playing from somewhere. And then the dancers started to float up into the ether.

The ropes made the illusion extremely unconvincing: from where she was standing, the two men holding them were obviously working as hard as they could in making this deception real. Then they relaxed, and Eliza understood that the system did not depend on them, that they were there as an extra layer of protection. Something else, probably very clever and theatrical, worked the ropes and levers to create the illusion of the dancers floating over the wooden boards. Of course they must also sense it in their bones, feel it in their muscles as they climbed, up and up, into the studio's heights; and the girls looked free, unattached, giggling away.

A strange buzzing started over their heads. Instinctively, Eliza turned in its direction, and saw it was a beam of light, directed towards the dancers. She thought it must be some kind of illumination, and was immediately confused by the idea: why a green light, when everything was monochromatic in the studio? Besides, hadn't Alice said that Méliès didn't use any lighting at all, hence the huge crystal construction? But there was no doubt whatsoever: a green-yellow light was now bathing the dancers. Then, they started moving their limbs strangely, jerking almost; and then they relaxed again. Even from the floor she could see them, their faces completely calm, but it was an odd calm, unnatural. Their faces looked bigger; and then she realised as she squinted upwards: their eyes and mouths were open unnaturally wide. Were they acting? Was that eerie huge smile part of the repertoire of films? She remembered Miss Bustelo's exaggerated faces when she explained about movie acting, but somehow this did not seem to be what was happening here.

What was that? Eliza wondered. Were her own instincts perhaps taking over, just as Helena had anticipated?

On cue, the ladies started floating more lightly than before, as if they themselves were made of light. The ropes were no longer taut around them.

It could not be possible.

The light, which had been pale, intensified, acquiring the viscous density of a cloud.

She looked around: everyone had stopped paying attention. Why did nobody else see it? They must see it. Perhaps they chose to ignore it. She could not be sure if she wasn't imagining it all either, or simply wrong. She wasn't as versed in the crane system and fraud and theatrics as Helena was. She lacked her kind of expertise. Perhaps the ropes around the dancers could look lax to her and still be performing the miracle. One thing was clear: Méliès's illusion was one cut above anything she had witnessed in vaudevilles.

8

INTO THE NIGHT GARDEN

21st March – Later. Trianon Gardens

Eliza found a map in the office, and she wondered if she could borrow it, on the pretext of wanting to go for a walk during lunch. Still, she was not very good at reading maps, and she had no idea how long it would take her to go to Versailles and back. Then she had a better idea:

'Gaston, I am not feeling very well. I think I ought to stop for the day.'

'But of course, my dear. You go home and take care of yourself.'

Strangely, Eliza seemed to have miscalculated the timing, and she got to the gardens at dusk. In fact, it seemed as if her first day at the strange studio at melted away somehow, and she had no idea where the hours had gone. After a whole day of flying dancers and star-women, and Méliès's mad contraptions defining what was real and what not, she wasn't feeling herself. Lunch that day had been quite heavy, consisting of cold roasted small birds, stewed potatoes, rich meats and cheeses, and all those sauces that they so freely pour over her plate; so many other things that Eliza would not normally have associated with communal eating in England.

Still Eliza tried to keep her wits about her. The Trianon was a beautiful place, and she wandered for a while aimlessly, just enjoying the fresh scent of the flowers and cool shade of the trees. But she realised it then: there were no birds singing, no crickets chirping. Everything was silent, and unnaturally so.

This at once brought to mind her pointless search for the tern in Norfolk a year or so ago, when she and Helena had met. Somehow, it wasn't a good recollection. There had been an unnatural light floating around in Norfolk as well – was that what was happening in Star Film Studio? Whatever she had seen that morning, it wasn't just a play of luminescence, it wasn't simply some colours dancing on the air. It was as if a hidden current had crossed the room, making itself felt. And an acute sensation had overcome Eliza: attraction, mixed with dislike.

Eliza heard someone, and, despite her being so untrained as yet, she remembered some of Helena's words on the subject of surveillance, when explaining 'soft but unmistakable advances, that seemed to be muffled or stop altogether when you try to hear them'. She could see a flashlight as well, moving widely around despite the fact that there was still some dusky light, as if there was some confusion about the time of the day from whoever was using it. Eliza's instinct was to hide; rather melodramatic, she thought, but hide she did. Night was now falling a bit faster than she had anticipated, or than she thought was possible at that time of the year, which brought to mind Carroll's Tulgey Wood. Then she saw them: a strange procession passing by, people dressed in old-fashioned robes, perhaps a theatre troupe?

But they looked, or felt, to her wrong somehow, as if they were not meant to be there. She thought of her first private reaction to the misses' mystery – maybe it was possible that the closeness of the studio meant that there were workers in costume having a picnic there. She had not dared to put this to Helena, but she was now secretly hoping to have been correct. Still, they did not look from the studio: they were not made up in grey colours, the distinctive black and white required for the orthochromatic film to work properly. Their garments had colours, if faded.

In her mind there was no reason for those people being there, and she felt stupid, unworthy of Helena's trust in her. What was happening to her? Was Eliza now coming to terms with those lines in Bram Stoker's novel, the one that Helena had recommended so imperiously to her?:

> It is so hard to accept at once any abstract truth, that we may doubt such to be possible when we have always believed the 'no' of it.

Eliza kept crouching down on the grass, feeling confused and disorientated. She hardly managed to get herself to the station at Versailles on her rented bicycle, where she jumped on the first train back to the capital.

21st March – Early evening. Hotel Lirriper

'Miss Waltraud! You look as if you have seen a ghost!'

Eliza's day was not over yet. Miss Charlotte Moberly and Miss Eleanor Jourdain were waiting for her in Mrs Lirriper's parlour, a cheery fire burning behind them, the ladies partaking of the nice sherry in company of the Misses Winningham.

The irony of this visit was not lost on Eliza. She privately cursed her luck. She had still felt disoriented on the train, incapable of processing what had happened. She had several theories, all involving groups of people that belonged to the twentieth century, thank you very much. But she had still not managed to conclusively prove them to herself. She ought to manage a greeting, but all this was pressing too much on her. She would have preferred to have this particular encounter after processing her recent experience. Alas, it was not to be. Eventually, she spoke:

'Miss Charlotte, Miss Eleanor. What a pleasure. What are you doing in Paris?' It came out rather more forceful than she had intended, but the two ladies did not notice.

'Charlotte is lecturing at the Temperance Society here, and had the courtesy of inviting me along,' said Eleanor.

'I hope it is alright for us to have come unannounced: Miss Helena informed us of where you were staying.'

'Yes, of course,' muttered Eliza unconvincingly. She found a chair and collapsed in it.

'Oh dear. You do look tired. We were going to invite you to a gathering tonight; we thought you may find it interesting.'

'What, the lecture? It would be a pleasure—'

No, the ladies were shaking their heads.

'My lecture is scheduled for tomorrow afternoon, Miss Eliza. We were hoping you would be so kind as to come with us to a rather different gathering. A séance.' Something must have changed in Eliza's face, for Miss Charlotte quickly added: 'We would like your scientific opinion, of course.' This pricked Eliza's interest. 'In fact, we were hoping you would be able to help us with this matter. One of our good friends has fallen under the spell of a medium, and frankly we can't tell if she is being duped or not.'

Surely she is, thought Eliza. To the ladies she said:

'Of course. Please let me change my clothes, and I will come with you.'

Eleanor clapped her gloved hands, while Charlotte exclaimed: 'Excellent!'

Eliza went upstairs to change her dress and clean herself a little. She was tired, but also intrigued; and going out on an errand would mean she did not have to interrogate very closely what had just happened to her, the silly way in which she had lost sense of time, and got lost, and had hallucinations in the gardens. Yes, that was it. She had hallucinated the whole thing. She ought to go back and look at the plants there. Even better, peruse the planting plans in the helpful guide Helena had lent her. Wasn't the herbal garden close to the English garden, if she remembered correctly? Perhaps there was something in the air… Yes, that would do. She was happy to have thought of something, something concrete that she could check on later.

————•—•————

21st March – Evening

They arrived at an elegant building of Lutetian limestone, its regular lines and gilded balconies forcing Charlotte to double-check that they were at the correct address.

'I wouldn't want to force a viscount from his soup!' she chuckled before ringing the bell. But indeed it was the right address for Mademoiselle Calvé, and a skeletal maid guided them inside, into a palatial vestibule in the middle of Paris. They were taken into an even grander reception area where other people were also waiting. There was a round table right there – they would sadly not have the chance to trespass onto more of the palace – and they were instructed to sit and, unusually compared to the séances that Eliza had attended with Helena, introduce themselves. The participants included a Spanish grandee, a foreign mystic, another well-known medium, a marquis, two lady scholars from the town of Oxford, England, a young gentleman who introduced himself simply as 'a poet', and Miss Eliza Waltraud, from London, England.

It later transpired they had attended, for Eliza unwittingly, Lady Caithness's famous salon; but as the Spanish-English lady was away in her London mansion, so her favourite medium that season, Mademoiselle Calvé, had been tasked with keeping the salon going for milady's friends and those wandering souls who passed by the highest Paris society each season. How the misses had got themselves an invitation to such a select gathering was a mystery. Later on, Eleanor would have to come clean: she had heard about La Calvé, and had decided to risk getting into the salon; a strategy which, as the salon was composed of different people who happen to be in the French capital each week, had proved to be worth taking the chance.

But, before Eliza could get any of that, they were regaled with an evening of levitating furniture followed by broken furniture, trances and spirit guides; and when La Calvé revealed hers, Eliza nearly fell off her chair:

'She is here at last! Welcome, my queen!'

Marie Antoinette herself was, allegedly, Mademoiselle Calvé's spirit guide.

There was no commotion about this, as the rest of the sitters seemed aware of the impossible situation; but Eliza had questions. Many questions. She could not break the circle, but she looked inquisitively to the smiling misses. La Calvé sat up on her chair. Her face had the hue of Mediterranean ladies many generations back, but her countenance had completely changed now: her posture straight as a board, her demeanour intimidating. Her mouth was twitching, as if she despised even the Spanish grandee; and her brows had shot up a whole inch at finding herself in the company of these vassals. She was transformed, suddenly regal – there was no other way to put it.

'My dear misses,' she said in French. 'I am so glad to see you again. For you *looked into my time*. Pray tell me, how did that feel, to peer, from the confusion of this epoch, into the benevolent past? To look beyond and see your queen?'

Marie Antoinette was not the misses' queen, as they were English subjects, but Eliza's inner protestations went further than that. She was fuming. Next to her, Miss Charlotte and Miss Eleanor beamed like little girls. The Spanish grandee was looking at them with obvious distaste, as if they smelt funny, the woman's nose subtly moving left and right. As for Eliza, her anger was only ballooning now. She was about to explode.

According to the spirit, a 'timeless window' had opened in the Trianon that evening in August, from their day all the way back hundreds of years earlier. She clarified that it had taken place many years before her death; and then she seemed to get bored of the misses.

'This is the France that the French deserve! This era of irresponsibility is of your own making!' wailed the medium; her head jerked backwards, and her mouth opened widely, too widely, unnaturally so, as the spirit guide finally left her. Was this the medium's particular trick? Eliza wondered. Her face looked unnatural, her dislocated jaw grotesque. Her screams made everyone shiver in their seats. Everyone except for Eliza. That did it. She got up from the chair, breaking the circle, and some of the sitters looked at her in horror.

'Enough!' she shouted. 'You do not sound at all like a queen, and this is nothing but a sham! How is it possible you cannot see it?' She was now looking around the table. Promptly, Mademoiselle Calvé's reticule of helpers invaded the grand salon, and Eliza and the misses were escorted out and firmly put on the street, with the tall, grand door that kept the location of the sumptuous mansion invisible to the average Parisian passer-by shut behind them with finality. The misses were incensed:

'How dare you?'

'How dare I? How dare *I*? You brought me here under false pretences!'

The women flinched at this.

'Miss Eliza, you would not have come if we had told you the real motives that had brought us here this evening. But I am sure you understand: we wanted confirmation, and now we've got confirmation!' Charlotte announced proudly.

'We did see into the past; we saw the queen!' This was Eleanor. 'She herself has confirmed it!'

Eliza could not believe what she was hearing.

'You cannot be serious. Is that what you think has happened here?'

'You heard it yourself! How else was she going to know to talk to us about "timeless windows"?'

'My dear ladies, your incident is infamous by now! Everyone on both sides of the Channel knows about it!'

Charlotte laughed at this:

'We are aware of that, Miss Eliza. But pray tell me, how could Mademoiselle Calvé possibly know that we would attend today, and prepare her little performance?'

'Very simple: it must be well-known – except to me, it seems – that her spirit guide is none other than Marie Antoinette, the protagonist of your... strange happening!' She was talking louder than she really wanted to, and tried to calm down.

'Don't you see? She must have known that you would make your way to her salon at some point, and was ready for it.'

The faces of the misses went ashen. Eliza continued: 'Actually, now that I come to think about it, if the story about your "friend in need" was not true, then pray tell me, how did you come to be here today? Who suggested you should attend this particular spiritualist circle, and no other?'

The ladies did not reply, but looked at each other. Eventually, Eleanor started sobbing, loudly. Eliza felt immediately guilty.

'Please, Miss Eleanor. I am doing my best here to find out what happened. What *really* happened, which is what you both said you wanted.'

'Are you?' snapped Charlotte, who was protectively hugging her friend. 'We have not received a single report from either you or your employer. For all we know you may not have been to Versailles at all yet!'

Eliza wanted to object: she had indeed visited the Trianon, that very afternoon as it happened. However, thinking about how little she had accomplished with the futile visit, she held her tongue.

She had more questions that she wanted to put to the misses: for example, Beatrice's report on their Oxford scandal. But she thought that it wasn't the right moment. All she could do was to reassure them that she was working on their case.

'My dear ladies,' she started, 'it's been only a few days since I got here. I am working as quickly as I can, but there are a variety of angles that have arisen, a lot of ground to cover, and new information that needs to be evaluated.' The ladies were listening, but she felt she was not really communicating much. 'You should talk to Helena,' she said. 'I have never known her to leave anyone without answers. She will have one for you eventually, I am sure about this.'

'Very well,' said Charlotte. 'And, if we still want to believe that we've just had confirmation from the queen herself…'

'Then please, believe whatever you want to believe. I am not interfering with that.'

Everyone calm now, they tried to hail two cabs to go their separate ways, Eliza back to the Lirriper, and the misses to their own lodgings; but there were not two cabs to be found at that hour, and they had to share one. Once in the cab, Eleanor had stopped crying, and presently closed her eyes. Eliza thought she was sleeping. Perhaps it was the time to talk more with Charlotte. She didn't want to antagonise her by mentioning the Oxford scandal, but it was an opportunity too good to pass up.

'Miss Charlotte, I'm afraid I must ask you something,' she started, her voice low. 'Some questions have arisen out of our enquiries…'

'Ah! I was expecting this. I must apologise: we should not have insulted your intelligence by withholding information from you.'

Eliza was not expecting this extraordinary statement, and let the lady speak.

'In fact, you are right. We did not share everything from our experience. Not in our interview, not in our statements.'

Eliza sat up. 'What do you mean, you did not share it all?'

Charlotte Moberly sighed. She looked like a little girl, caught up in a lie.

'The green light,' she started. 'A light emerged out of nowhere. It was a green, viscous thing. It looked liquid, or as if it could stain our dresses. I had felt disgusted just thinking it would touch me. It was shining in rays, glowing up between the trees. It seemed to come from one place. And then it condensed. There was a peculiar force to it, a sort of wicked energy. This light anticipated our window into the past. This light opened it. Once we were safely outside of the haunted place, we looked back: everything was normal now; the strange yellow-green light was shining through the copse from which we had just come.'

Eliza listened to this strange statement. Then, like a lightning bolt, she remembered: weren't the flying dancers at Star Film Studio enveloped in a green light?

Shortly after, the cab drew up by the Lirriper, and it was time for Eliza to go.

'Why did you not tell us this before?' she said, as she alighted.

'Because that light, Miss Eliza… that green, viscous, horrid thing,' Charlotte was now visibly agitated, 'it gave us both nightmares of strange people, and strange places, for months to come. It was some sort of 'evil' energy, showing us things that it did not have any reason to show us. It wasn't a force from nature, *our nature*, our world. We decided we could not speak of it. An evil light! Can you imagine how absurd that sounded? We thought that people would think us mad! Little we knew they would decide that anyway.'

Back in her room, Eliza needed to get a message over to Helena as soon as possible, but could not do that without access to a telephone, which the Lirriper lacked. How she wished for one second that they could talk by some unknown means, in the 'spiritual dimension'. Or, even better, that someone scientifically minded and bent on banishing all this medieval obscurity and superstition from the world had already invented some way of telephoning all the way from Paris to London. Sadly, neither of those two options was possible. There was only one course of action: to get everything down as quickly as possible, so as not to forget anything of what had transpired. Eliza started writing furiously in her casebook, the pen pushing against the page, starting with the unexpected turn the misses had taken towards the supernatural, which, in Eliza's opinion, only reinforced how unreliable they were as witnesses. They had given the detectives a completely opposite idea of how they were, of what they believed in, when, in truth, they were as gullible as the next spinster. But perhaps this was unfair. In order to give an honest account, she had to recount her own strange visit to the Trianon as well. Pixie-led, she thought it was called. Tomorrow, she would walk to the nearest telegraph office, and send a lengthy telegram to Helena – it would cost her a fortune – summarising these points. A green light? How was she going to explain that one?

INTERLUDE

When had reality shifted for Helena? Probably in Norfolk. But this reality had never shifted for Eliza. And this was causing problems between them.

The case, right after Norfolk, had been, on paper, already strange enough. That should have constituted a warning.

Something wasn't right in a central London home. It had taken some time to come to light, because the supposed haunting took place in an old unused part of the house. The room in question, a nursery, had been shut since time immemorial, and the current owner did not have much information to share. Avoiding that part of the house was already a custom firmly in place as he was growing up, and the long-serving housekeeper had retired to live with her sister, and died a month after finding herself at leisure.

The door was located up a narrow passage, up the last flight of attic stairs. It was dark at the end, even during daylight hours. And even carrying a candle, or an oil lamp, the passage never appeared illuminated. One had to walk up it, step by step, until the door itself was suddenly revealed at the end. And it was low; an adult would have to bend to pass through it. The play of shadows, the darkness, it all conspired to make the seemingly normal wooden door, once it appeared in view, an off-kilter, slightly unexpected thing.

The door that no one wanted to remember was there.

The undercurrent of fear had been reinforced with the hiring of new maids, modern girls who had chosen service when they could have chosen shop work, trained to be stenographers or typists. The young and modern girls would not allow the incongruity: a place no one acknowledged, and yet in plain view, with a mysterious story behind it: something lived up there, and it was understood by everyone that it left them all in peace. As long as, from time to time, there was an offering, a small rabbit, or a kitten perhaps. Their tale was one of utter impossibilities – a small sacrifice to be undertaken, performed, in the middle of the city of London, the most modern city in the whole world. So the young, modern girls complained, when no one had complained before, and Helena and Eliza were brought in by a very bemused new housekeeper.

The girls would simply not accept this state of affairs. Offerings of dead animals? They had to live in this place. They had demanded a solution, or else threatened their immediate departure. And good maids were like golden unicorns these days, you see, explained the housekeeper, almost impossible to find anywhere. A species in danger of extinction.

How did it all happen? The door would appear one morning a little bit ajar, and they – the older members of the household – would know what was expected, and they would procure it, no questions asked.

What could be done?

Eliza spoke of finding the 'actual' reason, a trapped animal, perhaps. Helena said nothing and set to work, asking the cards and moving a pendant from place to place within the room, its purple glass stone sending little dancing luminescences, a cheerful sight that did not tally with the seriousness of the faces who waited downstairs.

In the end, there had been no terrible monster unveiled in the old abandoned nursery, of course, no monster that Helena and Eliza uncovered, only a sad hidden room; and yet, filled with the bones of offerings throughout the decades.

As usual in these cases, their conclusions had been so different from one another's as to be opposite. For Helena had acknowledged a liminal space in which something not quite human might lurk, coming and going, whereas Eliza had preferred to blame rats, or even pigeons, for the carnivorous exertions.

It was Helena who pieced it together in her sitting room, shuffling her cards once again; while Eliza had remained in the dark nursery counting skeletons of small animals, looking for fungi, a gas leak. She saw a young nursery maid, she had explained, falling to her death from a window above. A force that was pulling her, an old, dark energy. It could not be stopped. Helena felt her pain, she herself felt like jumping… She decided against it, or, rather, the force that embodied Helena decided against it. That force, whether ghost, or energy, or demon, was evil. Helena had sensed that much.

So much pain was pain at a disappointment, the pain and the agony of surprise, at discovering your lover was not who you thought. The baby was born up there, in secrecy, and she died. A tale as old as the world.

Helena was certain that the maid was killed by this evil. That she would not have jumped. The baby gone, the nursery maid dead.

Had Helena solved the riddle?

She was forceful about it. She simply knew, she insisted, and Eliza would have to trust her in this.

But did she?

Eliza remembered her in the little room, moving the stone up and down. And becoming overwhelmed, and bending down, grabbing a chair. Helena gagged, violently, but nothing came up.

And then she went into a trance. Her eyes went blank, her head flung back, jerking unnaturally. The uncanny moment was more than Eliza could stand. Her basic training kicked in, and she rushed next to Helena to make sure she did not crack her head against the wall. She held her tight, and remained like this until the fit had passed. Helena had been so cold.

When she came out of it, Helena did not know what had happened, or that anything had indeed occurred in Eliza's presence. But Eliza knew, and had known since then, what Helena was experiencing. And she also understood that Helena was not confiding in her.

Helena explained to the solemn faces downstairs: something remains, trapped by the pain itself, in its own time-warp, a repetition. They might have found an answer, but did not know how to break the cycle. They thought that the monster-ghost-shadow, whatever it was, would remain there forever, unless they consulted another kind of expert. Helena suggested a priest. For now, the lock on the door would have to remain.

Eliza tried to contain her emotions, and took a moment to centre herself: whatever happened, whatever they found in her investigations, she would have to keep her wits about her. She could not say this to Helena, not yet; she would have to play along a little longer. But she was resolved not to be taken by this madness. Everything was an illusion that could be explained away.

Eliza noticed how she had been included in the answer – *we have found, we thought* – although she had not agreed with any of it.

9

THE SHAMAN UP
THE MOUNTAIN

London, 19th March – Early morning

Miss Jocasta Webster left her lodgings and headed towards the underground. She was looking forward to calling at Chaffins's Antique Collectables again, but before that she had one visit to pay.

Webster was not her real name. She had decided upon it during the journey. Since she was coming to London, where her brother now lived, she decided the best course of action was to adopt his new name; it might be possible that they would need to introduce themselves as brother and sister. It had been providential that her new employer had not required to see her references, and she felt a pang of guilt: she was an honest person who hated deceit, and the only reason why she had lied to Helena was out of survival.

She was terrified of the prospect of returning to New York. After her last conversation with her stepfather, it had become clear to her, not just that his intention was to forbid her from working, but also that, were he to get his hands on her, he would do even worse than that, would lock her up in the big ugly house on Fifth Avenue that her mother had insisted on building, and that her late father had hated so much. The idea of losing her independence, perhaps even her freedom, had been too much to bear. She had therefore become Miss Jocasta Webster, and had fled on the first boat going east. She hadn't even had time to telegraph her brother of her imminent arrival, and had done so from the boat.

By then, Jonas Webster had been in London for nearly a year. Jonas being Jonas, he was spending all his time with a rather idealistic but not very respectable crowd. Anarchists, to be precise.

She had really hoped to be wrong. However, after he came to find her and took her to stay in the rooms he had arranged for her – for he said that staying with him was, at least for now, too dangerous – he had happily, even proudly, admitted to it: he was now a revolutionary, putting his intellect to the service of those who had nothing, something that their father on his deathbed, before he passed, had made them both promise. Jocasta felt that memory was highly selective. After all, the man had only asked them 'to never forget who they were', and that, in their case, could mean a number of things.

But nothing would be more like her brother than adopting a lost cause, notwithstanding how positively dangerous that was in their current predicament. She feared that they were not entirely clear yet from the tentacles of their stepfather. Although he had not gone after Jonas, Jocasta knew that it would be different with her. He had made it a point of honour, and would find her and drag her back, even if it was simply out of stubbornness.

Mr John Cartwright, king of the steel railways, a self-made man, as he liked to call himself, and a smaller-minded millionaire than his position as one of Mr Edison's financiers would lead one to believe, had simply not abided her friendship with Miss Carlyle, a fellow library worker. Even if theirs had been an innocent affair, far removed from true love. No, *that* had not been love. She knew that now.

London had been the obvious place for her to go, for she missed Jonas. She also missed her father: soon it would be the fifth anniversary of the sad morning when they laid him in his grave. And she missed, especially, the life they had all had together, before he passed and their mother remarried. She missed, she thought, the simpler times now long gone of childhood, before life got out of her control and became so complicated.

Jocasta and Jonas had been brought up in a peculiar household, after being adopted by a family of New York socialists; they were a rare breed, but existed nonetheless. Their parents had been kind, and, on hearing that Jocasta had a twin brother, they had insisted on not separating them. Their natural parents had died, Jocasta's father in a factory accident, and their mother shortly after giving birth to another boy who, sadly, was stillborn. The philanthropic couple, unlike many of their fellow New Yorkers, were known for putting their care and effort where their mouth was, and, on hearing about the uncertain fate of the babies – they were then little more than one year old – had promptly stepped in. They were middle-aged, and by then had given up hopes of raising children, or of their huge townhouse and their summer retreat in Newport ever filling with the sounds of little feet and laughter. Although they had come into their parents' lives under such tragic circumstances, Jocasta and Jonas had been a blessing.

Indeed, their parents' socialist tendencies had taken them further, and when a tutor had been hired to educate Jonas, and Jocasta had been asked what she wanted, she had said that what she most desired was to attend lessons with her twin. Their parents had not denied her the possibility of receiving the same private education her brother had. She had loved libraries from very early on, had grown up fascinated by this particular room in their household. The cedar wood of the bookcases was a deterrent for moths and other unsavoury fellows, and her adoptive father, a lover of languages and word games and mathematics, had decided at some point to devise a system to classify the books himself – with the help of little Jocasta. The girl had been hooked since then. Her happiest childhood memories centred around the beloved room: reading and writing comic songs and poems, a corner between the fire and the French window set with cushions and blankets for her personal use, playing chess with her father or her brother with the heavy ivory set.

Even if she had been the first one attracted by the game, soon her brother had taken to it, and overtook her completely. If Jocasta was the female chess champion for New York State, her brother was a chess prodigy. From an early age his mathematical ingenuity had baffled his personal tutors just as later it had stumped the best-known scientific minds of the city. Indeed, this had been the problem: during his first year at Harvard – as much as she had wanted it, Jocasta had not been able to follow Jonas in that particular dream – an unusually violent incident regarding a fellow student, who did not like being beaten at chess by a black person, had led Jonas to challenge the youngster to a duel. As a result Jonas had had to flee, the threat of expulsion floating ominously over his head, a fate that had not been shared by his fellow duellist. Jocasta had no doubt that it was the colour of Jonas's skin that informed the college's decision. In her opinion it was better to understand where the real problem was, in order to get on with life. She looked upon it all with a clear, practical mindset. Jonas did not seem to mind the loss of college, which infuriated her. It seemed that he had taken to the life of advocating for workers' rights as a fish to water.

By then their adoptive father was long gone, and their adoptive mother had quickly remarried a rather sinister type, younger than the old lady, and clearly an expert at manipulation. And much, much worse was his treatment of Jocasta: she could have sworn that the man looked at her with something more than step-fatherly intentions, which made living in the family home awkward. Worse still had been when he had learnt of her true inclinations, and had decreed that the worst thing that could have happened to Jocasta was to be given an education, and that she would not set foot in a library again for as long as she lived under his roof, and certainly not while the Carlyle woman worked there.

Fleeing had not been easy. She had not really been away from the axis that ran between the family house, the Columbia professional school and the New York Society Library, and did not know much of the world outside of those spaces. At home she was known by friends and neighbours; here, she felt a bit of an oddity: since arriving in London she had been wary of certain looks, wary of the mistrust that she could only annul with her choice of expensive attire; somehow, looking elegant disarmed orderlies and shopkeepers and tram drivers and the usual populace. They could not place someone 'like her' with that kind of wealth, and therefore they did not know how to react. It was a good way of defending herself, she decided: her expensive clothes, all the chic outfits that her mother had forced upon her, now used as a protective armour. However, it also reminded her of something that had saddened her since her days as a student at the Columbia Library School: that she was forced to make more of an effort with her general appearance than her fellow students, that she needed to behave in a much more respectable way, that she could never commit a single tiny transgression, however minimal, for she was measured against rather harsher standards than the rest of her cohort. They in turn could dress shabbily, speak badly and not submit their assignments on time, for they were forever forgiven. This knowledge, although it gave her an escape route, a way of behaving that anticipated problems, served also as a constant reminder of how different things were for Jocasta and her brother.

In London, she had another piece of armour: her American accent. As soon as she spoke, she saw people visibly relax: she wasn't something entirely unexpected they had no idea how to deal with; she was simply an American, and they did things differently, with more well-to-do people of colour there; after all, many industrious, enterprising black men and women had made huge fortunes after Abolition. Being American, in short, was the perfect shield, and she had no problems using it.

Still, Jonas's fate was unfair. She knew he would be missing college despite his protestations, or at least a life of study. He had been destined to become an important mathematician. So why leave all that behind because of these unfair standards that followed them everywhere? She had been trying to convince him to return since her arrival, even if this meant that she might be found, or forced back. But she had not been successful, and it wasn't the kind of conversation that her twin wanted to have.

Jocasta arrived at a building in the vicinity of the docks and, from the outside, could hear the printing press, and smell the ink and the heavy-scented machine oil. He had written the address for her on a piece of paper, and she knew that she was in the right place.

She went in, unannounced and without knocking. The plaque by the door was dirty, and simply declared the building to be the headquarters of 'The Humanitarian Press', whatever that might be. She ought to keep her emotions in check: she knew that Jonas was proud of the place she was finally visiting.

There were four printing presses working at a fierce rhythm, boxes with finished chapbooks and pamphlets, and some youngsters snapping papers with enormous and terrifying cutting machines. It looked as if one of them could lose a finger any second. She read some of the pamphlets in passing, which proclaimed:

BOYCOTT! To All Friends of Organised Labour: Support the Dock Workers!

'Great,' she said to herself. Some people stopped what they were doing to look at her. She spotted her twin brother at the back of the room, perched on a table, studying a printed pamphlet and in animated discussion with two other youngsters. He saw her, and jumped off the table, beaming:

'Little sister! How good that you found us!' He beamed, walking towards her with his arms wide open. 'What do you think of my kingdom?' Instead of embracing her, he lifted her, bear-like. Jonas was heavier-built than Jocasta, but had the exact same dark brown eyes and dimple in his left cheek.

'Put me down this minute!' she complained. 'And, just so we are clear, what do you possibly mean, little sister?'

'I was born ten minutes before you!'

'Horse-pucky!'

'Everyone! This is my clever little sister.' At this Jocasta hit him. 'Miss Jocasta *Webster*.' He carefully pronounced their shared fake surname.

She was polite and smiled hello, but she was eager to have a private conversation with Jonas. Five minutes later they were sitting alone in the back office, where Jonas produced hot coffee and two suspicious-looking pies that had been bought from a little shop by the river shore. Jocasta cut to the chase.

'Have you given any thought to our last conversation?'

'Which conversation? Oh, don't be a bore! I am perfectly happy here,' he said, encompassing the filthy surroundings with a wide arm movement. 'That printing workshop you just saw: I put that together in less than a year, and now we are fully operational. Why would I want to abandon all this?'

'Why indeed?' she rolled her eyes.

Looking around her, she could not help thinking that her brother, the mathematical genius, did not belong here and had absolutely nothing in common with those people she had just seen.

'You had the chance to study mathematics, go to college. I didn't. It is not fair that you threw all that away. You owe it to both of us.'

'But Harvard is not everything. I can study mathematics anywhere I want.'

'Says who?'

'Godfrey Hardy?'

Jonas explained he was the happiest he had ever been, pretty much in love with London, and with the young Cambridge don he had been exchanging letters with. She knew her brother meant that metaphorically, not literally, but she said:

'Jesus, I had no idea we were going to have this kind of conversation.' Many thoughts were racing inside her head. She had also met someone recently, someone she liked. But it was too soon to mean anything. Still, her twin brother knew her well. 'Why are you looking at me like that?'

'Absolutely no reason!' he smiled. He got up, went around her, and embraced her.

'Let me go!' Jocasta protested.

'Haha! Alright,' he beamed. '*Come to my arms, my beamish boy! O frabjous day! Callooh! Callay! He chortled in his joy!*' he chanted from their favourite childhood poem, while more bear-hugging of his sister ensued.

'Let me go! I am late, anyway. I have to get to work.'

'Ah! You got a job already? Excellent! A library, I suppose?'

'A detective agency,' replied Jocasta. He seemed surprised. 'So now you know, if you misbehave at all, even one foot out of line, I will find out.' He laughed at this.

'Of course you will.'

Before she got to the door, she looked back, and said, 'Before I go… I need a new place to stay.'

'I see. Well, in that case, I think it will be better if you came and stayed with me.'

'I thought you said it was too dangerous. You know, all eggs in one basket, and all that.'

'About that. I've since thought about it. We will get new rooms elsewhere, together. We have been separated long enough. And I don't have anyone good enough to play chess with in the evenings,' he said, smiling. Then he added: 'You are still carrying dad's fob watch.' She came closer to her brother and they hugged again: just like that, a missing piece of her life was back.

'Goodbye, little brother,' she said. And she left before he could protest.

London, 19th March – Morning

That same morning, Helena headed to the British Museum early. The previous day she had placed a query about the societies funded by the philanthropy of the Society for Psychical Research, and she was hoping to have something to collect. As an afterthought, she decided to look again at the date of the misses' incident. Helena was not yet contemplating the possibility that the misses had seen a ghost, but was willing to keep an open mind.

Versailles had been first attacked by the revolutionary mob as early as the 20th of June. It had been a surprise violent attack. The king, queen and their children were allowed to remain together, and, as the commemoration of the fall of the Bastille on July 14th approached, many schemes were entertained for taking the family to safety. She then read how the queen dismissed them all, one by one. The history books did not speculate on her possible reasons, but Helena interpreted that the queen believed that her family would be safer staying where they were, rather than venturing into the provinces.

Inside the hot Reading Room, Helena read how the 10th of August was also a hot, sultry day in the Tuileries. As the family heard mass, the crowd gathered to attack them. It was not pleasant reading. After the children went to sleep, the adults were kept appraised of reports of the imminent assault. It was early morning when it happened, and it was bloodier than anyone had anticipated. The family was taken elsewhere to await their fate. But they knew by then what was in store for them.

Still, something was clear: Marie Antoinette had not been 'playing farms' in the Petit Trianon on that day in August; hence, the possibility that they had seen a ghostly apparition diminished greatly – at least according to spiritualism's own rules.

It was nearly time for elevenses – she had not had much breakfast – when she exited the Reading Room. She didn't know if the new information would amount to much, but felt darkly that she hadn't had a good morning: the information she had sought about the SPR appeared to be restricted. She had flinched at this: that information belonged in the public record, but of course the powerful SPR knew how to cover their tracks at each turn. She would have to find some other way; how to call herself a detective otherwise?

She reflected that, although she had been doing detection for a long time, she had never called herself that, a detective. Had she been hiding because she was unsure of her abilities? Or because she was a woman? She always noticed certain looks coming her way when she entered the museum library; but she wasn't the only lady there, and there were always a few whispers here and there whenever a lady entered the Reading Room.

Later that afternoon she would go with Aurora to see the shaman as promised. She wondered if she really had time for a recreational outing, when she ought to be preparing to join Eliza in Paris. What a bore she was becoming! But, in truth, she knew there was more to her afternoon of fun, as it would give her the chance to see the SPR's and the Dawn's efforts to ingratiate themselves with the public after the previous year's scandal. She left the female reader's cloakroom directly into the Room of Inscriptions, and, as she was coming towards the museum's entrance hall, a figure emerged from behind a Doric column to intercept her.

'Detective.'

Detective O'Neill looked at her and smiled in the direction of her leather casebook. She instinctively clutched it closer to her chest.

'Miss Walton-Cisneros.' He pronounced her full name for the first time and, somehow, this made her skin chill all over.

'You find me at a busy time. I am sorry, but I cannot stop to chat,' she excused herself, trying to get around him. He delicately manoeuvred her to stop in front of him.

'Police business, madam, if you are so kind.'

'Oh, I *am* lucky.'

He could not hide a laugh, but did his utmost to appear serious again.

'It has come to my attention that you have been asking questions about...' he checked a slim notebook with a dirty and chewed pencil hanging from a rude cord, 'financial contributions by the SPR to scientific expeditions and philanthropic endeavours.'

For a second, Helena could not find a snappy reply. She was stunned. How was it possible that the police possessed such intimate knowledge of her current enquiries? And so quickly?

She felt violated that it was happening where it was happening: the museum, and the Round Reading Room, had always been a refuge for her. Until now, that was. There was only one explanation for this: her movements, and with all probability those of her known associates, were being monitored. In other words, she was being spied upon.

She laughed, a long and crackling sound.

'Miss…?'

And, as a reaction to O'Neill's confusion, she laughed more. Visitors to the museum were now noticing them: a mad-looking woman, laughing openly in the middle of the foyer, and the confused-looking policeman – no one could have mistaken O'Neill for anything else – next to her.

Eventually, Helena calmed herself enough to speak: 'I am sorry, it is just… pathetic. Yes, I think that is the word I am looking for.'

'I beg your pardon?' This wasn't the reaction that Detective O'Neill had expected.

'How threatened you all feel. Why are you so scared of a bunch of women asking questions? What is it that you fear so much?'

'Fear, madam?'

'Look, the agency is now open. We comply with all regulations. You cannot prevent us from taking clients. You would have no reason to do so.'

'Do you really think so?'

Helena instantly regretted her words, her damn impetuousness. She was happy Eliza was not here to witness her outburst. Her words had sounded like a dare, and she knew what happened with men when they were dared to do something. She would have to try and fix it.

'What I mean is, Detective… Look. We can be valuable as well, to you.' It was O'Neill who laughed now. She insisted, 'We can help each other. I have worked many times for your predecessor, and we—'

'Times have changed, madam.'

'Isn't that obvious?'

What had she just done? Had she just given this man, if not the ammunition, then at least the spark to close her agency, ruin her life, everything she, and Eliza, had worked so hard to achieve during the last year? To her surprise, the whole demeanour of Detective O'Neill changed now. It was almost imperceptible, but there.

'If I may. A friendly piece of advice.' Helena tried to suppress an eye roll. 'You ought to be more careful of the company you keep. That is all I am going to say.' He touched his hat as he moved away. 'Good day to you, madam.' And he left, leaving her more baffled than she would have expected.

London, 19th March – Afternoon

Shamanic Paths, Session One and Two:

'Ritual for Good Luck' and 'Make a Shamanic Journey'

Beware! Do not join if you fear good luck in your life!

'Why in heaven have you brought me here?' Helena asked, half-mockingly.

'Oh, no silly shamanic journeys for us today!' Aurora winked. 'I already did that one yesterday, in the slot for ladies. You lie down, somebody beats a drum, and asks you to visualise going up a mountain, and there you are meant to meet your shamanic teacher. A huge disappointment.'

Helena remembered that the shaman's presence had not been advertised until today, and wondered if Aurora had had access to another, secret gathering.

'What, you did not find your teacher up the mountain?' she asked.

'Indeed I did not. And some of the other ladies present fell asleep! I could hear them snoring.'

'Oh, so why come today?'

'For the pleasure of your company, of course. And, oh well, a bit of good luck has never done anybody any harm, don't you think? We will try Shamanic Ritual Number Two. This one was full yesterday, but I took the precaution to book us in advance.'

Helena read the event description. The ritual was called *ikenipke*, which was apparently a Siberian tribal word meaning 'singing and dancing', which should have given her a clue of what was about to happen. Words like collective ritual ('*all members of the audience are to take part*'), dancing, jumping and wrestling ('*the purpose is to imitate animals*'), fertility and virility, jumped from the page.

This is a ritual that epitomises the relationship of man with life-giving supernatural entities, animals, instead of gods. The imitation of animal behaviour, through the medium of dancing, chanting and movement, effectively aligns man and animal, making man similar to them, that is, destined to be eaten.

'Eaten? How grim! I'm sorry, Aurora, but I do not see how any of this is connected with luck.'

'The ritual is some sort of symbolic hunt. The shaman performs the hunting of an animal, and it is intended to bring luck for the hunt. Indeed, if this ritual is not performed yearly, the community cannot hunt at all.'

Helena surrendered herself to the inevitable.

'But first, we have time to sample some refreshments.'

They walked towards a long table set with sandwiches, cold meats, buns, biscuits, cake, tea, wine; and, as Aurora was healthily heaping a china plate with delicately cut finger sandwiches and slices of Victoria sponge, Helena was sent to find a bottle of bubbly.

'I do hope you are not planning on drinking that all by yourself.'

She turned, an apologetic smile on her face. How she disliked it, to be taken unawares, and by none other than Mr Woodbury, the director of the SPR. The man he was talking to turned to face her. It was Detective O'Neill. She'd now encountered him twice in one day. What rotten luck.

'Miss Walton!'

'I see you know each other already,' said Mr Woodbury rather unhelpfully. 'Of course you do. Detective, I imagine Miss Walton-Cisneros has already been able to assist you with some tricky investigation? Let me guess, one of those affairs that defies a "logical" explanation.'

Helena did not like the tone in which Woodbury had delivered this, particularly since he had no right to belittle her work or the paranormal – he was the director of the SPR.

'Mr Woodbury. Of course you are here. Let me reassure you, Detective O'Neill has little time for me.' Her tone did not dispel what she thought about the old man, or about the younger one. She turned her back.

Woodbury chuckled loudly, whereas O'Neill looked hurt, of all things. But Woodbury was not going to let her off so easily.

'I trust you are enjoying our little festival.'

'It is quite the event, I must admit,' offered Helena. Woodbury beamed. Somehow this made him look even less trustworthy.

'Indeed!' he said. 'We have many more things planned, my dear. Do you remember my little bookshop?' Woodbury was referring to The Little Haunted Bookshop, a shop dedicated to occult literature he kept in Charing Cross.

'Yes, I do. Are you still publishing those pamphlets on how to unmask female mediums?' she put in.

Woodbury replied: 'Ah! Those! We are expanding now, my dear lady. We are planning a series of fairy volumes, for children of all ages.'

'I see. Get them soon to the cause, is that it?'

O'Neill looked like he was enjoying himself; Woodbury looked lost for words for a moment.

'Woodbury!' Thankfully, Aurora joined the group. 'I have brought Helena with me, are you being mean to my dearest friend?' Aurora had no control over how she spoke, or care for how she was perceived, and, for once, Helena was happy about this. Woodbury was flushing, albeit only a little.

'I can assure you, my dear Miss Chaffins, that I am the very image of civilised conversation. Isn't that true, Miss Walton-Cisneros?'

Helena found herself unable to conjure a timely retort. Then she realised. The reason was none other than O'Neill's eyes, locked on hers.

'Miss Walton-Cisneros...' He took a step towards her. 'I was wondering if you had had a moment to think about our conversation from this morning?' He steered her slowly away from Woodbury.

'Detective O'Neill, I don't need you to help me. Thank you.'

'I was in fact curious, so the question stands.'

'I certainly had no idea of what you meant in the library.'

'Miss Webster.'

'Oh! I see. Pray tell me, what is the problem here, exactly: that she is black, or that she is a foreigner?'

To his credit O'Neill's face turned a deep red.

'My dear miss, neither one nor the other. Were you aware that Webster is not her real name?'

This was indeed a surprise to Helena, but she hid it well. The last thing she wanted was for O'Neill to have a reason to mock her abilities at detection; and indeed, what kind of detective could she be if she didn't know this? Instead she said:

'Many people change their names, for all sorts of reasons. It is not a crime, as far as I am concerned.'

'I see. Well, perhaps I should let you know how she has come to be under the radar of the Yard. Her brother is mixed up with a rather dangerous group. Anarchists.'

Helena was taken aback. It was her turn to redden.

'I see. I beg your pardon. You mean here, in London?'

'Yes. Here, in London. It is all rather unfortunate. Mr Webster seems to be some kind of mathematical genius, a student at Harvard, now mixing with the most despicable, and dangerous, men in all of London. He is wasting his potential, that much is clear. However, that would be the least of his worries, if he contrives to land himself in jail.'

She could see he was serious; but Helena knew that, nine times out of ten, these 'revolutionaries' were not as dangerous, or as disruptive, as the Yard claimed. Still, the real question here was: why was he sharing this information with her? Was he trying to ingratiate himself? Could she have been wrong about him? She doubted it.

'I see. I... I admit I didn't know she had a brother.' She had shown her cards on purpose, expecting his mockery, but O'Neill didn't take the bait.

'It would be a real shame, someone so promising. You would do well advising Miss Webster to make sure her brother stops playing revolutionaries, especially if he has no intention of boarding the next ship going west.'

Could all this be true? Was she now harbouring someone connected to the anarchists? She had to confess to not having followed their politics, but, whatever their ideals, these were people who used bombs in order to achieve their goals. Meanwhile, what was the nature of this unexpected interaction with O'Neill? What was that in his face? Could it be genuine concern for her?

'Thank you, Detective O'Neill. I confess this is a surprise to me. I am in your debt,' she said, just to see his reaction. To her surprise, he smiled at her.

'Please, there is no need. And, if you are ever in need of help, or assistance, I hope you will let me know.' And after that extraordinary statement, he left her. Aurora was soon back at her elbow.

'Forget about Woodbury, what a bore! What did the handsome policeman want?'

Helena did not reply. Miss Webster had come into her life by Aurora's mediation, and she needed to learn more about the situation before knowing what to do. One more mystery to solve.

They consumed their refreshments and walked around a little longer. In one of the rooms, a beam of light flickered over a white sheet, and, to the audience's admiration, images began to move across it.

'I wasn't expecting this,' Helena commented. To her surprise, Aurora elaborated: there were some in the Golden Dawn who were seeing the value of film-making, in particular to record their rituals.

'Since young Aleister Crowley had the audacity of publishing them in *Two Doors*, not only making them public, but also, apparently, heavily distorting them in his image, the idea of finding a way of documenting what truly happens has gained adepts, even among some of the most senior members of the Golden Dawn. Mind you, as long as these films remain for private consumption...'

'I see,' was all Helena replied. But she was wondering how on earth Aurora was so knowledgeable about all this. She now realised that her friend seemed very up to date with the Dawn's activities, when, as far as Helena knew, she had left the organisation a long time ago. Indeed, her friend had not finished:

'You see, words can be misleading. Even photographs may not tell the whole story. But if someone shoots a ritual with a camera exactly as it is, then it is preserved, as it is meant to be, forever.'

Helena felt the need to say something.

'Aurora, please forgive me, but you sound awfully informed about all this.'

'Well, I did not want to tell you, not after our last conversation.'

'Tell me what?'

'I have been invited to attend the Vernal Equinox tomorrow. They invite me year after year, and I have always said no. But tomorrow, I will be there.'

'Oh no, Aurora.'

'Yes.'

'But why? I thought you didn't want to associate with them anymore.'

'That must have been true at some point, but things are not so simple.'

The two friends had now stopped wandering around the exhibits, and had sought a more secluded spot to talk.

'You ask why,' started Aurora, 'but surely you see, Helena, we are not winning this battle.'

'Which battle?'

'The SPR controls everything; it's involved in everything. Someone needs to be close to the source, in order to understand their motives, learn their plans, and anticipate their steps.'

Helena thought for a moment. She noticed now O'Neill looking at them while pretending to consider some magic rocks on a nearby stand. He was doing a really poor job of it. Aurora followed her gaze.

'Think of him, for example,' she said, pointing at the detective. 'Don't you think he is in the pockets of the SPR? He always turns up everywhere, tonight escorting Woodbury himself. A Scotland Yard officer!'

Helena could not deny any of this.

'Very well, but still, what are you trying to achieve? Infiltrating the SPR strikes me as the bravest thing I have ever heard anyone doing,' Aurora smiled, Helena continued, 'but also the most dangerous.'

'We will talk more about it later, I promise. The ritual is about to begin.'

———•—•———

The shaman's aide started beating the drums steadily, rhythmically. It would have been hypnotic, but Helena had trouble letting her mind go. Aurora's words were preying on her mind. She did not trust the SPR, she did not trust Woodbury, and she did not like the Golden Dawn. And those three things were proving to be one and the same. Without even mentioning the ubiquitous O'Neill.

As she was losing herself within these dark thoughts, she fell at last under the spell of the rhythm, which seemed to imitate an anxiously beating heart. She did not see the shaman, slapping his legs to the beat, or the animalist dancing; she had no chance to see anything. For as soon as she let go properly, she dropped to the floor, limp as a rag doll.

It was out of her control now. In her mind the little bell was furiously chiming.

Helena could see the other world, the world beyond the veil, the portal that led there; figures and monoliths and forests, enveloped in mist.

And she knew the meaning of the ritual, 'man destined to be eaten', and she knew that it wasn't the flesh, but the soul. And that there were many ways in the world in which this could happen. She could not breathe, and everything was green under her eyes, not black.

'Helena?'

Aurora was hovering above her as she slowly came around. She felt embarrassed that this had happened in public.

'The shaman fell to the floor, as if he were dead, and so did you.'

Behind Aurora's worried face, another figure hovered: Detective O'Neill.

'Everyone! Give her some space, for God's sake!'

Before she could protest, O'Neill had gathered her in his arms, and was walking away with her, crossing the rooms, shouting at people to let them pass. She could hear Aurora's protestations; she herself wanted to object, put him in his place. But all the energy had left her body, and she resigned herself to wander in and out of consciousness. When she came around again, she found herself inside a hansom. She recognised the route, the buildings, and understood that O'Neill must know where she lived. Still, she could not find the strength to protest. She dozed for the rest of the journey, and then woke up lying on her own ottoman, a blanket covering her. O'Neill was at her side, holding her hand lightly.

'Please don't move,' he said, letting her hand go. 'I have sent for Miss Waltraud. My men are trying to locate her, either her or another of your associates.' He obviously did not know that Eliza had crossed the Channel the previous day.

'I don't remember what happened,' Helena began.

'You fainted, at the same time as the shaman fainted. There was a bit of a commotion. You could not be awoken for several minutes, not until the drums stopped. The stupid man in charge refused to break the chant; he said that would be worse, and that you might not wake up.'

'Where is Aurora?'

'She stayed there. She is quarrelling with the shaman, with Woodbury, and, in general, raising hell with the organisers. She said she would come later to see how you were.'

Helena had no energy to form a reply. Still, why was this man here, in her parlour? He might be a police officer, but he was also a stranger, darkly connected to the SPR, to Woodbury. Helena remembered Aurora's plan, and felt momentarily sick: how deep had her friend's past involvement with London's occult societies been? And how well connected had she remained to them, all this time? Helena knew it was not possible to come 'in and out' of the Dawn, not like that. Aurora had to have powerful friends within the order still. Momentarily, she tried to sit up and found a horrid nausea overcoming her.

'Please, don't…'

'Detective O'Neill,' she gathered all her strength to formulate her thoughts, 'thank you so much for your assistance, but I am very much recovered now, and my friends are on their way. I would like you to leave now, please.'

'I don't feel that leaving you is wise.'

'I don't know what you mean, but I want you out of my house.' She tried to sound forceful.

'Why?' he insisted.

'Because I don't trust you.'

'You don't trust me?' He seemed to find this amusing, for some reason. He was still perched on the side of the ottoman, terribly close to her. He could easily murder her, and no one would know. But Helena did not feel in danger. She felt a current of pure electricity through her body, towards her hand, now so close to his that the tips of their fingers were millimetres apart. But the energy seemed to pass on from the tips of her fingers to his nonetheless, as if moving through air, at least until he pulled his hand away and got up, firmly placing his hands in his pockets as if to protect them.

'You don't trust me,' he repeated.

'You are working for the SPR, admit it.' She tried to muster as much finality in her words as she could. He looked at her.

'Is that what you think of me?'

He managed a pitiful smile, found his hat, and left. As soon as she was alone, Helena felt something similar to regret. Perhaps she had gone too far, perhaps Aurora was wrong about O'Neill. But it was too late for Helena to find out.

10

INTO THE WOLF'S MOUTH

19th March – Evening

It was but four days since she had received in her not-yet-opened offices two ladies who swore they had experienced a vision of the past – a vision that her partner would have called a 'hallucination' – and Miss Lowry, Mina, after them; an awful lot had happened in such a short space of time. Eliza was now in Paris. Helena had received one telegram, informing her of a safe arrival, as well as one letter in the post.

Helena had not been idle. She had now read Emily's letters to Mina several times, but had gathered very little from them. Had the letters been completely useless? She felt particularly guilty about this, as Eliza had risked so much to get her hands on them. She still had one hope: that they contained something pertaining to the Dawn, something that someone adept to the Dawn's inner workings may be able to interpret for her.

Aurora had finally arrived, and was fussing with the brandy decanter, the tea produced by Dottie all but ignored.

'Do you want to talk about what happened?' she asked.

'The elephant in the room...'

'I beg your pardon?'

'Aurora,' started Helena, 'what is happening to me?'

The older woman sighed.

'Your inner eye is opening, and you are seeing beyond.' A pause. 'This is a privilege, my dear child, a gift.'

Helena could not share her mentor's enthusiasm. Her stomach was tied in a painful knot.

'I fainted in public, Aurora. And I have no idea of what indications I give: I simply move, as our Golden Dawn friends would say, from this realm, into another, and then switch back again. Nobody says anything about what transpires; but this only makes it worse. And to top it all, O'Neill was there.'

'The handsome detective.'

Helena felt herself reddening.

'So, you are worried that you will need to explain yourself soon?'

Helena had no idea of how she was going to explain the little chiming bell, the premonitions, the apparent dreams that provided timed answers, the notions and ideas and inspirations that were deposited in her mind now whenever she looked at a spread of colourful cards, seemingly offering her, for some reason that she could not explain, the answers as to the hows and whys of the whole universe.

As always, her senses felt heightened after the episode, but she did not like what they were suggesting to her. They were pointing at Aurora, her friend and mentor, to whom she owed so much. Helena looked at her, and saw her wrapped in some sort of dark, angular shadow; she resembled a gigantic black bird, that could gobble her up as if she was a tiny worm. She shook herself, and looked again: it was all normal.

Helena got up slowly and went to a painting of a Romany princess, and slid it to one side to reveal a hidden safe. She turned the dial clockwise and anticlockwise a couple of times, pulled the door open, and took the bundle of letters from the safe. It was obvious that even this little exertion had been a lot for her.

'Are you alright?' asked Aurora.

'I will be.' Helena managed a short smile.

'Well, you should rest,' replied Aurora. 'You need to stay put. You haven't even let me, or Dottie, call a doctor!'

Helena moved towards a little mahogany card-playing table on which cards had never been played, and that she had really acquired to repurpose for tarot readings.

'If I don't want you to call a doctor, it is because you know as well as I do that there is nothing physically wrong with me. At least nothing that a doctor can look into. Aurora, I need your help,' she said, indicating the bundle.

Aurora approached the table, two tumblers of brandy in her hands.

'Are these the famous letters from the missing girl?'

'Yes. Look, they may contain something... something I may have missed. We have no idea what Emily might have witnessed while in Paris. I am therefore asking you to look over them as a consultant in these matters to the agency. Are you alright with that?' she asked.

'That suits me well. Where do you want me to send my bill: here, or to the agency?' They both laughed; although the night had taken such a sinister turn in the exhibition, it was good to be able to recover their spirits.

'Right. We need to hurry with this,' Helena explained. 'Miss Webster must be en route, and I would like to have this finished by the time she gets here.'

'Right-o!'

They started their search. The letters spoke merely of the day-to-day life of a young woman out in the world, living by her wits. They interrogated the new smells, sounds, and even food available to her in the Parisian suburbs. Emily seemed to have kept mostly to herself: the few character studies that the letters contained belonged to students and teachers from the art school, or workers at Star Film Studio. A few outings to the theatre with girls from work, watching some of the films made at the studio or elsewhere. Subtly, the topics changed, showing an increased focus on activities in Star Film Studio. As the letters progressed, a new sense of urgency built up in the accounts, mostly related to Méliès's magical illusions.

Perhaps sensing that her fears ought to be unfounded, Miss Emily started getting more and more interested in how the effects themselves were created, and in the strange machines owned by *le patron*. There were descriptions of crane systems, with half a letter dedicated to the hard work of the seamstresses, their role in making the impossible seem possible by concealing ropes and levers. Then, out of nowhere, the mention of a mysterious contraption, one which seemed to have allowed *le patron* to significantly improve the effect of flying in his movies. There was a pencil sketch of something that looked like a wooden box, from which green rays, painted over the pencil with watercolour, were escaping, together with the following description:

> *We are hard at work shooting* The Journey to the Moon, *and the troupe is so worried! I think they fear they will go up and up to the sky, and disappear altogether… I am counting the days till you come and visit, my dear friend, for I am having the most horrible nightmares.*

'She didn't really think this would happen, right?' Helena said.

'Hmm. It is difficult to tell, isn't it? The tone in a written letter is not easy to decipher. Is she being serious? Or funny?'

'Serious, I think: she sounds scared.'

Emily's letter continued to explain how she had experienced something that could only be understood as an out-of-body experience:

> *I am, dear Mina, absolutely terrified by one thing: I am not sure if this has been a dream or not! I went to Paris, I am sure it was Paris, for the Eiffel Tower was still there, but my body continued in my bed! There were flying machines dropping bombs and turning everything into fire! A ray of light was coming out of the tower itself.*

'What is going on here?' asked Helena.

'I think she is talking about some sort of astral projection, or travel.'

'Like with the shaman?'

'Exactly. Remember what I said to you? You reach these dream states with trances and meditations, according to Woodbury… or other substances, according to Mathers. And when the substances don't work anymore, you search for another form of energy. Remember?'

'We go back to the energy theory,' said Helena. 'Is that what you think these rays are, some form of energy?'

'My dear, I have no idea. These letters are raving mad. All I know is that this is what everyone is after right now, here in Paris and in Timbuktu! You can have all the shamanic trances that you want, take all the drugs that you want, but in the end, people are going to fall asleep with the shamans, and the drugs are going to wear off. Then what? Something else, something more efficient, easy to produce, with no side effects, is what is needed.' Aurora was becoming more animated, and Helena had the feeling that she had said more than she wanted. Was it now the time to ask how on earth she knew all this? But Helena did not dare to put the question to her.

'An otherworldly amount of energy,' she offered instead, echoing their last conversation on the topic.

'Exactly. Energy produced by something, or released while doing something. Either way, there is nothing in the world capable of that.'

Helena considered this for a moment.

'Or is there? If these letters talk about anything, it is about machines.'

They looked through Emily's letters again, and indeed, as they got progressively more erratic, they were also filled with unusual drawings and spoke more freely of strange machinery, described in a frenzy, the drawings competing for space with the spidery writing, rays of light cutting through the written word. The rays of light had all been coloured a vivid green with the same watercolour.

The letters began mentioning a visit to Paris from New York by a friend of Méliès's, Nikola, who had come to service the boxed machine, and of a horrible row the two friends had. The references to Nikola, or Niko, by Emily were filled with affection.

My dearest friend, I am so happy to have found my Niko, for he is the only one who understands my fears! He is so worried of what le patron *might do with the machine, a machine that he only created as a force for peace. He would now like it back, but there is no way to convince* le patron! *He has thrown Niko out of his house, and Niko is staying with me now. I hope you don't find it too shocking! I have been so lonely. In any case, he will not be here by the time of your visit, as he has urgent business in New York. But he has promised that he will always remain my friend and protector.*

They now moved to the last letter of the bundle. It was written on the back of old drawings the artist had turned around in order to re-use the paper.

'Why do you think these women are swimming? Is that another Dawn thing?'

'I don't think they are swimming, Helena. I think they are levitating.'

'Levitating? Helped by the "energy" of the machine and the rays?'

'It's possible.'

There was nothing else in the letters, and eventually they put the bundle away. Why had Mina been so sure that they could endanger her life? Helena had suddenly many more questions to put to her. She would be paying her a visit at Chaffins's soon.

The fire had been put up, a small meal improvised, and a further teapot of strong tea produced, after Miss Webster arrived. Good old Dottie was huffing and puffing around Helena, complaining that these strange occurrences – the fits and the fainting, all those moments when her mistress seemed to go away but stayed there – were now happening more often; that her mistress was obviously overworking herself; and that, if she insisted on going down that road, she ought to look after herself a little bit better, and so on and so forth. At last, Aurora assured the good woman that Helena was well looked after, and Dottie disappeared into her realm of kitchen and back rooms with plenty more huffing and puffing.

Aurora had taken over the distribution of the tea, and was simply talking about her day: the fertility figurine she had sold to a curator from the British Museum, right out of one of the crates in the docks she had inspected the other morning; the shipment of quartz stones that needed polishing; and even referred to some gardening that, March looming to an end, she could in truth not postpone any longer, no matter how much she hated doing it. Miss Webster was keeping to her own counsel for the time being. She was sipping her tea, smiling now and again. Helena felt sorry she had been caught in the drama; but she had been at the agency when the message from Detective O'Neill had arrived. She ought to find a moment to discuss with her O'Neill's revelations; her instincts, enhanced as always after a fugue-moment, were telling her that she could trust the new addition to their group.

'Aurora, how was Miss Lowry today?' she asked, and noticed Miss Webster's ears prick up at the mention of Mina.

'In good spirits, I think,' declared Aurora. 'She has taken to life in Montague Road like a fish to water. She has been writing non-stop for the past couple of days, a story in the Gothic Romance fashion, she tells me, about a cursed gemstone hidden among the thousands of exhibits of a national museum.'

'That is excellent news,' said Helena. 'I am very glad to hear it. I should come by tomorrow and give her an update on her case.' She noticed Aurora looked towards Miss Webster, smiling. 'We have found something,' Helena announced. 'Miss Webster, if you would be so kind. It would be good if what I am about to report is put in writing and sent to Eliza. It is important that she reads it soon.'

'Of course.' The young woman got into motion, producing a ledger from her bag. She sat at the card table, where the letters were still spread, and opened her ink pot.

Helena summarised their findings, including the drawings of the machine, the rays emanating from them, the endless drawings of flying ladies. She pointed at the letters to show some examples.

'Of course, the references to flying in them may be… merely symbolic,' continued Helena. 'They may be referring to some form of trance, for all we know. But the energy from the machine seems to be involved in the outcome, in attaining this state,' she concluded. 'Miss Webster, how quickly do you think we can send this information to Eliza?'

'The fastest post is two days. She will receive this on the twenty-first, if I go immediately, as soon as they open.'

'I wonder if that is quick enough?' wondered Helena out loud.

'I noticed the letters mention the name of the machine maker, Nikola, or N.T. Shall I find out who he is?' asked Miss Webster.

'By all means. In fact, I wonder why Miss Lowry did not mention him before. Whenever a woman disappears, the most logical first step is to look into the man she left behind.' But Miss Webster was not paying attention. She was lost in thought, and suddenly stood up. 'What's the matter, Miss Webster?'

Instead of replying, Miss Webster went to the table, where the Discovery Lectures programme was lying, one similar to the one that had fallen from the thug's pocket in Mina's room. She passed it to Helena but, instead of opening it, she turned it over. On the back there was an advertisement. It was a promotional image for something called the 'magnifying transmitter'.

'What on earth is this?'

'Have you heard of Mr Tesla, Miss Walton? Mr *Nikola Tesla*? *N.T.*?'

Miss Webster explained briefly what she knew about the inventor. She admired his unconventionality and flair for experimentation, which she took for a sign of his genius.

'He is really famous in America. It says here that Tesla is touring the European capitals to raise funds for his next project, the Wardenclyffe Tower.'

Helena got up, still with difficulty. She examined the advertisement for this Wardenclyffe Tower. The proposed machine was depicted in the promotional image with rays of light shooting crudely out of it. The similarities with the drawings in the letters were clear. It looked as if it generated some kind of energy, a surge of unknown power.

'Look,' she said to Aurora and Miss Webster, indicating the tower from which the rays of light came out in Emily Peter's drawings: 'they are the same tower. She was not drawing the Eiffel Tower, but this tower! There is no doubt – Niko must be Mr Tesla. And this tower is somehow connected with the energy generated by the machine. But how?'

'Perhaps it increases the energy?' suggested Miss Webster. Aurora and Helena exchanged a significant look. 'I mean, if the machine generates some energy, maybe the tower multiplies it at a massive scale...?'

'My, oh my!' Even Aurora was excited with the new theory.

'According to the letters, we know that Tesla and Méliès fought. It is clear what we ought to do next. We need to look into this Wardenclyffe Tower, make sure we understand what it does. This is excellent work, Miss Webster. I think we are finally getting somewhere. We need to get this news to Paris as soon as possible. Eliza needs to find out what kind of invention Nikola left to his friend Georges, what it does exactly, and why he wanted it back so badly.'

'Absolutely.'

'Now, excuse me, but I need to rest. Please, do feel free to stay in the guest bedroom, if you don't fancy crossing London again so late.'

Miss Webster accepted the invitation, but Aurora said she would return home, as she did not want to leave Mina alone.

London, 20th March – Morning

Mina had spent the past few days and nights in the back and attic rooms at Chaffins's Antique Collectables, working on a new story. Having something to work on had helped immensely. She normally liked to cocoon herself away to write, otherwise, the many distractions of life contrived to get in the way. The usual type of hideouts she escaped to, which, due to her circumstances, could not be more than a little cottage, or some cupboard room in a sad seaside town, tended to be much more claustrophobic than the place where she found herself now. Therefore, she wasn't feeling particularly trapped, considering the circumstances. The rooms were comfortable, and Aurora's company, whenever she wasn't in attendance at her shop or out hunting for pieces to add to her stock, was friendly and warm. All in all, she was lucky. Aurora even had a little garden at the back of her house, hidden from the street, where Mina could take a stroll morning and evening after a day working at her writing; hardly a prisoner's life.

She had also started waiting with certain anticipation for the visits of Miss Jocasta Webster. For now, she refused to let herself think of what this might mean, or exactly what she might be expecting to happen. Any consideration would be fruitless; at the moment it was just daydreams. She was also trying not to think about Paris, the SPR, and other things that might make her feel guilty. She had been nothing but honest when she had said to Helena that her life was in danger; she had been less forthcoming in revealing the real reasons for this, namely, that she had betrayed the SPR, and the Dawn. The prospect was terrifying. It did not bear thinking of.

Mina's best course of action was to concentrate on her writing for now. She had found that the best place to do this was the attic room. There was a little table and a chair below a round window. She could sit and write, she had some light from the window, but she was not in view from the street. She had felt embarrassed to have to ask Aurora for ink, and the woman had tutted at her, but had given her access to an unexpectedly large supply cabinet, with inkpots and neat stacks of cream-coloured sheets of paper, telling her to help herself to anything she wanted.

'I wanted to write myself, for a while,' Aurora said that morning.

'Really? What did you want to write?'

'A treaty on cartomancy, the art of divination through cards.'

'What happened?'

'Oh, well. I had already written most of it, in fact, and then I realised.'

'What?'

'That certain things cannot be taught in a book. Or learnt in a book.' Mina went oddly silent. Aurora continued: 'You go and write your gothic romance, my dear. I love those! That is precisely the kind of thing that books are for. Off you go, you write. Not to worry, I will let you know if Jocasta comes to see you.'

Mina felt a blush creeping up her cheeks.

'Miss Webster?'

'Oh, yes, dear. You know, in case she brings a message, or any communication from Helena.' Aurora's eyes lingered on her stomach, and only then realised that she had been cupping it during their conversation. 'Since it seems that she has been appointed as our liaison with Marylebone.'

'Yes, of course.'

Mina escaped to the little attic room as quickly as she could, secretly hoping that Miss Jocasta Webster would indeed grace them that morning with another visit, but scared to let herself hope, every chime at the door setting her heart racing. Then, at mid-morning, her wish came true.

They were drinking tea, when Jocasta said:

'Does it not spook you a little to be among all these weird things?'

It had been meant lightly, but Mina considered the question in all seriousness.

'Look, all these things, and all the occultist societies that use these objects…'

'You mean the Golden Dawn that everyone is talking about?' Jocasta said. 'I have been asked to write a report on Mathers, the founding member who lives in Paris.'

'Yes, the Order… I would like to think that all these societies are created for the greater good, with the idea of "doing good". Or at least that is what I hope. So, no, I don't feel spooked around the artefacts.' Mina had spoken without thinking, and now wondered whether she had revealed her cards too clearly. Why had she defended the Golden Dawn? 'I mean to say… that is what I would like to believe. Surely it must be the reason why people join them in the first place.'

Jocasta was considering her closely now. Mina wished she had bitten her tongue.

'Well, I am sorry to tell you this, but none of these organisations will do any good for absolutely anyone.' Jocasta took a large gulp of tea.

'What do you mean?'

Jocasta thought for a minute, and eventually said:

'You have to forgive me, but I do wonder if any of you have actually thought about the implications of these "syncretic" religions and societies. Why always these "exotic" cultures and places?' Jocasta used air quotes around the word.

'I am not sure what you mean. Why is that relevant?'

'I'll try and explain,' Jocasta said, taking a deep breath. She looked as though she was slightly embarrassed, while at the same time accepting that some things needed to be said. 'Can you please explain to me why a mystic society, founded in England of all places, doesn't have druids at its centre? English spiritualism, and occultism, is the same as everything else that has come out of the empire: a dream of colonies and colonising.'

Mina was all ears.

'I had never thought about that,' Mina said. 'I remember, two years ago, in Paris – Egyptomania, absolutely everywhere. It was like some sort of frenzy.'

Jocasta beamed.

'But,' Mina continued, 'Aurora says that occultists' main objective is to demonstrate that human consciousness is alive after death, to be able to see the unseen. Isn't that the kind of solace that religion has offered until now?'

'That may be the case, but ultimately it is a project of substitution: modern rational thought at the service of the common good,' said Jocasta. 'Or rather at the service of justifying a certain moral code, and a universal order: empire. And empires,' she added, 'have never done any good. For absolutely anyone.'

Jocasta looked up worriedly towards Mina. She had let her thoughts run free in a way that she hadn't done with anyone for a long time. She felt comfortable with Mina, but wondered if she had gone too far. She need not have worried:

'You are extremely well informed.' Mina was looking at her with admiration. And she was relieved that her inclinations towards the Dawn weren't too obvious.

'We librarians tend to be,' Jocasta replied simply, and sipped her tea to avoid the need to say more. Eventually, as the silence extended, she asked: 'What are you writing about?'

Mina felt nervous.

'Oh, it's nothing. A story. A Gothic romance.'

'I thought you wrote fairy stories?'

Again, Mina's eyes wandered to the floor. 'I only did that for a bit… I am not writing fairy stories anymore.'

Later on, Jocasta would reflect on this. Her own outburst had not made Mina uncomfortable, it had been this last part of the conversation. What she could not understand was why. And then she remembered something; it was from Helena's casebook: Woodbury's printing business expansion plan. *They would branch out into popular stories for boys and girls, told in the fairy fashion.*

20th March – Evening

It was nearly eleven in the evening when Aurora entered Helena's sitting room. She poured two large drinks.

'Thank you for what you are going to do, Aurora.'

'It's not a problem. How are you? Are you ready for this? Are you ready to climb into the wolf's mouth?'

Helena was sitting in front of a small dresser, applying make-up. She paused, brush in hand, 'Much better than yesterday. And yes, absolutely.'

'Good.'

'What can we expect to happen tonight?'

'It's difficult to tell, I haven't been a part of that crowd for quite some time. The ritual space will be consecrated, and we will witness some members of the Inner Circle perform a certain type of higher magic. Maybe the Hexagram Ritual. And everything will be decorated with symbols that you may find familiar. Oh! And the coffin used in most Rosicrucian rituals.' It seemed to Helena that Aurora was looking forward to the evening. 'But what I do know is that all the usual subjects have decamped in town from their cosy country retreats. The Inner Circle. Annie Horniman.' This was the main leader, their Magus, after Mathers' messy dismissal a couple of years earlier. 'Yeats, Bram Stoker.'

'The writer?' With a paste of her own creation, Helena had applied a fake layer of skin on her face, on which she carefully sculpted the under-eye bags and wrinkles of a septuagenarian.

'Indeed. He is now, if I am correct, in the process of gaining access to the Inner Circle, from what I hear.' Aurora lit one of her pink cigarettes before continuing. She went on to explain the ritual that she anticipated would take place, but it was too complex for Helena to follow. The hierarchy was incredible, and Helena became lost among the Neophyte, Zelator, Theoricus, Practicus and Philosophus. The one thing that piqued her attention was learning that the highest grade in the Outer Order, the grade that mediated between the Outer and Inner Order, was called *Portal*. The amount of occult material that needed to be studied to advance from grade to grade sounded vast, and the formal examinations required thorough. The person who had historically progressed fastest had of course been Crowley.

Helena asked Aurora's opinion about the film projection they'd seen at the exhibition.

'I know you said it will help the Order "fix" the rituals into some kind of certain steps, but I am really surprised that they are putting their faith in something so modern as moving pictures.'

'Maybe its modernity that attracts them, the fact that it cannot be to everyone's taste.'

'What do you mean?'

'I will tell you something for nothing: I imagine they like moving pictures because, unsurprisingly, it divides the adepts in two. And they absolutely love being divided in two, let me tell you. They thrive on that kind of drama, which I found so tedious.'

'What do you mean, "divide" them?'

'Because I imagine that it would seem as something rather good for some, whereas others would think it dangerous.'

'Dangerous? How so?'

'As you know, the Order is rooted within the tradition of Hermetic Magic, and, as such, the most important thing for its members is secretiveness. If they record their rituals, and those recordings were to be found by someone, well, a lot of people would not be very happy.' She downed her drink. 'Come on, time is of the essence.'

Helena's hair had been neatly tied back, encased into a net. Now, she took a wig from a bust, a white hair bun, and carefully placed it on top. When she got up and turned, she was another person.

'My goodness! Who is this beautiful creature? I would not have recognised you in a million years!'

Helena had transformed herself into an old lady, complete with stooping shoulders and a frail walk.

'Come on, let's go. I am ready to attend my first vernal equinox,' she announced in a weak and unrecognisable voice.

London, 21st March – Early hours of the morning
The Vernal Equinox

It was incredible, almost ludicrous, that Aurora was attending the equinox with a 'plus one', but that was exactly who she was. Helena had assumed for the evening the persona of a wealthy unmarried heiress, looking for suitable philanthropic societies to which she might donate her vast amounts of money, and as such was greeted as a valued guest. The entry was into a sort of ballroom, and, apart from the fact that some of the attendees were dressed in the peculiar fashion of the initiated, and that the only illumination came from torches, she could have been in a regular society gathering. There was even a string quartet merrily playing on a balcony – although they were wearing rather ominous animal masks – and canapés and champagne were being distributed as people chatted and mingled.

Then she saw him: O'Neill was among those present, wearing a rather fetching garment, a black robe with golden symbols, chatting with a group of giggling young ladies. She indicated to Aurora to look in his direction.

'My oh my, the handsome detective,' she said.

'What is he wearing? Do you think he will take part in the ritual itself?'

'My dear, that garment, as you put it, is not for merely participating. Some lucky fellows get *initiated* during the equinoxes. It is a great honour.'

'And that is an initiation garment?'

'Exactly.'

Helena's heart sank. His hurt the previous night must have been all pretence. She was furious, remembering his little game at being offended when she suggested he had sold himself to the Dawn. Even worse, to think that she had been very close to believing him. Rather, she had to admit to herself, she had wanted to believe him.

The heavy vapours of incense impregnated the hall as the complex structure of the ritual got under way, with many involved, their roles completely obscured from Helena's understanding. When she saw O'Neill approaching a kind of coffin, which acted as an altar, someone offering him a goblet to drink from and him willingly taking it in his hands, her heart raced inside her chest. She could not breathe properly; she felt hot and clammy, standing in the circle with dozens of people. She took off her gloves and untied the clasp that held her shawl together, and then forced her way out of the masses of people to hide in a corner, where Aurora found her long after all the chants and antics were over.

'Where were you? Come, there is someone I would like you to meet.'

Aurora took her by the arm, and delicately steered her among the crowd. She stopped next to another old lady, the real thing this time. They were introduced.

'Lady Ashford, pray continue telling me what you were saying.'

'Oh, yes, my dear. The Paris temple!'

This animated Helena greatly:

'You have seen the Order's Paris temple?' she started in her fake voice.

'I heard it is formidable,' suggested Aurora, grabbing some more champagne as a waiter steered flute glasses around them.

'A dream!' exclaimed the lady. 'I have never seen anything more beautiful. The "Iris Movement", he calls it. I trust they let good old Mathers return, he was always full of fresh ideas.'

'We know that the internal struggles here have always been many and various. But I myself have been part of many a society, and believe me, those of the Dawn certainly top them all.'

'You are right,' encouraged Aurora. 'Mathers was one of the best at creating strife. Now, tell my friend here what you told me. What was Mathers doing in his temple that so caught your eye?'

'Moving pictures! He was filming rituals, like the one we just performed. There was this funny little French man who was helping him.'

'A funny French man,' said Aurora, looking at Helena and opening her eyes very wide. 'How fascinating! What was his name again?'

'Melisandre, or Meliandre, or something like that…'

'Méliès? Georges Méliès?' prompted Aurora.

'That's right! Ah,' beamed the woman, 'the lobster is being added to the buffet. Excuse me, would you?' And she left.

'There you have it, Helena: a clear connection between two men in your enquiries. Have I delivered?'

'So, it is possible that he will wish to preserve the rituals for posterity, and that Méliès is helping him.'

'I am not surprised at all,' commented Aurora. 'One of Mathers's major problems was Crowley, altering how the rituals had to be performed. That young man did a lot of damage in a short space of time. From what I know of Mathers, he is traditionalist enough to want to preserve the rituals in their "true" form, whatever he may think that is, and also scientifically minded enough to think that the answer may be in some sort of recording machine.'

Suddenly, O'Neill was beside them.

'Miss Chaffins. How delightful of you to come. I know Woodbury would be particularly enthused by your presence.' And turning to Helena. 'Will you introduce me to your friend?'

'Mr O'Neill, this is my good friend, Miss Violet Burton.'

'Miss Burton,' he said, taking her hand to delicately kiss it. Her hand, which suddenly looked incongruous to her eyes: Helena had taken off the gloves when she had felt overheated among the crowd, and had forgotten to put them back on. There was no doubt, he was looking now from her youthful hand to her eyes, quizzically.

Helena felt herself redden. But there was no reason to believe O'Neill could recall the exact shade of her eyes. As far as she knew, he believed he was looking at an old woman.

Unless. She knew it, then. That he knew her eyes by heart, and that despite her disguise they both knew they were staring at each other.

Thankfully, Aurora muttered an excuse, and they were soon gone. Helena let herself be taken out and into a hansom, no time to interrogate her feelings about everything that had transpired: O'Neill was the enemy, or at least one of them. And he cared about her.

London, 21st March – Morning

Helena was trying to write an account of the Vernal Equinox as she had witnessed, with a view of increasing their knowledge of the Golden Dawn. She had referred so far to a carefully curated setting, prepared to make everyone feel that they were attending some extraordinary event; but she was far from being able to point at any supernatural occurrence. Mass hypnosis would perhaps have been more accurate. The lighting and the shape of the room, and even the music and some plant that may have been burnt somewhere, it all had contrived this.

Of the ritual, little could she write, as she did not understand much of it, and had left it halfway. Any attempts from Aurora to enlighten her had ultimately gone over her head. Helena ended up limiting herself to writing a dispassionate account of what transpired.

Two or three things were more valuable to her: the confirmation that Samuel Mathers, Magus to the Paris chapter of the Dawn, and Georges Méliès, the filmmaker Emily Peters worked for, knew each other, and worked together, at least in producing filmed rituals. Detective O'Neill was firmly on the SPR's side. (And, no less important: next time she decided to disguise herself, she needed to make a better go of it.) The last point was of a more personal nature, for it seemed now clear to Helena that Aurora's knowledge of the Dawn and their factions – from London to Paris – pointed at something she had not wanted to believe until now: she was, in some way or form, still part of the Dawn.

———◆———

TELEGRAM, DR ARCHIE LAURIE (KING'S COLLEGE, CAMBRIDGE), TO HELENA WALTON-CISNEROS (LONDON)

Dr Walton suddenly taken ill. Heart weak. Come at once.

TELEGRAM, MISS HELENA WALTON-CISNEROS (LONDON) TO MISS ELIZA WALTRAUD (HOTEL LIRRIPER, PARIS)

My grandfather suddenly taken ill. Arrival in
Paris postponed. Please be careful.

11

THE GREEN FAIRY

Paris, 22nd March – Evening

The cottage where Emily Peters had lived was located in a forest close to Sèvres. Mina had provided Helena with the exact address. Eliza didn't think it was wise to undertake this task on her own, and asked Alice if she would accompany her.

It was dark when they arrived. From the outside it seemed disused, its French windows closed tight. Alice knocked vigorously on the door anyway, and, when there was no answer, she tried to open it: it would not budge.

'Now what?' asked Eliza. 'Hang on.' She went round, and located a smallish window with a rotten frame, which led directly into the kitchen. Careful with their clothes and hands – it would have been easy to hurt themselves on the rotten wood – they made their way inside. As soon as they did, they noticed the stench.

'What on earth?' protested Alice. There was food left out, now covered in flies and their writhing offspring.

The kitchen led into a small passageway with the staircase on the left, and leading into the main sitting area, on which the street door could be found. There was a small wood-burning stove there, and a couple of chairs around a French sitting table, the kind where old women would attach a burner close to their feet, and cover themselves and the table with a heavy round piece of fabric. The chairs were a little moth-eaten, but the floor looked clean enough. There were a couple of rugs.

'This place looks alright, in fact it looks very nice,' offered Alice.

'Alice, how much would you need to pay to live in a house like this?'

'I'm not sure, but I will tell you what: I could not afford it.'

On the staircase there were a couple of cheap-looking watercolours, a crucifix and a little stained mirror with a candle attached to it, which they lit. Upstairs, a small room with an armoire and a washing unit. The armoire still contained clothes and other necessities. On a little table in one corner, a small pile of books, paper and ink. It truly looked as if the occupant of the place was about to return at any moment, which was disquieting, Eliza thought.

They went down again.

'Don't you think it is odd?' started Eliza. 'There are none of Emily's art works or art materials here.'

Alice, obviously more used to French houses than Eliza, lifted a little oval rug made of undyed wool, to reveal a trap door to the inevitable cellar space.

'Voilà!' she announced.

They went down to the cellar. The stairs were steep, and they had to climb down with their backs to the wall. Once downstairs, on the earthen floor, they found and lit another candle. The light illuminated a strange scene. All Emily's art materials seemed to have been kept down in the cellar. An easel was opened to reveal a black charcoal rendering of a face that it was hard to place, perhaps a self-portrait. But such a sad, melancholic face that Eliza's heart almost contracted.

There was something else: Miss Peters had filled all the walls of the cave-like space with flying women. Some of them had even sprouted wings. Some of them had rays of green light shooting from their chests, appearing to kill the people gathered to see them: they had '*fée électricité*' written next to them. Some of them were launching themselves from a tower-like structure, acting as a sort of lighthouse, with a ray of light pouring from the top. It was an eerie drawing, as if made by a child, which did not tally with the idea of a professional artist like Miss Peters.

'That Eiffel Tower is all wrong,' offered Eliza. She was feeling a little faint.

'That is not the Eiffel Tower,' answered Alice.

'What is it then?'

'Absolutely no idea… Look,' said Alice. She was holding papers and files; some looked as if they had been pinched from Méliès's offices, and had been partially burnt.

'Rotten luck,' commented Alice. But Eliza saw something else next to them: a tin of film – it seemed that Miss Peters had taken much more than papers from Star Film Studio.

'Are we taking it with us?' asked Eliza.

'Of course!'

'We have no way to project it.'

Alice laughed at this.

'I know many places and many people who would lend us a projector, don't you worry,' she replied. But Eliza thought that, despite her lightness, Alice sounded somehow unhappy.

23rd March – Morning

As soon as Eliza entered the studio she felt it: a changed atmosphere. Dark faces, even more so than usual. People silently moving around. In a corner, a commotion: the woman she recognised as the head seamstress agitatedly surrounded by a group of women. One of them was offering a bottle of something that could be brandy. But as soon as the lady took a sip, she crumpled down onto the floor, and they had to deftly manoeuvre her onto a chair. Eliza's mind was racing: laudanum? Morphine?

In the office, Gaston attempted to keep the morning light-hearted, and continued explaining the current legal situation. Eliza tried to remain casual, all the time surprised as to how much pretence being a detective entailed: she had never stopped to consider this, as she had been fixated on the idea of detecting as finding the truth. She did her utmost to appear interested. Still, having to dig deeper into the legal conflict had allowed Eliza to peruse Méliès's correspondence, which was meticulously arranged by topic and date, in filing cabinets marked as 'Patents' or 'Copyright'.

Eliza had received a communication from London. The report, typed by Jocasta, described a possible link between Méliès and the American-Serbian inventor Nikola Tesla, and made references to Emily Peter's letters and her drawings of machines emanating rays of green light. She knew now of a connection with regard to the misses, who had seen this green light themselves; but those in London did not. She had started her day sending a telegram to this effect back to London. She had been proud of herself, putting these two little pieces of the puzzle together. She had managed to achieve this one small thing, which went beyond the mere information gathering that Helena had expected. Besides, she now felt responsible for doing as much as she could, as Helena's telegram meant she had to delay joining her in Paris for a few more days.

As soon as she was capable, she perused the cabinets, filled with documents that referred to Mr Tesla, who was mostly listed as a witness in the litigious cases involving Mr Edison. However, one filing cabinet was marked 'Personal', and eventually she had had the opportunity to look inside, finding Mr Méliès's creative correspondence with his many associates. Here, also, there were letters between him and Mr Tesla.

Eliza had not been able to write this in the telegram, and was planning a letter that she would compose that very evening: Méliès and Tesla had become allies, because both inventors had their ideas and patents stolen by Edison. There were constant references to the 'machine' and the 'flying woman trick', but there was some kind of disagreement about them between the two men.

That morning, as soon as Gaston left the office, Eliza went to the filing cabinet marked 'Tricks & Illusions', only to find that the section for 'The Flying Woman' was empty. She feared it might have been the file stolen and burnt by Emily, so that was another dead end.

At midday, Eliza left the office, and headed for lunch. The mood around her was still subdued. She sat next to some of the crew members. By this point, the atmosphere was unbearable. Almost no one was talking, and those who were doing so were quiet, as if they were worried about bothering someone sick. The contrast with previous days was considerable.

'Hello,' she said to the person to her left, one of the dancers. 'Are you having a good day?'

But she thought that the woman did not understand her poor French, for she ignored her. Eliza now turned to the person to her right, a young carpenter.

'Hello!' she tried again. 'Are you—'

'Don't worry, I can speak English.'

'Oh!' She was embarrassed, but also thankful. They talked a little about this and that, until Eliza thought she would risk it.

'Why is everyone so gloomy today?'

'Ah! That would be because of Sandrine.'

'Who is Sandrine?'

'She is one of the dancers.'

'And, what is the problem?' Eliza was trying to sound casual, not gossipy; she lightly took some bread and passed the basket on to her left.

'No one knows where she is,' said the carpenter, leaning towards her conspiratorially.

'She must have left herself, right?' commented somebody. 'Maybe she had problems at home, or with a boyfriend, or maybe she simply hated her job.' Eliza was having problems of her own following all this in French, and asked the carpenter exactly what was being said.

'They think she left of her own volition,' he explained. 'But I put this to you: why do all the dancing ladies end up vanishing into thin air?' As he said this, the dancer who had been sitting on the other side of Eliza got up to leave. Her plate was left untouched on the table.

'What do you think happens to them?'

'Who knows. I wonder if we should ask *them*,' he said, darkly. Eliza followed his gaze: he was staring at Gaston and Georges. They were in the middle of the field adjacent to the studio, far away from the place, but in view through the gigantic glass walls. They seemed to be arguing heatedly, with Gaston pointing at a newspaper that he held in one hand. He kept waving the newspaper, and even pushed it against George's lapel. His brother had no intention of reading whatever it said, and just walked away towards the Méliès's family home. Gaston eventually walked in the opposite direction.

23rd March – Evening

As soon as Gaston was gone for the day, Eliza put her plan into action. It was late, the studio was dark and silent. There were a few more people around busying themselves, in anticipation of tomorrow's duties. The oil lamps burnt here and there, but most of the place was engulfed in shadows. She walked towards the wooden stair, carefully avoiding the other handful of studio workers, all worried with the final touches to their various tasks. Studio work never ended: she had learnt this soon enough.

She felt a bit guilty: Gaston Méliès had proved to be a good boss and colleague. Several times during the day he had entreated her not to work too hard, and had even playfully chastised her for being so efficient. At each turn Gaston kept insisting that the piles of letters were very well where they were, that the filing could wait, and that surely there were more interesting things he could show her about the business of making movies? This had immediately made her think that he did not want the problems with Edison to be resolved, which had led her in turn to wonder: since when had she started to think the worst of everyone? Gaston did not deserve it. Much worse, she had stolen from him. It was hard for her to believe it, but that was exactly what she had done: she simply had needed to get her hands on the newspaper that he and Georges had been arguing about. It was now crumpled at the bottom of her leather bag.

Compared to those actions, sneaking up to inspect the system of levers and ropes that made the dancers fly did not seem too terrible, or was it? Of course it was. It was much worse. If she was caught, she would be exposed, her mission would be over, and with all probability Helena would have to end her investigations. They would never find what happened to Emily Peters. Still, she needed to see what happened up there. The illusion was simply magnificent, much too magnificent. Monsieur Méliès was a fair master but endlessly demanding, allowing no distractions to impede his ultimate vision. The ladies would indeed dance, would levitate, would perform their daring manoeuvres while floating in mid-air, and everyone involved in the illusion would work hard to please him. And still, something else was going on here.

She climbed the wooden stairs; her heart was racing. To go farther, she would have to be extra careful: after the wooden landing ahead, she would need to negotiate two sets of ladders, and very narrow platforms. But she needed to see, if only to understand the quality of the illusion, to be able to reject what it was that her heart, if not her brain, wanted her to believe. For there was something very wrong about it, that much was clear. It was something magical happening there, right in front of her eyes. Except that magic did not exist in the world. The only magic possible was the kind happening everyday in the studio, those tales of fairies and kings and travellers to the moon, those stories that *pretended* that magic was real. As a logical mind, her problem was how to deny what her eyes were seeing. When she had seen the ladies being pulled up by the ropes, something had switched on somewhere, a delicate buzzing, almost imperceptible. And the light, which had been a pale shade, engulfing the ladies, had intensified, acquiring the density of a cloud. Instinctively, she had looked towards the beam of light: it was green now, there was no mistake possible. It was eerie-green, and yellow and bluish, oceanic. Exactly as Charlotte had described the light they saw. On cue, the ladies started floating lightly, as if they themselves were made of air, the ropes and pulleys lax around them. She was certain about this last fact.

Had no one noticed? The ladies themselves must have, if they were aware of the effect the light had on them. From the first time she noticed it, their faces, all wrong; those grotesque expressions, fixed in permanent grins that hid the fear. The lady dancers, who spent longer than anybody else under the light, and did not like it. They knew it, she was sure of this. She knew she could not be the only person who felt its eeriness. That gluey quality, awfully wrong, that emanated from it. As if you were about to be covered in sludge. But no, it was only a luminescence. Why then did it feel so obstinately repugnant? What had Charlotte said? *I had felt disgusted just thinking it would touch me.* Yes, thought Eliza.

What she was suspecting was this: that the harnesses and the ropes and the levers were put there by Monsieur Méliès, *le patron*, for mere show, a very cleverly thought-out distraction. What about the other witnesses? The studio was filled to the brim with workers. Was she imagining it all? Or were they avoiding the truth? They might have simply chosen to do so: they needed their jobs.

She was up on the wooden platform now. From there, the glass doll house looked strangely small. There was nothing there. In a corner, under a canvas cover, she found a sturdy oak box with a lid. She went towards it. She had no idea if that was what she was looking for, except that she was feeling lightheaded just touching it, strangely sick. She had to pause, compose herself, and take a long breath to hold down her nausea. The sensation brought some sense of déjà vu, and she recollected the scene in a London theatre a couple of weeks ago: Mademoiselle Carrière extending her limbs, a powerful stench emanating from her and pouring over the audience, and Eliza's conscious attempt to hold her last meal inside her.

The box was locked. Thankfully she had remembered her lock-picking tools. However, it was impossible for her to open it. Her lack of experience was showing, and her hands were shaking with emotion. She knew how to manoeuvre the tools, but she felt as if her hands weren't responding, as if she could not control them. On a wooden crate next to the box, there were several broken bulbs. Eliza could see that their filaments were of a powerful and shiny green colour. All the filaments seemed broken. She did all she could do in the circumstances: she inspected the box as carefully as possible, its smooth surface, the unbreakable lock. It had a small logo at the back, claiming that, whatever it contained, had been manufactured by the Tesla Electric Company, NY.

'What are you doing up here?'

She turned around, scared, to find one of the young under-assistants from the lighting crew.

'Oh,' she tried to think on her feet, and, taking up a broken bulb in her hand, said: 'I have been told to order more of these from New York.' She smiled faintly. Would he believe her? 'I am new, my name is Eliza. I deal with all correspondence in English.' She was pronouncing each word in French as carefully as possible, which was difficult, as her heart was racing in her chest. But he seemed to understand.

'You are the new English girl?'

Eliza smiled. 'Yes, I am the new English girl.'

The boy laughed. She did not know if it was at her accent, or if she had mispronounced something.

'I was counting them, trying to work out how many we get through each time?'

Would this work? She remembered one of the first psychology lessons with Helena: if the person you were interrogating suspected that you knew what you were talking about, they could be persuaded to share what they knew themselves, filling in your gaps. Incredibly, it worked, for the teenager started talking in fast French about the bulbs, and *le machine*, asking her to, please, she thought he said, *lose the order*, and never bring the bulbs back at all.

That was nothing if not curious.

Later on, this is what she recollected in her casebook in a desperate attempt to remember what he had said, despite the gaps in her French, her tiredness, and the time that had passed between their conversation (she had not dared to keep her ledger in the studio itself) and Eliza being back at her desk in the Lirriper:

Le machine lived inside the box. The platform had been cleared of odd bits of rope and remnants of *papier-mâché*, and then given a good clean, the floorboards shiny with soapy water. He had been involved in taking it up there: extra care had been given to this task, with *le patron* constantly scared that it was going to fall and break into pieces.

The next day, a further man had come, tall and gangly, with a thick moustache. This man and *le patron* had locked themselves in the big office, and there had been shouts and the noises of a heated argument. *Le patron* had popped his head out at some point to ask for a decanter of brandy to be refilled, and, eventually, both men had emerged. Monsieur Méliès's friend had then tended to his machine, for he was the inventor of the contraption. They had locked themselves up again, this time together with Gaston, *le patron*'s brother. The youngster liked Gaston more than George, as he, unlike his brother, remembered everyone's names.

After a while the funny tall man had left.

No one knew what the machine was for. It seemed that it did something special to the lighting, and Monsieur Méliès explained in a little speech that, from now on, all their illusions would seem so much more real once they were projected. He did not give any details as to how this would happen, or what it was exactly that the machine would do to the light. Monsieur Gaston was put in charge of the machine. The operators who dealt with the lighting weren't pleased about this, and their manager, the boy's uncle, threw his hat on the floor in desperation.

But they had nothing to fear. Their roles would not change, and their jobs would not be lost to a new automatised system.

That wasn't what the machine was there to do. Monsieur Méliès would still need to carefully explain his vision, demonstrate the techniques that they were expected to replicate, in the incessant experimentation that was the day-to-day in the studio. They continued to operate all the major lighting, and worked the oversized drapes that covered the glass ceiling and walls of the studio, carefully positioning the shadows where *le patron* expected them.

None of that had changed. Then what was the light for, exactly? And how had the misses seen it all the way back in Versailles?

23rd March – Later

Back in the Lirriper after dinner, Eliza shared some sherry with the other guests, and sat next to the fire. Eventually, when it was time to retire for the night, the crashing of furniture and opening and closing of doors began again. As per the previous instance, everyone in the room ignored the noise coming from the attic rooms and continued with their activities. Miss Bustelo was reading a fashion magazine in a corner. Miss Lamont was playing chess with one of the Scottish ladies, her sister having retired for the night.

This time, Eliza did not move. Next to her was the newspaper she had taken from Gaston. It was a copy of *Le Monde Illustré*, still folded open on the page that Gaston had tried, unsuccessfully, to make Georges see.

It was a short report, titled '*Le magasin hantée de la rue d'Enfer*'. It told the story of an *épicier* who had his shop in said street, close to an access to the catacombs, and who had been attacked by a green 'devil', '*la fée verte*', who had climbed out of the municipal ossuary. The devil, or fairy, had been throwing skulls at all and sundry, and had even broken his fruit display. The gendarmerie had been called, but had found nothing, and thought that some local youths had played a trick on the shopkeeper. The report concluded:

> The Catacombs, whose construction dates back to the eighteenth century, when the city needed to find some solution to the overcrowding of the local cemeteries and the epidemic diseases this caused, have always been surrounded by similar stories. A famous anecdote about a green creature, a long-tailed half-demon, half-man who lives in them, seems to be the basis for this strange incident.
>
> These mass graves have forever been shrouded in mystery, as the many pits and quarries constitute a veritable labyrinth, something which has been often used to criminals' advantage. It said that demonic Black Masses and occult rituals are performed in them. Several Rosicrucian societies and at least two Masonic Lodges based in Paris are known to have kept sacred spaces underground.

There was a green fairy or demon living in the Paris Catacombs. Eliza remembered one of Helena's first lessons in detection: there are no coincidences.

Later, when Eliza was in her room, she reflected on these latest developments: the key was the light, a green light, shiny, with yellow tints, and a viscous quality to it. It was still there when she closed her eyes, tiny dots floating and dancing. She was now in bed, trying to sleep, and all she could see was the light. It brought with it strange dreams. She came out of her strange reverie, only to fall into an uneasy sleep. There were flying ladies, all around her – some of them dressed in white ghostly chemises, like the inmates of a lunatic asylum, some of them looking like old-fashioned milk-maids – and they endlessly crossed the sky over her head. She woke up feeling uneasy about the day that faced her.

INTERLUDE

Philothée was looking forward to seeing the interior of Maison Méliès, where she and the Matherses had been invited to attend a small gathering. They rented a hansom all the way to Montreuil, a considerable expense. Samuel Mathers was expansive, and Moina Mathers had made herself particularly beautiful, as she always did when Georges was in attendance. Philothée was extremely curious. She had often seen *le patron*'s house from the outside, as the studio was located in the fields next to it. A very pretty maid opened the door for them and took Philothée's new light spring coat. They were directed to the sitting room, where a cheerful group of people was mingling around a fire, consuming light drinks. Méliès was all congeniality, and asked them what they wanted to drink, before instructing Gaston to get it for them. She looked around the room. There were chess and backgammon sets opened and ready to play on little tables, and on the walls and up on the huge mantelpiece a great number of puppets were displayed, obviously a lovingly gathered collection. She turned to find Méliès next to her, and felt a shiver.

'Ah! Mademoiselle Gaimard! I see you are admiring my little collection. Puppetry was one of my first loves. I have always been blessed with some special talents, for drawing, puppetry, magic illusions. If my father had allowed me to join the École des Beaux-Arts, perhaps I would have succeeded in becoming a painter. But alas! It was not to be.'

'I am so sorry. What did you do instead?'

'As with many other young men, I had to join the family business, I am afraid. Shoes! Can you believe it? Still, my father sent me to London to study for my trade, and I fell in love with it as well.'

'London?'

'Indeed. I am extremely fond of London, for my life changed completely. Pantomime. Magic. It was all there for the taking, such endeavours, so suited to my personal talents. I saw many "pantos": *The Golden Ring, Red Riding Hood, Cinderella*...

'But then nothing in London can equal what I experienced in the Salon des Indiens, here in Paris in 1895. I truly was forever changed that day. I had not come across any method of performance that would give such a thrill to an audience. Yes, my dear, I was there at the Salon des Indiens when that marvellous new invention, the cinema, was shown for the first time! And to think that I complained to the man sitting next to me that it would all be a waste of time – nothing was so far from the truth. The whole of life was there, playing in front of our eyes, the hustle and bustle of the street, the trams, the passers-by – we were truly spellbound. Moving pictures don't need to replicate nature, my dear, they can do so much more!

For example, show us what we *can't see* in nature with our own dull earthly eyes – things that are there, but hidden!'

'So is that your – aesthetic vision? Not to replicate reality, but rather to unveil, to show, what we miss from reality. To reveal the occult?'

The filmmaker smiled.

'My dear Mademoiselle Gaimard, you put it so exquisitely. But of course Mathers tells me you are a wonderful addition to our cause. A very apt pupil indeed.'

'So, are you saying that you put fairies in movies because you believe in them?'

The filmmaker let out a crackle of raucous laughter.

Samuel's tall figure approached them.

'Mademoiselle Gaimard and I are discussing the possibilities of our new science. She agrees with me on one particular: movies have the power to unveil the occult!' Had she said that, she wondered. Men tended sometimes to interpret an encouraging look, or a vague repetition, or a smile, as complete acceptance of their ideas; she had already noticed this with Samuel. Still, there was nothing else to do but carry on smiling prettily.

'Ah, Philothée here is a fellow believer, my friend.' Mathers seemed to expect an answer. What could she possibly say that was sufficiently vague?

'I like to think that.'

The two men were smiling but soon forgot about her, and were talking among themselves. Philothée carried on sipping her wine, looking down demurely, and trying very hard to appear as innocent as possible, while listening to what was said, even if she did not understand much of it.

'I have already started experimenting with the two chromatropes, like we said, moving them and dissolving them into one another,' Méliès was explaining. 'Very similar to the *Pantomimes Lumineuses* in the Musée Grévin, you know the ones? But the thing is, no one had thought about recording, and then recording back over the same film that had already been exposed. Simple but so effective.'

But Philothée had sensed a change in the tone of Mathers' responses, and she tried to give the impression to moving away from the men, while she tried to remain closer enough to hear them. She feigned being very interested in the table setting that she was now inspecting, but at the same time not moving too far, so as to be able to carry on listening to their conversation. It was a difficult balance to strike.

'Do you think it will work?' Mathers was now asking somewhat coldly.

'It cannot hurt to try.' There was a begging note in Méliès's words.

'The problem, my friend, is that we are running out of time,' Mathers complained bitterly. This took her off-guard. She thought she knew everything that happened in the Mathers household: she was tasked with the minutiae of the everyday, from running the Matherses' appointment diary to the extraordinary – such as putting on a theatre show that explained the Isis Cult to neophytes. Most things passed over her table. What were the two men discussing then?

'Things are being reported, even as we speak,' a rather cross Samuel was now shouting. 'Yes, Georges! This week's *Monde Illustré*!' Mathers was furious, but kept his voice lowered, while checking that their interaction was not being noticed. 'You tell me what you are doing about this, as it is your mess!'

And with that, Mathers moved away and Méliès was left looking at the newspaper that had been thrust at him, all joviality lost. Then he put it in his pocket, forced himself to smile, and walked back to his guests.

Philothée had absolutely no idea what that was about. She wished she had more confidence for what she was about to do. As soon as she was able, she discreetly went out into the corridor. Here, a number of doors presented themselves. She would try a couple; she could always claim to be looking for the ladies' room. She ought not to have been so alarmed, as several people passed her by without giving her a second look, servants with trays, and laughing couples who were looking for a secluded spot. She opened a door, and suddenly she was in an office. Georges or Gaston? The puppets hanging from the walls gave her an answer. They looked at her eerily as she entered the room.

The first thing she saw were papers in the dying embers of the fire, mostly burnt. She went over, took a poker and moved them about. They seemed to be files. She manoeuvred them: two or three files, and, underneath them, what looked like a black journal. The leather of the journal seemed to have protected most of the pages, which were only singed on their corners. She removed it, displacing some of the ash, looked around herself, and found a cloth to wrap it with.

She did not know why she was doing this, only that she had come looking for some answers, and there seemed to be something here that *le patron* had tried to dispose of. That did it: her hands and her skirt were now covered in soot. There was nothing else to lose. She took the poker, and tried to move the files around. They were mostly lost, but she could still see, using the poker to open them over the ashes, that they were each headed with an individual's name. Why did Georges have files on people? They might be employees, she reasoned, as they were similar to the ones the Mathers household kept for people on their payroll. One had the name E. Peters. She had never heard it. The paper beneath had the name M. Calvi. Maria Calvi was a name she knew. She had been one of the dancers who had disappeared shortly before her arrival. She had heard talk about her, and about little else in fact, when she first set foot in the studio.

She heard steps outside, and went on her knees to hide under the solid mahogany desk. Someone entered the room. She could see their legs and shoes, and she was sure it was Georges. She covered her mouth with her hand, and tried not to move.

Georges went directly to the fireplace. He cursed at seeing the fire petering out and set about building the flames up again, until there was a fire roaring inside and he was satisfied. Then he left with a loud bang of the door. She came out, tentatively. The fire was now at full blast: whatever was in those files would be lost forever. And Georges had left something else on the pile, now being consumed by the fire:

that week's issue of *Monde Illustré* that Samuel had thrust on him furiously.

She decided to have a last quick look, poking around and opening some of the small drawers: one of them contained a notebook clumsily marked as *Grimoire* in Georges's childish handwriting. She took it out, almost suppressing a laugh: serious magic textbooks did not look like this, a penny notebook displaying its contents to the world in clumsy writing. She remembered her first assignment, between Georges and the Matherses, bringing back Samuel's real magic book. Was this Georges's clumsy attempt to compile his own magic compendium? She knew she ought to be moving, but decided this was worth a look. She opened the so-called *Grimoire*.

There were random notes, all concerning the idea of Artist as Alchemist, or Artist as Magus, that she had heard Samuel and Georges discussing often, in which poetry and theatre, and perhaps films themselves, would matter more than the invocation of demons, or spiritualist séances. If Mathers believed that occultism should concern itself with the practice rather than the study of magic, he genuinely thought that the English Dawn's failure was due to a failure in creativity, and consequently he surrounded himself with many artist friends, actively sought authors, and poets, and painters, and dancers. Producing art and producing magic as one and the same thing: what he called the Apotheosis of the Artist. Artists as the definitive Magus who would open the secret door to the mysteries of the universe. But more importantly, a Magus capable of influencing significant matters on earth, public opinion, anything that the Cult of Isis desired. But this was new to her – influencing people. She had never understood why Samuel, the leader, the Magus *per se*, shared the symbolic importance of his office – for he had never shared real power – with his artist friends, Georges occupying a special place in the hierarchy.

What exactly had Mathers hoped that Georges would do for him, and how was his friend failing him? She had no time to muse about this: she ought to find somewhere to clean the tell-tale soot from her skirt before returning to the party, the small journal safely hidden underneath her clothes. She had a quick look in a little mirror that hung by the side of the door, and carefully rearranged her shawl to cover her secret further. How she was going to go through the rest of the night hiding the journal she did not know, as she kept feeling it, cold against her skin.

12

UNEXPECTED ALLIES, UNEXPECTED ENEMIES

London, 23rd March

Finally, it was beginning to feel like spring. Ever since the awful night of the Vernal Equinox, Helena had been feeling as if the ghoulish members of the Golden Dawn, all the Yeats and the Stokers and even the Chaffins, had somehow stolen the date from her. Their ministrations had decidedly made the season darker, and she felt the crisp days of flowering were long overdue. It didn't help that she had spent the last two days at Cambridge, making sure her grandfather was well looked after. They had been quiet days, ill health overstretching the hours, and setting all the members of the household into some sort of limbo, herself included. She had not heard from Eliza, but knew that one letter had arrived at the agency. While in Cambridge, she had not seen any of her old haunts, not even one of the bookshops; but at least she had been able to go for her usual walk along the river as it turned into isolated canals at the edge of the town, the occasional cow and magpie the only witnesses to her hiking efforts. She always felt strange back in Cambridge, as if she was a rebellious teenager again. She had only agreed to return to London once her grandfather, recovered and with the worst of the attack behind him, had insisted that she should. She had been touched by his worry for her and her business, and eventually, only after discussing it with his doctor and securing the services of a competent nurse, she had returned home on the promise of telephoning every night and coming back if there was any change for the worse.

She had also asked the cards, waiting for the chime of the little bells while in her childhood room – that was, after all, the first place where they had visited her – and, while the chimes had not come, at least the cards had assured her that everything was fine with her grandfather, and that he would make a full recovery – on this occasion at least.

London had received her while displaying its more beautiful face for her. It was incredible what a couple of days of uncertainty, a couple of days lived in her past, as it were, and with the dread of worse looming over her, could do to the spirits. She revelled in all the smells, and the views from the hansom, the usual crossing of the bridge on her way home, and read it all as a narrative of belonging. This was her chosen city; she had decided to embrace this place, to make it hers. It was her home.

Dottie opened the door, and was quickly busy arranging for bags and cases to be brought in.

'I am so happy to see you, madam. I will have a bath ready for you in no time. Meanwhile, I have arranged for some late lunch in your sitting room.'

'Thank you, that is exactly what I need,' said Helena, looking behind her for a moment. She knew everyone in her street, and there was someone who decidedly did not belong out there, kicking pebbles and making a really bad show of reading the newspaper. The Yard, as clear as day. 'Has everything been okay?' she asked as they were entering the hall. 'Any unexpected visitors?'

'No, madam, nothing at all to report.'

Helena left the woman to organise the unpacking of the valises, and went directly to her cold meats and chutney, and later on to her bath.

That night, after everything was done, and Dottie and Janet, the maid-for-all, had turned down all the gas lamps around the house, Helena was sitting in her favourite kimono-dress, her hair pinned precariously while drying, next to a small fire lit for this very purpose, very awake, despite the late hour. She was writing in a notebook that she kept at home, a diary. Many of the dates were not filled in, as she was an irregular diary-keeper. But she turned to it from time to time, in an effort to find clarity. She inspected the last pages, blank for many weeks. She knew she had been going more often to the cards for the purpose of finding clarity than to writing, and she felt a slight guilty pang.

Helena was deliberately not going to bed, for she was expecting a night visitor. No one had announced themselves, or their intention to come to her home. She had received no letter, no telephone call, no telegram. But seeing the clumsy surveillance type from the Yard had made her understand the situation: her leaving of London had been sudden, and there was someone who now was looking to have a private word. She suspected who this person might be, and felt restless as a result, incapable of concentrating on anything. She would soon be proved right about the identity of the visitor.

Detective O'Neill appeared behind the pair of French doors that led into the garden. He was standing there, out in the spring dusk. When she saw him Helena got up, crossed the kimono-dress over her, tied it in a firm knot, and placed herself directly in front of the glass doors. She wasn't going to make it easy for him.

O'Neill looked at her through the glass, for seconds that stretched an eternity. Wasn't he going to ask to be let in? He seemed content just looking at her, standing on the other side. With a long sigh Helena gave in and opened the double glass doors. The cool air of the night hit her, and she shivered a little.

'You were waiting for me,' was his greeting. She could not parse his tone. Was he amused, or impressed?

'Your surveillance men are pretty obvious. No offence.'

'None taken,' he entered the room after her, closing the double doors behind him. Helena's hairs were prickling on the back of her neck. She was trying to interpret the scene, but drew a blank. She checked the room: the dagger was where she had left it, under a heap of papers – she might need to defend herself. She went to stand on the further side of the small writing table, within easy reach of the weapon, and with the piece of furniture between them both as an extra precaution.

She noticed at once: he had guessed the motives behind her chosen position. He suppressed a laugh, that much was obvious, but a small smile curved up his face as he considered her. She hated being looked at, interpreted. Again, she could not entirely guess if he was appreciative of her or simply mocking.

'To what do I owe this honour?' Helena started. 'Police matters again? Or perhaps this time you're here on the orders of the Hermetic Order of the Golden Dawn? Tell me, Detective, which one is it going to be today?'

He did not take the bait, but his expression changed. His smile had disappeared.

'I knew it was you,' he simply said.

Helena felt acutely the embarrassment that was probably displayed on her face at that moment.

'I haven't the slightest idea what you are referring to.'

'*Miss Violet Burton.* Good disguise. But something gave you away.'

'Don't worry, Detective, you don't have to tell me. I am perfectly aware. I expect you will want a drink, or are you on duty?'

He followed her now towards the little drink cart to the left of the mantelpiece. Helena had another weapon concealed in a vase atop it.

'It was not what you think,' he said. 'It was your eyes. You half-close them when you are deep in thought, or considering something. Didn't you know? There, you see? You are doing it again.' He was smiling again, at his private joke perhaps. She looked right to the mirror over the mantelpiece, and saw her expression. A memory floated inside her mind, of being very small, and someone pointing out that she was frowning when doing a puzzle.

'It is a very endearing gesture,' he continued. It was the combination of two things: the deepness of his voice, that slow-motion way in which he delivered information, and the choice of words. Endearing. Whatever it was, she felt again the same current that had vibrated between their fingers the day she fainted, but that now moved all over her body, making it impossible for her to think clearly. She had to make it stop.

She moved away from him with a sudden flourish, and positioned herself on the other side of the room. Expertly, she had taken the dagger in passing, and now pointed it at him.

'Why are you here?'

His countenance became serious, more serious than she had ever seen it. His whole demeanour had changed: he looked worried now.

'I just needed to explain, that's all,' he said, both hands up in a placatory movement.

'Explain what, exactly?'

'What you saw the other night.'

Helena laughed at this.

'You have absolutely nothing to explain, I can assure you. You can join all the occult societies in London that you want to, as far as I am concerned.'

He ignored her mocking tone.

'And I was also worried. You just disappeared.'

He was *worried*? Helena said nothing. He continued:

'I trust your grandfather is feeling better now. He must, or you wouldn't be back.' Helena said nothing. He knew it all, every one of her movements. She didn't know how to feel about this, but was confused at not being angrier. 'Just promise me,' he was now saying. 'Promise me that you will be careful. That is all.' And with that, he started moving back towards the glass doors.

'Enough with the riddles, please. Why do I need to be careful?'

He doubled back and found himself right in front of her; instinctively, she lowered the dagger; this took her by surprise.

'Because I could not bear anything bad happening to you. And you are climbing into the wolf's mouth.'

Helena frowned, despite herself. Wasn't that the same expression that Aurora had used?

'Leave, please.'

'Helena, listen, I beg you. I wasn't joining the Golden Dawn. I have no desire to join the Golden Dawn. I was *infiltrating* the Dawn.' She said nothing, and, although she had lowered it, she still held the dagger firmly in her hand. 'You don't believe me.' It wasn't a question.

'Why would I?'

'Because it is the truth. It was all part of an operation that it has taken us almost a year to organise. I don't give a damn about the Dawn! The only thing that I care about is to bring it down.'

'Prove it.'

'Very well. Aurora and Mathers.'

'What about them?'

'They were lovers.' He let this sink in. 'She hasn't told you, has she?'

'And why is this relevant?' she said, despite knowing that she herself had suspected it, had thought that Aurora was more involved than she was letting on. Still, O'Neill tried to explain:

'It is relevant because *you* are investigating Mathers.'

'But again, I ask you, why is this something that she ought to have shared with me, or with anybody? She has told me everything that may be useful for my investigation, when she didn't need to in the slightest. What she chooses to share or not from her past, it is none of mine, or indeed your, business!'

She could see this had not had the desired effect – although she wondered if she herself believed it – and that he was looking for something else to say. Eventually he did, although it seemed to be a great effort for him to articulate the words:

'The Dawn is interested in harnessing some form of energy. We understand that the SPR was involved in some similar scheme a year ago, and… you stopped them, didn't you?' It was admiration now, she was sure. He was getting closer.

'The truth is, they have found something else now. There is something out there, man-made, not supernatural…' He was very close, barely inches from her face, looking at each one of her features, as if he were trying to memorise them. 'An energy which, they imagine, can be harnessed into a source of unimaginable power.' He touched her hair, delicately. 'They are not going to stop at anything, Helena, and are prepared to kill for this. They have allies all over the world, powerful allies. Tell me,' he concluded, 'have I shared enough of our theories? Do you believe me now?'

'I…' she could not bring herself to speak, or even to breathe.

He moved away from her, and walked again towards the doors.

It happened then, in a flash of mutual understanding, perhaps instigated by the current that had contrived to unite them, little by little, enacting now its final pull. Helena let the dagger fall to the floor, and the noise made him turn towards her, the energy in the room changing with each one of their movements. It was at that moment when they rushed towards each other.

24th March – Morning

The next morning Helena opened her eyes, a shadow gradually visible. O'Neill was still there, sitting on the side of her bed and watching her.

'Good morning,' he said.

'Good morning,' she replied, still too sleepy to react, but not so sleepy as not to make sure that she was properly covered. It was daylight now, and she felt a rush of guilt, but not too much. She could still remember flashes of what had transpired during the previous hours, and the energy she now knew so well electrified her skin at the mere recollection. 'What are you doing?' she asked. He smiled at her.

'Looking at you,' he said, as if this was the most natural thing in the world. 'Helena,' he started. And she could see it on his face, all the questions. She knew exactly what he was going to ask next: 'What happened during the shaman's ritual?'

'Do you mean why did I faint?' He looked at her silently, his expression encouraging her to continue. 'I think you know the answer to that,' said Helena, as she got up and donned her kimono, turning to look at him. 'This is all so new to me. Aurora, she has been helping me.'

He nodded.

'And has she? Helped?'

'More than you can imagine. But there is not much I can explain myself. I am still learning my way,' she said. 'What about you? What have you learnt about the Dawn?'

He lay down on his back, looking at the ceiling.

'They are in trouble, or think themselves in trouble. With Mathers gone… Woodbury took over the reins from the SPR.' There it was, Helena thought, confirmation of her theory. 'But they can all sense it will not be enough. There will be a war, Helena. "Fail not of an heir"… That is a primary Rosicrucian adage. Everyone is at pains to demonstrate that they are in contact with a "higher authority". But they are like children, playing in the mud.'

'What do they want this heir to do?'

'To help their cause: exercise influence and power. The times are catching up with them, though. They can sense they are living at the end of something. They have benefitted immensely in this era of irresponsible experimentation, disregard of values, dilettantism and in general the uncommitted attitudes to common sense; not to mention the drug taking and delusions of utopia. But, at the same time, they believe they are part of this landscape, and contributors to it. Hence, contributors to their own demise. They are both the shadows and the embers of these dying times.'

Helena was speechless. Detective O'Neill was a poet.

'Why do you think they are so adamant in curtailing women?' he continued. 'They have sensed it, more than once. That their true heir could be a woman. They would throw themselves on the pyre of history rather than accept that as a possibility.'

Helena was silent, contemplating his words.

'I need to go now,' he said, sitting up.

'I know,' she agreed: her maid would soon knock on the door with her morning coffee.

'But before I do,' he said, 'there is something I need to do.' He came closer to her, until their faces were touching, and he kissed her slowly and deeply.

Then he got up, took his jacket, and, with a last look at her, climbed smoothly out of the window. Helena lay there for a while unable to think, until Janet brought the coffee and drew open the curtains. She got into motion – there was so much to do. She would think about O'Neill later.

After a quick bath, she went to the small square room that housed her costume collection. It contained open wardrobes occupying the main three walls that she had specially made so that she could view everything at once. She had not thought of transporting any of the costumes to the agency, as they were for her personal use and the majority made to measure. She was thinking about O'Neill's morbid reflection. Was he accusing the Dawn of being reactionary, or simply morally indifferent? She wondered why the Yard had become so interested in an occult society as to launch an impossible year-long infiltration, and could only think of one reason: the Dawn were no longer just displaying their well-known hostility to established government, religion and society in general, but potentially looking beyond, into more far-reaching and dangerous areas of influence. What these could be, Helena dreaded to contemplate.

Eventually, she selected a pale grey outfit, unassuming but elegant, its only concession to chic a number of silk flowers sewn at the hem of the skirt. She matched it with a complicated hat that told the story: exaggerated plumes, strange bird-like ornamentation: new wealth. Then, with the hat in her hands she went down to breakfast.

'Dottie,' she called while eating, 'as soon as it is office hours, I'd like you to call here,' she passed on a paper with a scribbled telephone number, 'and say that Mrs VanderMair, of Fifth Avenue, New York, would like to arrange an appointment this morning, as she is very interested in investing in Mr Tesla's new invention.'

'Leave it with me, madam,' said Dottie, who was used to this kind of request from Helena.

Shortly after nine o'clock Helena arrived at Tesla's offices in London, and was surprised by their shabbiness. Her own situation in Marylebone was far more comfortable. There were a good number of clerks working in rows at copying tables, of the kind that were fashionable a few years ago. But the place boasted a boxed telephone on a wall, and one or two lady typists here and there. Helena handed in her false visiting card to the clerk at the reception window.

'Mrs VanderMair. Please, do come this way. Mr Franklin is expecting you.'

Indeed, Mr Franklin, a short and roundish man, bald and bespectacled, was obligingly waiting for her; he ushered her to the most comfortable of the chairs in the room, and ordered coffee and 'the good cake, Jenkins. None of those crumbling slices!' Imparting these instructions once she was already in the room, instead of having organised it beforehand, indicated nonetheless that the man wasn't a natural salesman. There were two large-size renditions of the proposed Wardenclyffe Tower in Long Island hanging in the wall, plus one studio portrait of Mr Nikola Tesla himself. Helena took the opportunity to inspect it. It portrayed him reclining on a desk, in a showman's pose, almost like a magician – it seemed a strange choice for a scientist. In fact he looked very little like a scientist. But her attention was quickly diverted, for Tesla's London agent was now indeed treating her to the full sales pitch, detailing the advantages that the proposed tower would bring to the world.

'Do not be alarmed, dear lady, if I say it again, that the Wardenclyffe Tower will change the world as we know it.

There will be a before and after its construction, do not doubt it for one second!'

'That is so interesting, Mr Franklin. Pray, tell me, how will the tower do this, exactly?' she said, in her most charming American accent.

'I am so glad you asked.' The man looked a tiny bit at lost. 'Ah! Good!' He had been saved by the appearance of the coffee and the 'good cake'. Looking at the slice that was put down next to her chair, Helena worried about what the 'bad cake' might entail. Meanwhile, Mr Franklin had used the moment to check some notes that he had fetched out of the chaos of his desk. He now read: '*The tower will work as a magnifier of waves.* And it will transmit messages, of course. That's right! I always forget about that one,' he confided cheerily.

Helena feared for poor Mr Tesla's business sense: if these were his agents in London, it would be very difficult for him to raise any money here.

'Fascinating! And how will it magnify the transmission of these messages?'

'Like the telegraph, my dear lady, but a very powerful one. Mr Tesla's inventions already allow us to send the sound of voices, and even images, across the Atlantic. The tower will enhance the speed with which this is done. The energy will be multiplied tenfold!'

Helena's heart missed a beat: energy multiplied tenfold was music to her ears. What she was hearing fit perfectly with her ongoing puzzle.

'*The ultimate goal will be to create a wireless system of global communication, encompassing the whole planet.* It's all very scientific, if you allow me to say so,' he concluded. But Helena wasn't thinking of science. To her, it sounded exactly like magic.

———— ·•· ————

PROMOTIONAL LITERATURE – WARDENCLYFFE TOWER
TESLA ELECTRIC COMPANY, NEW YORK, 1901

Imagine a man from a century ago, so bold as to design, and in fact build, a large tower with which he intended to transmit the human voice, music, newsreels, and even energy. He would have been burnt, either financially or else at the stake. Mr Tesla's superior intellect hasn't produced a fabulous wonder in this transmitter, a machine to send wireless energy.

∽

There is no mystery, and this is no magic! His historic North American patents and his scientific articles explain the method that he uses. The transmitter is the result of a lifetime's work. The tower will transmit photographs, text, sounds in a completely wireless manner. It will also transmit moving images from one side of the globe to the other!

∽

The costly wire will be rendered irrelevant! A system of towers around the world that will send information everywhere will also transmit cheap energy. The scarcity and high cost of energy will be a thing of the past!

When Nikola Tesla started building the Wardenclyffe Tower in Long Island earlier this year, he was one hundred years ahead of his time. The Tower will make this transmission ten times more effective, ten times faster, ten times more powerful! By investing in the Wardenclyffe Tower you can now help Mr Tesla bring forward the future!

Wardenclyffe Tower–Now building in Long Island.

Helena missed Eliza; even reading and re-reading the promotional leaflet, she felt that she only understood half of what was there. One idea at least was clear: whatever Tesla was doing, it was hoping to make possible some form of energy enhancement. If O'Neill was right, and if Aurora had been correct regarding the Dawn's latest interests, there was something here that tied with the main theory that was now forming in her head. Energy was one of the major preoccupations of Mr Tesla: producing it cheaply, and giving it for free – she imagined there might be people who did not like this, hence his problems with Mr Edison, which had created a friendship with French filmmaker Georges Méliès. They knew all this thanks to Eliza's reports, at least the ones that had reached them. Furthermore, if Mr Tesla's experiments were... unusual, could it be possible that he had tapped into some form of energy unknown before to man, one which could be used by the Dawn, for example, to increase the power of their magic rituals? Even if he hadn't, it was clear that he was in possession of an energy-making machine, and that his current endeavours were designed to build a system of towers around the world that would make energy more powerful. Somehow, along the way, his interests and those of his friend Méliès had diverged, and the Frenchman had stolen an energy-producing machine from him.

How did Mathers fit into this? Mathers wanted energy himself, to enhance his occult rituals. It was possible that he had had little interest in Mr Tesla's inventions; that was, until he heard about the projected system of towers. Could any of this be true? It all seemed to fit, for the first time.

She forced herself to go through the usual motions before escaping, so as not to raise suspicions, including praising the frankly stale cake, commending Mr Tesla for his ingenuity, and Mr Franklin for his vivid descriptions; and, of course, promising to be incredibly interested, and to want to race home solely in order to write a fat cheque without further delay, which she would put in the post at the first opportunity. Mr Franklin was very happy with his success. He went as far as walking her to the door. There, a tall square-built man moved away courteously for them to go by and she left.

But Helena paused on the landing of the office building.

Something had pricked her senses, but her brain was scrambling to hold it. She had seen the promotional images of the proposed tower before. Mr Tesla had more closely resembled an illusionist, with his handsome face and thick moustache and long hands, than a scientist. She was aware of the confusing properties of déjà vu. It wasn't that either. The leaflet had sounded strangely antiquated. No, it wasn't any of that. Something was surely pricking at her tongue, the taste of recognition… And it certainly wasn't the horrid cake.

And then it struck her: the heavy-built man who was entering the office, casually looking at the posters on the landing, just as she exited, who moved away courteously, a hand to his hat, and who had resumed his way to chat to one of the clerks as she was leaving. That face.

They had not had the chance to try the suspect portrait system invented by Eliza very often. And yet, the man had been the spitting image of their last attempt. The man chatting to a clerk at Tesla's London offices and the man who ransacked Mina's room were two peas in a pod, or were twin brothers, or, simplest of all, were the same person.

There was only one way to find out who he was and what he was doing there: she would have to follow him. She cursed: her current attire was not very appropriate, not for the kind of place he would go into, the kind of transport he would take. She would have to move quickly. First, Helena found a discreet place for surveillance, around a corner from the office entrance. She took off her jacket, turned it inside out: it was now black and nondescript, the visible sewing affording her a shabby and unkempt appearance. She next took out a pair of scissors, and cut out the silk flowers at the hem of the skirts, transforming it into a plain skirt. The hat she was particularly upset to part with, but there was nothing else to do. She approached a posy seller, a young girl who looked at her quizzically as Helena advanced in her direction:

'Hello. Would you be interested in swapping your bonnet for this hat?'

The girl merely nodded, took the hat, removed her bonnet, and left.

'Thank you, miss!' She had thrown the posies on the floor; the expensive hat was worth a month of her trade. Helena had a sudden idea, and picked up the posies: she was the seller now. A quick visit to the small garden opposite the building, grubbing earth and rubbing with it her hands and face, and a quick dishevelment of her hair under the bonnet, concluded her new outfit. She now paced round the park gate selling her flowers, never losing sight of the entrance to the office building. From her position she could observe the children at play, the dogs running after the squirrels, the older boys with their trousers tucked up, looking for fishes on the pond, and, of course, the entry to the building itself.

Soon the thug emerged, accompanied by the clerk; they seemed to be the best of friends, when she guessed they had just met. She made a mental note of the marvellous skill displayed by the man. He must be a conman, or a well-trained criminal. By sheer bad luck it was at roughly the same hour when most clerks left for their lunches. Thankfully, he moved slowly. The first thing he did was to abandon the avenues for the flea-infested streets where he continued at this leisurely pace. The two men entered a pub, and Helena quickly followed them into a crowded space, and ordered a drink herself. After drinking a couple of pints, the man left the pub, now on his own, with Helena in hot pursuit. Now he was walking quickly; she assumed he was going to a meeting, perhaps to pass on whatever information he had just learnt from the unassuming clerk. Eventually, he entered another pub, this one a couple of degrees below the first in respectability. He moved into the back rooms of the establishment, and sat himself heavily at a table with other men. A game of cards ensued.

Helena was beginning to despair. It seemed as if all she was going to get out of this man was a tour of the most notorious pubs in London. Just as she was thinking this, he moved again, and, after turning a corner, they were by the riverside. This was more appropriate territory. He located a small boatyard and entered. Helena positioned herself in a way in which she could see what was happening: he was moving towards the adjacent building, using the boatyard as some sort of decoy. This was promising.

Helena realised that the people working would not flinch at her presence; there was simply too much going on. She kept close to the wall, and slowly worked her way to a small door that was connected to next door's commercial premises. There were a number of rooms, the first one containing some unused brewing equipment. There were voices in the next room. She moved on, trying to keep to the shadows. This wasn't like the busy boatyard next door: if they found her here they would drown her in the river.

She edged her way onwards, painfully slowly. There were boxes everywhere, more like storage than headquarters. Eventually she positioned herself by the doorframe. The thug was sitting at a table, talking with two other men who looked as dangerous as himself. They were talking routes, distribution, payments. Helena moved back, and considered again the boxes. Could she open one without being heard? It was worth a try. She had got this far and needed to know how this gang of criminals was connected to these cases. She moved around the room like a shadow, looking for a crate with a top already opened or dislodged. Here. Perfect.

She wasn't sure, not without running tests, and she took a small quantity in a pouch for later analysis. But it seemed to her that the crates contained hashish: enormous quantities of it.

24th March – Afternoon

'There is a little matter that we need to discuss.'

'Of course.' Miss Webster did not look worried in the slightest, and Helena wondered what she imagined it might be about.

Helena had now washed herself, and donned one of her own dresses that she kept at the agency. They had been going over Miss Webster's latest piece of research: after placing a foreign information request at the Patent Office Library in Chancery Lance, Miss Webster had confirmed that both Georges Méliès and Nikola Tesla had ongoing legal battles with Thomas Edison of Menlo Park, New Jersey. On her letter sent on the 20th of March from Paris, Eliza had reported on Méliès's creative and financial issues with Edison regarding copyright. Now, Jocasta had found that, as well as feuds involving patents, and violations of authorship in Tesla's case, there was also an unresolved financial issue that had been filed with the courts: Edison had failed to pay Tesla fifty thousand dollars for solving a major engineering problem for one of the American's electrical systems.

'Forgive my ignorance of American law, but I am frankly surprised that Mr Edison can legally do what Eliza explains, and simply show his competitor's films as if he has made them, pocketing all the proceedings,' said Helena.

'Well, his argument is that he owns the first American *patent* for the film-making equipment, and therefore he is somehow entitled to control all film production and showings in the country. I do not know a lot about the law either, but this sounds ridiculous to me,' explained Jocasta.

All this was very informative and useful, and worthy of addition to their casebook. Next Helena moved on to tackle the issue that she felt she needed to discuss:

'I am sure you realise that you seem to have gone from archivist to detective in a matter of days. As I said, a certain amount of research was to be expected in your role, hence my need for someone with your skills. I am happy to say that you are exceeding my expectations already.'

'It is kind of you to say so. But let me reassure you, I am not interested in praise. I find puzzles interesting, a challenge, very much like a game of chess.'

Helena indicated that Miss Webster ought to sit in the little chair that Helena kept for visitors by her desk.

The younger woman sat down. 'But. I'm expecting a "but". There is a "but", am I right?'

Helena sighed.

'Look, I have no right to ask about your private affairs,' Miss Webster's face went pale on hearing this, 'but I have been made to understand, from a rather reliable source, that your brother is in London, that he is a rather promising young man, academically speaking, and that he is putting his whole future in jeopardy by running along with a politically challenging crowd. Please, take this as a friendly – warning is perhaps a rather crude word – piece of advice?'

To Helena's surprise, Miss Webster seemed relieved at this.

'Oh, that...'

'And also, it may be better if I knew your real name.'

That did it. On hearing this, Miss Webster started breathing heavily and with difficulty.

'Are you alright?'

The younger woman could not speak, and Helena got up and crossed the room at a run to fetch the jug of water and the glasses that they had put on a silver tray for visitors.

'Here.'

Miss Webster drank. Slowly, she composed herself, but it was still a good couple of minutes before she could say anything.

'Who... who talked to you about us?'

'Scotland Yard.'

'Oh dear.'

Miss Webster got up, and started nervously pacing the room. Helena felt she ought to say something:

'Look, as I said, I have no right to demand any kind of explanation. But I need to know who I am employing. That is all. I am very happy to have Miss Jocasta Webster with us, for the foreseeable future. But, your brother... the possibility of that particular group ending in jail very soon was commented upon. Perhaps a raid is being planned at some point? Miss Webster,' she continued, 'forgive me, but I need to ask. Are you in any kind of trouble?'

'Only with my stepfather. He found out about my involvement with... a friend, another librarian.'

'I see.'

'He said he would lock me in the house. I had to flee. I need to be who I am.'

Helena crossed over towards Miss Webster, and posed her hand lightly on her arm.

'I understand that. I respect that. And your brother?'

'He is just playing revolutionaries. He could have gone back to Boston, but he is very proud. He told me about a new friend, some Cambridge don, and said that he didn't need to study maths back home.' Miss Webster was trying to contain the tears. 'They will find me.'

'Who?'

'The men my stepfather sent after me: Pinkertons. I haven't seen them in a while, not since the boat, but they will find me eventually. My only hope is that he gets bored and forgets all about me.'

Helena thought for a second. Then she said:

'Miss Webster, if I may. The Pinkertons are a rather efficient lot. Are you sure they followed you to London? I doubt they would not have caught up with you already. Is it possible that your stepfather has given up the search for you?' Miss Webster considered this for a second. Helena could see it: hope, as well as doubt, clouding her eyes. But she still looked scared. Helena continued: 'I've had an idea: why don't you and your brother go away for a while? My grandfather has a little house in Grantchester, a village next to Cambridge. You can stay there for a couple of weeks. No one will find you there: believe me, I have many contacts, and Cambridge and the villages that surround it are but a small area to cover. We would know at once if they decamp there. Meanwhile, your brother can enjoy the company of this maths don. What is his name, do you know?'

'Godfrey Hardy.'

'Doesn't ring a bell. But I am sure Grandfather knows him.'

Miss Webster calmed a little.

'One more thing: has your new… identity been compromised with these men, as far as you know?'

'I don't think so. I definitely saw them waiting for me when I alighted the boat, but I crossed under my real name. Stupid, I know.' Helena wondered how she could be sure of this, but let her speak. 'I took lodgings under this name, and they have not reappeared since then.'

'Why this name, if I may ask?'

'This is the name my brother adopted when he left the family – he was the first one of us who wanted to disappear. And my stepfather never bothered to go after him. I doubt he ever found out Jonas's new surname.'

'In that case, stick with it for now.'

Miss Webster nodded.

Helena told her to go back home, talk to her brother and start getting ready for their trip. She needed to telephone her grandfather. Before leaving, Miss Webster said:

'Jocasta is, in fact, my real name. So, maybe you can call me that for now?'

'It's good to know,' Helena said. The young woman did not move. 'Is there something else?'

'Maybe. I'm not sure. My stepfather is one of Mr Edison's financiers… I mean, this may be irrelevant to our case, as he is one of dozens, if not hundreds.'

'Yes? Forgive me, but I am not sure how we can use this, if you are not on good terms with him.'

'Well. He made Jonas, my brother, work in Menlo Park for a couple of summers. I wonder if he can tell us more about Mr Edison's affairs with both Mr Tesla, and Monsieur Méliès.'

'It's certainly worth a try. Thank you, Jocasta.' The young lady still did not move. 'Is there something else?'

'I am not sure if you are aware of this, but I've formed a friendship with Miss Lowry.' Helena nodded. 'This may not mean anything, but it has been nagging me for a while now. Remember when Miss Chaffins mentioned that the SPR was expanding their publishing business? Into fairy tales?' Helena nodded. 'She even mentioned the title of one of the books they were going to publish first.'

'Oh yes, I remember… *The First Little Haunted Fairy Book*, was it?' Woodbury would not be getting top marks for creativity, Helena thought. 'What about it?'

'Miss Lowry's notebook, one of the two that Miss Eliza recovered from her room. I noticed it the other day, while we were having tea. She had some of her writing things around her, she had been taking notes before I arrived. One of her notebooks was out, and had that title written across the marble-paper cover with ink. And then it had been crossed out, a single straight line right through.'

London, 25th March

Helena was sitting across from Mina at the back of Aurora's antique shop and the conversation had halted abruptly.

'Walton & Waltraud,' said Mina. 'It is not a usual name. Jocasta confirmed that it was indeed a Miss Eliza Waltraud.' Helena flinched. 'Please don't be upset with her. She didn't know of our past. She was merely confirming a name that I said out loud.'

'I apologise, Mina, I truly do. I should have come to see you days ago, in fact as soon as I knew what had happened. But I, we, have been extremely busy. And believe me, it was an honest joke of fate, nothing else.'

'I understand. I confess I was shocked when I confirmed

it. How likely was that? But then life sometimes brings you these surprises,' she concluded.

'You seem… extremely accommodating of all this.'

Now it was Mina's turn to surprise Helena.

'I am expecting, Helena. I am going to be a mother in the autumn. An event of this magnitude puts everything in perspective. Things long past, no matter how painful, find their level, and don't affect you as much.'

'That is a very sensible way of looking at things,' said Helena. She was surprised by the revelation, but it had nothing to do with her or the investigation. 'And, may I add: congratulations.'

'Thank you.' Mina served herself more tea. 'More? Yes? Excellent. I am sure, Helena, you have not come to talk about Eliza. I know she is in Paris now, so I imagine that many leads are being followed at present. Is there anything I can help you with?'

'In fact there is,' said Helena, who was impressed at Mina's no-nonsense approach; she had come a long way in a few days. There was no trace left of the nervous creature she had met in the agency. This Mina exuded confidence. This only made Helena more suspicious: Mina had not been entirely honest with her, and her demeanour made it obvious that she thought she was in control of the situation, and held all the cards in her hand.

'Before I go to Paris, I need to ask you a few more questions, things that have arisen in the course of our enquiries.'

'Of course, by all means.'

'I am curious: since your friend lived so close to Versailles, did you ever visit the palace, or walk in the Trianon Gardens?'

'Why do you ask?' she asked with a slight frown.

'Oh, just double-checking something, it probably means nothing.' Helena didn't enjoy lying to clients, but she was determined to get to the bottom of a couple of things, and the Trianon was one of them.

'Well, we went during my first visit, in early summer last year; we behaved very much as tourists then, and yes, we saw Versailles. But we didn't return during my second and last visit to Emily.'

Helena made a grimace: this was the first time Mina mentioned having been in Paris on two different occasions.

'And did you notice anything strange while you were there?'

'No, I didn't, but Emily was spooked by something that had happened to her in the gardens, and she insisted that we not go again.'

'What happened? Do you know?'

'It was during the visit of her friend Niko.' Tesla, thought Helena. 'They went there; he was testing some apparatus he had invented. She didn't gave me any more details, but, when I pressed her, she said that the machine had made her lose herself? She fainted, or something along those lines. She woke up back in her cottage. Niko did not really explain what had happened, only that the machine had something wrong with it.'

Helena had one sudden idea.

'Do you know when this took place, this visit with Niko?'

'Oh, he went there shortly after my first visit. It must have been around August, then?'

'August 1901?' asked Helena.

'Yes, that's correct,' confirmed Mina, sipping more tea.

Helena's heart missed a beat. This connected the misses and Tesla's inventions: indeed, one had apparently been tested in the gardens at the time when the two ladies were visiting the place. Did the ladies have their strange experience as a result of this testing, and was that the same day when Emily was 'spooked'? Could these two incidents be connected? They had to be. This had to be the bulb-activated contraption Eliza had written about.

'I am surprised you managed two visits within a year.' Helena was subtly asking, how could she afford this?

'Well, the second visit wasn't planned. But Emily's letters started becoming stranger. She was more and more scared at work – that much was obvious – and they hinted about strange happenings in the studio.' Helena knew: she had read the letters. 'The fraught state of Emily's mind was one of the reasons why I decided to pay her a second visit.'

'Do you have any idea as to why she was scared at work?'

'No, sorry, nothing clear.'

'But Niko wasn't there when you got to Paris that second time. Had he left any of his inventions with Monsieur Méliès, perhaps the one they had tested in the Trianon in the summer?'

'Yes, now that you mention it, Emily was furious with her boss. I think Méliès and Niko had fallen out over it. Something about Emily's boss borrowing it, and then not wanting to give it back.'

'I see. This is all most interesting. Thank you so much for your time.'

'Anything I can do to help, of course.'

'Mina, did you meet Monsieur Méliès during your stay?'

'Indeed I did! In fact, I worked on a little project for him. I am sorry, I didn't mention it before as I did not think it relevant.' Sure, thought Helena.

'And what were you doing for him?'

'Some research on French fairies: folklore and literature. I can try to remember in more detail, if you want, and put it in writing for you.'

'That may be useful, thank you. Did you meet any of his associates? Did you ever cross paths with a Mr Mathers?'

As if on cue, Mina put Aurora's delicate china cup on its saucer with a clatter. In a split second Mina was holding her belly, and bending down in pain.

'Here!' Helena's brief medical training kicked in. She made Mina lie down and put her feet up; then she asked where was the pain, doing a quick evaluation. 'I don't think it is the baby. Do not worry. I'll fetch you something for the pain.'

'No!' Mina was shouting in her direction. 'I don't want anything! I don't want to pollute my body and the baby's, please!'

Helena stopped in her tracks. What an extraordinary thing to say. And, much more, what a *Golden Dawn* thing to say! Somehow, Mina had given her alliance to the Dawn, then she had travelled to Paris, where she had got mixed up in the ritual substance-induced ways of the Paris chapter. It seemed that now she had managed to kick her habit, perhaps due to the baby, or at least was fighting with teeth and claws to do so.

Helena still wanted to help her, but she needed to press on. She hated this, but there was no other way to do so. She had to do it for Mina. She also had to do it for Eliza. It had been her fault that she had found herself in such a dangerous predicament in Mina's rooms; and now she had gone alone to Paris, perhaps with not enough experience to protect herself. They all needed to know: what other information might Mina be withholding? And what did that indicate about her possible role in all this? It was impossible that she may be involved in Emily's vanishing, for she was far too scared, and Helena was certain that she cared for her friend. The possibilities raced through Helena's mind in seconds, her detective training kicking in as beautifully as her medical one:

(a) Mina had been perhaps playing the detective herself, and, after reading about the misses' experience in Versailles, thought that they might hold the key to the mystery. Hence, she followed them, was followed herself, and stumbled upon the agency.

(b) Mina was working with whoever vanished Emily, and then got spooked, for what she'd done to her friend, or, indeed, what could now be done to her.

(c) Mina was connected with the Dawn, as simple as that. While working for Méliès she had met Mathers in Paris, and either been drawn into the Dawn, or forced to work for it. Mathers could even be the father of her child? That seemed too far-fetched. Perhaps she had been approached by the Dawn, or the SPR, to spy on her friend and her partner, in exchange for... what, exactly? What could Mina want that she didn't have, that the SPR could give her, and that made it worthwhile to betray a friend? Helena remembered Eliza's words: 'At that point, she was desperate. She would have sold her soul in exchange for getting published.' Then, she remembered Jocasta's words: her notebook. It all clicked beautifully. Jocasta was right, and the answer was staring at her.

Helena wanted to ask more, but waited for Mina to calm down. She had drunk some water, and was breathing more regularly.

'Are you feeling better? Shall I ring for the doctor?'

'No, no doctors!'

Helena could see now this particular puzzle in her mind's eye, its beautiful resolution: Mina must have accepted work from the SPR or the Dawn; had come to regret it; and, in a moment of lucidity, had decided to free herself from their clutches, putting herself in danger. But then, why not go straight to their enemies in Paris for help? Why not simply move to the other side?

It was (c). Mina had gone to Paris to work for Woodbury. But once there she had decided to work for Mathers instead, and sadly become addicted to some trance-induced substance. Mathers had probably asked her to keep an eye on Emily's comings and goings. In all probability, Mina did not think this was too bad. However, when Emily disappeared, Mina got cold feet about the whole thing, and started to feel guilty. It was clear what Helena needed to do: she put all this to Mina.

'Who is after you, Mina? Is it Mathers?'

The younger woman started crying loudly.

'It will be okay, Mina. I promise he won't find you, or the baby.'

It was obvious that she wasn't going to say much, but Helena took her silent acknowledgement of her facts as an admission of guilt. Finally, Helena felt she had solved this one particular riddle.

Aurora walked into the room then.

'Whatever has happened here? Is she alright? The baby…?'

'The baby is fine. Do you have anything herbal, at all, for her stomach? She needs something to help her with her withdrawal from those… substances.'

Aurora understood at once: 'Of course.' She went quickly to the kitchenette. A few minutes later she emerged with something foul-smelling, that she forced Mina to gulp down. As soon as she could move a little, the two women took her to bed. Soon Mina was soundly sleeping, all the nervous intensity of the scene a surge of energy that had burnt itself out as quickly as it had started.

Energy. Everything was, once again, connected to it. Who possessed it, what to do with it, who to share it with or not.

Helena had experienced different kinds of energy surges recently, like the one that burst out of her whenever she found herself close to O'Neill; who could say that there weren't other kinds of energies that did extraordinary things? It was all perfectly possible.

'Aurora, we need to talk. I need to know about Mathers.'

'Mathers?'

'Yes, Mathers.' Helena indicated the room where Mina slept with a movement of her head.

'You don't think that…'

'Yes, I do. And I think she fled him, and he is the one she has been hiding from.'

'Oh dear. I had assumed he would mellow with age! How disappointing.'

'What I need to know is, how dangerous is this man, from zero to ten?'

'I've no idea. I haven't seen him in years.'

'I believe you, of course. But what I cannot believe is that you don't have any information at all that could help us now. Mina is terrified.' She could see the guilt on Aurora's face. 'Please, anything you can think of. You know where to find me.'

Helena went directly home. She felt exhausted. The afternoon had taken a sour turn very quickly. But still she had made huge advances. What a pity that they had come at a cost to Mina.

London, 26th March

Helena did not have a good night. She kept turning in bed, feeling guilty. There was another feeling there, one as unwelcome. She had tried not to think about O'Neill and their night together. This had not been difficult: her work had kept her busy enough. She had had no time at all to think through what had happened, and now it was too late for reflecting. She could not help feeling slightly enervated that he had not been in touch, and felt somewhat upset by this. They were two adults who had shared something, perhaps that was all that had happened. She hated feeling like this. No, it was too late to let him wander into her head. She resolutely shook him out.

She decided she needed another busy day, and was already dressed and at the door when a hansom cab stopped in front of the house. She parted the little curtains, and looked through the entry-hall window. To her surprise, Aurora alighted. Before her friend had walked to the door and rung the bell, Helena opened the main door.

'Look what the cat dragged in…' she said, throwing the quip back at her friend, who smiled for all reply. 'Good morning.'

'Good morning. Are you leaving? I am so sorry for coming unannounced. Do you have time now?'

'I always have time for you,' Helena said, and gestured for Aurora to come in. They both took off their outer garments, and went and sat in the little sitting room where Helena did her card readings. Aurora sat heavily; she looked tired.

'I wanted to come as soon as possible. The poor child was writing this last night, ignoring my protestations.' She handed Helena a page:

Memorandum By Miss Carmina Lowry

I am writing this at the request of Miss Walton-Cisneros, although I am not sure how it may help in the investigation of the disappearance of Emily Peters. I am a writer by trade, I write mostly fairy tales and tales in the fairy fashion; and, after Emily introduced me to Mr Méliès, and explained what I do, he decided that my visit was providential, and that he could use my help, if I was at leisure. I am not ashamed to say that the fee he offered was handsome, but, more importantly, the assignment was interesting, at least for me.

He wondered if it was possible to believe in fairies in the modern era of electricity, and how to make an audience believe in them.

It is perhaps important to understand that the fairy tale in the French tradition was an educational tool as much as an entertainment one. Perrault's tales were written to reinforce moral codes, and, whenever women were present, to educate them about the expectations of their feminine roles. These tales had been in circulation from the sixteenth century onwards, with multiple editions of Perrault's works and Madame d'Aulnoy. Méliès was a fervent admirer of these tropes, as fairies were presented in these texts as a nostalgic look into France's rural past.

Mr Méliès wanted me to look into a very specific piece of fairy folklore: how to dispose of, or kill, a fairy. To be precise, his exact instructions were how to kill off a fairy, changeling, or someone 'turned into the wrong thing'. I had no idea such folklore existed, but agreed to look into it. I spent a very happy couple of mornings in the Bibliothèque National, and indeed located an answer for him: fairies could not be killed off by human hands; instead, they were thrown into caves underground when too bothersome; this in turn could have been the reason for the folklore associated with fairies living 'inside mountains'. Fairies needed to be tricked into going into these underground spaces, where they became lost in the dark, and could not come out again.

None of this satisfied him, and indeed he didn't pay me.

'I hope it is of some use?' asked Aurora.

'I am not sure yet, but thank you for bringing it in. And please thank Mina for writing it.' Still no acknowledgement of her connection to Mathers, Helena thought.

'I will do so.'

Helena said nothing else, allowing Aurora the time she needed to speak, and they sat together in companiable silence. Eventually her friend and mentor said:

'I am sorry I didn't mention my liaison with Mathers. As far as I knew, he was as removed from the Dawn as it was possible to be.'

'Rivals?'

'Exactly. But, you see, that was what made me think of something. Remember when I mentioned how much the Dawn thrives on drama?' Helena nodded. Aurora had mentioned that more than once in the last few days: 'I recalled something last night. Mathers was an incredibly jealous man, you know.'

'I see.'

'This may have been the reason Mina fled. But it also points at something else: if the Golden Dawn is after something, Mathers will want to get there first.'

Helena offered her theory about Mina, how she had been offered something she could not reject, by Woodbury.

'If Woodbury approached Mina,' suggested Aurora, 'and Mathers' London informants knew of this – don't look so surprised! I assure you the Paris and the London chapter of the Dawn keep a close eye on one another – it is no wonder at all if he came knocking as well. I imagine Mathers promised Mina much more than the publication of some stories.'

'Poor Mina. To find herself in the middle of these two…'

'Do you think it became too much for her?'

'It certainly ought to have contributed to her eventual decision to break free. Mathers vs. Woodbury? I cannot even start considering how unbearable it must have been.'

Helena thought about this. Perhaps once she found out she was pregnant, Mina thought closely about what she was doing, and sought a way out. She said:

'We have never had any doubt that she was following the misses – now we know why. She was acting under instructions.'

'Either Mathers' or Woodbury's…'

'Then, when she found herself in a detective agency, one that helped women, she felt it was providential, and acted on instinct.'

'She saw her chance to escape, and took it. It was an incredibly brave thing to do.'

'And don't forget what she said the night she met me: by then, she already knew she was being followed. Woodbury knew of her desertion, and had sent his thug. And now, taking this further step…'

'She was betraying both parties. My god, Helena!' Helena nodded. 'In that case,' continued Aurora, 'she's as good as dead.'

Helena briefly summarised the energy theory; she left O'Neill out of her narrative. She could not find within herself where exactly he fitted, not yet.

'The first time I came across Woodbury… the SPR, together with the Dawn, they were trying to resuscitate a source of energy by the Norfolk coast, something dangerous, which was hurting the environment. We put that to ground. But now, here we are, a year later, and they are involved in something similar. It is clear they *need* to find some new form of energy, for some occult purpose. Your theory of this making magic more potent now makes sense. But also,' she added, 'it would be a way of achieving all their goals…'

'Powerful magic, astral travelling, world domination…' put in Aurora.

'Exactly, without needing to resort to the hallucinogenic substances that the London chapter despises so much.'

'There is something else,' said Aurora.

Mina had kept one of the letters from Emily in her notebooks, as a personal keepsake. She had only admitted to this the night before, and gave it to Aurora to show Helena and include in her casebook. The two friends looked together at the letter.

Unsurprisingly, it was by far the strangest. It was sent to Mina shortly before she travelled to Paris for her visit, and it did not contain any reference to Méliès, or his mysterious friend Nikola, but a recipe for home-made ice cream, of all things, together with what looked like detailed instructions on how to build an ice-cream maker for home use. This, however, was described in the oddest language imaginable:

Please follow the steps below to make your ice-cream maker, and remember: ultimate success will depend upon the completeness of the study of the subject and the correctness of the observations, alerting to certain peculiarities of the phenomena.

i) *Replace the tinfoil coatings of the jar by rarefied gas and exciting luminosity in the condenser thus obtained by repeatedly charging and discharging it.*

ii) *The ice-cream maker consists of a large glass tube sealed at one end and projecting into an ordinary incandescent lamp bulb. The primary well-insulated copper sheet is inserted within the tube. This forms the apparatus.*

iii) *As to the number of turns which gives the best result, it is dependent on the dimensions of the apparatus.*

iv) *Before the disruptive discharge takes place, the tube or bulb is slightly excited and the formation of the luminous circle is decidedly facilitated. To excite luminosity in the tube it is not absolutely necessary that the conductor should be closed.*

v) *A curious phenomenon may be observed; namely, two intensely luminous circles, each of them close to a turn of the primary spiral, forming inside of the tube, and connected by a faint luminous spiral parallel to the primary and in close proximity to it.*

vi) *It may also be noted that when the primary touches the glass the luminous circle is more easily produced and is more sharply defined. But the circles are always in close proximity to the primary and are considerably easier to produce when the latter is very close to the glass.*

vii) *I think that the feeble luminous effect referred to has been noted by many cooks, but in my ice-cream maker the effects were much more powerful than those usually noted.*

Signed: N.T.

They looked at each other.

'What on earth is this?' asked Helena.

'I have absolutely no idea. But let me tell you what it is not, for sure: instructions on how to build an ice-cream maker. It looks like instructions for something else, to build something that would produce, or release, an otherworldly amount of energy, perhaps?' suggested Aurora.

The two friends left together, and shared a hansom into town. Helena alighted in Marylebone, and Aurora went on, enigmatically saying she 'had a call to make'. Helena went up the stairs to the new offices. She knew Jocasta would not be there, and dreaded a whole day on her own. She would be travelling to Paris that night, and needed to organise her casebook and tie a few loose ends. That would surely keep her occupied: she didn't want a certain person to creep into her thoughts. Just as she was thinking about this, still removing her jacket and bonnet, the bell rang, and she walked over to the front door. She opened it to a boy, with the biggest bouquet of white flowers that she had ever seen.

'Helena Walton... *Zisnegos?*' he asked, unsure of the pronunciation.

'Thank you.' She collected the flowers and went back inside. The first thing that came to her mind was that they could be a threat: they looked a lot like funeral flowers. Then she saw the card. It was unsigned, and simply said: 'To my endearing friend.' For once, she did not have a theory about this.

Paris, 24th March – Afternoon

Alice was as good as her word: she had found a place where they could see the film they had found in the cottage. She took Eliza to a small empty theatre, where one of her friends had set up the camera-projector for her.

Once again, the light flickered, Eliza secretly hoping this was the last time she would have to witness those shadowy images.

The image revealed a dark space, some sort of lamp showing its roundness. Eliza thought it was a chapel, until Alice announced, 'The catacombs!' And then Eliza saw it, the back wall in which hundreds of skulls, placed one on top of the other, rested.

They both tried to interpret the images: three people appeared on the screen and were positioned in what Eliza interpreted to be the north, east and west. A man in robes said some words, and everyone bowed. Then he fell convulsing to the floor. Another man, dressed as some kind of officiant, passed a knife over the palm of his own hand, and poured blood on a woman. The woman disappeared – at first she was there, and then not.

'Good trick!' commented Alice, approvingly. 'It was seamless: faultless even.'

Now, the first man started hovering in mid-air, while everyone around him threw their hands up to praise the miracle. Presently, the others fell to their knees.

'Do you think Méliès shot this?' asked Eliza.

'Absolutely. It has all his trademarks. Think about the elaborate arrangement of the scenery. Georges always relies on costumes, sets and all the illusionist tricks he can dream of.'

'But, are you saying we just saw a fiction?' she asked.

'What else?'

'I think it looked like a ritual, a filmed ritual.'

Alice laughed. 'Are you joking? Someone vanished! And another flew in mid-air.'

Precisely, thought Eliza. Had Alice been asleep during all the days she had helped her? She had shared with her every idea, every suspicion, every clue.

The filmmaker realised Eliza was put off by her reaction, and said: 'Listen, I think I know where this place in the catacombs is.'

'What? How?'

'I have seen it before, I am sure of it. I think we ought to go there.'

'What will we gain? We may get lost.'

'We won't. I know how to find my way down there. It's exactly like you said: this is about putting a puzzle together. What if we find something down there that makes sense?'

Rather reluctantly, Eliza agreed.

It was one thing to imagine going down the Paris Catacombs, another thing entirely to actually do so. The dark wasn't the worst, but the sense of damp, the smell of rot. They both covered their noses and mouths with handkerchiefs. They hadn't walked for long before Eliza thought that she had no idea where they were, or how she was going to get back if she lost sight of Alice. And the filmmaker was not waiting for her.

'This way! Come now, Eliza!' and she was gone after a turning, only to emerge at the last second in which Eliza had been about to scream for her. 'Come on! Follow me!' And again, she pressed on, Eliza slowly trying to find her way. The floor was uneven; it was difficult to walk in the dark, and she was falling behind.

'Alice! Wait, please!' Nothing. Then, Alice would appear, a smile on her face.

'You *are* slow!' she protested.

Alice was not going slower, and, at times, Eliza was only following the sound of her steps and the orange flicker of the torch ahead.

They had arrived in the area where the ritual, or the movie, was filmed, deep in the catacombs. It was a circular room, with several openings into the darkest corridors she had ever seen. Eliza was not thrilled that Alice held the only source of light for them both. She trusted her, but she could get lost anyway. Why had she not insisted on carrying her own? Some nagging instinct was telling her that had been a really stupid mistake. *Instinct…* She thought of Helena, and missed her. She would be proud of her, she thought, even if her instincts were telling her something was not right. And then it dawned on her:

'Alice, how did you know of this place?'

She smiled at this.

'I told you: I've done all sorts of things for Georges. No one would finance my movies, because I am a woman.'

'I know. I am sorry. Did you shoot that movie?'

Alice did not reply. Somehow this was far scarier than having had a shouting match.

They heard a noise nearby, and Alice popped her head into the utter darkness of one of the corridors. Someone, or something, came charging at them, out of nowhere. A woman shining the purest green, with long yellow teeth, terrifying red eyes and a disproportionately large jaw. Or at least this is what Eliza saw before fainting on the spot.

13

ON THE NATURE OF MAGIC

Paris, 29th March

There was a certain light that hung close to the window. If Eliza squinted, it moved, gaining consistency. Then, a face emerging.

The translucent head, elegant, with a long white neck and a horrid dead smile, looked like no one she had ever seen. As the lady vanished in mid-air, Eliza semi-consciously wondered whether it was the elusive Lirriper ghost who had come to pay her a visit. She fell asleep again, dozing into oblivion. Things continued like that for what felt like a long time. In reality Eliza had been ill for a couple of days, seriously ill for another two or three before that. It had been touch and go for some horrid hours; but thankfully she was not aware of this. Only weeks later, on receipt of a letter from two Misses Winningham, she would realise this fully. When the fever finally broke, she woke up to a strange bed, clammy limbs, her nightdress stuck to her body. She did not know where she was. In close proximity to her unknown bed, a wash-basin, dirty clothes on the floor around it, some vases filled with unknown potions. The general shape of the room, the wallpaper, the particular tone of the wood in the furniture, made her conclude that she was still in France. Paris, then. It was an anonymous room, but things had that certain suggestion of foreign places, alternative ways of approaching the same daily tasks and objects. This was an acute observation; she didn't know yet, but she was turning into a detective. Otherwise, the anonymous room could have been anywhere, belonged anywhere.

There was no one in the room. She was alone.

She spent some time like that, and then she dozed again. She longed to get up, clean herself, change her sweaty garments. But she could also recognise a particular tiredness that anchored her body: her legs in pain, from toes to knees, heavy as after a hike, a heaviness mixed with a certain amount of ache.

A memory flared of her mother, who used to say that she could never reply to doctors about whether she was in a little or too much pain. How to know that? When you had gone through childbirth, anything seemed like a lesser pain.

The pain seemed to be concentrated mostly around her hands, and she considered them: they were bandaged, and she could see a little blood seeping through the white. She followed the same pain, and pulled up the sleeves of her nightdress to reveal small cuts and bruises on her forearms. She had no recollection at all of how she had got those.

The door opened, and a face flashed up and left promptly. Then Eliza knew that she was in the Lirriper, as she thought she recognised one of the little maids who helped at the establishment. But she wasn't in her room; that much was certain.

The next faces were more welcome: the two Misses Winningham entered the room, and approached her bed.

'We are so glad you are finally awake! My dear Eliza, we have been so worried.'

And then her sister added:

'There is someone here who flew to be by your side as soon as she heard what had happened. Let us not be suspenseful: it is Helena!'

Eliza had hardly any time to accept the news when Helena appeared by the door, with much fuss trying to suggest that she should rest, and they would talk later. But a sense of urgency was overpowering Eliza.

'Please! I have rested quite enough, I think. Can you please let me know what has happened?'

'We'll leave you two to get on with it, but do let us fetch you something to eat first. What would you prefer? Sweet or savoury?'

Eliza realised she was in fact very hungry. The misses left the room to arrange food with Mrs Lirriper, and Eliza and Helena were now alone.

'You should really be proud of yourself. It is outstanding what you have achieved here, on your own, and in such a short space of time,' Helena began. Eliza could see her casebook open on the mahogany desk, and guessed that Helena had been making herself acquainted with its contents. She flinched at her partner's words.

'That may be so, but…' she started.

'But what?'

'I feel like an idiot. Did Alice leave me there?'

'Not exactly… We don't know. Alice is missing.'

Eliza's stomach contracted at this.

'How was I found?'

'They found you unconscious at one of the catacomb's street entrances, close to the Louvre, feverish and making no sense. But it was clear that someone, or perhaps even yourself somehow, had dragged you there, to that particular entrance, precisely in the hopes that you would be seen by some passer-by and rescued. The small cuts all over your hands and your arms, and the state of your clothes, seem to confirm that theory.'

Eliza processed this information.

'And how did I get here?'

'Luckily, you were carrying a piece of paper with the Lirriper's address and monogram, and the gendarmerie brought you here.'

'Do you think it was Alice who brought me to the entrance?'

Helena flinched.

'I don't think so, Eliza. New information has emerged in the past few hours. It looks like Alice was secretly working with Thomas Edison to sabotage some of Méliès's productions. We think that Edison promised to produce her movies, promised her a career in America.' Helena let this sink in. 'I'm sorry, I did send you to Alice. I arranged that she would help you. This is all my fault. Again.'

Eliza considered this. Helena got up and said:

'There is much that I need to explain. But I will leave you to rest now.'

Eliza could sense that there were far more horrid revelations than Alice's potential betrayal and flight.

'Look, Helena. I am fine. And I don't want to wait in this bed. I want to hear it all. Now.'

'Very well.'

She was called Philothée Gaimard, and she was a young woman in her early twenties. By the time she had stumbled upon Eliza's unconscious body at the catacombs entrance, she had already formed a theory of her own.

'We've had a very long chat. It seems that we are investigating the same occurrences, and that perhaps our preliminary conclusions coalesce with her findings. In fact, once I got her to trust me, and we put together the information we had, it was clear to both of us that our findings not only matched, but in many instances filled the gaps of each other's.'

Helena went on to explain about the green light, the machine, and Philothée's observations of the dancers. She crossed the room to the desk, and took Eliza's casebook in her hands.

'By then, I had read your observations; in fact, I could now understand better some of the facts you relayed in your letters.'

Eliza felt a pang of guilt. There hadn't been many letters. Time seemed to have gone so fast once she found herself in what Helena called 'the field'. She apologised.

'I understand – there wasn't much time at all to write to each other, and for the letters to cross the Channel! But putting together what you sent, and what you collected for us here, I have been able to complete the picture I was forming with my own findings, and that picture seems to match Mademoiselle Gaimard's almost like for like.'

Helena now put to Eliza that the machine, and the green light, had some unexpected effect on the dancers; the same dancers that Eliza had mentioned as 'vanishing' in her first letter after talking to Millie, her predecessor at Méliès' studio.

'Note this, Eliza: vanishing. Exactly like Miss Peters,' she pointed out, and then continued: 'The reason why Méliès was interested in his friend's invention is because it rendered his "effects" more realistic, in particular the flying trick. However, the machine had not yet been properly tested, and it also had unexpected effects on the dancers. While he was here, Mr Tesla tried to fix it, and took it for a test run far away from the Studio, to the ample gardens at Versailles. He was trying to figure out what the problem was. The machine's primary role is to be an emitter of energy, of source unknown. Unfortunately, something else happened.'

Eliza let this information sink in.

'Are you saying that there is a… *scientific reason* for… No, wait. Are you saying that the misses *did* look into a portal open to the past? And that *a machine* did that?'

'Talk about the murky ways in which science and magic may be confused with each other, interact with each other,' observed Helena. 'Whatever happened in Versailles was due to the faulty machine. Mr Tesla was trying to fix it, but didn't manage before returning to America. Despite the problems, and Tesla's warnings, Méliès at some point got his hands on the machine, and refused to give it back.'

Eliza could see the story unveiling in front of her: the problems with this strange energy emitter, both in the way it generated energy by secret means, and by Méliès's failing to control its power, seemed to have been at the centre of what had happened at Versailles and Star Film Studio.

'How do you know all of this?'

'Here.' Helena brought a black leather journal over to the bed. It was singed at the corners, as if someone had tried unsuccessfully to burn it.

'This journal belongs to Mr Nikola Tesla. Mademoiselle Gaimard found it in Georges Méliès's house. We don't know how Méliès got hold of it, but he probably stole it. He must have been trying to figure out how to solve the machine problems as well.' Helena gave it to Eliza, who saw several pages marked with pieces of paper. She went from one marked entry to the next, and read:

JOURNAL, MR NIKOLA TESLA.
FOUND BY PHILOTHÉE GAIMARD

[No dates, just a series of entries. N.B. The beginning of the journal nevertheless states Paris, August 1901]

[*Entry #1*]

I am back in Paris! Beloved city!

How much I have missed the City of Light! How much I love this city.

It seems that my good friend G. invited me here in order to ask, once again, if he can borrow the Electromagnetic Tesla Battery. He insists he wants to try his idea in his filming, although I have impressed on him its higher purpose. I am completely sure that my electromagnetic technology will bring peace to the world. Why? Because it is, quite simply, the most ingenious invention ever devised by a human being. Once energy is free for everybody, available for everybody, without the need for faulty wires, without the limitations imposed by coal, a revolution will start! I will bring stability and peace to the world.

But I cannot put him off any longer. He has been so good to me.

[*Entry #2*]

G. reports strange happenings when using the machine, unexpected effects!

Problems: there is something wrong with the energy flow. The particles behave in an unexpected fashion. I needed to look into this. G. seems not bothered by this, wants to borrow the machine anyway. But he fails to understand its power!

I took the machine for a test. We got to the gardens at dusk. Miss E. was with me. Such a sweet creature.

I write the following as honestly as I can, for I am finding French lunches quite heavy. But, equally, there was nothing expressly wrong with me, and I certainly do not scare easily.

I switched on the machine.

Then E. stopped being there. There is no other way of writing this: she disappeared, right in front of me – a sort of window appeared where she had stood, showing me another world! Then the portal disappeared, and she was back. I asked if she had gone elsewhere, perhaps to the world inside the portal. But she would not tell me. She was understandably scared, would not sleep in the same building as the machine, so I had to take it back to G.

I have reported all of this to G., to make sure he understands that he cannot use the machine anymore.

[Entry #3]

I have diligently registered my inventions and discoveries in the Office of Patents, and I have been assured that the irrevocable rights to exploit those patents remain with me. However, it is also truth that judicial enterprise is so slow and could last years, according to G. and his unveiled threats; with the result that, meanwhile, anyone can exploit your efforts, establish themselves in the collective mind as the true father of advances that others have dreamed up first... One thing is to take my scientific advances, like Marconi did with his odious telephone, and another very different would be to put people in danger!

But G. does not want to return the machine. Only God knows what will happen.

I cannot stay here any longer. Building my Tower is now the priority, and I haven't managed to secure funding from many *sources. I leave, and who knows what I will find on my return. But there is nothing to be done – the next few months will be crucial.*

Eliza had finished reading, and Helena continued:

'We ought to lean towards the theory that the production of energy is what the Dawn is after; and that this green light is either a signal that the energy is happening, or a by-product of it.'

'In that case,' Eliza suggested, 'if the "time-slip" was in itself a by-product of this generation of energy, it may just have happened by chance.'

'Probably. What we know is this: the Dawn invited the misses to the autumn equinox, and asked about what happened in Versailles, at a time when they had not made their accounts public. Let's not worry now about how they got their hands on the incident: the case is, they learnt about it somehow. This obviously shows that they must have had some interest in their experience: otherwise, why bother? As the women did not want to play ball – that is, share what they saw – they sent their hounds, the SPR, to discredit their story.'

Eliza considered this.

'The misses got off lightly, considering,' continued Helena. 'Their experience was brief: one specific thing happened to them. The dancers were not so lucky. Their continued exposure to the green light would eventually damage them irreparably.'

'You mentioned that George wanted the machine to perfect his… "flying trick"?' asked Eliza. Helena nodded. 'What exactly did the machine do?'

Helena was now holding Eliza's own casebook.

'I think you know the answer to that, Eliza. You saw the machine in action yourself. You went to find the source of the light. Frankly, the observations of Mademoiselle Gaimard and yours are so close as to give credibility to each other.'

'Are you saying that… the ladies were really flying?'

Helena smiled. She did not give a direct reply.

'And then, what? It turns them into white rabbits ready for the magician's hat?' Eliza's tone wasn't entirely mocking. She sounded confused. Helena came to the rescue.

'What happened in the studio, while shooting the films, is not important. What we need to find out is how it is connected with the dancers vanishing. What were the secondary effects of exposure to this unknown source of energy?'

'Very well. But we have nothing, do we?'

Helena smiled.

'We may have nothing. But I did say that Mademoiselle Gaimard had… her theories.'

'Wait a second. Why was she investigating this as well? You have not explained to me who she is, where she comes from.'

Helena quickly summarised Mademoiselle Gaimard's connection to Star Film Studio, and her work for the Matherses.

'As you can imagine, she has been in the middle of it all. It has taken a toll on her, I dare say.'

'And *what is* her theory?'

Helena briefly conveyed the Matherses' performative and artistic brand of magic, and how this led Mademoiselle Gaimard to first assume that dancing itself was the key.

Were the dancers under any kind of spell, she wondered? She knew dancing was important for Moina Mathers in the performance of her rituals, but it wasn't all that was needed to transcend in this manner. The Isis Cult, the Parisian chapter of the Dawn, routinely uses drugs to enhance their trances and mystical experiences. In fact, this was a major reason for their break with the London Dawn. As far as Philothée knew, there was absolutely no substance-taking in the studio, but she wondered: was there a drug present, perhaps in any other form?

'The green light?'

'It is possible. Maybe some element in their performance, together with exposure to the light, took them too far in their… let's call it "trance", and some of them could not return later: Mademoiselle Gaimard had seen Samuel's and Moina's trances, aided by vapours, and drugs, and aromatic essences – what they call "journeying from the organically visible to spiritual vision". Who said that was not what happened to them as well? And what if that process went wrong?'

'Okay, so they experienced some… moment of transcendence when exposed to this energy?'

'Correct.'

'Forgive me, but all of this sounds a little far-fetched.'

'It is possible; but you yourself noted the strange effects that the machine had on you, and furthermore, that Méliès's body of work had on you. You wrote to me, after seeing the misses, about how the green light disgusted you. You mentioned a feeling of attraction mixed with dislike. Eliza, your instincts were correct. The dancers were being influenced by this energy in the most horrid fashion.'

'Yes, but flying?'

'We have another testimony now: "suddenly her rope broke, but she never reached the floor. Monsieur Méliès, *le patron*, he gave us a talk about some advance emergency levers that he had fitted himself. But no one had seen him doing it, or any emergency pulley activated."' Helena read.

'Where is that from?'

Helena did not reply immediately. 'All in good time. We have more pressing matters now. But before we go down, so you can meet Mademoiselle Gaimard, and we can decide what to do next, I need to apologise to you.'

Eliza was surprised to hear this. But that wasn't all.

'I am exceedingly sorry to admit to this, but I am not sure I trust Aurora completely. Recent happenings have confused me a great deal about where her loyalties stand. She went back to the Vernal Equinox this year, in order to help me get in and observe; now, that was helpful. But, on reflection, how did she walk in there as if nothing had happened? She had been protesting for a while that they had been inviting her for years, and she had always refused to go. She said something about "gracing them with her presence" to finally get rid of them, a very Aurora remark. But I am not sure that is all the truth.'

'Are you saying that she has stayed connected to the Dawn?'

'That is what I think, what my instincts tell me.' Again, the instincts, thought Eliza. But Helena was in fact getting at something a bit different. She went on to recount everything:

about the little chiming bells, waking up flustered, her instincts enhanced after each event. Eliza listened in silence.

'This has been happening for some time now. It has helped me, at times, to figure things out, to realise things. Like now, with Aurora.'

'I knew it. I knew that something was going on.'

'There is more.' Helena continued: 'Aurora tried to make me believe that she was "getting back at the Dawn" in order to help us. But she knows far too much of what is going on. Not just in London, but also in Paris.'

'The Matherses?'

'Precisely. She was involved with Samuel, perhaps with Moina too. She is very up to date with everything that has been happening on both sides of the Channel.' Helena paused. She got up from the side of the bed and started pacing the room. 'I considered that she somehow managed to keep herself informed via her old connections, but she is too well-acquainted for that. In fact, before coming here, I sent Miss Webster and her brother Jonas – that is a tale for some other day, believe me – to Cambridge, to a little house my grandfather owns in Grantchester. At the last minute, we went and packed all Mina's belongings, and I sent her with them.' She paused, and looked through the window to the overcast street. 'Aurora was furious when she found out.'

'But, why send Mina away?' Helena could hear the trepidation in Eliza's voice.

'I am afraid I may have put Mina in danger myself: Aurora and I discovered that she had kept a letter, as security. I'm sure you realise what it contained: the instructions for building a machine, a powerful machine.'

Helena quickly summarised her theory about Mina's involvement, including her pregnancy; that she had put to the young woman everything she had done, and how Mina had not denied any of it.

They were silent for a minute while Eliza processed all this.

Eventually, Helena said: 'Miss Lowry has had a terrible time. We ought not to be too harsh with her. When we are back, we are going to have to help her settle somewhere quiet, help her put all this behind her.'

Eliza nodded, and said: 'I don't understand, why exactly is she in danger?'

'What is this machine? The one you found, or perhaps an innovation from it, much more powerful? Whatever it does, this machine is extremely valuable, so much so that people are willing to kill to get their hands on that letter.' Eliza looked up. 'Don't worry, Mina is not in danger now. But my thinking is that she fled first the SPR, to fall on Mathers' mercy, and then fled Mathers himself, and now she is a poor lost lamb.' Another pause, and she turned around to look at Eliza. 'I don't think that Aurora would do anything to put Mina, or any of us, in danger, I want to be clear about that. But until she decides whose side she is on, fully, I think we ought to remove her from our operations.' Eliza wanted to smile, but contained herself.

'I'm sorry,' she said. It was a generous remark.

'You saw through the incongruities far earlier than I did.

It is I who am sorry, Eliza. I should have listened to you. And now Thomas Edison and the feud.'

'I did not think it mattered much,' Eliza said.

'I think you are right; however, it was a small but significant piece of the puzzle. If we had dug deeper, we might have understood Alice's position in all this. Besides, Eliza, it is possible that Edison was hoping to get his hands on Tesla's letters as well, or at least on anything that would place him above his competitor.'

Jonas Webster had worked for Thomas Edison while a student. The young man seemed to have met Mr Tesla, and they had liked one another.

'I got him to write me a memorandum about Tesla and Edison.'

'What did we find out with that?'

Helena summarised:

'Edison is the reason Méliès and Tesla know each other, even before their legal problems. Mr Tesla's first job was working for Mr Edison in Paris, where he became friends with Méliès. Tesla was so remarkable that Edison brought him to his labs in Menlo Park. Tesla spent nearly a year in Edison's lab in Menlo Park. Then followed the dispute Jocasta discovered: Edison and Tesla falling out over some unpaid services to the tune of fifty thousand dollars.'

'That is a vast amount of money.'

'Eventually, he founded his own company, and started working on a system of generation and transmission of electricity different from Edison's. He has had many successes, providing electricity to the city of Buffalo by alternating current, a system opposite to Edison's. By 1890 three hundred electrical stations were using the system.'

'I guess Edison did not like this.'

'This was when the whispering campaign, the plan to discredit Tesla, began in earnest. Edison did not lose time in launching his attacks. He publicised the fact that the alternating current needed thousands of volts, and it was therefore dangerous. Edison seems to have a flair for publicity, and staged several showcases in his laboratory in which he "demonstrated" this. In front of journalists, politicians and other curious people, they electrocuted several dozen dogs, lambs and even horses, claiming that they were using Tesla's energy system. But of course he wasn't.'

'What? That is sick!'

'It is worse than sick. But all of this is theatrical. The important thing for our case, Eliza, something that young Jonas impressed on me, is the fact that Mr Tesla's methods for generating energy are not very well understood, at all. Take this for example: a few years ago Tesla lectured all over London and Paris, in places with top-notch scientists,' she consulted her notes, 'the Royal Institution, the Institute of Electrical Engineers, and the Société Française de Physique in Paris. He generated a lightning bolt, which then transmitted more than 20,000 volts through his own body of alternating current. Since the energy needed to execute someone in the Electric Chair is a mere 2,000 volts, this created a commotion in the scientific community. Alternating current is safe, but Mr Tesla was less concerned with explaining that than with getting a performative effect. Even if the principles behind it are completely scientific, most of the people believed they were witnessing a magic performance.'

'What genius! And how stupid!' claimed Eliza.

'That "connection" to something seemingly occult, although untrue, constitutes good grounds for discrediting him. And then, young Jonas pointed out something else entirely, something that has obviously affected Tesla's ability to gain funding and investors. Something beyond eccentric.'

'What is it?'

'He seems to have been trying to find an energy so powerful that he would be capable of talking with the Beyond. Or even with civilisations that he believes may exists on other planets. Yes, Eliza. He claims all he wants is to help humanity, that his objective is to be able to offer free energy to anyone on the planet. But, believe me, his reasons are altogether more sinister.' She paused. 'Since 1899, Tesla has been doing research in a lab in Colorado. He uses a tower that is a reduced version of one he intends to build in Long Island. In July 1899 he claimed to have received a signal from Mars.' She let this sink in. Eliza was not moving, following the tale intently. 'I visited the offices of the Wardenclyffe Tower in London. The SPR series programme that your thug lost, that was what put us on the scent of this.'

'And what does this tower do?'

'We are not sure. Increasing energy, whatever this energy is or comes from. In view of the particulars we have investigated in this case, this seems to me entirely dangerous. I have instructed young Jonas to write to Mr Tesla in our name, and to explain to him our findings, in the hope he might reconsider. They only started construction of the tower in December of last year, so there is a long way to go, either to improve things, or to scrap it altogether.'

Eliza took a moment to take all this new information in.

'All of this is very interesting indeed, and I can see how everything is connected, all the work that we have done, together and separately.' Helena was nodding. 'And I look forward to meeting Mademoiselle Gaimard, and to thank her for saving my life.'

'But? I sense there is a but there, somewhere, about to pop up...'

'But. I am glad we have an answer for the misses. Somehow. I still don't understand very well these... scientific experiments of Mr Tesla. But we have failed in one major way, Helena. We are not any closer to knowing where Miss Peters may be. We know nothing of her fate, what could have happened to her. Surely, you agree that a life is more important than the reputation of two people, even if they happen to be the greatest authorities in female education in England. What? Is there something else? I know that look.'

'I haven't told you the most important thing of all. It went completely out of my mind!' Helena put her hands inside the pockets of her skirt, and took out a small folded piece of paper, which now she handed to Eliza. 'You were found with this, clutching it for dear life! Even unconscious, the Misses

Winningham had so much trouble getting you to let go of it!'

Eliza took the paper and unfolded it. It was a crude drawing of a flying lady, very similar to the ones in Emily Peter's cottage, but dirty and almost rotten after its stay in the catacombs.

'I trust you know what it is – I have read your casebook twice. I also recognised it myself: some of Emily's letters had drawings like this.' She paused, obviously affected by what she was about to say: 'Méliès's discarded dancers. Those who were so affected by the green light that they may not be entirely human anymore… We are working on the theory that Méliès takes them deep into the catacombs, and leaves them there.'

'Does this mean… what I think it means? He did it to Emily too?'

'She knew too much, about the machine and its uncanny effects. She needed to be disposed of, and I guess Méliès is not a killer. I think we need to contemplate the theory that Miss Peters has… ended up there, with the missing dancers. That means that we have to go back, Eliza. We need to go back to the catacombs to finish this. Don't worry, you do not need to come.'

Eliza practically jumped out of bed.

'What? No. I am definitely coming.'

Helena beamed. She felt so proud. To have ever thought that Aurora was brave, when the bravest by far of them all had been Eliza all along.

'Very well. I will be downstairs with Mademoiselle Gaimard. Come down whenever you are ready, and we can discuss our next move.'

Helena exited the room and Eliza dressed herself the fastest that she had ever done so in her life.

Mademoiselle Gaimard had told Helena that she was twenty-one, but Eliza had serious doubts about this. She looked fifteen. Which probably meant that she was somewhere in between, perhaps seventeen or eighteen years old. Now, torch in hand, her face illuminated by the orange light of the flames, she looked even younger. But Eliza had to hand it to her: she did not look scared in the slightest, at least not as much as Eliza herself was feeling.

'Miss Eliza, do you recognise this turn?' They had walked through the same entrance close to the Louvre where she had found Eliza two days previously, and now she was guiding them to the area that Mademoiselle Gaimard claimed was used by the Isis Cult for some of their rituals. 'I have been here before, more than once, with the Matherses,' she explained.

'It is difficult to say,' conceded Eliza. She looked around hopelessly. She felt useless; all the twists and turns looked exactly the same to her.

But Mademoiselle Gaimard was advancing confidently, and Helena and Eliza had little option but to follow her.

'*Le Royaume des Morts,*' she commented. The Kingdom of the Dead.

It was eerie down there. Whole walls, metres and metres of it, were covered in skulls piled high in the manner of bricks. Now and again, huge crosses with names and strange ornamentation broke the symmetry of the horrid angular grinning things. It was good that they were advancing cautiously but with certain speed, as Eliza did not dare look at them to take note of the names of who had ended up buried down there. *What a stupid thing*, she thought. The crosses weren't many in comparison with the hundreds, thousands of people, each of them represented by a skull, that had ended up in the horrid place. She could taste, as the first time she had descended with Alice, the intense smell: of earth, and of rot, and of the burning torches, all mixed up together, choking her throat. Ahead of her, both Helena and Philothée walked with the security of those who knew what they were doing. But Eliza was feeling out of her depth. Perhaps she was still tired from her recent ordeal. Perhaps she was not built for a life of detection. In the past couple of weeks, this thought had insisted on coming into her head. She did not know how she would communicate this to Helena.

'I don't understand,' Helena was saying. 'My contact in the gendarmerie assured me that Miss Peters' drawing was enough to mobilise them to come, and I explained which entrance they should take, as per Mademoiselle Gaimard's instructions.' Mademoiselle Gaimard stopped to look at Helena. 'Why on earth are they not here?'

'That,' the Frenchwoman said, 'is a very good question indeed,' and she continued walking ahead. Something told Eliza that she probably knew more than she was letting on. Was the police connected with some of the occult societies? It was possible. 'This way,' Mademoiselle Gaimard was now indicating.

They followed her into a new turn, and came up to a room. It was a round chamber. But here, contrary to the corridors they had just left behind, now eaten up by the darkness, there was not a dirt floor, but a crude round space covered by cement.

'Look,' Mademoiselle Gaimard bent down, and turned her torch to it, revealing marks. She moved the flames slowly, and Eliza could see it: a pentagram of some kind, with a myriad of symbols and letters, was carved onto the cement.

'What goes on here?' asked Helena.

'Believe it or not,' said Mademoiselle Gaimard, 'it is almost innocent – chants that take hours, long hours.'

'For what purpose?' interrupted Eliza.

Mademoiselle Gaimard looked at her, and responded with one word: 'Power. Nothing else and nothing more.'

Eliza laughed. It all sounded so basic; but for some, she knew, those chants would be of the utmost importance. Mademoiselle Gaimard was now up, looking through all the openings that communicated the circled chamber into adjacent corridors. She considered them all, went back to some of them a couple of times. At last she announced:

'This way.'

Helena moved at once, but Eliza asked, 'Are you sure? All those openings look the same to me. Where exactly are you taking us?'

'Exactly where I said I would. The place where I saw the woman.' The woman who, they all now suspected, might be one of the missing dancers.

They passed into the new corridor. Eliza shivered; she was conscious of how much further away they were getting from the entrance, and of the fact that she could not get back there on her own. This realisation brought a sort of vertigo over her. She stopped abruptly, refused to advance.

'Eliza, are you quite well?' asked Helena. The younger woman had started to breathe loudly. She signalled around them with difficulty.

'This corridor divides itself into ten or fifteen new partings. How can we be sure we know where we are going?'

Helena nodded, and took a step back.

'Leave that to me,' she announced. She took a pendant from under her dress, a long piece of carved quartz that had been resting on her bosom. It was the most striking blue that Eliza had ever seen, but within it seemed to shine with multiple colours beyond blue, even in the unfathomable dark where they found themselves.

Helena grabbed the rock tightly with her left hand, her right still holding her torch. She started muttering something intently under her breath. She took the rock to her lips as she muttered.

'What is she doing?' asked Mademoiselle Gaimard, fascinated. 'Is that a spell?' Eliza did not know, and hoped not; but inwardly she knew that the Frenchwoman probably had far more experience than herself in these matters, and that probably was what Helena was doing, in the open, in front of her and this stranger.

Then Helena's eyes opened wide, wider than seemed possible, and her hand dropped the stone. It went rigid in front of her, suspended in mid-air, the chain that went around Helena's neck the only thing that prevented it from piercing a skull-wall. Eliza saw a flicker of lights and colours. It was all making her sick, as sick as the green light-energy in Méliès' studio. The shadows around the corridor were unfolding with cruel intention. She wanted to close her eyes, was terrified of what Helena's spell was going to reveal.

Then Helena's eyes returned to normal, and the flicker of lights and the shadows stopped moving.

'This way,' she announced cheerfully. Was she even conscious of what had just happened? Eliza did not know.

Helena picked one of the openings emerging from the corridor, and the other two followed. They walked for a few minutes, until they came into a small chamber, no more than five by five metres. The smells were more intense here, of firewood, and rot; not bones or dirt, but a more fleshy rot, as of small animals and human waste. They moved their torches around, covering their noses, and revealing what looked like human-size cages, empty.

'Good God,' exclaimed Eliza.

There was little doubt that the cages had contained people. Around the room, and inside the cages, there could be recognised the leftovers of food and stained garments and dirt-rotten blankets, and even puddles of urine in dark patches in the corners.

One thing was clear. If this was the place where the women had been kept, they were long gone, or had been taken elsewhere.

'What now?' asked Mademoiselle Gaimard.

'We continue,' said Eliza. She did not know where her sudden resolution had come from. But seeing the cages had cured her fear: she was now furious.

The reality was, they did not know which direction to take, and walked aimlessly, Eliza marking with a soft chalk she had found the turns they were taking. Suddenly, a scream pierced the darkness and the three women stopped in their tracks.

'Where did it come from?' asked Mademoiselle Gaimard, visibly agitated.

Helena closed her eyes, grabbed her stone again. But this time she only touched it for one brief second before announcing:

'This way!'

Eliza had no idea why, but Helena had broken into a run, followed by an equally eager Mademoiselle Gaimard.

'Wait! I can't…' the darkness swallowed her voice. She was still feeling weak, and could not go as fast as them. She pushed herself, breaking through her pain, and took the turn they had; and could see them, ahead, taking another one; and she pushed herself once more, and, this time, she could only guess the flicker of their light, as they disappeared into yet more darkness. 'Helena!' she shouted in vain, and got there, her legs about to give way. 'Helena!' She was alone.

The scream was clearer now, and much closer than she had expected. It was also behind her, not in the direction that the others had taken. She felt disoriented after all the turns, left and right; she could possibly have been running in a circle, or even further into the maze.

The steps, and the shout, like an animal trying to communicate, were getting closer, and closer, and closer. Eliza looked at her hands: the blood was again seeping through the bandages.

Three women appeared and surrounded her. Eliza did not notice how short her breath was, how close she was to passing out. They were jerking their heads, considering her, as if some remnants of understanding flared under their horrid blank faces. She looked from one woman to the other, and to her hands; and understood that, somehow, the smell of the blood must have attracted them, as they must be famished. She realised then how they had been looked after in some fashion at the beginning, only to be left to die eventually. Whoever had come to feed them had not done so in a while. Their eyes told the story of what had happened. They were green and shone with ghostly hues, Eliza's scientific mind understanding that the deformity allowed them to see in the darkness. She would not stand a chance.

The women were forming a circle around her now in beautiful symmetry, each of them the same distance from her, and from each other, or so Eliza thought in her dream-state. She was about to pass out, in pain, in fear. One of the women knelt down carefully, almost delicately, and took her hand. She stuck out her tongue, and licked the seeping blood, and a horrid smile covered her features. She opened her mouth, showing her teeth. Eliza prepared herself. She would die here, and no one would ever find her.

'Emily,' a voice behind her. Helena and Mademoiselle Gaimard, who had come back looking for her. 'Emily. We are friends, Emily.' The girl looked up, her small head still jerking, confused. 'Emily,' Helena now took out a small piece of paper from her pocket: it was the drawing they had found Eliza with. Miraculously, the girl got up and walked towards Helena, still jerking her head. She took the piece of paper, cradled it like a baby in her arms. 'Emily, we have come to find you,' Helena was repeating softly, so softly, until the woman let herself be hugged, taken in her embrace.

The other two started wailing now, screaming and sobbing loudly, and this seemed to break the spell. Emily broke her embrace with Helena, and joined them.

'*Qui est là?*' someone was shouting.

'*Mon Dieu!* They are here,' announced a relieved Mademoiselle Gaimard, as the gendarmerie erupted in the scene.

It unfolded quickly then. The women were covered in blankets and slowly walked into the entrance; a stretcher was brought for Eliza, and she let herself be taken out. Once the light of the outside bathed her face, Eliza opened her eyes again. There were many people around the entrance, demanding to know what was going on, police vehicles parked everywhere, and nurses attending the three vanished ladies, the missing women that they had managed to find. Helena was speaking in French with the police chief, Mademoiselle Gaimard next to her, adding details here and there. Eliza felt happy in a way she had never felt before, as one does after a job well done. Eventually Helena approached her.

'Well, now we can go back home! We deserve a long rest, and an equally long drink,' she said, smiling. This is what it must feel like, Eliza thought, solving a mystery. It must be nice to feel like this regularly. Helena continued: 'The gendarmerie are getting in Méliès for questioning. He has much to explain.' Eliza smiled, but her face could not hide her true feelings. 'What is wrong, Eliza?'

'I am not coming home. At least not now, not immediately.'

'Why? Whatever is the matter?'

'There is something I have to do, Helena. The Lirriper. I want to solve that mystery too.'

Helena smiled, and bent down to embrace her.

'Well, we can still have a long drink, don't you think?' she asked.

Eliza, deep in thought, didn't reply for a moment. She had realised something rather unexpected: she did not feel sadness, or upset, at the thought of Mina. In fact, she was very much looking forward to seeing her again. Perhaps it was time to put the past behind them, and be friends. To Helena she said:

'Absolutely.'

ACKNOWLEDGEMENTS

Thank you to James Womack for being a constant point of stability. Quencher of anxiety attacks, wonderful parent to our children, cat wrangler, amazing chef, miracle worker, and unswerving first reader. Without you this book would not exist, and neither would any other.

Thank you to writer friends who gave advice when advice was needed, wrote a cheery email, sent a postcard, reached out via Zoom, read my future in the tarot cards. Charlotte Cory, Nina Allan, Vida Cruz, Martin Cahill, Priya Sharma, Sofía Rhei, Cristina Jurado, Helen Marshall and Vince Haig. You are all an inexhaustible source of inspiration.

Thank you to my agent Alex Cochran, who always knows what's best so I don't have to. Thank you to my editor Sophie Robinson, who has never failed to make a book a thousand times better, as well as Elora Hartway and Hayley Shepherd.

Thank you to Ian Boyd from Cambridge University for putting me on the trail of the green devil attacks in the Paris catacombs. I look forward to reading your thesis on underground spaces in the early French novel when it is finished. Thank you to dear Philothée for letting me use her name.

Thank you to the Tuesday London bookbinding gang and our fearless leader, Sue Doggett, for keeping me sane.

I am still incapable of writing without listening to Tori Amos, Joanna Newsom and Kate Bush. Thank you for the music.

Thank you to Oliver and Anita, the best possible children a mother could have. This book is for you two. I hope you will read it one day and decide that Mum wrote something fun.

AUTHOR BIO

Marian Womack is a bilingual writer of gothic, weird and science fiction. Her writing features strange landscapes, ghostly encounters and uncanny transformations. She has published the Andalusia-set novel *The Swimmers* (2021) and, in the Walton & Waltraud uncanny mystery series, *The Golden Key* (2020) and *On the Nature of Magic* (2023). Her short fiction has been collected in *Lost Objects* (2018) and in the forthcoming *Out Through the Window, Into the Dark*. She lives in East Anglia and works as a librarian.

For more fantastic fiction, author events,
exclusive excerpts, competitions, limited editions and more

VISIT OUR WEBSITE
titanbooks.com

LIKE US ON FACEBOOK
facebook.com/titanbooks

FOLLOW US ON TWITTER AND INSTAGRAM
@TitanBooks

EMAIL US
readerfeedback@titanemail.com